First Sight

Sasha stepped back as she turned around, bumping smack into a boy who stood behind her, also admiring Jefferson's portrait. "Oh excuse me!" she exclaimed.

"Excuse *me!* If anything, it's my fault. I — I should have gotten out of the way," the boy said, a trace of a southern lilt in his deep voice.

Sasha took a good look at him. His strong face and finely chiseled features were framed by short, straight dark hair. His eyes were green, deep-set, and fringed with long black lashes. Her gaze locked with his, and everything else in the room seemed to melt away. All that existed for Sasha at that moment was the boy, her nearness to him, and the pounding of her heart.

Books from Scholastic
in the **Couples** series:

Moving Too Fast

M.E. Cooper

SCHOLASTIC INC.
New York Toronto London Auckland Sydney

0-590-33394-1

Copyright © 1985 by Cloverdale Press. All rights reserved. Published by Scholastic Inc.

12 11 10 9 8 7 6 5 4 3 2 1   10   5 6 7 8 9/8 0/9

Printed in the U.S.A.   06

Chapter
1

"Can you believe it, Phoebe?" Sasha Jenkins tugged at her friend's arm, her large brown eyes shining with excitement. "You and me in college!" She smiled as she watched the students crisscrossing the beautiful campus, some stopping to talk to each other, others scurrying to get to class. All around them, the colonial-style buildings of the university rose majestically out of the winter landscape.

"Sash, don't you think you're rushing things, just the teensiest bit?" Phoebe laughed. "What about the year of high school we have to get through first?"

Sasha ran a hand through her long, wavy dark hair and nodded. "Yeah, I'll probably even miss Kennedy High once I'm out — no more lunches on the quad with the gang, no more spoiling our appetites for dinner at the sub shop. . . . But Pheeb," she waved the university catalogue vig-

1

orously, "look at the great courses you can take here. Kennedy doesn't have anything compared with this."

Phoebe took the catalogue from Sasha's hand and flipped to the section on dramatic arts. "It's true," she nodded, her red curls bouncing up and down. "And the theater looked pretty amazing, too." She paused, and her voice grew lower. "I wish Griffin could see it."

Sasha couldn't miss the note of sadness that had crept into her friend's voice. Phoebe and Griffin had promised to stay in touch when he'd moved to New York City to try to break into acting, but Sasha knew Phoebe hadn't heard from him in months. She gave Phoebe a hug. "Hey, you'll live," she kidded gently.

"Oh, Sash, sometimes I just hurt so much." Phoebe's blue eyes welled up with tears.

"I know," Sasha replied softly, with a sigh. But she wasn't certain she really did know. She'd never had a real boyfriend. Sure, she dated occasionally. But she spent most of her free time with friends, working on articles for the school newspaper, or helping out at the bookstore her parents owned. The right boy just hadn't come along for her. Sasha sighed wistfully. Sometimes she almost envied Phoebe's heartbreak. She hated to see her friend so blue, but at least Phoebe'd met someone who was actually worth hurting over.

"Sash, I know what that sigh means," Phoebe said, dabbing at her eyes with the back of her mitten. "But believe me, it's no fun breaking up. Chris says that the best thing for me to do is to forget about him. I only wish I could."

"Yeah, Chris is usually right about stuff like that," Sasha replied. She could picture their good friend Chris Austin: There she was, a serious look on her classically beautiful face as she doled out good, sensible advice.

"But if this was one of those romantic old movies," she continued, "just when you'd really lost hope, Griffin would come riding across the Kennedy quad on a white horse and whisk you away. Can't you just see it? You two galloping through the streets of Rose Hill into the sunset?"

Phoebe giggled. "Sasha Jenkins, your problem is that you're an incurable romantic." She gave her friend a playful push.

"Maybe," Sasha agreed, "but at least I put a smile on your face. Now promise me you'll leave it there."

"I'll try," Phoebe responded dutifully.

"Good. I just know that one way or another, everything's going to work out for you."

"For you, too, Sasha." Phoebe gave Sasha's hand a squeeze.

"So, girls, what do you think?" Sasha's parents had been walking a few paces behind them, and now Mr. Jenkins' deep, resonant voice carried through the crisp February afternoon air. "Does university life meet your expectations?"

"Sasha and Phoebe waited until the Jenkinses caught up with them. "Dad, it's so perfect!" Sasha exclaimed. Enthusiasm filled her voice again. "It's so, I don't know . . . collegiate, I guess! It's just the way I pictured it would be."

"What was your favorite part of the tour?" Mrs. Jenkins asked, coming over and putting an arm around her daughter's slender shoulders.

"Well, the library was pretty impressive," Sasha began.

"And it was great to be able to see the choir rehearsing," Phoebe put in.

"Visiting some of the dorms was neat, too," Sasha said. "Could you believe those two girls who were still walking around in their bathrobes?" She laughed. "It blows my mind to imagine sitting around the dorm all day when there are so many things to do on campus."

Mr. Jenkins agreed. "You girls are awfully lucky to have this opportunity; to learn not just physics and math — although they're certainly important — but to study, oh, say organic gardening, if it interests you, or the Egyptian pyramids. It's going to be a time for all kinds of new experiences."

"Sometimes I wish I had the chance to do it a second time," remarked Mrs. Jenkins. "Don't you, Paul?"

Mr. Jenkins smiled at his wife. "And get to fall in love with you all over again? Now how could I resist?"

Sasha rolled her eyes in mock exasperation. "Parents — you can't take them anywhere," she joked to Phoebe. Though she realized her parents actually didn't seem all that out of place on the University of Virginia càmpus — in their jeans, ski parkas, and boots, they looked like somewhat older versions of the college students who were milling about them.

Sasha felt incredibly lucky. When she thought of her friends, it seemed that so many of their

4

parents didn't understand them or respect their ideas. Phoebe's dad, for example. Sasha knew he was a loving father and a good man. But he was usually so involved in his law practice or the latest developments in the stock market, he had no time to find out what was going on in his daughter's life.

Sasha's parents, on the other hand, loved to discuss off-beat thoughts and theories with her. Not that she always agreed with them one-hundred percent, but at least she felt that they respected her point of view and encouraged her to have a broad view of life.

Then all of a sudden, a frown darkened her father's normally untroubled and open face. Sasha followed his gaze and saw a troop of ROTC cadets marching in formation on a section of the campus lawn. They were drilling with rifles over their shoulders.

Mr. Jenkins shook his head in dismay. "You know, that's one thing I don't think I'll ever understand. Training young people for the military, to fight and kill in wars — it's so bullheaded, such a waste. That kind of thing doesn't belong on a college campus, where people should be discovering and growing." He stroked his beard. "And I don't think it belongs anywhere else either, for that matter," he added.

"Well, Dad, neither Phoebe nor I are about to rush out and join the ROTC," Sasha joked.

Mr. Jenkins' expression didn't soften. Mrs. Jenkins moved away from Sasha and took her husband's arm. "Paul, I know how strongly you feel about this, and you know I share your feelings, but those kids have the right to be out there in those uniforms. They're doing what they believe in. Now what do you say to a little side trip on our way back to Rose Hill?" she asked, pointedly changing the subject.

"Where to, Mom?" asked Sasha.

"Well, Monticello's not far from here. We passed a sign for it on the way up."

"You mean Thomas Jefferson's home?" Phoebe asked enthusiastically. "I've always wanted to see it."

"Me, too." Sasha chimed in.

"Paul?" Mrs. Jenkins prodded. "How about it?"

Sasha watched her father's eyes following the retreating squad of cadets. Then he waved his hand, as if to put the whole issue behind him. "I think that would be lovely."

Mrs. Jenkins pushed up the sleeve of her ski parka and consulted her watch. "Well, according to that sign, there's a tour starting in a half hour. We can just about make it if we hurry."

Something about the portrait of the third President of the United States riveted Sasha's attention. Perhaps it was his red hair. Funny, she'd never thought that Thomas Jefferson might have the same color hair as Phoebe. It made him seem somehow more human — not just a marble figure in the history books, but a flesh and blood person who happened to have been President.

Sasha found herself wondering what it would have been like to live in post-revolutionary times, in this elegant old hilltop mansion. She pictured herself in a lace-trimmed, full-skirted gown, strolling the grounds of the estate, parasol in hand, as horse-drawn carriages pulled up to the doors.

"Sasha! Earth to Sasha!" Phoebe's voice drew her back to the present. "The group's going this way." Phoebe peered at her from the doorway to the next reconstructed room.

Sasha stepped back as she turned around, bumping smack into a boy who stood behind her, also admiring Jefferson's portrait. "Oh, excuse me!" she exclaimed.

"Excuse *me*! If anything, it's my fault. I — I should have gotten out of the way," the boy said, a trace of a southern lilt in his deep voice.

Sasha took a good look at him. His strong face and finely chiseled features were framed by short, straight dark hair. His eyes were green, deep-set, and fringed with long black lashes. Her gaze locked with his, and everything else in the room seemed to melt away. All that existed for Sasha at that moment was the boy, her nearness to him, and the pounding of her heart.

She tried to catch her breath, moving a few steps back. She took in the boy's broad shoulders, his muscular frame clad in a gray sweat shirt and jeans. She felt him drinking in her appearance, too.

The spell was shattered when two younger boys burst into the room, each grabbing one of his arms. "Hey, dingdong, are you gonna stand here all day?" the bigger of the two pestered. They pulled him toward the next room.

Sasha remained rooted to the spot. Her pulse raced and her cheeks felt flushed. Her fingers trembled. What was happening to her? If ever

7

there were such a thing as love at first sight, this was it!

"Are you okay, Sash?" Phoebe had reentered the room and was at her friend's side. She saw the boy and his two young companions as they turned to go into the room next door.

"Oh, Phoebe . . . yeah, I'm fine." Sasha's words sounded far away to her.

"That boy — do you know him or something?"

"No, I've never seen him before," Sasha replied, though she felt as if she did know him.

"I didn't notice him at the beginning of the tour," Phoebe commented. "Maybe he was late or something. But look, we're going to miss the next room if we don't keep up with the group."

Sasha followed Phoebe as if she was in a trance. By the time they caught up with the others, the boy was on the other side of the crowd of people. But she could feel his presence as if he were still right in front of her.

The guide was going on and on, explaining something about the period furniture, but Sasha barely heard a word of what he was saying. For her, the rest of the tour was like a picture out of focus. All she was truly aware of was the boy. Several times their eyes met, and Sasha felt heady and dizzy, and her knees grew weak. How could this be happening? she wondered. It's crazy. She didn't even know this boy's name. She needed to get some fresh air . . . to think. This was so weird, maybe the cold air would bring her to her senses.

When the tour finally ended, the guide encouraged the visitors to explore the basement kitchens and grounds on their own. Sasha took the opportunity to wander away from Phoebe and her parents, out into the brisk winter afternoon. She found a bench near the Jefferson family cemetery and sat down with her back to the huge house. She closed her eyes, listening to the wind whistling through the bare branches.

Then she heard his voice. "Do you mind if I sit next to you?"

Sasha turned her head. In that instant, she knew she didn't want to be brought to her senses at all. If this was a dream, she hoped it would never end. Unable to form a single coherent word, she simply smiled at the boy.

"It's very beautiful here, isn't it?" he remarked, taking a seat. "Makes you feel as if you're a part of your own history, if you know what I mean."

Sasha felt warm all over, despite the chilling wind that was whipping through the estate grounds. "I know exactly what you mean!" she answered excitedly. She had been thinking the very same thing herself when she was looking at Jefferson's portrait.

"It's so inspiring to be standing right where Thomas Jefferson once stood," she added. "Maybe I'll write an article about this place."

"You're a writer?" the boy asked, smiling shyly.

Sasha felt a blush tinting her pale skin. "I do a lot of writing for my school paper," she told him.

"Oh? What school is that, if you don't mind my asking?"

"Kennedy High. It's a few hours away from here, in Rose Hill. Just outside of D.C."

Surprise registered on his handsome face, but before he could say anything, the two little boys Sasha had seen earlier appeared on the lawn, madly waving their arms at him.

"My brothers," he explained. "I'm taking care of them for the day. I guess I'd better go." Sasha could hear the reluctance in his voice as he stood up. He took a step away from the bench, then turned back, and extended his hand. "It's been very nice talking with you. . . ."

"Sasha. Sasha Jenkins." Sasha took his hand in hers. An electric tingle raced through her fingertips and up her arm. She shook the boy's hand, grasped it for a second longer, and then let go. Their eyes held each other.

"Good-bye, Sasha," he whispered. Finally he turned to leave. Sasha watched him move across the lawn toward his brothers. She didn't stop looking until the three boys, who were headed down toward the parking lot below the estate, vanished below the crest of the hill.

Chapter 2

Sasha was curled up on the window seat in her living room listening to the drops of water beat against the shingled roof of her red, brick house. She, Phoebe, and Woody were supposed to be memorizing vocabulary for a French quiz, but Sasha couldn't seem to keep her mind on the words for more than a few seconds at a time.

"Okay, Woody, how do you say, 'It's raining cats and dogs'?" Phoebe was asking, reading from a mimeographed sheet.

Sasha watched Woody toy with his trademark red suspenders, his long gangly legs folded beneath him Indian-style as he sat on the braided colonial rug. "Let's see. *Il pleut*. That much I know. It's raining. Hmm, cats and dogs . . . *chats et chiens*, right? *Il pleut chats et chiens*."

Phoebe sent a gingham pillow flying across the room in Woody's direction. "No, silly. That's a direct translation. They don't say it that way.

Sasha, how about you? Do you know? You've been pretty quiet over there."

Sasha looked over from her perch at one side of the cozy room and sighed. "Sorry, Phoebe. I guess I'm just not in the mood for this today."

She shifted positions, but she couldn't get comfortable. She felt restless, as if she were waiting for something to happen — something new and exciting — and a French quiz was definitely not it.

Phoebe drew her eyebrows together. "Sasha, what is it? We all know about you and your daydreaming, but it's like you've been out of the earth's atmosphere this week."

"Invasion of the moon people," Woody cracked. "They look like your own friends, but don't let them fool you. . . ." He whistled a few notes of an eerie sounding tune.

Sasha forced a laugh, and it came out choked and tight. She wasn't fooling anyone, least of all herself. She knew the exact second when her funny feeling had started — when she'd turned around at Monticello and seen that handsome, dark-haired boy. Since then, she'd had the persistent, nagging sensation that there was something missing from her life. She needed an adventure. And she needed it with the dark-haired boy.

"Sash?" Phoebe was still giving her a funny look. "Are you okay?"

Sasha shrugged, toying with her long, dark braid. "Yeah, I guess." What else could she say? That a few minutes with some mystery boy had

12

suddenly made the rest of her life seem boring with a capital B?

"Well, then, how about telling me how to say 'raining cats and dogs'?" Phoebe persisted.

"Raining cats and dogs?" She rolled the "r," showing off her near-perfect accent, but it didn't make her feel any better. Studying was the last thing she wanted to do.

Phoebe seemed to sense that. "Come on, you guys. We're going to have to face this test first thing tomorrow morning. We've got to learn this junk," she insisted.

"Come on, Pheeb, I was almost right," Woody said.

"Yeah? Tell that to Madame Duclos," Phoebe responded. "Know what she'll say?"

Woody made a face. "I know. There's no such thing as 'almost right.'"

Phoebe turned back toward Sasha. "And you, Sash, aren't you the one who's always saying how romantic the French language is? I thought you loved to speak it."

"*Oui, c'est vrai,*" Sasha affirmed. She made an effort to smile. "But even we French experts need a study break now and then. Look, how about if we take a break for a bit, and I make us a batch of my wheat-germ granola bars?" If anything could cheer her up, that might.

"One of your infamous whole wheat concoctions?" Woody asked suspiciously.

Sasha felt a real, honest-to-goodness laugh escape her lips for the first time that afternoon. "Oh Woody, they're not going to kill you. In

13

fact, they're a lot better for you than, say, chocolate brownies. Besides, you might even like them. Your taste buds just have to get used to a different kind of flavor."

Woody groaned. "Don't even mention brownies. I don't want my stomach to get all excited over nothing."

Phoebe came to her defense. "Hey, Sasha's wheat-germ granola bars are really delicious. No kidding. I mean, whenever I try to cook that kind of stuff, I wind up with a disaster on my hands. Like one time Chris and I tried to make a health-food pizza. Boy, it was harder than a boulder." Phoebe groaned as she recalled their culinary disaster. "But when Sasha cooks she has some kind of magic touch."

"Ah, *oui*. Mademoiselle Sasha knows how to tame zee wild whole wheat berry, my *cheries*," Sasha joked with a thick French accent, trying to get a little spirit into her voice. It wasn't fair to her friends to have her mope around all afternoon. Besides, maybe if she acted like she was in a good mood she really would make herself feel better.

"Well, okay. I'll try your cookies." Woody gave in, as he followed her and Phoebe into the kitchen. "Anything to get away from studying for a while!"

He took a seat next to Phoebe at the round oak table, while Sasha bustled around the kitchen getting out ingredients. She took a jar of honey and a bag of wheat germ from the cupboard and then got a stick of butter from the refrigerator. Finally, she pried the lid off an antique cracker

14

tin and thrust her hand inside. Her fingers touched the bare bottom of the container.

"Oh, no," she wailed. "I can't believe it. There's no more granola left."

"After that big buildup?" Woody asked. "I was actually starting to look forward to tasting those things. But never fear — Woody and his trusty Volvo are here! We'll just have to take a drive to the health-food store for a refill."

Sasha noted the grin on Woody's face. "Uh-oh, watch out! Woody's found another excuse to show off his prize possession. Woody, tell us, exactly how much time have you spent sitting in the front seat of that car since you got it?"

"Let's see," Woody mused. "If you count the time Ted and I sat in his driveway listening to the Georgetown/St. John's game, I'd say a total of about one solid day since I picked it up last weekend. I wanted to throw my sleeping bag in the backseat and camp out in it last night, but my mother drew the line at that point."

"You're kidding, aren't you?" she asked, wide eyed.

"Who, me?" Woody returned, deadpan. "When have you ever known me to kid you?"

Sasha knew she'd been had. She rolled her eyes at Phoebe. "Okay, okay. So maybe I am just a little, teeny bit gullible," she admitted, giggling. "But I do make a great granola bar, so how about if I take you up on that offer for a lift, and we go get the ingredients I need?"

A few minutes later, Sasha was seated next to Woody in the used silver Volvo he had saved for

15

so long to buy. Phoebe stretched out in the back, humming along to the song on the radio.

"Just think about the sexy new image this car'll give you," Sasha teased. She had to admit that she *was* feeling at least a little bit better. It was nice to get out of the house and away from studying for a while. She patted the dashboard as she gave Woody a sly glance.

She could see Woody's cheeks beginning to turn red. "Maybe a new image wouldn't be so bad," he said.

"Okay, Woody, 'fess up," Phoebe demanded from the backseat. "Who is she?"

"Who's who?" Woody asked in perfect innocence.

"You know," Sasha said. "Who's the girl you want to change your image for?"

"Hey, no fair. Two against one," Woody pleaded.

"Look," Phoebe began. "You might as well tell us, because you're not going to get a moment's peace until we know."

"You said it," Sasha confirmed.

"Guess I can't argue with logic. Or the two of you." Woody sighed. "But really, it's no one. I mean, no one specific. That's exactly the problem. . . ." He made a right turn onto President Street, cruising past the spacious homes that dotted the tree-lined Park Heights section of Rose Hill.

"And even when I do meet someone, I always seem to come across as good old Woody, everybody's pal." He was quiet for a moment.

"Just once it might be nice to have a girl think of me as well — romantic."

An embarrassed silence filled the car. Sasha knew that Woody had always hoped his friendship with Phoebe might blossom into something more. But although he was one of Phoebe's dearest friends, she'd never returned those deeper feelings.

Sasha wanted so much to lean over and give Woody a comforting hug, but she didn't. Wasn't she just another perfect example of a girl who thought of Woody as a pal?

Phoebe was first to speak. "You know, Woody, there'll be lot of girls at that party Ted's throwing. Maybe it will be the start of something good for you."

Woody looked thoughtful. "Yes, you're right. It's as good a time as any." He steered into the mall and pulled into a space at one of the long rows of stores. "Any new kids going to be there?" He switched off the ignition and pulled up the emergency brake.

Sasha let herself out, and drops of rain splashed against her face. "Actually, I think that Kimberly Barrie might be coming," she heard Phoebe saying. "At least, I know Ted invited her. Have you met her yet? She just moved here from Pittsburgh. My mom met her mom at some school board meeting."

"I'm not sure. What does she look like?" Woody asked as they entered a store with a wooden facade and hand-lettered sign that read "Nature's Gate."

"Real athletic looking. Short brown hair, very cute. You might have seen her riding her bike to school," Phoebe answered. "I think she lives somewhere near you."

"No, I don't know who she is." Woody shook his head. "But if there's a pretty new girl at Ted's you can bet I'll make sure to talk to her."

The three friends made their way down an aisle lined with large lucite containers. "She's in my math class," Sasha put in, taking a metal scoop from a shelf and dipping it into a bin filled with granola. "She seems nice. But, Woody, I don't know if it's such a great idea to start making plans about someone you haven't even met yet."

"You don't?" Disappointment colored Woody's words.

"I mean, I'm not saying it might not work out," Sasha replied hastily, bringing her bag to the check-out counter. She put it down and fished around in the front pocket of her favorite worn-out jeans for a few dollar bills. "What I mean is that I think love comes when you least expect it, when you aren't looking." Like that boy at Monticello. She thought once again of his handsome face and lilting voice.

"Maybe." Woody shrugged. "But it couldn't hurt to find out a little more about this . . . what did you say her name was? Kimberly?"

Sasha and Phoebe nodded in unison.

"Kimberly. Right. If I just knew what she's interested in, it might come in handy as a conversation starter." He pushed open the door at the front of the store and stepped back out into the parking lot.

18

"Well, I know she's helping her mother start some kind of catering business," Phoebe volunteered. "You could talk to her about food."

"No, you guys," protested Sasha, climbing into the backseat of the Volvo. Hadn't they understood what she was trying to say? "You're going about this all wrong. Sometimes it's best *not* to know too much about the other person. Sometimes words aren't even necessary."

"Well if that's true, I'm in real trouble," cracked Woody, his usual playful manner surfacing again. "You know me, Sash. I can never keep my big mouth shut."

"I don't know if that's so terrible," Phoebe ventured. "I mean, that way at least the girl knows what she's in for!" She tousled Woody's curly brown hair as she seated herself next to him and fastened her seat belt.

"But, Phoebe, what good is romance without a little mystery?" Sasha asked from the back.

She couldn't seem to get the boy from Monticello out of her mind — his intense green eyes, his trim, muscular body. She kept daydreaming about him in the middle of her classes, or when she was supposed to be writing an article for the paper. And this afternoon she'd been imagining herself with him, arm in arm, walking through the gardens of Thomas Jefferson's estate.

Woody and Phoebe continued to discuss Kimberly Barrie and Ted's upcoming party, but Sasha was quiet. She was certain the boy from Monticello was that special one she could love above all others.

She'd always dreamed about the right boy for

her. They wouldn't meet in an ordinary way. It would be something unexpected, somewhere beautiful and romantic. Their eyes would meet. It would be love at first sight. And she would be able to tell that he felt the same way about her. When she closed her eyes she could practically feel him looking at her all over again, and a shiver ran up and down her arms.

In her dream, she and the boy would go off together, to some secret world for two. But that part hadn't come true. Sasha pressed her lips together tightly. What good did it do to think about him when she would never see him again? She didn't even know the boy's name.

Sasha blinked back a tear, staring out the windshield of Woody's car. The familiar sights of Rose Hill glided by in a wet, gray blur, as the windshield wipers moved back and forth with a steady, monotonous rhythm.

Chapter
3

Sasha chewed on the end of her pencil and stared blankly at the typed columns in front of her. Normally she didn't mind missing one lunch period a week with her friends to help do a layout on the school paper. But these days, the word *normally* didn't seem to have much meaning in Sasha's life.

Sasha had carried her secret around inside her for nearly a week, despite her friends' growing concern about her withdrawal and their playful teasing about what Woody kept calling the "moon people syndrome." After all, what was she supposed to tell them? That she was in love with someone who was no more than a memory, a fleeting encounter? Finally, however, the afternoon before, she had spilled everything in an all-out confession to Phoebe and Chris.

"So that's it!" Phoebe had exclaimed. "Well, why didn't you come right out and say so? If any-

21

one understands about love at first sight, it's me. I remember the first time I saw Griffin. . . ." A far away look had drifted across Phoebe's face. But she'd given her head an abrupt shake, and the expression disappeared almost immediately. "Well, anyway, that's history," she added gruffly. "I just meant that I know exactly how you feel."

Even Chris, usually so down-to-earth, had sympathized. "Yeah, I guess I felt that way about Ted when I first met him, too. I knew he was a guy I could share almost anything with, even though I'd barely said two words to him. But, Sash," she'd continued in her more practical vein, running a slender hand through her long, straight blond hair, "at least Ted and I had a chance to see each other in school every day, to go out on dates and really get to know each other. You met this guy over a hundred miles from here. You don't know the first thing about him. And it's not like you're going to run into him on the street or something."

Sasha had felt her dreams of romance shrink like a punctured balloon. A part of her had known all along that what Chris said was true, yet deep inside she'd nurtured a seed of hope, a feeling that such a strong attraction was destined to draw them together somehow. But Chris's cool logic had toppled her castles in the sky.

Hurt and disillusionment must have been written all over her delicate features, because Chris's tone softened instantly. "Oh, Sash, I didn't mean to make you feel bad. I just don't think you should go around thinking if you wish hard enough this whole thing is going to have a storybook ending. 'Cause if you pretend too long, you'll hurt even worse in the long run."

Now Chris's words echoed in Sasha's mind as she sat at her desk in the newspaper office. What her friend said made sense. On the other hand, Sasha didn't believe everything that happened could necessarily be explained by hard facts or scientific information. It was spooky with her. There were times when, for example, she'd thought about someone she hadn't seen in ages, and the next day she'd run into that person on the street; or she'd learn a new word only to find it a few hours later in the book she was reading.

She knew many people chalked this sort of thing up to mere coincidence, but she knew there were other theories, too. Her father had recently told her about one he'd called the cosmic design of nature, in which there was no such thing as a random event. Everything that happened had a purpose.

Sasha wasn't certain she fully understood all this, but she supposed it had something to do with fate. In that case it wouldn't be entirely out of the question for the dark-haired boy to come walking through the door to the newspaper office at this very moment.

Sasha knew a lot of her friends would laugh at the notion of cosmic design. Some of them had even told her she'd been born in the wrong decade, that she and her offbeat ideas belonged back in the sixties. Sasha sighed. Was she really some kind of free spirit who had been born too late? Maybe she should try to be more practical. She bent over her desk and forced herself to concentrate on her work.

It was no use. She looked up at the door again. Suddenly, the door knob began to turn. Sasha held her breath, but let it out in a disappointed groan as the door was flung open and Kennedy High wrestler John Marquette sauntered into the room. He was the farthest thing from the Monticello boy Sasha could imagine.

"Well, well, my favorite foxette," Marquette uttered harshly. "And how is my little lovely today?"

Sasha held her breath and silently counted to ten. It wouldn't do any good to let herself get angry. That was just what that humongous jerk wanted — to get a reaction from her. A few weeks earlier, when Sasha had interviewed him for an article on athletes at Kennedy, he'd tried to throw himself at her, all two hundred and fifty beefy, arrogant pounds of him. Now he must think if he hadn't gotten the reaction he'd wanted then, he'd might as well try provoking her.

Sasha composed herself. "Yes, John," she said cooly. "What can I do for you?"

Marquette walked over and sat down at her desk. He brought his face right up to hers. "My dear little lady," he said, his voice thick with sarcasm. "It's obvious you've been dying for me to walk in here, but you really don't have to look so totally overjoyed to see me."

"John, I have a name, and it's not little lady or foxette." Sasha tried to keep her voice level. "Now what was it you wanted to see me about?"

"You're so cute when you're all worked up,"

Marquette leered, his small eyes narrowing into slits as he looked her up and down.

"I'm not all worked up," Sasha replied, "but I do have things to do. So if you don't have anything to speak to me about, I'm going to get back to my work."

"Ah, yes. The busy little doll. But you're too pretty to be spending all your time on such important, serious jobs."

"Okay! That does it!" Sasha finally burst out. Her pale, translucent complexion grew pink with fury. "You just take your male chauvanism and rude remarks somewhere else, John Marquette!"

"Now, is that any way to talk to someone whose cousin's store practically supports your precious newspaper?" Marquette pulled a folded-up copy of *The Red and the Gold*, the Kennedy High paper, from his athletic bag and pointed to a full-page ad for Superjock Sporting Goods.

Sasha bit her lip in utter frustration. Superjock was the one reason why she had to control her urge to let John Marquette have it once and for all. Without the store the paper would lose one of their most valuable contributors. But there were other ways of dealing with people like Marquette. When it came to a battle of wits, he was a big hulk on very thin ice.

"Listen, John," Sasha began in honied tones, "you're right. I owe you an apology. So I guess you can stay here and talk to me if you want." There was a calculated pause. Marquette's face registered confusion at her sudden about-face.

"It's just that I'm awfully surprised that such an important man on campus has time to bother

25

sitting around here with me," she added off-handedly.

Marquette appeared to be thinking hard. "Maybe that's true," he said haughtily. "I mean, I've got better things to do than hang around here all day with someone like you." He waved Sasha off with his hand, as if she were no better than a fly, and puffed out his chest. He seemed to think he had come up with the ultimate put-down all by himself. Sasha almost laughed out loud.

Suddenly Marquette's brow wrinkled as it dawned on him he'd just volunteered to leave the room. "But don't think you're going to get off so easy," he roared, trying to regain the upper hand. "I'm going to be on your case until you finally print that interview you did with me. And it better be good. No. Make that *great*. Or else. . . ." He poked his finger at the Superjock ad once more.

Sasha nodded calmly. "Your interview will be printed in the next issue, and I'm sure you'll be satisfied."

"You better hope I am — foxie," he snarled, turning toward the door and strutting out.

Sasha let out a long, noisy stream of air and shook her head. So much for romance and the cosmic design of the world, she thought.

Sasha heard a knock on the door to the newspaper office. "It's open," she called out. "Come in." She looked up to see Janie Barstow and Henry Braverman. "Janie, Henry. Hi. Come on in." She patted the seats next to her, happy to see two real friends after the little scene with the wrestler. "Janie, what a great dress. You look fabulous!"

"I do?" Janie sounded surprised as she smoothed her hands over her pearl gray jumper, which was belted at the hips with a deep green sash.

"Of course you do," Sasha said matter of factly. Janie should be used to getting compliments by now. Everyone agreed that her new look was terrific — her wardrobe, sleek haircut, the whole way that she was now. But Sasha knew that Janie sometimes still had trouble imagining herself as anything other than the timid, drab little wallflower she had been for most of her life.

"I keep telling her the same thing," Henry said, looking tenderly at his girl friend. "Maybe if we tell her often enough, she'll wake up one morning and start believing it."

"Oh, you guys. . . ." Janie blushed happily.

"No, it's true," Sasha said. "You always look so good." And what was even more important, she added to herself, it looked as though Janie was feeling good these days, too.

It all started when Janie had stumbled in on Henry in the home ec room, secretly working on a design for a new dress. Janie agreed to try the dress on and model it. It couldn't have turned out any better, Sasha thought, if Janie had wished it all to happen. From that chance encounter had followed a loving romance and new kind of confidence for both her friends.

She smiled warmly at them. "So, is that one of your new designs, Henry?" she asked.

27

Janie nodded enthusiastically. "Yeah, this is his latest creation." She turned her tall, willowy frame around slowly, modeling her dress. "The buyer at Rezato liked it, too," she confided shyly. "She put in an order for a half dozen in different colors."

"You're kidding!" squealed Sasha. "Janie, that's amazing! Boy, this business of yours is really getting off the ground, isn't it?"

Janie and Henry looked at each other proudly. "You know," began Janie, "if anyone told me, a few months ago, that we'd be selling clothes to the chicest boutique in Georgetown, I never would have believed it. But ever since Henry and I met, well. . . ." Janie gave an embarrassed smile, running a hand through her dark hair. "What I mean is that I've been so happy lately that I'm almost afraid I'm going to wake up one morning and realize I've been dreaming all this time."

"But you haven't," Sasha said firmly. She took Janie's hand and squeezed it for emphasis. "At this very moment you are most definitely standing here in the *Red and the Gold* office talking to me."

"Oh, which reminds me," Janie said, pulling a white envelope from her roomy leather shoulder bag, "we stopped by because we were just in the principal's office, and one of the secretaries asked if we'd mind bringing this to you."

Sasha took the envelope and turned it over. It was addressed "Sasha, c/o Kennedy High School Newspaper Staff." "Hmm. Must be someone writing in response to one of my articles. I wonder if it's good news or bad." She put the letter down on her desk. "Thanks."

"Sure," replied Janie, moving toward the door. "By the way, Henry and I were just talking to Ted in the lunchroom, and he invited us to his party. You're going, too, aren't you?"

"Absolutely," Sasha replied.

"Great. So are we." Janie gave a little wave good-bye.

"See you, Sash," said Henry.

Sasha watched them leave the office hand-in-hand. Perhaps the right people did eventually find each other, she mused, as Janie closed the door behind them.

Sasha inspected the oddly addressed letter in front of her. Why hadn't the sender used her last name, she wondered, absentmindedly tearing open the envelope. And why had the letter come through the main office instead of directly to the newspaper room?

Dear Sasha, she read, *I hope you remember me. We met at Monticello last week. I was the one with the two brothers.*

Sasha began to tremble. She felt her face grow warm as her pulse raced out of control. Did she remember him? How could she ever forget him? She clutched the letter and continued reading.

This may sound weird, but I can't get myself to stop thinking about you. I've never written a letter like this to anyone before, but I had to try and get in touch with you again. I wonder if this will reach you.

Please don't think I'm too forward, but I'd like

to invite you to have dinner with me this weekend. There's a great Italian restaurant called Millie's not too far from you in Carolton. I'll be waiting there at seven o'clock on Saturday evening. I'm keeping my fingers crossed that you will meet me. But if you don't, I'll understand.

Until then, Wesley Lewis

Sasha clasped the letter against her body and took a few deep breaths. Then she read the letter again, lingering over each sentence. She ran her index finger over the closing signature. "Wesley. Wesley Lewis," she whispered to herself. Suddenly she knew exactly what Janie meant about being afraid she would wake up from a dream. Her heart soared like a jet at takeoff. "Wesley," she said again, louder this time, full of joy.

She'd been wildly hoping for him to walk into the newspaper office, but this was even better — a secret date for a romantic dinner. And it was real! This was actually happening!

Sasha didn't know how long she sat there, looking at the words on the piece of lined notebook paper, picturing Wesley's strong, handsome face. But before she knew it, the first bell for afternoon classes was ringing.

She took one last look at the letter. Then carefully, as if she were handling a fragile treasure, she refolded it and slipped it in between the pages of her biology textbook. She put her newspaper work back into its file and gathered her books. She hugged them to her chest, a smile of pure happiness spreading across her face. Well, Wesley Lewis, she said to herself, it looks like you have a date!

Chapter
4

"I thought I was the one around here who was supposed to be worried, not you," said Ted Mason. Chris Austin's boyfriend slung his arm around her shoulders.

Chris had to raise her voice over the noisy chatter and the music from their friend Peter's lunchtime radio program, which was blasting through two huge speakers at the front of the cafeteria. Now that the weather had turned cold, the crowd had forsaken their usual spot on the quad for the hectic, but considerably warmer, north corner of the enormous room.

"Well, Ted, if you refuse to get nervous about this party, then I'm going to have to do it for you." She tried to joke away her concern, but there was nothing she could do to keep the worried look out of her large blue eyes. "I mean, you've invited practically the entire school. Aren't you even the slightest bit afraid that things

31

might get out of hand?" She looked up at her boyfriend, his handsome face framed by a slightly unruly crown of curly light-colored hair.

"Hey, you know what they say, Chris. The more the merrier. Besides, am I Kennedy's top quarterback for nothing? If anyone steps out of line. . . ." He flexed his biceps, a lopsided grin on his lips.

Chris giggled. She loved that crooked smile. "Oh, I see. Nobody's going to mess with the big man, is that it?"

"You got it!" Ted speared an overcooked carrot on the end of his fork. "What do they do to these things anyway?" He wrinkled his nose.

"Maybe they subject them to Mr. Houseman's American history lectures until they wilt," suggested Woody. "Boy, I wasn't sure I was going to make it through his class today."

"Yeah, I had him last semester," commented Henry, reaching into the bag of potato chips he was sharing with Janie. "That guy is probably the only person in the whole world who could make the discovery of America sound about as exciting as an old, wrinkled up pair of pants."

Phoebe laughed. "And we all know that when it comes to pants — and shirts and dresses — you're the expert!" She tapped her hand on the plastic-topped table in time to the song Peter had just put on the air.

"Well, I've got this theory about Houseman," put in Sasha, polishing off the last bite of a carton of yogurt she'd brought from home. "See, I think he's invented this new thing: He can lecture and sleep at the same time."

"You and your theories," Chris teased. She was glad to see Sasha in such a good mood, but she was also a bit confused. Just a few days earlier her friend had been near tears when she'd explained to Phoebe and her that she'd let the perfect boy walk right out of her life without even finding out his name. But today Sasha was back to her happy self. In fact, she seemed even more exuberant than usual.

Chris's thoughts were interrupted by Peter's familiar baritone, booming out of the lunchroom speakers. "Hey, Cardinals, this is Peter Lacey at WKND. Hope you enjoyed that set from my all time fave, the Boss — Bruce Springsteen. And we've got a lot more for you coming up. Here's a new one from the Night Owls called "Go Out and Win." I'd like to dedicate it to the hockey team, which as you all know, has a big game coming up a week from Saturday. And don't forget the victory celebration afterward. Your favorite quarterback and mine is taking advantage of his off-season to play host to our men of ice."

Chris groaned as the Night Owls' opening chords came over the speakers. "Honestly, Ted. Doesn't Peter have more sense than to go around making public announcements about this party? Your house is going to end up like an overcrowded zoo if you're not careful." She shook her head, her blond hair swaying from side to side.

Ted shrugged good-naturedly. "Don't sweat it, Chris. I promise — you have my word — everybody's going to have a great time."

* * *

Woody hurried after Phoebe as she carried her lunch tray away from the table. "Pheeb!" he called out. "Wait up, okay?"

Phoebe slowed down and Woody fell in step alongside her. "There's something I've got to tell you," he said.

"What's up, Woody?" They walked over to the far side of the lunchroom, and Phoebe dumped the rest of her soggy carrots into the garbage can and placed her tray on the conveyor belt to the kitchen.

"Well, I wanted to talk to you alone," he began as they exited the lunchroom and headed toward the rows of lockers at the end of the corridor. "My parents are going to take a five-day trip to New York City so my mom can see some of the new Broadway shows.

Phoebe nodded. She knew Woody's mother worked for the Arena Stage in Washington, D.C., and frequently went to New York to the theater.

"I'll have to miss a few days of school." Woody continued, "but Mom and Dad said I could go with them."

Phoebe listened attentively. New York City. That's where Griffin was. He'd risked everything to move there and try to make it on the stage as an actor. And he had actually landed a job as an understudy in one of the new shows. Phoebe had it all worked out how she would visit him in New York and help celebrate his success. But then, suddenly and totally unexpectedly, she'd gotten that phone call. Griffin had told her he wouldn't be able to see her anymore. No explanations.

Phoebe blinked furiously to hold back her

tears. It still hurt so much to think about Griffin. Had the big time really changed him? Had he met someone else? Or had he never actually loved her at all? Griffin always used to say they had to be open and honest with each other. What could have possibly happened in a few short months to make him forget all that? She slumped against her locker.

As if reading her mind, Woody reached out and squeezed her hand. "Phoebe, I know how badly you must want to find out about Griffin. That's why I thought I should talk to you in private. I saw my mom's ticket order form. Griffin's show is on it."

Phoebe let out an involuntary gasp. "It is? Oh, Woody, do you think he'll be there? I mean — I don't know — do the understudies have to be at every performance?" She nervously twirled a strand of curly red hair around her finger.

"Whoah, Pheeb, back up a minute." Woody's brown eyes were full of concern. "I should have finished explaining before I got your hopes up like that. We won't know if we're really going to his show until the tickets actually come in the mail, but I promise I'll keep you posted on what happens."

Phoebe did her best not to appear disappointed. "I know you will, Woody," she said softly. "Thanks." She smiled gratefully at her friend. If he had been any other kind of guy, he might not have said anything to her. But even though she knew Woody was jealous of the way she felt about Griffin, he didn't let his romantic feelings get in the way of their special friendship.

"How come I'm lucky enough to have a friend like you?" Phoebe asked, looking up at him.

"Just incredibly good luck, I guess," Woody kidded gently. "Are you okay?"

Phoebe nodded.

"Good. Well, I better get to my locker and grab my biology book before I'm late to class, or Mr. Patriano will threaten to turn me into one of those specimens in his dissection lab." Woody was back to being the class clown. He gave a goofy little wave and disappeared around the corner.

Phoebe tried to steady her hand as she dialed the combination to her lock. Griffin Neill. She'd been trying so hard to forget him, to get over the hurt she felt at the mere mention of his name. But if the Websters did get tickets to his show, there was a good chance Woody would be seeing Griffin, talking to him about old times . . . Rose Hill . . . maybe even Phoebe, herself. And what if he did talk about her? Could Griffin ever become part of her life again?

Phoebe thought back to the first time they'd met at an audition for the Follies, the annual variety show Woody had directed. Griffin had asked her to help him rehearse a song, and when she joined in with him their voices had blended so sweetly, so perfectly, it was as if they'd been singing together all their lives. And then there was their nightime walk down to the old railroad tracks. And their first kiss. . . .

No! Phoebe thought furiously. You've got to stop doing this to yourself. Griffin had sure made it clear he didn't want to see her again. Whatever his reasons, Phoebe couldn't let herself go around dreaming about him all the time. If he didn't need her, she was just going to put him out of her mind — whether Woody saw him in New York or not.

She gathered up the books she needed for her afternoon classes, slammed her locker shut, and strode down the hall.

Chapter
5

"Sasha dear, it's supposed to rain tonight, so please drive carefully." Mrs. Jenkins put the keys to her white VW Rabbit into her daughter's outstretched palm. "We ought to be home from this party around eleven-thirty. You'll make sure to be back before then, won't you?"

Sasha nodded. She felt a twinge of guilt for not telling her parents the truth about where she was going. But as understanding as they were, she knew they wouldn't be overjoyed at the idea of her driving off to another town to meet a boy she hardly knew. She'd told them all the kids would probably be hanging out at the sub shop, which was true, but she'd neglected to add she didn't plan on being there with them.

"Okay then, see you later," her father said, pulling on his coat. "Have a good time, darling."

Sasha looked down at the living room rug, tracing the coiled braids with her big toe.

"Thanks. You, too," she replied, unable to meet her parents' eyes.

When the door shut behind them, she breathed a sigh of relief. She felt so bad about fooling them like this, but she didn't see that she had any other choice. Besides, there was something so romantic about this secret rendezvous. Not even Phoebe or Chris knew about her date.

She felt a tiny shiver of excitement as she ran upstairs to her room to get ready. She slipped on the lavender dress Henry had designed for her, then studied her reflection in the mirror. The dress fell softly around her small, slender body, and the color complemented her pale skin. She pulled on the patterned stockings she'd bought to go with the dress and a pair of gray suede boots that folded over at the ankle.

Sasha almost never wore makeup, preferring a natural look. But this was a special occasion, so she whisked a light touch of pale pink blush across her high cheekbones. As a final touch, she put on a pair of handworked silver earrings and brushed her long black hair so it flowed down her back.

Glancing in the mirror one last time, she picked up her purse and headed back downstairs. It was only after she had gotten her hooded wool cape from the front closet that she paused, her stomach fluttering with nervous anticipation. She remembered the first time she'd had one of her short stories published in the school paper. The day it had come out felt like this — happy, scared, and out-of-breath, all at once — a sensation of being on the brink of a wonderful new adventure.

Sasha opened her tooled leather purse and took out Wesley's letter. Just seeing the letters of her name traced in his neat script made her heart beat even faster. She pulled on her mittens and hat, checked once more to make sure she had the car keys, and stepped out into the foggy night air.

"Phoebe, phone call!" her mother yelled from downstairs.

Phoebe stuck her head out of the bedroom door. "Okay, Mom," she shouted back, hurrying into the den to pick up the upstairs extension. "Hello?" she said into the receiver. She heard her mother hang up.

"Pheeb? Hi, it's me, Woody."

"Oh, hi, Woody. How're you?" Phoebe settled into the reclining chair next to the window. In the beam of the street lamp, she could see that a light rain had begun to fall.

"I've been trying to get you all day," Woody said. "Where have you been?"

"I was over at Jeannie Seidman's house practicing the new piece we're doing in chorus."

"Oh. Well listen, Phoebe." Woody's words came out in an excited rush. "My mom got the tickets today. We *are* going to see Griffin's show."

"You are?!" For one unrestrained moment, Phoebe's exuberant tone of voice matched his. "I mean, oh, that's nice," she said checking herself quickly, reining in her enthusiasm.

There was an awkward silence. Finally Woody spoke up. "Do you still want me to go backstage and try to find him?"

Phoebe bit her lip. "I guess," she replied.

She heard Woody let out a long breath. "Hey, Phoeberooni, I'm really sorry," he said gently, using his special nickname for her. "I'm beginning to think I was a dummy to bring this whole thing up in the first place. Maybe you really don't want to know about him."

A single tear stung Phoebe's cheek. It was no use pretending, with Woody, or herself, either. "Woody, I do want to know about him. But I'm afraid. He hurt me so badly. I don't want to go through that kind of pain again. I can't and I won't." Phoebe gathered her strength as she spoke. "But you — well, I know he'll be glad to see you. He always liked you a lot. You should definitely go backstage."

"Yeah, I'll do that," Woody said softly. "And Pheeb? One more thing?"

"Uh-huh?"

"It's about my car."

"What about it?" Phoebe didn't know whether to be unhappy or relieved to be off the subject of Griffin.

"It has to be looked after while I'm gone. In this cold weather it needs someone to start it every day — you know, give it some exercise."

"You mean you want to leave your most prized possession in my hot little hands while you're away?"

"Well somebody's got to take care of the Webstermobile. Might as well be good old Phoeberooni. Maybe you'll even have some fun with it — you know, driving around. It's a great car."

"Well, okay, sure, Woody," Phoebe agreed.

"Great. Then it's a deal. We're leaving the day

after Ted's party, so I'll make sure you get the keys before then. See you at the sub shop later?"

"Maybe," replied Phoebe. "Right now, I have to see how much work I get done on this composition for Pearson's class. I might go over there later."

"Good. And, Phoebe — I'm sorry if I upset you."

"No problem, Woody. I'm fine. Really. I mean, you were right to think I'd want to know about this. And listen, if you do get to see Griffin, tell him . . . tell him I send my best."

Phoebe said good-bye and put the receiver back in its cradle. For a long time she sat without moving, staring out into the foggy, wet night.

Sasha pulled the Rabbit into the lot behind the rustic neighborhood restaurant. She climbed out of the car and took a few steps. The fine, misty rain caressed her face and the blanket of thick, dark clouds above added to the glorious mystery of the evening. She breathed deeply, closing her eyes for a moment to compose herself.

"Sasha?" a male voice behind her whispered.

Sasha turned. Wesley was standing next to her: tall, broad-shouldered, and every bit as handsome as she remembered. She looked into his deep-set green eyes, his gaze holding hers. No words were spoken.

Slowly, hesitantly, Wesley reached out and put his arms around her. Sasha felt she was melting and burning at the same time. Her head swam as she wound her arms around the small of his back and tipped her mouth up toward his.

42

Gently, Wesley lowered his lips to hers. He kissed her sweetly, softly, then more insistently as Sasha feverishly responded to his embrace.

Finally they drew their lips apart. "Sasha, you got my message. You're here." Wesley laid a gloved hand on her flushed cheek.

"I'm so glad you got in touch with me," Sasha whispered breathlessly. "I was afraid we might never see each other again." She covered his hand with hers.

"I hope you don't feel too uncomfortable about meeting me this way, but I didn't know how else to find you." Wesley held her in his gaze.

"Wesley, this is perfect." Sasha spoke his name to him for the first time. "I couldn't imagine anything more romantic."

Wesley smiled, his eyes crinkling at the corners. "The food's good here, too."

"Great! I was so excited all day I hardly ate a thing." Sasha's words came out easily and naturally. What was it about this boy that made her feel so relaxed and yet so excited, so alive?

Wesley kissed her cheek, his lips warm in the rainy winter air, and they headed for the restaurant door.

Inside it was warm and cozy, with candles on each table and a crackling fire in the massive stone fireplace. "It's lovely," Sasha said, breathing in the delicious aromas that filled the simple, comfortable room. She slipped her cape off. Wesley took it from her and hung it on the old-fashioned coat tree near the door. Then he unbuttoned his heavy overcoat. As he removed it, Sasha's eyes opened wide, and she felt her jaw drop in shock. It was all she could do to keep from gasping out loud. Wesley was dressed from head to toe in a military uniform.

Numb, Sasha followed him to a table in a secluded corner of the restaurant. He pulled her chair out for her, and she sat down stiffly, like a wind-up doll going through automatic motions. "Your — your uniform," she finally managed to get out.

"I'm a cadet," Wesley explained, a note of pride in his voice. "I go to a military academy."

Sasha felt herself grow weak. She clutched at the edge of the table. Wesley reached out and covered her hand with his. "Is anything wrong?" he asked, his deep voice filled with concern.

Sasha looked up and met his gaze again. She felt the panic draining from her body, and as his green eyes held hers, she turned her palm up to take his hand. Suddenly she knew she didn't care if he went to military school or anywhere else. She had never felt so strongly about a boy before.

"No, nothing's wrong," she replied, her voice sounding more certain now. "It's just all so strange — I mean, I don't know anything about you, but. . . ."

". . . But it feels so right, somehow," Wesley finished, a smile illuminating his face.

Sasha nodded. It was true. She felt some kind of irresistible attraction to this soft-spoken, handsome boy. And no uniform could change that. "Did you come all the way up from Charlottesville just to see me?" she asked.

Wesley's brow creased in puzzlement. "Charlottesville? Oh, I see." He laughed. "You thought

I lived down there. Well, my parents do. I was visiting them when we met. But I live at school — Leesburg Academy, between here and Rose Hill. That's why I was so surprised when you told me where you came from. It was too perfect."

But Sasha's emotions took another nose dive and alarm was racing through her again. Leesburg? That was Kennedy's biggest rival. Only a few months before a fight had broken out at a football game between the two schools. Afterward, the Kennedy guys had poured paint all over the academy's statue of Robert E. Lee.

Since then it had been all-out war between Kennedy and Leesburg. She knew that many of her friends automatically thought of any Leesburg boy as an enemy — and here she was having dinner with one of them. What would her friends think? But that was a minor problem compared with what her parents would think. They'd made their disenchantment with anything having to do with the military quite clear.

Whatever her parents might think, they'd also drummed into Sasha the importance of making her own decisions, forming her own opinions, and trusting her instincts. And right now, looking into Wesley's clear green eyes, she knew they could share something that went way beyond whether or not he was a cadet. Besides, Sasha prided herself on being broad-minded and receptive toward new ideas. Didn't that mean she should at least give him a chance to express his point of view?

Sasha took a deep breath. "Wesley, tell me

why you're going to Leesburg." She prepared herself to listen openly to his response.

"Well, here goes, Sasha. I've always wanted to be a pilot; a Navy pilot." Sasha nodded as Wesley continued. "My father's a commander in the service — head of one of the Navy's top squads, so I've been around planes since I was old enough to walk. I don't think I've ever doubted for a moment what I wanted to do with my life." Wesley's tone was earnest and certain. "As for Leesburg, it's the best, and I want to be the best."

Sasha couldn't help admiring Wesley's determination and drive. She sure didn't have her life planned out the way he did. In fact, she felt very strongly about exploring a wide variety of possibilities before deciding to devote her life to any one thing. But, she agreed with him on one thing: Whatever she ultimately chose, she wanted to be the best at it.

"Leesburg is my stepping stone to Annapolis," Wesley added. "And then Pensacola. That's where most of the best flyers get their training."

Sasha listened quietly. Wesley's whole life was the military. He had been born into it, his peers at school were part of it, and he was determined to make it his future, as well. What would he think when she told him about her background? After hearing just this little bit about him, she knew nothing could be further from his experience. Sasha's delicate face clouded over with worry.

"Sasha?" Wesley was responding to her expression with a puzzled look of his own. "Did I say something wrong?"

46

Sasha was on the verge of plunging into an explanation, when a heavy-set woman, her dark hair shot through with streaks of gray, approached their table, menus in hand. Sasha felt as if, having been asked an impossibly hard question in one of her classes at school, she was barely saved by the bell.

"I didn't see the young couple all the way back here," the woman said, a faint trace of an Italian accent in her voice. "But I guess you wanted a little privacy, no?"

Wesley smiled at the waitress, and then, shyly at Sasha. Sasha felt some of her concern about him begin to melt away again. He hardly seemed to be the kind of overbearing person she had always associated with the military. Sasha felt a sharp sting of guilt as she realized that, perhaps, she had been harboring a prejudice she hadn't even been aware of. Maybe this new friendship would turn into a learning experience for both her and Wesley.

The waitress put a menu down in front of each of them. "In addition to what's listed, we also have a nice pasta and bean soup, a rigatoni dish with chicken and broccoli, and *calamare* in garlic sauce."

"Cala-what?" asked Sasha.

"*Calamare*. Squid," the waitress explained. "Now I'll just leave you two alone, and you let me know when you're ready to order."

"Squid!" Wesley made a face.

"I don't know, I think it sounds interesting," Sasha returned. "In fact, I think I might try it. I don't usually eat a lot of meat or seafood, but since tonight is kind of an adventure, I figure I ought to be daring and order something adventurous!"

Wesley laughed. "Maybe you're right," he said, looking through the menu. "But I think I'll stick to chicken parmegiana with a nice big side order of spaghetti."

After they had ordered, Wesley's face grew serious again. "Sasha, you were about to tell me something before the waitress came over. What was it?"

Sasha sighed. "I don't know, Wesley. Maybe it's not as big a deal as I think."

"What's not?"

Sasha toyed with a bit of hard wax that had dripped from the slender red candle in the center of the table. "I'm not really sure how to explain this," she began, "but I have to tell you something about me and my family. Wesley, while your father was teaching you about fighter planes, I was going to demonstrations and marches with my parents."

"Demonstrations? About what?" Wesley looked confused.

"Anti-nuclear stuff, mostly," Sasha explained. "And protest rallies against parts of the government's foreign policy."

Wesley was silent for a moment, his expression stern. "You know, Sasha, our government might not be right one-hundred percent of the time, but it's the best one in the world, and it's our duty as good citizens to stand behind our leaders no matter what." His words rang with conviction.

"Even when they're wrong?" Sasha shook her

head vehemently. "No, I think it's our duty to make our government better, and that doesn't happen by blindly agreeing with everything it does."

"I don't mean that people should just blindly agree." Politely but firmly, Wesley rose to the challenge. "That's what elections are for. The way to change is through electing new people to office, not through demonstrating and trying to cause trouble."

"It's not a matter of trying to cause trouble." Sasha's tone grew heated, but more from excitement than antagonism. Her opinions were definitely at odds with Wesley's, yet she found she was enjoying the discussion. It sure beat her last date with Eddie James, a boy in her math class. All they could think of to talk about was the previous night's homework assignment.

"Elected officials are human, too," Sasha went on, "and sometimes they need a little coaxing. Or a lot."

She waited for an argument. Instead Wesley laughed. "I can't say I agree with you, but you sure make a good case. It's fun arguing with someone with some brains for a change."

Sasha felt positively exhilarated. "You're not going to believe this, but I was just thinking the exact same thing about you."

Their eyes met again. "So we agree to disagree?" Wesley asked softly.

"Something like that," Sasha replied. Cadet or not, she knew she had fallen in love with Wesley Lewis.

Chapter
6

As the evening progressed Sasha discovered she and Wesley actually had more in common than she had thought at first. For starters, they both loved going to the beach in the wintertime.

"Who needs it in the summer — I mean, you get so hot and sweaty that all you want to do is run for the nearest patch of shade and flop down," Wesley said. "Give me the ocean when it's rough and the weather's all raw. You can really feel alone with nature."

"Yeah, I remember this one winter day when my parents and I drove down to Virginia Beach. It was all kind of foggy and windy. We were so bundled up. We walked for miles and miles. . . ." Sasha could almost feel the salt air stinging her nostrils. ". . . I kept pretending I was the heroine of some spooky old English movie on the moors. I love old movies."

"You do?" Wesley's face lit up. "You know,

I've seen every movie Humphrey Bogart ever made."

"You're a Bogey fan, too? Wow!" Sasha reached across the table and grabbed Wesley's hand excitedly. "Did you know *Casablanca* was just on *The Late, Late Show* last month?"

"Are you kidding? I wouldn't have missed it for anything. I was down visiting my parents that weekend. Fourth time I've seen it!"

"My fifth," said Sasha, feeling a bit smug. "I've got you beat there!"

Wesley grinned. "I guess that makes you the expert, huh? So what's your opinion — should he have left Ingrid Bergman at the end or not?"

"Well, I think it *was* kind of rotten of him to assume he could make all the decisions for both of them."

"You do? Not me. I think he was absolutely right," Wesley said emphatically.

"No way!!" Sasha knew her voice was rising. She took a breath and gave a little shrug. "Agree to disagree, right?"

Wesley laughed. "You got it!"

Sasha shifted to a more neutral topic, telling Wesley all about her work on the newspaper and her writing. Did she want to make a career out of it? he wanted to know. She explained she wasn't ready to make any hard-and-fast decisions yet, but writing was one of the most important things in her life at this point.

Over the main course, Wesley told Sasha about all the different places he'd lived while he was growing up. Sasha sat spellbound. She knew how hard it must have been to have to pick up and move every time his father got stationed in a new place, to make new friends, and get used to a new home. But she was also a little bit envious of Wesley, he had had the opportunity to see exotic things all over the world. He could speak French, some German, and even a few words of Japanese. And he described everywhere he'd been in such rich detail that Sasha almost felt as if she were taking a trip around the globe with him.

The food at the restaurant was delicious, and Wesley even summoned up the courage to taste a bite of squid, after much prodding from Sasha.

"Look, Wesley, someone who's traveled as much as you have must have tried a lot weirder food than this," she coaxed.

"Well, see, we usually lived on an Air Force base wherever we were," he explained. "They all had a PX, that's like a supermarket for the service families, that stocked American products. Once in a while, we did eat the local food. But, I'll bet that for the most part I ate the same kinds of meals you did every night."

Sasha had to laugh as she thought about her mother's carrot-zucchini health loaf and her father's special meatless chili. "I doubt it, Wesley. I seriously doubt it."

All in all, Sasha couldn't have imagined a better evening. Nevertheless, in the back of her mind there remained the nagging question of how her parents and her friends would react to Wesley. And the more she found herself entranced by this boy, so different from herself, the larger the differences between them seemed to loom.

She finally broached the subject over a dessert of chocolate cake a la mode. "Wesley, I've told you what my parents are like, and I guess I've described them as pretty open, accepting people. But there's one thing they're totally not accepting about." She bit her lip.

"What's that?" Wesley arched an eyebrow.

"The military. Cadets and all that. . . ." Sasha paused. "People like you." Her voice wavered. "Wesley, what are we going to do?"

Wesley put down his fork, looking puzzled. "Sasha, I've really had a terrific time this evening, and I — I mean I'd really like to see you again. That is, if you want to."

Sasha nodded. "Oh, I do want to — I have ever since I turned around and saw you standing behind me at Monticello," she admitted.

"I felt the same way." Wesley reached out and touched Sasha's cheek. "So, I guess your parents will have to meet me and try to see me as a person, not as a part of some military machine they think they don't like."

"Some military machine they know they don't like," corrected Sasha.

"Whatever. I don't think we ought to let that stand in our way."

Sasha pushed away her half-finished piece of cake. As delicious as it was, she didn't think she could eat another bite. "Well, okay, somehow I'm going to work up the nerve to tell my parents about you and get you invited over for dinner." Sasha played with her ring, nervously twirling the slender silver band around and around her finger. "But, Wesley, there's something else, too. What about this whole dumb rivalry between Kennedy and Leesburg?"

Wesley's strong, handsome face darkened. "Well, I've got to say that pouring paint all over our statue was a pretty sleazy thing to do."

Now Sasha was starting to feel defensive. "Hey, you guys didn't exactly act like officers and gentlemen on the football field that day. Maybe you deserved what you got."

"Whoah! You think that was our fault?" Wesley's voice rose. Then he inhaled deeply. "Wait a minute." He made a time-out motion with his hands. "What's more important — a stupid feud between our two schools or us?"

Sasha calmed herself. She looked into his eyes.

"Us," she replied. "But I can't guarantee that my friends are going to feel the same way. Are yours?"

Now it was Wesley's turn to look grim. "I don't know."

"Of course, we don't exactly have to advertise where we go to school," Sasha suggested. "At least not until we've all gotten to know one another better."

A look of uncertainty passed across Wesley's face. "Sasha, maybe it's not such a good idea to start out telling people lies," he said in his soft southern accent. "Maybe this is a cliché, but I've always really believed in that old saying: 'Honesty is the best policy.'"

"But they wouldn't be lies," Sasha said. "We'd just wait awhile before telling them the truth." She wished her words didn't sound so hollow.

She'd been skirting the truth a lot recently, with her parents and with her friends, too. And she didn't feel good about it. But she was determined not to let anything get in between her and Wesley before they'd barely had a chance to get to know each other.

"Sasha, even if I agreed with you, there's one big problem with your idea." Wesley's brow was still furrowed.

"There is?" Sasha felt her heart sink. Wesley just had to be accepted by the people who meant the most to her.

Wesley fidgeted with a metal button on his regulation jacket. "Look, one of the rules of my school is that you have to wear your uniform all the time. Except vacations."

Sasha felt a wave of despair break over her. "Weekends, too?"

"Weekends, too," he confirmed.

"Couldn't you break the rules? Just once?"

The look on Wesley's face was all the answer Sasha needed. "I was afraid of that," she said. "And maybe it was wrong of me to suggest it, but Wesley, I think the answer to our problem is for my parents and friends to find out who you are before they find out *what* you are. I mean, after they've already decided they like you it'll be a lot easier for them to accept where you go to school, what you want to do, and all that."

"Sasha, try to understand. What I want is part of who I am. I'm beginning to feel as if I'm supposed to be ashamed of the whole thing." Sasha detected a note of anger creeping back into Wesley's voice.

"I'm sorry," she relented. "I didn't mean to get you so upset. And, of course, obviously, I don't mean that you should be ashamed of yourself. But think of it this way." She had to try to explain how she felt once more. "What do you think would happen if you went back to school and told your friends that you'd had this date with a girl from Kennedy?"

Wesley paused a moment to consider Sasha's question. "I guess I'd have to take a lot of flack. They'd probably ask me why I couldn't find a girl from somewhere else."

"And if they met me before you told them where I went to school . . . ?" Sasha reached across the table and took Wesley's hand.

He responded to her touch, closing his fingers around hers and studying her face. "Well, obviously, if they had any sense at all, they'd think you were terrific. Okay, Sasha, you win! I know when I've had it." Beneath his teasing was a genuine warmth and tenderness. "Once, just once, I'll do it. I'll sneak out in civilian clothes to meet your friends. But only because it's you."

"Yippee. Oh, Wesley, I knew you'd do it!" Sasha leaned across the table and gave him a noisy kiss. "I promise, you won't be sorry. Now, there's a big party next Saturday . . . a good friend of mine is giving it. . . ."

"So, a week from tonight — the big night!" Phoebe watched as Peter Lacey slapped Ted on the back, then slid into the orange plastic booth where she and some of the gang were sitting at the back of the sub shop.

"Big's the right word for it after your birdbrain comments on the radio the other day," Ted replied. But the good-natured smile never left his face.

"Guilty, as charged," Peter admitted, pulling his dark sunglasses over his eyes and pretending to hide behind the collar of his Hawaiian-print shirt. "I'm so psyched for this party that I guess I just got a little carried away."

"Mr. Cool, carried away?" Phoebe teased. "Oh, no!" After a hard couple of hours working on her essay, she was enjoying the chance to relax with her friends. "I thought Peter Lacey was always the mellowest man around."

"Well, with Lisa coming home on vacation the same night as Ted's big bash. . . ." Peter let his sentence trail off.

"Oh, that's right." Phoebe nodded. Peter's girl friend, Lisa Chang, who had left for Colorado several months earlier to train with one of the country's top Olympic skating coaches, was flying back to Rose Hill. "How's she doing out there, anyway?"

"Pretty well, I think. Sometimes it's hard to tell, though. She works so hard that by the end of the day when I get to talk to her, she's so beat she can't wait to get right into bed. But she says it's worth it, that she's learning things there she never could have back here in a million years."

"Wow, that is so interesting!" Chris echoed Phoebe's own sentiments, pausing to take a bite out of the salami-and-cheese hero she was splitting with Ted. "Just think how fabulous it'll be if she gets in the next Olympics!"

"She'd better make it," Peter remarked. " 'Cause I can already picture myself at her side when the press beats a path to her door. 'Tell us, Ms. Chang, what is the secret to your perserverance and success?' " Peter grabbed a salt shaker and held it up to his mouth like a microphone.

"Then she'll say, 'I owe a lot of it to the young man at my left, who ran up the world's biggest phone bill to keep encouraging me.' " He imitated his girl friend's soft, high-pitched voice.

"Lacey, get lost!" Ted exclaimed playfully.

"Well, maybe I will go get myself a sandwich. Anyone want anything?" Peter offered.

"A ravishing young princess?" Woody suggested. Peter flashed him a wry look and headed for the counter at the other side of the crowded room.

"Boy, is he ever in love," Ted commented after Peter had left the table. "It's funny. Until he met Lisa I don't think Lacey ever looked at all the hundreds of girls who kept throwing themselves at him. Too busy with his beloved radio station."

"Speaking of being in love," Chris whispered to Phoebe, "where's Sasha tonight?"

"I don't know," Phoebe whispered back. "To tell you the truth, I've been kind of worried about her lately — you know, after she told us about her mystery boy." Phoebe knew Sasha had always been highly emotional, but since that day at Monticello her moods had been even more extreme than usual.

"Hey, you two, what secrets are you keeping from us over there?" Woody blew the wrapper from his straw at them.

"Oh, we were just wondering where Sasha was," answered Phoebe. "That's all."

Woody shrugged. "On Friday I asked her if she was going to come out with us, and she said she had other plans." He pulled on one of his red suspenders. "Now, I ask you, what could possibly be more important than us?"

The waitress brought the check to the table, and Wesley took it. Sasha reached into her leather bag and brought out her wallet. "What did it come to?" she asked.

A look of astonishment flitted across Wesley's chiseled features. "Excuse me?"

Then Sasha saw him catch sight of her wallet. "Oh, I see. Look, it's nice of you to offer, but it's my treat," he said, holding the check out of her reach.

"Wesley, I don't believe the boy should always pay for the girl. There's something totally unfair about that arrangement." Sasha pushed a few bills across the table.

Wesley shoved them back. "But I *want* to take you out. It's my way of saying thank you for the best evening I've had in ages."

"You're sweet." Sasha smiled. "But I really wouldn't feel comfortable about it. Besides, I should be the one thanking you. I mean, I could've ended up with Eddie James, talking about our boring algebra homework."

"Eddie James?"

"Oh, he's just this guy from my math class. Perfectly nice, but kind of on the dull side." Sasha laughed softly. "It's really not important."

"But he let you pay for half your date?" Wesley asked.

Sasha shook her head. "Actually, I had to go through the same thing with him that I'm going through with you. Guys can be so stubborn."

"So can girls." Wesley quickly motioned to the waitress and, before Sasha knew what was happening, he paid the bill by himself.

"Look, let's make a deal," Sasha finally conceded. "You treated me this time, so next time I'll treat you. Okay?"

Wesley looked skeptical. "That's not the way I was brought up," he protested.

"Sorry, that's the deal. If there's going to be a next time, it's going to be on me. And I'll tell you something, mister. You just better be prepared to enjoy getting taken out, too!"

"Well, in that case, it looks like I don't have much of a choice," Wesley said lightly. "Because I absolutely intend that there'll be a next time." He got up, came around to her side of the table, and offered her his hand. As she stood, he slipped his arm around her slender waist and drew her close to him. Sasha could feel the electricity racing between their bodies.

"By the way, I haven't told you how beautiful you look tonight." His breath was warm against her face. "That dress seems as if it was made especially for you."

"It was." As they got their coats, Sasha told him how Henry had designed the outfit for her. "He's started a business with his girl friend, Janie. You'll meet them at Ted's party." As soon as Sasha had slipped into her cape, she moved back next to Wesley and wound her arm around him, feeling the heavy wool of his coat.

Together they stepped out into the brisk night. The rain had stopped, and a tiny sliver of moon was peeking out from behind the clouds. "Did you drive here?" Sasha asked, staying close to his side and breathing in the fresh air.

"Uh-uh. A few of the guys were driving into D.C. for the evening, and I asked them to drop me off. I was kind of hoping you might be able to give me a ride back to campus."

"And I was kind of hoping you might need a lift," Sasha admitted softly. "I don't want the evening to end any sooner than it has to."

Wesley pushed up his coat sleeve and took a look at his watch. "I've got another three quarters of an hour before my eleven o'clock curfew. If you're interested, there's a spot I know about down the road from school that has a great view."

"You're on." Sasha led the way to her parents' car. "Just point me in the right direction."

She started the car, every nerve in her body aware of Wesley's presence next to her. She didn't have to actually touch him to feel the tingle of exhilaration he stirred in her, just being with him was like a constant caress.

It was clear Wesley felt the same way. As they stopped for a red light, they were immediately drawn toward each other for a lingering embrace. Sasha's thoughts spun wildly as she gave in to the softness of Wesley's lips. Only the honking from the car behind them kept her from being overpowered by the sweet sensations.

They drove for a few minutes in silence.

"There's a small road up ahead," Wesley finally said, his voice quiet, as if he didn't want to break the spell. "We turn right there."

They wound upward as Sasha followed the narrow road, which had a thick forest of pine trees on either side. As they pulled up over the crest of the hill, they approached a plateau of bare ground, behind which the earth dropped off sharply, plunging into the valley below. The lights of Rose Hill and Carolton twinkled beneath them and above, the sheerest veil of clouds created a rainbowlike ring of brilliant hues around the moon.

"Oh, Wesley, you were right!" Sasha pulled the car over to the side of the road and turned off the ignition. "It's beautiful here. And look! I think you can even see my house! See, four streets over from the lights of town hall," Sasha gestured with her hand. "I live right in the middle of that block! I can't believe I never knew about this place before!"

"Well, now that you do, maybe you'll have to come here more often . . . with me." Wesley cupped her face with his palm and tilted it up toward his. He gently traced the contours of her cheeks with the tips of his fingers, then her eyebrows and her lips. He planted a whisper-soft kiss on her forehead, stroking her long hair. Sasha let out an intoxicated sigh, as her mouth found his.

She was aware only of Wesley as his lips searched hers with a hungry tenderness. One kiss was sweeter, more passionate than the last.

They lost all sense of time, and suddenly, unexpectedly, eleven o'clock was only minutes away. They fought back the yearning for another embrace and pulled apart unwillingly.

"Sasha, I have to go," Wesley said breathlessly. "If I'm late, they'll take away my off-campus privileges."

"When can we see each other again?" Reluctantly, Sasha started the car, still tingling from Wesley's touch.

Wesley ran his hand through his short hair. "I'm only allowed to be away from school on Saturday night and Sunday, and my parents usually come up on Sundays." He pointed to a road on the left. "Here. The entrance is at the end of this road."

Sasha steered left. "So I guess Ted's party is the next time, huh?" She couldn't keep a note of disappointment out of her voice. She wasn't sure she could wait a whole week before she saw him again.

"I guess so. God, I wish there were some way it could be sooner." Wesley's tone echoed her sentiments. "But rules are rules. I'd like to call you, though, if it's okay."

Up ahead, wrought-iron gates loomed up out of the darkness. Sasha pressed down on the brake and put the car into park. "Maybe it's better if I call you," she hedged. "I mean, until I figure out some way to break this to my parents."

"Sasha, you'll just have to tell them outright." Wesley spoke softly. "I don't see that there's any other way."

"I know. But I need to get up my nerve . . . you've got to give me a little more time. . . ."

63

Wesley nodded, his features etched in the beam of light from the entranceway that flodded in through the car window. "How can I say no to you?"

He searched around in his coat pocket and pulled out a stubby pencil. "Do you have something to write on? I'll give you my number at the dorm."

Sasha found an old envelope in the glove compartment and watched as Wesley wrote down the numbers in his neat, round hand. "This is a hall phone," he explained, "so you'll have to ask for me. I'll give you my address, too. Since you like to write," he added.

"Great. And you can write to me at school again, if you want." Sasha found herself studying his face, trying to memorize it to carry her through the week ahead. "I guess you'd better go," she said with a great reluctance.

"Yeah, I'll be in hot water for sure, if I don't." Wesley drew her toward him pulling her close again. "Sasha I think I'm falling in love with you," he said huskily.

"Oh, Wesley, me, too. I think I'm in love with you, too."

They held each other for a moment longer. Finally, Wesley let himself out of the car. Sasha watched him sprint toward the gate, running as fast as his legs would carry him. Just before he disappeared inside, he turned around and blew her one last kiss.

Chapter
7

"Oh, Woody, look. There she is!" Phoebe grabbed Woody by the arm of his navy, down parka.

"Who? Where?" Woody looked around, trying to follow Phoebe's gaze.

"Over by the bike rack. Kimberly Barrie — that new girl Sasha and I were telling you about, remember?"

Woody's pulse sped up. Kimberly? Where? He whipped around to see a pretty girl with short brown hair about to sling her leg over her bicycle. She was wearing a bulky Icelandic wool sweater. He felt short of breath, but he made certain not to let on to Phoebe. "Oh, yeah, that's right." Woody formed his words with studied casualness. It would have been way too embarrassing to admit just how vividly he remembered that conversation about Kimberly Barrie. Considering she was someone he had never met, he had thought about her an awful lot.

"Come on, we've got to catch up with her before she takes off." Phoebe gave Woody a tug. "I'll introduce you."

But Woody's red hightop basketball shoes remained firmly rooted to the ground. It was one thing to daydream about Kimberly; it helped keep him from getting too sentimental about Phoebe. He knew he had to stop pretending that someday Phoebe would wake up and realize he was Mr. Right. If thinking about other girls would help, then that was what he would do. Besides, he did wonder when it was going to be his turn for a little romance.

But now that Kimberly was right there within sight, he felt awkward and shy. What if she didn't live up to his expectations? Or worse, what if he made a bad impression on her. It was easier just to dream.

"Woody? What's wrong?" Phoebe pulled on his arm again. "I thought you wanted to meet her."

Kimberly pushed away from the bike rack and began to coast across the parking lot. "Kim, wait!" Phoebe called out. She waved to attract the brown-haired girl's attention. Kimberly turned, spotted Phoebe, and waved back.

"Woody, you never cease to amaze me," Phoebe said, coaxing him forward. "Most of the time no one can figure out how to keep you quiet, and now all of a sudden you've decided to go all bashful and tongue-tied on me. What's so scary about meeting some girl you don't know?"

Woody took a hesitant step as Kimberly wheeled her bicycle toward them. "That's exactly it. She's a girl I don't know." He hoped that maybe he could joke off the problem.

"Well, then, maybe you should try pretending she's just one of the guys."

Woody gave her a dubious grin.

"No, I'm being perfectly serious," Phoebe insisted. "Don't think of her as a girl. Think of her as — well, a human being." Phoebe giggled. "I guess that sounds pretty dumb, doesn't it?"

"It sure does," Woody responded. Because as Kimberly got closer, he could see a pretty oval-shaped face and long, lean legs in a pair of tight fuchsia jogging pants. Sure, just one of the guys. He grew even more nervous.

"Hey, Phoebe, what's up?" Kimberly smiled easily.

"Just wanted to say hi," Phoebe said. ". . . See how everything's going."

Woody hung back, wishing he could somehow assume Phoebe's casual manner.

"I appreciate it, Phoebe. That's really nice of you," Kimberly was saying. "You know how it is — it takes some getting used to, being the new girl at school. Things are pretty good, though. Thanks."

"Glad to hear it," said Phoebe. "Oh, by the way, I'd like you to meet my friend Woody Webster. Woody, Kim Barrie."

"Hi," Kimberly said cheerfully. She extended her hand.

Woody felt Phoebe give him a little nudge forward. "Hi," he heard himself say. His voice was tight, and he hardly recognized it as his own. He took Kimberly's hand and shook it, feeling self-conscious as their fingers met.

"Woody. Right, I've heard about you," Kimberly remarked. "Aren't you really involved with the drama department or something?"

"I help direct some of the plays we put on here," Woody replied modestly. "Act in them sometimes, too." At least that was a subject he was comfortable with.

"Have you heard about the Kennedy High Follies?" Phoebe supplied. "The program of one-acts and music, and dance numbers, and stuff, that we do every fall?"

Kimberly nodded.

"Well, that's Woody's show!" Phoebe said proudly.

"You're kidding!" Kimberly sounded impressed. "I'm sorry I wasn't here to see it this year. I used to do some theater stuff at my old school — mostly the backstage end of things. I mean, not like actually getting up and performing."

"Really?" Woody began to loosen up in spite of himself. "That's good to know, because my stage manager for the Follies is graduating this spring. I'll be looking for someone to help me out next year." He looked into Kimberly's big blue eyes for the first time. "Have you ever stage-managed before?"

"I was assistant stage manager once, for a production we did of *Cyrano de Bergerac*. But most of what I did in drama was to help with the costumes and build sets," Kimberly explained. "Plus, I did all the cooking for the cast parties. I think that's probably why they put up with me clunking around and getting in everyone's way during all those plays. I'm not such a great stage-hand, but I'm a pretty good chef." She laughed. "That's really what I'm interested in."

"Yeah? Well, I'm kind of interested in food, too. On the eating end, that is." Woody gave himself a mental pat on the back for managing to pull off a joke. The conversation was going more easily than he had imagined. Kimberly acted so relaxed and natural it was hard to stay tied up in knots with her for too long.

Kimberly laughed. "I'll keep that in mind the next time I need volunteers to sample my latest experiments."

"Count me in, too," Phoebe said. "Except if it's something irresistibly fattening. I'd say Woody can handle that better than I can. The lucky stiff." She nodded at his tall, thin frame.

"Speaking of cooking, I've got to get home now and help my mom with some catering work, but maybe we can get together after school some day, Phoebe. And, Woody, it's really nice to meet you. Maybe I'll see you soon, at Ted Mason's party?"

"Definitely. See you there." Woody grinned. He had managed to survive the conversation, and he hadn't even done that badly!

"So?" Phoebe asked, after Kimberly had driven away.

"So, it wasn't that bad. I guess she wasn't exactly the way I'd pictured her, but. . . ."

"But what?" Woody could feel Phoebe studying him.

"But . . . well, she's nice," Woody finished. He nodded, more to himself than to Phoebe. "Yes. In fact, she's really nice."

Sasha gazed at a jet as it streaked through the sky overhead, leaving a thin white trail behind it. A week ago she never would have given it a second glance, but now she could almost imagine Wesley sitting in the cockpit, the world beneath him, maneuvering the huge silver bird with grace and power.

She'd received a letter from him at the newspaper office that afternoon, describing a flying lesson he'd taken earlier in the week: the feeling of triumph as he defied gravity, the speed and sleekness of his craft as he whistled through the clouds. She could picture his strong hands at the controls, his face taut with determination.

"Sasha!" Next to her, Phoebe's voice cut into her thoughts. "Yoo hoo, anybody home?" Sasha felt a tug on her dark braid. "Where are you today?"

Sasha came down to earth with a thud. "Oh, I was watching that plane," she explained to Phoebe and Chris, as the three friends walked home together after school.

"What plane?" asked Chris. "Sash, are you feeling okay today?"

"It was just some plane," Sasha mumbled. "Up

in the air. . . ." She made a vague gesture with her hand.

"You know, Chris. Like, up in the air: It's a bird, it's a plane . . ." said Phoebe, ". . . it's spacey Sash!" She gave Sasha an affectionate poke.

Chris remained somber. "No, really, Sasha. Remember us? We're your friends. We're called Phoebe and Chris. You can talk to us." She looked Sasha straight in the eye. "Is it that boy you told us about? You're not still dreaming about him turning up out of nowhere, are you?"

Sasha had to make a quick decision. There was something exhilarating about the secrecy of her new relationship with Wesley, something so romantic about their concealed meeting, the letter they'd exchanged, their tender, though too brief, phone calls. Sasha behind the locked door of her parents' study, Wesley in his bathrobe and slippers in the hall of his dormitory.

She did want her friends to know about Wesley, to meet him, and to like him. But she'd been imagining a really dramatic introduction: Wesley showing up on the doorstep of Ted's house, the handsome mystery guest, and she, Sasha, coming over to take his arm and welcome him to her circle of friends. It was the kind of introduction that seemed in keeping with the way they'd met.

Now Chris was asking about him directly. If she told her friends about Wesley now, it would take some of the drama out of her plan, but on the other hand, she didn't want to lie. She'd hidden enough already. And Wesley was right. Starting a relationship with lies and half truths was not the way to go. She was certain he would want her to tell her friends about their date.

"Well, are you, Sasha? Are you still thinking about him?" Phoebe asked gently.

Sasha stopped walking and shifted her books to her other arms. "Yeah, I am," she admitted. "But listen, you guys, it's not the way you think." She couldn't stop the grin from spreading over her face. Boy, were Chris and Phoebe in for a surprise. "I do know who he is. And we went out on a date last week."

"You did!" Phoebe squealed, grabbing her arm, and jumping up and down. "Sasha, you're kidding. How did that happen? How'd you ever find him?"

"Actually, he found me." Sasha turned to face Phoebe and Chris. "See, when I saw him at Monticello, I happened to mention that I wrote for the Kennedy High newspaper. So he wrote me a note there and asked me if I would have dinner with him."

"Where?" Chris asked. "What's he like? I can't believe this."

"Believe it, Chris. He's the best, the absolute best," Sasha exuded. "We went to this incredibly romantic little Italian restaurant in Carolton." She remembered how Wesley had looked that night sitting across the table from her, his face glowing in the candlelight. "It was so perfect."

"And then?" Phoebe demanded.

"Well, there's this beautiful view on the top of a hill. Wesley showed it to me."

"Wesley. Kind of a distinguished-sounding name, don't you think, Chris? So this guy, Wesley, took you to a place with a great view," Phoebe said.

"Only I guess we didn't concentrate all that hard on the scenery," Sasha admitted, her cheeks growing pink.

"Uh-oh," Phoebe intoned. "Sounds serious to me. What do you think, Chris?"

"I think I finally understand why Ms. Jenkins here has been such a space case this week. This is *too* incredible. Sash, why didn't you tell us before?"

Sasha shrugged. "I sort of wanted to surprise you by introducing you to him at Ted's on Saturday." Then a new thought occurred to her. "You don't think Ted'll mind if I bring him, do you?"

Sasha noticed a worried frown flit across Chris's all-American features, but she made an effort to brush it away. "I must admit that I don't want the party to get too big, but the people I'm nervous about are the ones who might get out of control. I'm sure Wesley's not in that category."

Sasha shook her head vigorously. "No, he's a real gentleman."

"Well, then, I can't wait to meet him." Chris's face relaxed.

"Me, too!" Phoebe's voice was filled with excitement. "Sash, it's so neat that you two found each other again! It almost seems like it was supposed to happen, like someone's watching over you. I know that sounds kind of weird, but. . . ."

"I know," Sasha agreed dreamily. Maybe her cosmic universe idea wasn't so off base after all.

73

"So what's he interested in?" Chris asked. "And how does he know about all these places near Rose Hill?" she continued.

"Yeah, how does he?" Phoebe echoed.

"Hey, hey." Sasha put her hand up in a gesture of mock surrender. "I'll tell you whatever you want to know, but one thing at a time, okay. He's about Ted's height, and he has short, dark hair, and the most amazing green eyes. He's gorgeous."

"Naturally," Phoebe giggled.

"And he's interested in airplanes. He wants to be a pilot."

"Wow, really?" Chris's big blue eyes got even bigger. Then, all of a sudden she slapped herself on the forehead. "Oh, now I get it. That's why you were getting so weird about that plane!"

Sasha nodded. She kept telling her friends details about her date until she came to the turnoff to her house. As she waved good-bye to Phoebe and Chris, she felt a rush of relief mixed with a pinch of guilt. They'd been so eager to hear all about her night out with Wesley that she'd managed to avoid explaining how he knew the area around Rose Hill.

Sasha would tell them soon enough — about Leesburg and how Wesley wanted to be a Navy pilot, and all. But first, the most important thing was for them to meet him. Once they discovered for themselves how terrific he was, everything else would fall into place.

Chapter
8

Sasha zipped up her favorite black jeans and pulled on a Mexican white cotton blouse edged with lace. She'd given Wesley explicit instructions how to get to Ted's, and he'd promised to be there, in civilian clothes. Still, she felt jittery, and her palms were moist. What if something went wrong? What if he got caught trying to sneak off campus out of uniform?

Sasha didn't think she could stand it if Wesley didn't show up. She'd waited a whole week for this evening, thinking about it almost nonstop. She sat down cross-legged on her bed, closed her eyes, and took a few deep breaths in a meditation exercise she'd learned one summer at camp.

When she felt calmer, she opened her eyes again and stood up, her toes sinking into the purple shag rug that covered the floor of her room. She finished getting dressed, brushed her long, wavy hair, and secured it on either side with matching tortoiseshell combs.

She took a look in the mirror. All set. Now all she had to do was try to keep her mind off Wesley until he showed up at the party. It wouldn't do any good to worry about him, and she knew it. Besides, even Phoebe had said it seemed as if someone was looking out for her and Wesley. She had to have faith in him. He would make it to Ted's without any trouble.

She pulled her boots on and went downstairs to wait for Woody, who was giving her a ride to the party. She had to stop feeling so nervous. Wesley had told her he knew about a back way off campus, so there shouldn't be any problems. And certainly, once he was at the party, everything would be fine. In fact, better than fine. With Wesley at her side, how could Sasha's evening be anything less than perfect?

Woody pulled the Volvo up in front of the Jenkins' red brick house and honked twice. He tapped his hightops in time with the tune blasting from the car radio. He was full of energy and couldn't wait to get to Ted's and let loose. He was also looking forward to getting to know Kimberly Barrie better. This time he vowed not to be tongue-tied.

He honked once more, and the Jenkins' front door flew open. "Bye, Mom, bye, Dad," he heard Sasha call. She came running down the front walk, her long hair flying out behind her.

"Hi, Woody." Sasha opened the passenger door and climbed in. "Ooh, good song." She bounced

76

up and down in her seat, humming along with the music, as Woody pulled away from the curb.

Woody joined in, doing the harmony.

Sasha's singing grew bolder, so did Woody's, until they were shouting above the music, laughing crazily. Sasha's spirits soared. There was always a feeling of electric exhilaration before a big party, and tonight the thought of seeing Wesley made the excitement almost unbearable.

"Get set for the bash of the year!" cried Woody, steering the Volvo around a turn. Another song came on the radio, an old Rolling Stones hit, and he turned the volume up a notch.

Sasha snapped her fingers to the beat. "I heard Ted went all out on munchies for tonight," she said above the sound of the radio. "Chris was telling me they were going to spend most of the day cooking up cocktail franks, making dips, and all kinds of stuff."

"That's good," Woody shouted back. "With all those guys from the football team there, he definitely won't have any trouble finding takers." Woody swung onto a wide street with spacious, manicured lawns visible in the glow of streetlights. A long line of cars flanked both sides of the road.

"Wow!" exclaimed Sasha. "It's a good thing the Masons have all that room. They're going to need it tonight. I just hope Chris isn't freaking out over all these people."

"Nah, I wouldn't worry. You know how much Chris has loosened up recently. I mean, even though she was on Ted's case to keep the numbers down when he was planning this, I bet when we get inside she'll be having as much fun as everyone else."

Sure enough, as soon as they went in, they saw Chris in the living room, dancing with one of Ted's teammates. Next to her was her sultry, dark haired step-sister, Brenda, and her boyfriend Brad Davidson, the student body president.

"Sash! Woody!" Chris waved wildly, but she didn't stop dancing for a second.

"See, I told you," Woody remarked to Sasha.

Sasha took her coat off and looked around the living room. All the furniture had been pushed out of the way, and the large room was filled with people. She spotted Janie and Henry in one corner, talking to Peter and Lisa. "Woody, I'm going to dump my coat in the other room and go see how Lisa's doing."

Sasha couldn't wait to talk to her old friend again and find out all about her skating and her new life in Colorado. She was so proud of all Lisa's hard work and courage and knew that one day soon it would all pay off.

"Okay," Woody replied. He was looking toward the refreshment table, where Kimberly Barrie was talking to another girl. Sasha caught his eye and gave him a knowing smile before he moved off.

There was a different crowd in the den, mostly Ted's football pals and some of their girl friends. As Sasha added her cape to a pile in the corner, she recognized some of the kids from other sports teams at Kennedy, as well. She stopped to talk to Emmie Stern, who worked on the newspaper with her and also swam freestyle on the girls' swim team. Then she started making her way back to the living room to find Lisa and wait for Wesley to arrive.

As she stepped out into the hall, she felt a heavy hand on her shoulder. "Hey, foxie lady." She whirled around to face John Marquette, a lewd grin on his lips.

Oh no, she thought, this is not what I had in mind for tonight. "Hello, John," she said icily.

"Come on, baby, loosen up," Marquette leered, grabbing Sasha around the waist and pulling her toward him. "I know you've been dying to give me another try." Sasha could smell beer on his breath, and his eyes were bloodshot.

"Get off of me, you big oaf!" she yelled, pushing him away with all her might, and twisting free of his grasp.

"Why fight me?" Marquette persisted. "Deep down you want me." He lunged for her again.

Sasha jumped aside, barely escaping his meaty hands. "Now, listen, John," her words seethed with anger and she could feel her face growing hot. "I want you to get something through your big, dense head once and for all. I'm sick of having you push me around because your cousin owns Superjock, I'm sick of the way you treat girls like things instead of people, I'm sick of all your clumsy passes, and I'm especially sick of your dumb, piggy-eyed face!" At that moment Sasha couldn't have cared if Marquette's cousin owned every inch of Rose Hill. She had had it.

Marquette's obscene smile crumpled into a sneer. "Is that right," he snarled fiercely. He pressed Sasha against the wall and put his huge, powerful arms on either side of her. "Well, before you know it, you're going to be very sorry you ever opened your mouth. Very sorry." His eyes flashed with fury as he kept her pinned in one spot. Then suddenly, he moved back abruptly, and disappeared into the den.

Sasha exhaled loudly. She wasn't afraid of Marquette's boastful threats, but still it was a relief to be free of him. She wished Wesley would hurry up and get to the party. Maybe then Marquette would leave her alone.

Sasha had found out all about Lisa's new life in Colorado, helped Peter choose a few good records to dance to, talked to Brenda Austin about their latest English assignment, danced once with Woody, and still no sign of Wesley. She'd helped Ted restock the refreshment table, sampled the party snacks herself, and spent some time out on the back porch talking to Phoebe.

She was beginning to think Wesley was never going to show up. "Sash, don't worry," Phoebe consoled her, adjusting the collar of her new jade-green knit jumper. "Try to enjoy yourself. He'll be here soon."

Sasha nodded, but she couldn't relax. Phoebe didn't know the risk Wesley was taking, sneaking off the grounds of Leesburg out of uniform. Right this instant, he might very well be standing shame-faced while some stern, tough commandant meted out a terrible punishment. Or perhaps Wesley had decided on his own not to come.

After all, he'd been loud and clear on how he felt about breaking rules.

Sasha reached for a handful of potato chips from a bowl on the coffee table at the far end of the living room. She popped a few into her mouth, but she barely tasted them. Wesley just had to show up. The evening would stink without him. Should she call his dormitory and try to find out where he was? No, if he was in trouble that might only make things worse.

Sasha glanced toward the door for what seemed like the thousandth time. What if all the attention he had paid to her was phony? Maybe he didn't actually like her enough to face an entire house full of kids from his rival school.

Stop! Sasha commanded herself. Quit feeling sorry for yourself! In fact, she thought, Wesley was the one who might be out on a limb at this very moment, all because she had insisted he leave his uniform behind, because she didn't want him to come to the party as the cadet he was so proud to be.

It was the first time she'd thought about it that way, and a blush of shame stained her cheeks as she realized how selfish she'd been. Suddenly she knew that she would never blame Wesley if he didn't show up tonight.

"Phoebe, it's my fault if Wesley doesn't make it," she said. It was as if a light of understanding had just flicked on in her head. She was ready to spill everything to her close friend. The time had come to stop hiding the truth from everybody. She owed Wesley that much.

"Sasha, what are you talking about?" Phoebe's forehead wrinkled in confusion. "How could you stop Wesley from coming when you're here and he's — well, wherever he is. You never did say where that was, by the way."

"Phoebe, you don't understand." Sasha looked down at the wood parquet floor. "There's something I didn't tell you and Chris." There was a long pause, filled with party noises, laughter, and loud music. Sasha didn't raise her head.

"I'd like to hear what it is," Phoebe said gently. Sasha looked up at her friend and suddenly saw her expression change. "But I think it might have to wait," Phoebe said, with a gleam in her eye.

Now it was Sasha's turn to be confused. "Why?" It wasn't going to be any fun explaining Wesley's situation, but now that she'd made up her mind to do it, she wanted to get it off her chest as quickly as possible.

"Because. . . ." Phoebe's tone of voice made Sasha look up as she pointed toward the door. "From the way you described him, that sounds like it could be the guy you've been waiting for."

Wesley stood in the doorway, talking to Chris, but searching the crowd with his eyes. He saw Sasha and gave a big wave. "Wesley!" Sasha bounded over to him, leaving Phoebe behind. She raced to the door and gave him a huge hug.

"I'm so glad you're here!" Looking into his face again, she felt a warm tingle go from her head to her toes. She wished they were alone so she could greet him the way she really wanted to, but Chris was still standing there, and the room was swarming with partygoers.

"Chris, this is my friend Wesley Lewis. Wesley, my good friend Chris Austin."

Wesley smiled broadly. "We just got finished introducing ourselves. Chris was explaining where I could put my coat." His gaze never left Sasha.

"I'll show you," Sasha said. "Chris, will you excuse us for a minute? We'll be right back." She took Wesley by the hand and led him toward the den.

"I was so worried about you. What happened?" she asked, as soon as Chris was out of earshot. She kissed Wesley's fingers, still cold from the winter air outside.

"Sasha, I'm sorry. I had trouble getting out without my roommate seeing me. He kept asking me a lot of questions and hanging around . . . but, anyway, I finally made it. I'm here, with you." He wrapped his arms around her and kissed her tenderly.

Sasha felt heady with the same sweet sensations she'd felt on her last date with him. All the worrying she'd done about the evening vanished.

They entered the den, and Wesley took his coat off. He was wearing a pair of softly faded jeans and a crisp white button-down shirt. He looked wonderful, and very unmilitary. But she had finally realized how unimportant that was. She loved Wesley. That was all that mattered: not whether he wore his uniform or not, or what opinion her friends or even her parents had of him. It was what she felt about him that counted.

Wesley put his coat down, and they left the room. "Wesley, I realized something, when I was waiting for you to get here." Sasha's voice was solemn, as she looked into Wesley's green eyes. "I realized how unfair it was of me to expect you to cover up who you really are just to make it easier for me to introduce you to my friends. There's no excuse. I can't believe I didn't see how pig-headed I was before. I'm sorry. I'm really sorry."

Wesley opened his mouth to speak. "Wait," Sasha continued. "I'm not finished. If you want me to tell my friends about where you go to school and everything, I will. Right now, as soon as we go into the living room and I introduce you. . . ."

Wesley touched Sasha's cheek. "You're really special, you know that?" His voice was gruff with shyness. "Sasha, I realized something, too. I was trying to tell you. When I walked in here, I was glad that I — well, looked like everyone else." Wesley indicated his clothes.

"Don't get me wrong. I want everyone to know I'm a Leesburg cadet after they get a chance to find out what I'm like without my uniform. Sasha, it's as important to me as it is to you that I get along with your friends, and if I had come here in full military uniform, I would have stuck out like a sore thumb. I would have been uncomfortable, and everybody else would have been, too. So don't apologize, okay? I think this was a good idea."

Sasha felt a warm rush of happiness spread through her. Wesley was so sweet and understanding. She could barely believe how lucky she was to have met him. "You mean you're not mad?"

"At you? No way." Wesley's smile was like the caress of an ocean breeze. "I'm really glad to be here."

Sasha returned his smile. "Me, too. I'm glad you're here, too." The words weren't nearly strong enough to convey what she actually felt, but she was sure Wesley knew just what she was thinking. For a moment she was aware only of the two of them gazing at each other, their eyes locked.

A loud chorus of laughter from the living room broke the spell, reminding both of them that there was a full-scale party going on out there. Sasha didn't have to say a word. Together, she and Wesley turned toward the large room and went to join the crowd.

Chapter
9

Woody kept his promise to himself. Kimberly Barrie was so intelligent and such fun to be with, she made it easy for him to be himself. As a new tune came over the stereo, they launched into their fourth dance in a row together. Woody bounced up and down, pivoted on one heel, and executed a series of fast, fancy steps. Kimberly followed his footwork, adding a jump in the air as she clapped her hands above her head.

Woody reached for one of her hands and spun her around. He'd gotten over the worst of his shyness — panic, to be more precise. It was the beginning that was hard: meeting someone's eye for the first time, looking them over, and feeling that you were looked over in return. But once that was behind him, and he started getting to know someone, Woody was able to go back to being his usual outgoing self.

The song ended, and another one began, a big

hit from the early days of rock and roll. Woody tucked his thumbs under his arms, flapped his elbows up and down, and started doing an old sixties dance a cousin of his had taught him called the Mashed Potato.

"Hey, you know that one, too?" Kimberly laughed delightedly and danced along. "And how about the Swim, can you do that?" She wriggled her arms out in front of her and bobbed her head.

"Or this one. What's it called?" Woody's whole body rose and fell, his weight shifting from one foot to the other as he moved his arms vertically in front of him.

"Oh, yeah! The Monkey!"

"Shake those bones, Webster!" Ted yelled from across the room as he and Chris launched into their own version of the Twist.

"Uh-oh, I think we've started something," Kimberly laughed.

When they had gone through the whole repertoire of sixties dances they knew, Kimberly showed Woody some breaking and popping moves. By the time the song was over, they were both laughing, out of breath, and ready for a cold drink.

"That was great!" Kimberly exclaimed, dipping a ladle into the big glass punch bowl and filling a paper cup. She handed it to Woody and filled another one for herself. "Where did you learn those steps?"

Woody told her about his cousin. "He's sort of like the older brother I never had. He's a lawyer in Boston. Just got married to this woman he went to law school with. So in case I ever get in trouble

87

with the law . . ." he kidded. "How about you? How do you know all those old dances?"

Kimberly took a sip of punch. "We had this class at the school I used to go to, a dance class. Actually, it was after school, taught by a woman who used to be a dancer on Broadway. Every week we learned dancing from a different decade — thirties, forties, fifties." Kimberly and Woody moved toward the couch that was pushed to one wall of the large room. "I liked the sixties stuff best."

"Sounds like a fun class." Woody sank into the plush red upholstery. "Too bad they don't have something like that here at Kennedy."

Kimberly nodded. "Yeah, I miss it. I miss a lot of things about Pittsburgh." There was a note of longing in her voice. "But now I've got more time to concentrate on what's really important; my cooking and this catering business my mom and I are starting." Kimberly's tone grew more cheerful. "So maybe this move wasn't so bad after all."

"Still, it must be hard to have to start all over again in a strange place," Woody sympathized.

"It isn't starting over that's so bad," Kimberly shrugged. "In fact, in a way it's kind of nice to be able to begin with a clean slate. You know, where everyone hasn't known you since you were a baby, and you can be who you are, not who you used to be." She paused. "The hard part is leaving people behind who care about you."

Woody surprised himself by leaning over and giving Kimberly a hug, to show her that there were people in Rose Hill who cared, too. It felt like the natural thing to do. But a peculiar expression clouded Kimberly's blue eyes, and she pulled away.

There was an uncomfortable lull in the conversation. Finally Kimberly began speaking again. "Woody, I think it's only fair to tell you that I have a boyfriend back in Pittsburgh." Her voice was low and tinged with something that sounded almost like regret.

Woody's shyness and insecurity crashed back over him like a tidal wave. "Oh," he managed woodenly. *What a jerk Kimberly must think I am,* he lamented silently. *Throwing myself all over her, when she's still thinking about some guy back home.*

"But, Woody," she continued, "I've been having a terrific time with you this evening, and I don't want it to stop. I hope we're going to be very good friends."

Woody nodded. "Sure," he said flatly. *Okay, so they'd be friends, just like he was with Phoebe. All the fizz had gone out of the evening. This was exactly what he'd been so afraid of. Here we go again, folks. Meet Woody, every girl's pal.*

Kimberly steered the conversation to a new topic, and Woody followed along, but his heart was no longer in it. All he could think about was that history kept repeating itself for him. Everytime he started to like a girl, something went wrong. He yanked on his suspenders and let them snap back against his chest. The only solution was not to give in the next time he felt himself falling for someone. He had to keep his distance. That way he wouldn't get hurt.

* * *

Sasha was beginning to wonder why she'd ever been worried about Wesley fitting in with her friends. Right now the two of them were sitting on the couch with Phoebe, Lisa, and Peter, with Wesley's arm draped comfortably around her shoulder.

"You mean you've actually flown a plane all by yourself?" Phoebe was asking, awed.

Wesley laughed. "Well, not exactly by myself, I don't even have a license yet, so I always have to have an instructor with me. But I have handled the controls several times."

"You're a pilot?" asked Henry who had just joined the group with Janie.

"Well, I want to be one," Wesley answered.

"I used to dream about flying a plane when I was little," Peter remarked.

"Well, Lacey, everyone knows you're always up in the ozone layer anyway," Henry teased. He ducked aside as Peter tried to pelt him with a kernel of popcorn.

"So, Wesley, you've piloted a real jet?" Janie asked.

"Yes, but not a big commercial plane. Usually, I fly in a little Cesna: a two seater."

"I'd be terrified to go up in one of those tiny things," Lisa put in.

"And I'd be terrified to perform with a whole rinkful of people watching me," Wesley replied, "so I guess we're even."

Lisa shrugged humbly. "Oh, that's different. I've been skating practically since I was old enough to walk."

"And she's a real champ," Peter said with pride in his voice, giving his girl friend an affectionate squeeze. "World class. Don't be fooled by her modesty."

Lisa opened her mouth as if she were about to protest, but then something caught her eye across the room. Her face took an expression of distaste, and she grabbed Sasha's arm. "Uh-oh, don't look now, but here comes trouble."

Sasha followed her gaze. John Marquette was bulldozing his way through the throng of people, a can of beer in his hand, and a scowl on his face. Sasha rolled her eyes. "As if I hadn't had enough of him already tonight." It seemed that seeing her with another guy was not encouraging Marquette to keep his distance, after all. Why was that big hulk so set on ruining her evening?

But as he lumbered over to the couch, his attention was focused not on Sasha but on Wesley. "Hey, you! Your face looks kinda like I've seen it before." Marquette's voice was at top volume and his words slurred. "Don't I know you from somewhere?"

Wesley shook his head. "No, I don't think so," he replied mildly.

Sasha waited for Marquette to leave, but he continued to tower over them as they sat. "Are you telling me I'm wrong?" He spoke threateningly. "And what are you doing with my favorite little foxette, anyway?" he demanded, leaning down and pinching Sasha's cheek.

Wesley was on his feet in a flash. "I doubt that Sasha appreciates that kind of attention." His tone was still even, but Sasha noticed that his hands were clenched at his side. "And you are mistaken about knowing me."

"So you're calling me a liar, is that it?" Marquette was quickly making a spectacle of himself, his voice booming over the sound of the stereo.

Wesley's veneer of restraint cracked. "I'm simply saying that I don't believe I've ever seen you before." Anger colored his words now. "And I'm also saying that I want you to leave my girl friend alone."

"Your girl friend, huh? Your girl friend? So it's official. Little foxie-woxie went and got herself a guy." Marquette turned to Sasha. "Well, don't go putting on airs and thinking I wanted anything more from you than —"

Wham! Wesley's fist was in Marquette's stomach. Somebody in the room screamed as Marquette doubled over.

"No!" cried Sasha. But before she could get between Wesley and Marquette, the bully had straightened up and was retaliating with a jab to Wesley's jaw. In his drunkeness he barely grazed Wesley's face.

"Some punch," Wesley taunted.

"Oh, Wesley, just leave him alone," Sasha begged. She saw Chris on the edge of the crowd that was gathering around them. This was exactly the kind of scene Chris had dreaded happening.

Now Wesley faced Sasha. "But he insulted you, and he insulted me, too. And he picked this fight. You can't expect me to just walk away."

Sasha was about to tell him that fighting was no solution to anything, but as soon as he'd turned to talk to her, Marquette seized the opportunity to charge at his back. He caught Wesley in a flying tackle and the two boys fell to the ground, exchanging blows.

Sasha made a vain attempt to pull Wesley up, but he continued to lash out at Marquette. "Please, Wesley, you can't do this! Stop! You have to stop!" she begged. She looked around for help and saw Chris running from the room.

Chris returned a few seconds later with Ted, who raced over and pushed through the crowd, using all his quarterback strength to pry Wesley and Marquette apart. Some of the other football players stepped in to keep them from going at each other again.

Ted sized them up. "I should have known you were involved, Marquette." He turned to Wesley. "But you," he said, "I don't even know who you are or what you're doing in my house." His normally calm voice was filled with anger.

Sasha tried to speak up, but only choked sounds came out of her mouth. She was trembling and tears rolled down her face. Why did something awful have to happen just when her friends were starting to like Wesley? She took in huge, noisy gulps of air.

"Wesley is Sasha's date," Chris told her boyfriend quietly. Sasha could hear the disillusionment in her friend's voice. It occurred to her miserably that on top of everything else, she might be on pretty shaky ground with Chris after this.

Ted stepped directly in front of Wesley. "With all due respect to Sasha, no guest in my house has the right to come in here and behave like

93

some kind of animal. Nobody." His voice was controlled now, but his words were clipped. He looked Wesley hard in the face.

Suddenly an expression of surprise stole over Ted's classically handsome features. "Now wait a minute! I think I *do* know who you are." He kept looking at him. "In fact I definitely do. You were one of those guys from Leesburg who was in that fight on our football field." Ted put a hand on his hip. "Look, buddy, that little show was bad enough, but there aren't going to be any reruns in my house."

Hearing Ted's words, Marquette yanked free of the linebacker who was holding him and made a clumsy swipe at Wesley. "I knew it! I knew you were the enemy the minute I saw you!" he yelled. Two more boys grabbed hold of Marquette again and tried to keep him quiet.

Wesley paid no attention to Marquette. Instead he faced Ted and spoke up in his own defense. "It's true, I'm from Leesburg, but I was one of the guys trying to stop that fight on the field."

"Oh yeah? But you think it's okay to start one in my house? No, it won't wash." Ted looked from Wesley to Sasha. "Listen, Sasha, I'm sorry but I'm going to have to ask your friend to leave."

"Good idea!" bellowed Marquette.

"You, too, Marquette." Ted folded his arms across his chest. "Get your coat and get out."

"Fine. I'm tired of this boring party anyway." Marquette just laughed. "So long as these two get what they deserve." Somebody handed him his jacket and he made a cocky exit. "So long, foxette," he said to Sasha as he left, leaving the door wide open behind him.

Sasha wasn't sure precisely what happened next, but somehow, in a fog of humiliation and hurt, she managed to find her cape and Wesley's coat. As she made her way to the door, where Wesley stood waiting, she passed Chris.

"Sasha, I'm really disappointed." Chris's blue eyes flashed with anger. "I would have expected more of your new friend."

"You! Chris Austin, just who do you think you are to be passing judgment on everybody? You spend the whole evening trying to play the perfect little hostess at your boyfriend's party, and you end up with big red 'F' in my book!"

Sasha grabbed Wesley's hand and they made their way out into the quiet, dark night. They scrambled down the Masons' front walk and immediately fell into each other's arms.

Sasha held on to Wesley with all her might, as if by letting go, he would be taken away from her. "It wasn't supposed to happen that way," she sniffled, through her sobs. "It's not fair! It's not fair!"

"Oh, Sasha, I'm so sorry," Wesley whispered, stroking her soft, wavy hair. They stood entwined, feeling each other's unhappiness.

Chapter
10

Moonlight spilled onto the lawn in front of Ted's house, and the sky was filled with stars, but Phoebe barely noticed. All her concentration was on the two forlorn figures huddled together at the end of the walkway. "I bet you guys could use a friend right now," she said softly as she approached them.

Sasha whirled around, her cheeks stained from crying. "Phoebe?" It sounded almost as if she didn't believe her eyes. "How come you're not mad at us like everyone else in there?"

"Don't be silly," Phoebe said gently.

"But all those kids. . . ." Sasha let her sentence trail off. "I thought they were my friends. Phoebe, what are Wesley and I going to do?" Her brown eyes were rimmed with red, and her voice wavered out of control.

"Sasha, it's been a rough night," Phoebe began. "Maybe you should both go home and get a good night's sleep, and forget about this for now. You'll probably feel a lot more together in the morning."

Sasha shook her head back and forth in despair, her hair swirling around her shoulders. "I couldn't even think about sleeping right now." Her lower lip trembled and the tears threatened to fall again.

Phoebe sighed. She remembered the night Griffin had told her he was going to New York. She'd thought her whole world was collapsing around her. Right now, she knew Sasha was thinking the same thing, and her heart went out to her friend and her new boyfriend. She didn't approve of what Wesley had done, but John Marquette had been such a creep it was hard to blame Wesley too much.

She took a step closer to Sasha and put a consoling arm around her shoulders. "I know how you must feel, but standing here in the cold's not going to help. Come on, I'll drive you home. You, too, Wesley."

Sasha raised her shoulders in a gesture of helplessness. "What difference does it make anyway?" She let Phoebe lead her and Wesley to her parents' cream-colored station wagon.

The three of them piled into the front seat, Wesley holding Sasha close to him as Phoebe started the car. "Wesley, you'll have to direct me, okay?"

Wesley nodded, his face tight.

They drove in silence for several blocks. Then Sasha let out a tiny, heartbreaking sigh. "Wesley, what's going to happen to us?"

"Well, I guess we're not going to be going on too many double dates with your friends from school," he joked weakly.

"I beg your pardon," Phoebe returned lightly, trying to relieve some of the tension in the air, "but doesn't yours truly count as one of Sasha's friends from school? I mean, I wouldn't mind a double date every once in a while — although I can't for the life of me think of who I'd get to take me out."

Sasha managed a lukewarm laugh. "Thanks, Pheeb." Then her voice grew strained again. "But did you see Ted's face or Chris's? They're never going to accept us together. They're not even going to accept me alone anymore."

Phoebe couldn't deny the fury she'd seen on Chris's face, or the disgust on Ted's, but she was certain their anger would subside. They couldn't stay mad at Sasha forever.

"Sash, don't be too hard on them," she said. "They'll come around eventually. I think they overreacted. But fights are pretty ugly things."

"Come on, John Marquette deserved it," Sasha asserted. "Phoebe, did you hear the stuff he was saying?"

Phoebe was silent. Normally Sasha was the first person to condemn violence in any form. As far as she was concerned, the peaceful solution was the best one. But that attitude seemed to have gone by the boards in her defense of Wesley.

"Anyway it doesn't matter now," Sasha continued, pounding her hand against the dashboard in frustration. "The point is that it's going to be almost impossible for us to go out around here without bumping into some of the kids who were at that party. And there's no way they're going to be as understanding as you, Phoebe. Plus there's my parents to worry about . . . I don't know, I wish there was some way for us to just get away from all this craziness. . . ." Sasha sniffed back a sob.

"I'd like to help." Phoebe could feel Sasha's pain. "But I'm not sure there's much I can do. I guess you two are going to have to weather the storm somehow and keep a low profile for a while."

"But, Phoebe, how can we keep a low profile and manage to see each other, too?" Sasha's voice rose desperately. "It's not like we can have a date in Wesley's room. And my parents don't know anything yet, so we can't go there. That doesn't leave us many places to go if we want to stay out of sight."

Phoebe was beginning to see Sasha's point. Maybe the problem was bigger than she'd realized. Meeting on Wesley's turf was out — there was no way a girl could get into the dorm of an all-male military academy — and after tonight, Sasha's turf was just as bad.

They drove in silence for a while. "Hey! I've got it!" Phoebe exclaimed. "Why didn't I think of this before?"

"What?" Both Sasha and Wesley sounded a hopeful note.

"Listen. My parents don't have any plans to go up to our cabin until spring break. There's no heat, but there's a wood-burning stove . . . Sash, you remember it. Maybe you guys could take a bus up there one day next weekend." Phoebe smiled to herself. It was so simple.

"Really, Pheeb? Do you think so?" Sasha sat up in her seat. "Oh, Wesley, you'd love it up there. It's in the mountains, right in the woods, and it's so cozy."

Phoebe stopped at a traffic light. "You could spend a quiet day in the country, just the two of you." Wesley and Sasha exchanged a hug of anticipation.

"No problem," Phoebe returned, pressing back down on the gas pedal as the light changed to green again. The station wagon rolled forward. "Anything to keep you two from looking like the doom and gloom couple of the year."

"Oh, Phoebe, I'm sorry," Sasha said. "We didn't mean to dump all our problems on you."

"I know," Phoebe replied. "I volunteered for the job. I don't mind." Wesley motioned for her to turn right.

"But we took you away from the party," Sasha said apologetically.

Phoebe sighed. "That's all right. Everybody was pretty much paired off, anyway. Peter had Lisa home for the first time in months, and Woody seemed to be getting along great with Kimberly Barrie. And there were Chris and Ted and Henry and Janie. And Brenda and Brad — "

Phoebe bit down on her lip as she spoke this last name. She and Brad had been a long-standing couple before she'd met Griffin. And though she was happy for Brad that he'd found somebody else, she still felt a little strange about the whole thing. Especially now that Griffin was gone.

100

"Pheeb, give it time. Things will work out for you okay." Now it was Sasha who was offering the consoling words.

"I know." Phoebe forced her voice to sound cheerful. She had to stop feeling sorry for herself. If she thought positively, things were bound to get better. "Anyway the point is, I really didn't mind leaving the party to take a drive with you guys. It's such a nice night."

"Phoebe, you're a good sport," Sasha said warmly. "How come I rate a friend like you?"

"Aw, shucks," Phoebe kidded.

"I mean, if you hadn't come along, Wesley and I would probably still be standing there outside Ted's house feeling like it was the end of the world. Like, there's no question that we made a huge mess of things tonight, but. . . ."

". . . but you've really helped make us feel better," Wesley finished. "Plus, your cabin's probably the ideal place to get things back on the right track. Phoebe, if there's any way I can thank you. . . ."

"Maybe a ride up in one of those little planes when you get your pilot's license," Phoebe suggested lightly.

"It's a deal! You'll be the first one I take up. After Sasha, that is. Oh, hey, you've got to turn left here," Wesley instructed. "With everything that happened I almost forgot about having to sneak back in." He and Sasha explained the problem with his uniform.

"You mean you've got to wear it all the time?" Phoebe was incredulous. "Like in the Army or something?" The fact that Wesley was a Leesburg

101

cadet really hit home with her for the first time. Phoebe had been so wrapped up in the drama that had taken place at Ted's that she hadn't really stopped to take in the full implications of Wesley's being in military school, right now.

If she tried, Sasha couldn't have came up with a boyfriend less like what Phoebe would have expected. The fight with Marquette aside, Wesley was obviously a decent guy, but he and Sasha stood for such completely different things. That old saying popped into her head: Opposites attract.

The station wagon rattled up a narrow dirt road. "This is it," Wesley told Phoebe. "If I take that path up ahead, I can get in without being seen." In the flood of moonlight, she could just make out a spindly trail snaking through the woods. She stepped on the brake.

Wesley sat in the front seat, buttoning up his coat. "Thanks again, Phoebe. I can't tell you how much I appreciate everything. See you soon, I hope." They said good-bye, and he climbed out the passenger side.

Sasha slid over toward the door. "I'll just be a sec, okay, Phoebe?"

"Sure," Phoebe nodded, running a hand through her red curls as Sasha followed Wesley out. She waited patiently while they said their good-byes.

When Sasha slid back in next to Phoebe, the smile that stretched across her face could have lit up the entire town of Rose Hill. Maybe, thought Phoebe, maybe Sasha and Wesley are just right for each other.

Chapter
11

"I just can't figure out some of the dances you kids do nowadays!" said Mr. Webster, shaking his balding head. "What's all that about, Woody?"

"What, Dad?" Woody put a hand to his ear. "I'm sorry, I didn't hear you." In front of him a crowd had gathered on a street corner in New York City to be entertained by a group of young boys doing electric boogey moves to the tune that blared from a portable cassette deck.

"I was wondering what I'm supposed to think about all this," Mr. Webster repeated, above the loud music.

"Oh, Harold, you're not supposed to *think* anything," Mrs. Webster chided. "You're supposed to see it and feel it."

"Oh, I see." Mr. Webster gave Woody a wink, and they turned back to watch the boys. Their arms snapped in and out of geometric poses as they moonwalked around a slab of sidewalk that seemed to be as smooth and slippery as ice. Woody tried to mimic them, but his feet kept sticking to the ground.

Then he remembered the steps Kimberly had shown him at Ted's party, and he went through the process in slow motion. So that was the secret — you had to keep one foot flat on the ground while you slid it behind the other. He picked up a little speed.

"Not bad, Woody," his father laughed. "Did you ever think of putting on your own sidewalk show?"

Woody grinned. "I learned that from a new friend of mine." He wondered what Kimberly would think about how the kids danced here in the city. But he made an effort to cut off all thoughts of her.

It would be all too easy to daydream about being with Kimberly in New York, to pretend he was watching the endless stream of people with her: the style-conscious dudes; the rich and famous, hiding behind the darkened windows of their limousines; the kids with their green and purple spiked hairdos; and the young couples ready for a night out on the town, all parading beneath the shimmer of lights.

No, if Kimberly thought about taking a trip to New York City at all, it would be with her boyfriend from Pittsburgh by her side, not Woody. He was determined not to develop another hopeless crush on a girl. He watched the rest of the breakers' routine and put some loose change into the hat they passed around.

As he and his parents resumed their walk to

the theater, Woody continued to study the sights and sounds and people around him. This was one of the most exciting cities in the world, and he didn't intend to spend his vacation here moping about someone who wanted to be just another one of his pals.

Kimberly Barrie hung up the telephone receiver and stared off into space. She'd had a perfectly nice talk with David, but she felt a funny sort of emptiness, and couldn't quite figure out why.

She went over the conversation in her mind. David had told her about his latest win on the debating squad. Nothing new there. Kimberly had gotten him up-to-date on the most recent developments of Earthly Delights, the catering business she and her mother were starting, and David had offered his usual bits of sensible advice. Again, nothing out of the ordinary at all. Before saying good-bye, Kimberly had asked about some of the kids back in Pittsburgh, and David had filled her in. She was happy to hear that David's best friend, Hank, had gotten back together with his old girl friend Elise. But she had to admit to herself that the news seemed less important, less immediate than it might have a few weeks ago.

Already some of the memories of day-to-day things in Pittsburgh were getting blurry. It was easier, for instance, to imagine Mr. Hardin's nasal voice as he read off the names of the kids in her Rose Hill homeroom every morning than to remember how any of her teachers back in Pittsburgh had sounded. It was more fun to think about how neat Ted's party had been than to wonder what some of the parties she'd missed back in Pittsburgh had been like.

It was too bad Ted's had been interrupted by that awful fight, though. She felt sorry for Sasha, who seemed so nice, but Kimberly had had a good time anyway. Best of all, she was starting to feel that she was finally becoming a part of the Kennedy High social scene and getting to know some new people, like Woody Webster.

Was that why she was feeling so peculiar? Because Pittsburgh was her past while Rose Hill was her present, and future, too, probably? But David was still a part of Kimberly's life. She spoke to him on the telephone several times a week. She had plans to visit him sometime later in the month. And if certain voices and faces were growing harder to call up in her memory, David's was not one of them.

She could visualize perfectly his serious, angular features, his sandy-colored hair, always carefully combed, his tall, slender body and his neat, though casual, manner of dressing. Furthermore, she could always trust David to call when he said he would, to remember special days like the anniversary of the first time they'd gone out together, and to be there when she needed him. Good old dependable David.

Of course there were usually no surprises with David, either, and sometimes that bothered Kimberly. She sometimes wished that just once he would do something totally crazy or unexpected.

She found herself thinking about Woody Webster again. Now there was a guy who really knew how to let loose. True, he'd seemed a little stiff and shy at first, but Kimberly had worked hard to put him at ease, sensing there was something special about him. And she'd been right. Pretty soon his jokes and goofy theatrics had made her almost forget about Pittsburgh. She remembered what he'd done at Ted's party, grabbing some plastic fruit from a bowl in the den and giving everyone a spur-of-the-moment juggling show.

Kimberly firmly believed you had to give up one thing to get another. David might not be the most spontaneous person in the world, but he was certainly one of the most stable. And it was nice to have a boyfriend you could count on. She got up and walked away from the telephone. This funny feeling was probably nothing more than a temporary case of the blues — Friday night in a new town with nowhere to go. She pushed open the door to the kitchen. She had discovered a rec- ipe for Mexican cornbread in the *Post* and she wanted to try it out.

Testing out new cooking creations was a sure- fire cure for a not-so-great mood. Shrugging off all questions about Pittsburgh, David, and her new friends in Rose Hill, Kimberly set to work.

"Can you believe this?" Woody asked his mother, staring at the gold-leaf encrusted mold- ings and sweeping overhead arches of the elab- orate theater lobby. A crystal chandelier was suspended gracefully from the ceiling, and fur coats and black ties were in evidence everywhere. It was amazing to think that Griffin was working in the midst of all this splendor.

The Websters gave their tickets to a man in a bow tie and black vest, then climbed one flight of red-carpeted stairs to the first balcony. The inside of the theater was even more spectacular than the lobby, with art deco carvings flanking the stage and gold-leaf gilding on the ornamental woodwork.

Woody breathed in the air of excitement. He always felt a rush of exhilaration when he was in a theater, but this was something extra-special. This was Broadway.

The usher checked their ticket stubs, showed them to their seats, and gave each of them a program. "Not bad," Mr. Webster commented. From their places in the balcony's front row, they had a perfect view of the stage, at least they would once the heavy velvet curtain was raised.

Woody settled into his seat and thumbed through the *Playbill*. He skipped over the advertisements, the articles, and even the list of scenes and acts in the play itself. He would read all of that in a moment. His first concern was to find Griffin's name in the program. He turned to the page where the cast was listed, followed by a who's-who section giving a brief blurb about each person involved with the performance.

Woody felt a shiver of anticipation as he ran down the list, moving his index finger over the glossy paper. Imagine, a friend of his, listed in a real, live Broadway *Playbill*. It didn't even matter that Griffin wouldn't actually appear on stage. To be an understudy for this play was enough of a thrill.

Griffin Neill, Griffin Neill. Woody looked for

his name. His finger reached the bottom of the column. Maybe he'd missed it. He went over the page again. No luck. He consulted the program more carefully, reading the names of characters as well as the names of the actors. Understudies. There it was. Timothy Berkley and Jana Henderman. But Griffin's name wasn't printed.

The corners of Woody's mouth turned down. Strange, it must have been a mistake. Woody knew that when something had been left out or changed, you often found a separate page with the correct information tucked inside the program, but maybe they didn't do that for understudies.

Woody was still searching for Griffin's name when the lights dimmed. Oh, well, he thought. There has to be some logical explanation. He closed the *Playbill* and put it in his lap. He'd try to ask some questions after the performance, but right now there was something even more important to concentrate on.

A hush fell over the audience. All eyes were riveted on the front of the theater. Slowly, majestically, the curtain was going up.

Chapter
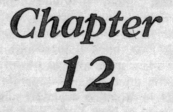

"I'll bet after the play Woody and Griffin will go to some big-deal place in the middle of New York City," Sasha theorized excitedly as she lay on her back on her purple rug. "Maybe they'll even sit next to some star. But Griffin won't pay any attention. He'll be too busy asking Woody about you — how you're doing, whether you still think about him every once in a while. . . ."

Phoebe picked at a loose thread on her old boy scout shirt. "Nice fantasy, Sash," she said gloomily. "Too bad it's a few thousand miles from the truth."

"Hey, come on, Pheeb. Give yourself a break," Sasha said, propping herself up on her elbows to look up at her bed where Phoebe was sitting. "You have to think positively."

"Sasha, be serious." Phoebe reached for an Oreo from the bag next to her and dipped it into her glass of milk. "You know what he told me:

110

that we couldn't see each other again. So it's just plain dumb for me to keep thinking about him."

"But he also told you he loved you, and that he'd always love you."

"A whole lot of good that does me when he's too busy with his career to find time for me."

"You mean you don't believe him?"

"I don't know what to believe anymore." Phoebe polished off half the cookie. "When we were together, I never would have thought in a million years that he'd go off and disappear on me this way. I mean I can definitely understand his wanting to go to New York. With his talent and everything, it makes total sense. But I was so sure he meant it when he promised to keep in touch. We really loved each other, at least I thought we did." Phoebe sighed.

"I don't know. I used to think I was pretty sensitive to what other people were feeling and thinking," she continued. "It's hard for me to believe I only imagined what we had going for us. But I guess I was blinded by my own feelings."

"Phoebe, it could be that once he gets used to being in New York and his new life and everything he'll come to his senses and realize that none of it's any good without you."

"Sasha, I've said it before, and I'll say it again." Phoebe stretched out on the bed. "You're my true friend, but you're also a hopeless romantic. This is real life. Things don't always have a happy ending the way they do in fairy tales."

"Sometimes they do." Sasha's voice grew dreamy.

Phoebe clicked her tongue in annoyance.

When was Sasha going to come down out of the clouds? "I'll bet you didn't think everything was so rosy and perfect when Wesley was rolling around on the floor with John Marquette."

The minute the words were out of her mouth, Phoebe was sorry. She saw Sasha's face fall. "I shouldn't have said that. I apologize, Sash." Phoebe hung her head. "Maybe I'm a little envious because I don't have a guy like Wesley around to stick up for me the way you do," she added softly.

"It's okay," replied Sasha. "I understand." She swallowed hard. "And besides, you're right. I felt pretty horrible when those guys were fighting. Worse than horrible, I was absolutely terrified. You know how much I hate violence."

"I do know. But what I don't understand is why you didn't call Wesley on it." As long as they were on the subject, Phoebe figured it was as good a time as any to air her feelings. "I mean, you were acting as though you thought he did the right thing."

Sasha flopped over onto her back and stared up at the ceiling. "I was so mad at that jerk Marquette, and just so upset in general, that I guess I wasn't really thinking straight. My first impulse was to defend Wesley no matter what, and that's what I did."

"Uh-huh." Phoebe pushed the box of cookies out of arm's reach. "You know, Sash, I think most people would have done just what Wesley did under the circumstances, and I'm not even so positive it was wrong. It's just that I know you're really opposed to fighting and all. It's kind of weird to see you compromising your principles because you've got this new boyfriend who has different ideas than you do."

"I know. It's hard to admit it, but I've been thinking the same thing all week, and I definitely have to let Wesley know how I feel. But I'm sure he'll understand. Phoebe, for two people who are as different as we are, it's really amazing how well we connect." Sasha's tone became more animated.

"I'm glad, Sash. But listen, take my advice and don't rush into anything, okay? I mean, I really liked Wesley. He seemed like a pretty good guy, but, remember, you've only had two dates, and one of them wasn't exactly ideal."

"I'll keep the motherly advice in mind," Sasha said dryly.

"All right, all right." Phoebe laughed. "I don't mean to butt in to what's none of my business, but I really hope everything goes right for you."

"And I appreciate it," Sasha said. "Don't think I don't. But I suppose I feel like I've got enough people watching out for what I should or shouldn't be doing."

"You mean Chris, don't you?" Phoebe asked.

Sasha nodded and sighed. "Pheeb, I don't know what to do about her. We've been avoiding each other all week."

"I know." Phoebe measured her words carefully. There was nothing worse than being stuck in the middle when your two closest friends were conducting their very own cold war. "But you guys are going to have to work this one out sooner or later, and it might as well be sooner."

Sasha pouted. "Well, she's not exactly going

113

out of her way to talk to me, either, you know."

"Sash, she's still pretty freaked out by what happened," Phoebe said gently. "It was the one thing she wanted to avoid at that party. You know how worried she was."

"Yeah, I know. But look at it my way. One of my best friends gets her boyfriend to kick me out of his house and turns all the kids against Wesley before they've even gotten a chance to know him."

Phoebe drained her milk glass. "Maybe you and Chris are being a little rough on each other," she suggested. "Don't you think you'd both be happier being friends again?"

Sasha considered Phoebe's question before answering. "I guess." She exhaled noisily. "Well, okay, sure. Of course I'd rather be friends. I mean we *are* friends. We're just angry friends." Then she seemed to hear her own stream of words, and let out a giggle. "Pretty stupid, huh?"

Phoebe didn't answer. She didn't have to.

"You're right," Sasha conceded. "I'll talk to her first thing Monday morning. I bet after spending all day with Wesley tomorrow, I won't even feel like being mad anymore."

"Oh, speaking of which," Phoebe said, "let me give you my set of keys to the cabin, before I forget." She reached down under the bed and felt around for her knapsack. From the side pouch, she pulled out two keys. "The silver one is for the top lock, and this one is for the bottom. They turn in opposite directions." She held them out for Sasha to take. "You remember how to get there from the bus stop, right?"

Sasha nodded as she got up and tucked the keys away in her top dresser drawer. "Phoebe, this is so great of you." She plopped down on the bed and gave Phoebe a big bear hug. "I can't thank you enough, not just for the cabin, but for being honest about Chris, and . . . well, just being here. . . . You're the best, Pheeb!"

"Thanks." Phoebe returned Sasha's hug. "Now, listen, I hereby order you to have a fabulous time."

"I will. And Pheeb?"

"Yeah?"

"About what we were talking about earlier — if Griffin doesn't miss you like crazy, the guy's a nut case!"

The theater thundered with applause. The cast bowed again and again. The young actress in the lead female role stepped forward and took a solo bow. The two actors who had played opposite her came out and joined her, one on either side, and the trio took several more bows. The curtain dropped. Then it came up once again and the entire cast took a final bow.

After the curtain had been lowered for the last time, the house lights came back on and the chatter of the audience began filling the room. People stood and gathered up their coats.

"So what did my son, the budding Broadway director, think?" Mr. Webster asked, as the family made their way toward the aisle.

Woody felt his face grow pink. "Aw, Dad, I don't know if I'm ever going to get this far." He turned his palms up. "Well, maybe if I work incredibly hard and get some really lucky breaks. The acting was so great. The set and costumes and lights, too. I mean, the play itself wasn't that deep or anything, but it was so well done that I've got to say it was one of the best things I've seen." If he had the chance, only once in his lifetime, to work with actors of such high caliber, Woody would know he'd really made it.

He could see himself breezing in through the stage door, fans fighting for a chance to say hello to him. Of course he'd stop and be friendly, always remembering his humble beginnings. In front of the theater, his name would be at the top of all the posters — directed by Woody Webster — the W's stylized in fancy letters. Girls would be dying to meet him. No more old-pal Woody stuff anymore.

Woody gave his head a hard shake. The excitement was making him giddy as if he'd been drinking champagne all night. If he kept getting lost in daydreams instead of actually working toward his goal, he was never going to get anywhere. Besides, now he had to come back to reality and figure out what had happened to Griffin.

He explained the problem to his parents and asked if they'd mind waiting a few minutes while he tried to get backstage to ask some questions. They agreed to meet out in the lobby when Woody was through.

He hurried toward the stage but didn't get any farther than the entrance to the wings before he was stopped by a security guard. "I'm looking for a friend," Woody told him. "He's supposed to be understudying one of the roles in this play."

The guard looked dubious. "I'm sorry, but we can't let just anyone wander around back here."

"But I don't want to wander around. I want to find my friend." Woody could see he wasn't cutting any ice with the guard. "The truth is, I'm worried about him," he added, putting on his best serious expression.

The guard shifted uncomfortably from one foot to the other. "I really can't let you back here. . . ."

At that moment, a young man Woody recognized as having played one of the minor roles rushed past them, nimbly sidestepping the props, lighting cables, and equipment that littered the wings. "Excuse me," Woody boldly called out to him.

The young actor stopped in his tracks and swiveled around. Woody wriggled his fingers in a goofy little wave. "Over here," he said. The actor took a few steps toward Woody and the guard.

"I'm looking for a guy named Griffin Neill," Woody said. "He's one of the understudies."

The young man's brow wrinkled. "You must have the wrong play. There's nobody here by that name."

The guard flashed Woody a smirk that clearly said I told you so.

Woody ignored it and kept talking to the young actor. "Are you sure? He auditioned about two months ago, and I know he was hired."

The actor shook his head. "That's impossible. I auditioned at about the same time, and I don't remember anyone else getting a part then. Grif-

117

fin, you say his name was?" He stroked his narrow goatee. "What does he look like?"

Woody described his friend as carefully as possible, from his straight, brown hair to his impish smile.

Suddenly a glimmer of recognition appeared in the young actor's eyes. "Hey, wait a minute. You know, there was somebody who fit that description auditioning before me. I remember because they kept him in there so long, I was sure he'd gotten something." He paused. "It's possible that he was put into one of the road companies that are touring the play. A lot of actors who are just starting out get their break that way."

Woody nodded. "That's got to be it. You don't have any idea how I can find out what city he's touring in or how I can get in touch with him, do you?"

The young actor shrugged. "I guess you could try asking one of the secretaries in the producer's office. They must know something."

"Well, thanks very much," Woody said. He was sorely disappointed that Griffin wasn't right there behind the scenes, hanging out with the actors and actresses he had watched in tonight's performance. But at least now he had a clue about where to find him. Phoebe might be trying to pretend she didn't care about Griffin, but Woody knew if he came home without any information that she would be very upset.

A half hour later he was back in his hotel room, taking one last look out the window at the nighttime skyline. The top of the Empire State

Building was lit up in a crown of red, white, and blue. The hotel manager had explained that the colors changed depending on the holiday or time of year. Near it, the Chrysler Building was majestically ornate, patterns of white lights gracing its tapered spire.

He stood for a few minutes, drinking in the panorama, and then pulled down the window shade and got ready for bed. He was still thinking about Griffin as he brushed his teeth and slipped into his pajamas. Why had Griffin told Phoebe he was performing in New York City if he'd actually been sent on the road? He had always thought of him as the kind of guy who couldn't tell a lie even if he'd wanted to. Woody wondered if he was a less astute judge of character than he thought.

It occurred to Woody that perhaps there was another girl involved. Still, he knew for a fact that the hardest part of Griffin's decision to move to New York had been leaving Phoebe behind. Woody climbed into the luxurious king-size hotel bed. It didn't make sense. Why would Griffin say one thing and then do another?

The last thing Woody did before turning out the light was to reach over and get the *Playbill* he'd brought back with him. He turned the pages until he found the credits again. Then he circled the producer's name with a red felt-tipped pen. He was going to follow every lead until he tracked his friend down.

Chapter
13

Sasha was in Wesley's arms again. "I thought this week would never be over," she told him, her fingers tracing the contours of his face. "I missed you so much."

"Not as much as I missed you." Wesley breathed deeply, pulling Sasha closer and kissing the top of her head.

She tilted her chin upward, and their lips met. She felt light-headed, the softness of Wesley's mouth and the spicy scent of his aftershave drowning the worries that had crowded her mind recently. Her parents' view of the military life, her problem with Chris, the fight at the party — all these problems were washed away by the sweet urgency of their kisses.

Sasha ran her hands up and down the lapel of Wesley's uniform, clearly visible under his open coat. He looked every bit the cadet today, but she didn't care. If people in the bus terminal thought they made an unlikely couple, Sasha in a pair of faded jeans and hiking boots, Wesley in his regulation khakis, they could stare all they wanted.

Around them, people hurried in all directions, some toting suitcases or wheeling carts loaded with baggage. Two boys about their own age were carrying ski equipment, huge packs strapped to their backs. The loudspeaker crackled with information about arrivals and departures, as travelers lined up at ticket windows.

Wesley looked around, his gaze settling on a large clock on the center of one wall. "We ought to find out what gate we're leaving from and get seats." He took Sasha's hand and they walked over to the departure board.

Sasha scanned the lists of destinations. "There it is. Gate nine." She gave Wesley's hand an excited squeeze. She loved bus terminals, airports, and train stations — the throngs of people headed in all different directions. Usually Sasha pretended she was journeying to some exotic, far-away place, making up a story about why she was going there, and who would be meeting her at the other end.

Today, however, there was no place she'd rather be going than to Phoebe's little cabin, and no one she'd rather be going with than Wesley. They found gate nine and boarded the old Greyhound, giving their tickets to the driver, who smiled and gave Wesley a little salute. It was as if Wesley's uniform represented pride in America, and the bus driver was part of that same patriotic spirit.

Sasha knew her parents would say that patriotism was not just about uniforms. But there was no denying that Wesley's outfit had created an instant bond between him and the driver, and there was something special about that. Somehow she would have to get through to her parents and show them that theirs was not the only way of looking at things.

But what her parents thought was not important right now. What was important was having Wesley next to her and the bus rolling out of the station, taking them away together.

"Sasha, I'm so happy we're doing this," Wesley said ,the buildings of downtown Washington, D.C., gliding by. He snuggled closer to her. "It was so nice of Phoebe's parents to let us use the cabin."

Sasha sat straight up. She had a funny feeling Wesley wasn't going to like what she had to say. "Mr. and Mrs. Hall have no idea we're going up to the cabin. Phoebe gave us her own keys."

Sure enough, the smile vanished from Wesley's handsome face. "Don't you think that's dishonest?" His intent gaze demanded a straight answer.

"Well it's not like they said we couldn't, and we're going anyway," Sasha hedged.

Wesley's silence was worse than any reply he could have given.

"It was so important for us to be able to spend some time alone," Sasha added hastily. "What if we hadn't been able to do this?"

Wesley answered her question with another question. "And your parents, do they know where you're going? You did say you'd tell them about me as soon as you figured out a way to break the news."

Sasha looked out the window. The large buildings had given way to private homes surrounded by large lawns and trees. "I still intend to," she mumbled.

"But you haven't. So I guess that means you lied to them about where you were going today." Wesley's accusatory words stung Sasha's ears.

"I told them I was going over to my friend Janie's." Her voice was low and shaky. This wasn't how their day together was supposed to start.

"I don't like it," Wesley said emphatically. "Not at all."

Sasha felt her cheeks grow hot. "Well, would you like it any better if I hadn't been able to come?" Her words burned with anger. What good was playing by the rules when the rules only hurt you? Were regulations more important to Wesley than she was?

"Sasha, of course I wanted you to come, but I also want you to start telling people the truth about me." Wesley's voice rose, and the gray-haired man across the aisle frowned disapprovingly. His next sentence was softer, but no less biting. "You know, it's starting to seem as if you're ashamed of me."

"Maybe I should be," Sasha snapped. "You've got your head buried so deep in your book of rules that you can't see anything else."

Minutes of icy silence seemed to stretch out like interminable hours. Sasha's head pounded and her throat felt raw. This trip was supposed to be a clean start for her and Wesley. Out of the corner of her eye, she looked over at him. His lips were tight, his eyes blazing angrily. How could it be that only a short time ago, those lips were kissing her softly; those eyes searching hers lovingly?

Sasha knew that all she really wanted was to make up. She couldn't bear even a second of bad feelings between her and Wesley. She had intended to talk to him about the fight with Marquette, as she'd promised Phoebe she'd do, but it would have to wait. Bringing that up would only cause more trouble, and right now, all she wanted to do was erase the last ten minutes.

"Wesley," Sasha began.

"Sasha," he said at the same instant, turning toward her.

"You first," she offered.

"No, you."

"Look, I don't want to fight. I'm sorry." Sasha held out her hand. "Maybe I shouldn't have lied to my parents, and maybe it would have been better to get the Halls' permission to use the house."

"And maybe I need to learn to be a little more flexible." He took her hand in his. "But please, let's not argue anymore."

Sasha smiled, her brown eyes full once more with warmth and tenderness. "Remember when we agreed to disagree?"

"Mmm," replied Wesley, his mouth already firmly on hers.

* * *

124

"Griffin Neill? No, the name doesn't even ring a bell." The thin, high-pitched voice came over the telephone line.

"Are you positive?" Woody asked, sinking down onto the edge of the bed. "Maybe there's some kind of list you can check."

"Look," the woman on the other end said. "It's Saturday. I'm not even supposed to be here, but I had some extra work I had to finish. You're lucky you got me at all, and now you want me to go rummaging around the office for some non-existent list."

Woody held his breath as he silently counted to ten. He had to be nice, he had to be polite, or he wasn't going to find out a shred of information. "Ma'am, I really appreciate your taking the time to talk to me," he said, "and I realize that someone who comes into an office on a Saturday morning must be awfully busy, but it's urgent that I find my friend. Someone suggested that he might be in one of the touring companies. I have to find out. Please."

"Look, the touring companies and the main stage production are part of the same operation, and your friend's not in it. I told you already, there's nothing I can do. He's not with us, and never has been."

"Maybe if I call back Monday. . . ." Woody sighed.

"Nobody on Monday's going to tell you any differently," the woman snapped. "I'm the book-keeper. I make out every single check to every single person employed throughout this company. If this Griffith person were with us, I'd know it."

"Griffin," Woody said.

"It's all the same to me. Now if you don't mind," she said nastily, "I have things to do."

"Yes, of course," Woody responded. "And thank you so much for your trouble."

He heard the receiver being slammed down. "Have a nice day," he added sarcastically, even though the line had gone dead. "You old witch."

He flopped back on the bed and ran a hand through his curly hair. So Griffin wasn't in the play at all. Now what?

"Look! A deer!" Sasha pointed through the bare branches as the long-legged creature bounded gracefully across an open patch of land and disappeared into the forest behind it. "Wesley, isn't this wonderful?" She pulled her wool cap farther down over her dark hair as a snap of cold air blew down the narrow road.

"*You're* wonderful." Wesley circled an arm around Sasha's waist.

They passed a farm. Smoke was rising from the chimney of a rambling old white house next to the barn and a few brave cows ventured out of their stalls to graze in the winter air. Farther down the road, on the other side, was a long, narrow field speckled with several gnarled oak trees, their twisted branches scratching the gray sky.

"I remember that field," Sasha said excitedly. "The cabin ought to be right around that next bend." She quickened her pace, pulling Wesley along with her and giving a few little skips.

The first thing she saw was the old rooster weather vane, peeking up from behind some trees.

She remembered Mr. Hall saying that those old stamped-tin weather vanes, which used to be as common as a bag of nails, had become something of a collector's item now, a kind of folk art.

As they got closer, the shingled roof came into view, and then the wooden cottage iteself. "Isn't it the cutest?" She jumped up and down, remembering all the good times she'd had here with Phoebe and her parents. Plus there'd been one fabulous weekend last summer of late-night giggling, super munch-out sessions, and long games of Truth or Dare, when the Halls had let Phoebe, Sasha, and Chris go up to the cabin by themselves.

Sasha felt a twinge of bitterness as she thought about how close she and Chris had been that weekend. And now this silent feud. Phoebe was right. They had to come to terms with what had happened and try to put it behind them.

But first, she and Wesley had a whole day ahead of them in this wooded paradise, with nothing to do but be together. This was not the time or place to get worked up over Chris again. Sasha reached into her jacket pocket and felt around for the keys. Eagerly, she led Wesley up the twisting gravel path and unlocked the front door.

It was cold inside, but logs and kindling were stacked up next to the Franklin stove, so they could start a roaring fire. The knotty pine rooms beckoned cozily, and Sasha ran from one to the next, showing Wesley around. "Here's Mr. and Mrs. Hall's bedroom," she said, pushing open one of the doors and poking her head into an L-shaped area with large windows on two sides, exposing the peaceful rolling hills behind the house. "And this is where Phoebe sleeps. Not that you couldn't guess," she laughed, showing Wesley a room with colorful posters for various musicals and theater festivals taped to the wood walls, candles, and a whole collection of windup toys covering the top of the bureau.

They went back out to the living room. "And see up there?" Sasha asked. "That trap door in the ceiling? If you pull it open, a ladder comes down and you can climb up into the attic. Phoebe and I found all these old snapshots up there of her parents when they were first married. But here's the best part of the cabin." She took Wesley through the tiny kitchen. Off to one side of it was a large screened-in porch, an airy, open room in the middle of a wooded glade, connected to the rest of the house by a short hallway.

"They added this after they bought the place," Sasha explained. "I guess it's going to be too cold to use now, but in the summer it's great. That's where — " She broke off in mid-sentence, the corners of her lips turning down.

"What?" Wesley asked with concern.

"Phoebe, Chris, and I had this jacks marathon out there last summer." Her voice was low. Why did Chris have to keep popping into her mind at just the wrong moments?

"You and Chris are having a pretty rough time of it, huh?" Wesley noted.

Sasha gulped hard and nodded. "Ever since the party."

"That's too bad," Wesley said sympathetically. "The whole thing's too bad." He paused. "Starting with the fact that that ape Marquette was at the party at all."

Sasha sank down on one of the kitchen chairs. It seemed their little talk about the fight was unavoidable. "Wesley," she began, keeping as calm as possible, "I would rather not have seen John Marquette there, either. But since he *was* there, did you have to be so quick to fight with him?"

"Me, quick?" Wesley sounded incredulous. "Sasha, you heard him. If that guy wasn't provoking me, I don't know what you'd call it. What was I supposed to do?" He sat down across from her.

"Ignore him?" Sasha suggested in a small voice. It came out more like a question than an answer.

"You must be kidding." Wesley was getting worked up again.

"No."

"So you wanted me to sit there and just take his insults? *You* wanted to take his insults?" Wesley's voice echoed in the small kitchen.

There was nothing to do but come right out and say what she felt and hope it wouldn't turn into another explosion. "Fighting doesn't accomplish anything." Sasha held her breath.

"I don't believe this; I just don't believe it!" Wesley banged his fist on the round kitchen table. "You mean to tell me that this guy had every right to bully us and push us around?"

Sasha felt her chances for a peaceful discussion dwindling to zero. Her own temper was rising, and she found herself shouting over Wesley's words. "Now wait a minute. I never said he should have acted like such a jerk, but two wrongs don't make a right." Her hand shook and she felt a

129

stab of despair in her chest. Why did Wesley insist on driving her to this? All she wanted was to talk.

"I wasn't wrong! Maybe you nonviolence types don't realize it, but anyone with any sense knows that when the time comes you have to take a stand, show your opponent you mean business."

"Oh, so now I don't have any sense?! Is that right?" Sasha's last reserve of patience was quickly evaporating. The last thing she wanted was another fight, but she felt so frustrated that her words just shot out.

"So what did you prove, anyway? All you did was create bad feelings among my friends, not to mention the fact that someone could have gotten hurt. And maybe you military types could learn a little something from us 'nonviolence types.'" She echoed his phrase bitterly.

"Sasha, I was sticking up for you! Maybe you'd rather find a guy who doesn't give a darn what people say about you!"

"Maybe." Sasha was beginning to feel it was hopeless to try to make Wesley see her point of view. Why couldn't he at least make an effort to understand? "I don't know what made me think you'd know about anything besides what they teach you in a school like Leesburg — fight, fight, fight." Tears sprang to her eyes.

Wesley leaped out of his chair and paced back and forth in the tiny room. His hands were clenched at his sides, his knuckles white. "You pretend you're so open-minded, but you have this totally false picture of my school stuck in your head and there's no way anyone's going to change it, big Miss Liberal. But the only opinions that count are your own. I guess you learned that from your parents, huh?" he spat out scathingly.

Sasha felt every muscle in her body go rigid. "You just leave my parents out of this, Wesley. If your idea of taking a stand means picking on people who aren't here to stick up for themselves, people you don't even know, I don't want to have any part of it." She pushed her chair away with a loud clatter, and stormed into the living room. Wesley had just pushed her past her limit.

She shivered, wrapping her arms around herself. Suddenly the cabin didn't seem so cozy, only cold and isolated. And the afternoon that had held so much promise stretched endlessly ahead. With the next bus home hours away, Sasha was beginning to wonder how well she really knew Wesley Lewis after all.

Chapter
14

The pungent aroma of tomatoes and wine sauce wafted in from the kitchen, as Phoebe stretched out on the living room couch and thumbed through the latest issue of the Kennedy High newspaper.

"I hope there'll be enough of this chicken to go around," she heard her mother say.

"Don't forget that everyone else will be bringing something, too," her father replied. "I've never been to a pot-luck dinner where there weren't plenty of leftovers."

Phoebe skipped over an article about the new computer the school was buying. After a whole semester of computer programming, she'd decided that her parents' little PC was enough for her. She continued to flip the pages absently, one ear on her parents' conversation.

"I wonder what Martha's going to bring?"

Mrs. Hall mused aloud. "If she makes anything as good as that chocolate souffle she served us at her house, I'm going to blow my diet."

Phoebe heard the sounds of clanging pots and of cabinets being opened and shut. Then her mother spoke again. "Len, you look preoccupied. You're not worrying about the Martin account again, are you?"

Phoebe turned another page and found an article Sasha had written about the new poetry elective that was being offered the following year.

From the kitchen, Mr. Hall cleared his throat. "I'm afraid so," he answered Phoebe's mother. "Jim Martin is one of our most important clients. We can't afford to lose him."

"But, Len, you're doing all you can," said Jean Hall. "You should try to relax and have a good time this evening."

"That's easier said than done. Jim and his wife are so hard to please. I can't help thinking about them up at the cabin. If they don't have the restful weekend I've been promising, there might be an awfully heavy price to pay."

Phoebe threw the newspaper aside and sat straight up. The cabin? What were they talking about? Her adrenaline racing, she got up and edged closer to the kitchen.

"Len, what good will it do to labor over it?" Mrs. Hall was saying. "There isn't a more peaceful spot for miles around. If they don't enjoy themselves, it's not through any fault of yours. Besides, once they change out of their city clothes and build themselves a fire in the Franklin stove,

133

I'd wager that even the Martins will loosen up. Mark my words. In a few hours Jim Martin is going to be smiling."

Oh my god! thought Phoebe. A few hours! That meant her father's clients were leaving this afternoon, maybe even right now! She had to warn Sasha and Wesley! But how? There was no telephone in the cabin, and the Halls' second car was in the repair shop with brake trouble.

Phoebe's stomach felt queasy as she pictured her father's stuffy client and his wife arriving at the cabin to find a teenage couple already there. And from what Phoebe had seen of Sasha and Wesley together, they'd probably be sharing a very private moment when the Martins showed up.

What a disaster! If her father was this worried already, she could be pretty sure this Mr. Martin was not about to be the understanding type. Phoebe would have no one to blame but herself if the firm of Hall & Olstein lost one of their most important clients.

Phoebe took a giant breath. She had no choice but to tell her parents the truth. Perhaps they could get to Sasha and Wesley before it was too late. Her steps were heavy as she crossed the dining area and peeked into the kitchen. "Mom? Dad?" Her voice trembled.

"Yes, dear?" Mrs. Hall turned around.

Suddenly Phoebe remembered Woody's Volvo. The keys were upstairs in her top dresser drawer! She made a snap decision. She'd take Woody's car and get up to the cabin as quickly as possible. If she reached Sasha and Wesley in time, no one would have to know a thing. Not her parents, and especially not the Martins.

Mr. and Mrs. Hall were still looking at their daughter. "Oh, I — um — just wanted to tell you to have a good time tonight. I'm going over to Sasha's for a while, okay?" Phoebe managed to say. She crossed her fingers behind her back.

"You have fun, too," her father replied.

"Yes, and say hello to Mr. and Mrs. Jenkins," her mother added, stirring the sauce on the stove. "I keep meaning to go by their store and pick up a copy of that new novel I want to read."

"I'll tell them," Phoebe fibbed, trying her best to sound calm and natural.

As soon as she was out of the kitchen, she sprinted up to her bedroom, grabbed Woody's car keys, and raced out of the house. She pumped her legs as hard as she could, panting as she reached Woody's house in record time.

The silver car sat in the driveway. Phoebe unlocked it and jumped into the driver's seat. She hoped Woody wouldn't mind her taking it all the way up to the cabin and back. She made a mental note to buy a full tank of gas when she returned to Rose Hill. Then she started the engine, and peeled away from the Websters' house. She didn't have a second to lose.

"It's nice and warm in here," Sasha said tentatively, taking off her mittens and untying her scarf. While she'd been out getting groceries at the tiny general store in town, Wesley had started a crackling fire.

"I thought you'd like it. I was hoping you

135

might take off your coat and stay awhile," he kidded hesitantly.

Sasha allowed him to take the grocery bag from her. "And I was hoping you'd ask." She accepted this uneasy truce as she peeled off her mittens and scarf.

"What's to eat?" Wesley poked around in the brown bag. "I'm starved."

"Stir-fried vegetables with rice," Sasha answered. "Why don't you bring that into the kitchen and we can start cooking."

Wesley followed her into the tiny room. "Rice and vegetables and what else?"

Sasha gave him a perplexed look. "What do you mean, 'what else?' "

"Like isn't there a main dish? You know, hamburgers, or chicken, or something?"

Sasha leaned against the rickety old stove. "Is there some rule that every meal has to have meat in it?" she asked, a trace of annoyance in her voice.

Wesley seemed to catch the meaning in her tone. "Oh, um, no, I guess not." He put the groceries down next to her and seated himself at the kitchen table.

Sasha took an onion from the bag and handed it to him. "Here, why don't you find a knife and chop this up?"

"Me?" Wesley raised his eyebrows. "But I don't know how to cook."

Sasha felt herself on the verge of losing control all over again. "I'm not asking you to prepare the whole meal, but I am asking you to help out.

Now would you mind telling me what's so hard about chopping a few vegetables?"

Wesley was quiet for a moment. "Sasha, I wasn't brought up the way you were. In my house the women made the meals while the men went out and worked. It's not that I mind giving you a hand, it's just that I'm no good in the kitchen. Nobody ever taught me what to do around food. Besides eat it." He laughed.

Sasha didn't find anything funny in his words. Her jaw tensed. "There's no time like right now to start learning a few new things." She scrubbed furiously at a carrot.

"Sasha, please let's not fight anymore." Wesley came over and stood close behind her, circling his powerful arms around her waist.

Sasha fought the temptation to melt into his grasp. That was what had gotten her into this mess in the first place, thinking with her heart instead of her head. She stood rigid, her body tense against his.

"Come on," Wesley whispered in her ear, his breath warm on her cheek. "I want to help. Believe me. I just don't know what to do. I mean, would you have known how to build that fire out in the living room?"

Sasha whirled around, breaking free of Wesley's hold. "As a matter of fact, I would!" she retorted.

Wesley sank back down at the table and rested his head on his arms. "I should have figured that."

Sasha wasn't finished. "Furthermore," she yelled, "even if I didn't know how, I would have learned how in a hurry." She handed him a paring knife. "So peel that onion and get to work."

She cringed at her own hard tone, but she couldn't seem to help herself. She'd tried as hard as she could to make allowances for Wesley's background. At first it had been easy. She'd felt so in love, that any contrary idea he'd offered had seemed like an exciting novelty. But the newness was beginning to wear off. Every time their opinions clashed, Sasha felt more like she had made a big mistake. Her anger was surpassed only by a deep, aching sense of anguish. She and Wesley had started off so beautifully. Why did everything have to go wrong?

Wesley gave her a sarcastic little salute. "Aye, aye, captain," he said grimly. He worked wordlessly for a while. Then he spoke up again. "Sasha, maybe you won't believe me, but I really don't mind preparing dinner with you. What bugs me is being insulted at the same time. I can't help what I learned when I was growing up."

Sasha measured out the rice, and put it into the pot of boiling water. "That's true. You can't," she replied "Once you're grown up though, you have to reevaluate what you've been taught. Otherwise you end up pretty narrow-minded," she concluded pointedly. She kept her back to Wesley as she spoke, busying herself with preparing the meal. Her pride wouldn't allow her to let him see how much she was hurting.

"Oh, and you think you're any different?" Wesley snapped. "Just because your ideas are liberal doesn't mean you're so open-minded. You've completely swallowed every single thing your parents told you, hook, line, and sinker."

"I wish I really had," Sasha shot back. "Then maybe I wouldn't be in this situation right now." What was she saying? Sasha couldn't believe the venom in her voice. She was so confused she didn't know what was coming out of her mouth anymore. She felt as though she was fighting her way through a dense, suffocating fog, and she couldn't get her head clear enough to think straight.

" 'This situation'? You mean being here with me?" Wesley's words rang with both hurt and fury.

Sasha gave a sigh swollen with resignation. "Well, can you honestly say you're having a good day here, either?" she asked softly. It was time to face the fact that their perfect afternoon in the country together was no more than a dream that had dissolved like a drop of rain in the sea.

"I wish I could." Wesley's voice was calmer now.

Sasha turned. A look of unhappiness clouded his handsome face. She felt the anger draining out of her, until all that was left was a grave sense of disappointment, and a hollow, empty feeling. "I wish I could, too," she echoed. "I guess we really blew it, huh?"

She sighed. Why hadn't she listened to Phoebe's warning about rushing into things? She'd been so willing to believe the old saying that love conquers all. But now she realized that with backgrounds as different as hers and Wesley's, it wasn't necessarily true. At least not if you went plunging into things without stopping to get to know each other first. Sasha glanced at Wesley, slumped over the kitchen table. Unfortunately, her realization came too late.

Phoebe screeched up to the cabin and slammed on the brakes. No sign of any other cars. So far so good. She turned off the ignition, jumped out of the silver Volvo, and rushed into the little wooden house.

"Sash? Wesley?" she called out. The Franklin stove was lit with a crackling fire, and the spicy smell of food cooking came from the other room.

"Sash?" she yelled again, heading for the kitchen.

"Phoebe!" Seated at the table, Sasha looked up in utter surprise. "What are you doing here?"

"You guys, I'm really sorry, but we may be in big trouble." Phoebe explained their predicament, the words tumbling out in a panicked rush. "We've got to clean up and put the fire out and leave as fast as possible. Mr. and Mrs. Martin could be showing up any minute!"

Wesley pushed his plate from him with a loud clatter. "Sasha, I told you!" he exclaimed. "We never should have come up here without permission from her parents."

Phoebe was taken aback by the anger in his voice. She was even more surprised when Sasha responded with equal venom. "You mean we never should have come here, period!"

What had happened between the two of them to make things sour so quickly? But there was no time for Phoebe to wonder, and even less time for Sasha and Wesley to argue. "Look, I don't understand what's going on here," she said, "but whatever it is, it's going to have to wait until we're in the car and away from here." She squeezed a jet of dishwashing liquid into the sink, and grabbed a sponge.

"Of course," Sasha responded, immediately getting up from the table, picking up a dish towel, while Wesley sprinted to the next room and started beating down the flames in the Franklin furnace.

"You two didn't exactly seem lovey-dovey just then," Phoebe whispered, as Wesley left the kitchen. "Is anything wrong?" She handed Sasha the wet frying pan and lost no time starting on the plates.

"Pheeb, it's such a mess," Sasha confided. "And now, I'm getting you in trouble, too. I feel so terrible."

"Don't worry about me," Phoebe said. "I'll be fine if you just keep drying and we get out of here in time." She thrust a plate into her friend's hands. "But you and Wesley . . . and here I was worrying about messing up your romantic day together."

"To tell you the truth, I think we were both kind of relieved to see you," Sasha admitted.

Phoebe was on the verge of asking for details, when Wesley appeared in the doorway. "Fire's out," he announced. "Now what?"

"Why don't you wipe the table?" Phoebe tossed him a sponge. "We're just about done here." Sasha's explanation of what had happened would have to be put on hold. There'd be plenty of time to talk once they got back to Rose Hill.

They finished cleaning up in record time, threw on their coats, and ran for Woody's car. Phoebe revved the engine and pulled out of the driveway like a race car driver gunning over the starting line. As she steered around the first bend in the dirt road, a large white Cadillac came into view. "That's them! That must be the Martins!" She pulled into a cutaway on the side of the road and let them pass.

In the rearview mirror, she watched the Cadillac disappear around the curve. "Oh, my god, talk about close calls!" Phoebe felt ill thinking about what would have happened if the Martins had arrived five minutes earlier. Her hands shook as she pulled back onto the road.

"Pheeb, it's okay, we made it. We're safe," Sasha assured her. Phoebe rounded several more bends. A light drizzle had begun, and she turned on the windshield wipers. The mountains glowed pink as the sun began to set.

"But we never would have been in that situation at all if we hadn't come up here without permission," Wesley reminded Sasha. Out of the corner of her eye, Phoebe saw him slump down angrily in the passenger seat next to her.

"So you've been telling me," Sasha said tensely from the back of the car.

Phoebe tried to tune out the squabbling, concentrating on the road, which was icing up as it grew darker and colder. She saw the old general store on her left; that meant they had gone only ten miles so far. She pressed down on the gas pedal as the car began climbing another hill. The arguing showed no signs of easing up.

Finally, Phoebe turned on the radio and hummed along, braking gently as they began their descent down the other side of the mountain. But Wesley and Sasha continued to fight above the music. Phoebe twisted all the way around toward Sasha. "Hey, would you mind giving it a rest?" she asked.

"Phoebe!" Sasha screamed at the top of her voice, terror written all over her face.

Phoebe whirled back around. The Volvo was skidding off the side of the road. She yanked the wheel in the direction of the skid, the way she'd been taught, but it was too late. She fought for control of the little car in a frenzied struggle to get back on course. The car would not respond. Phoebe gripped the wheel, staring out the windshield helplessly as the car twirled on the slippery road, slid downhill, and plummeted straight toward a huge tree.

As the tree trunk loomed in front of the car, Phoebe squeezed her eyes closed tightly, letting out a blood-curdling scream that mingled with the sound of crumpling metal and shattering glass.

Chapter
15

Phoebe felt the seat belt dig into her chest as she was hurled forward, her cries of fright meeting Sasha's and Wesley's. Then there was a terrifying stillness.

Phoebe gasped for air, the wind knocked out of her by the impact. She forced herself to draw in a long, deep breath. Her heart beat wildly, but she knew she was unhurt. She whipped around toward the two others. "Are you okay? Sasha, Wesley!!"

"What? What happened?" Wesley seemed stunned, but otherwise all right.

"We hit a tree," Sasha said. She, too, was unhurt.

Phoebe tried to calm down. It's okay, she told herself. No one is hurt. Everything is fine. She pushed open her door and got out of the car, her legs weak. She walked around the back of the Volvo and checked out the other side.

Suddenly, another wave of panic swept over her. Woody's Volvo! Everything was not fine. Both headlights were broken, the fender was irreparably bent, and the entire right side of the car was folded up like an accordion. The right tire was deflated, a useless piece of rubber.

"Oh, my god! Sash — his car. Look at Woody's car!" she moaned, as Sasha let herself out of the wreck.

"Wow!" Sasha uttered darkly, coming over to where Phoebe was standing. "Now what are we going to do?" She wrapped her scarf tighter around her neck, shivering in the chill of the quickly fleeing daylight.

Wesley joined them, his face grim. He poked around at the tire and stuck his head under the body of the car. "Do you think we can put a new tire on and somehow get ourselves home?" Phoebe asked him, afraid to hear the answer.

He slid out from under the silver car. "Not in this thing. To begin with, there's no place to put a new tire with the wheel all bent up and the fender crunched under like this. And anyway, we must have broken something in the engine, too. There's fluid leaking all over the ground."

Phoebe looked down. Wesley was right, a trail of oily-looking liquid seeped out onto the road. She leaned back wearily against the side of the car. This afternoon had gone from bad to worse to total disaster. "I guess we have to find a tow truck," she mused aloud. "But how, is the question."

"We can go down to the general store and use their phone," Sasha said.

Phoebe shook her head. "We drove by it at least ten miles ago, by the time we get there they'll probably be closed." The mountains were a deep purple now, and the sky grew darker with every passing minute.

"You probably won't like this," Wesley prefaced his suggestion, "but maybe we ought to go to the Martins and explain what happened. They could drive us somewhere to get help."

"No!" Phoebe's reply rang out. "That's even farther than the general store, and besides, I'd rather walk all the way back to Rose Hill. If we go bothering them and my father loses their account. . . ." She shook her head insistently. "Absolutely not!"

"The bus station?" Sasha proposed. "No, I guess it's in the totally opposite direction from the way we were going, huh." She dejectedly answered her own question.

Phoebe took another look at the crumpled front of the car and winced. "Seems like the only choice we have is to start walking toward the main road, and hope like crazy that someone drives by and picks us up." She pulled the hood of her ski parka around her face.

"And if not?" asked Wesley.

Phoebe shrugged her shoulders. "I don't even want to think about it."

It had to have been at least two hours since they'd started walking. Two of the wettest, coldest, most miserable hours Sasha had ever spent. "My parents are probably worried sick," she said, swinging her mittened hands to warm her freezing fingertips.

"Mine, too," echoed Phoebe. "Plus they're going to absolutely kill me if they find out what happened."

"You mean you're not going to tell them?" Sasha questioned. The dirt road in front of them seemed to go on forever, with not a single car in sight.

Phoebe sighed. "Yeah, I guess." She paused. "If they ask."

"Pheeb, don't kid yourself. We're not going to be home for at least a couple of hours, if we're lucky." Sasha kicked a pebble in her path. "Someone's bound to ask a few questions." Her voice was grim.

She knew she'd have a number of things to explain to her own parents — not only where she'd been, but who she'd been with. And that opened the whole Pandora's box of problems she'd been avoiding since the night she'd found out Wesley was a cadet.

"You two think you're in trouble," Wesley put in. "You won't have to face the Leesburg staff when you get back. They're going to have a field day with me when I walk into my dorm way past curfew." Sasha thought Wesley sounded just a touch scared under the bravura of his tough Navy-man attitude. "With them, there's no such thing as a good excuse," he added.

Sasha felt the urge to put her arm around him and give him some support. Besides, she was getting frightened, too. The three of them were alone in the middle of nowhere, the temperature was dropping rapidly, and the rain had turned to snow mixed with freezing sleet.

She took a step toward Wesley. But as pieces of their afternoon's conversation replayed in her head, she remembered how angry she was at him. She stiffened and moved away from him. This trip had been a terrible idea from start to finish. She kept putting one foot in front of the other. If they walked far enough, they'd have to find some signs of civilization.

Chris Austin heard the front door slam. "Hi! Anyone home?" Brenda yelled.

"In here, Bren," she called back. Her stepsister appeared around the corner, pulling off her knit hat and shaking out her long dark hair.

"You got home before me," Brenda remarked. She sat down and folded one lean leg over the other.

"Uh-huh," Chris nodded. "I just walked in a few minutes ago. Want some cheese and crackers?" She pushed a plate of wheat crackers and port cheddar cheese across the table.

"No, thanks. Brad and I stopped off for ice cream after the movie. What did you guys do?"

Chris shrugged. "Not so much. We watched a few TV shows at Ted's."

"Well that could be kind of cozy," Brenda teased. "If you know what I mean." She winked.

"Mmm," Chris murmured distractedly.

"You mean it wasn't?" Brenda asked with surprise.

"Oh, no, it was fine. We had a really nice time. I was just thinking about something else." Chris was picturing the hurt, angry expression that had been on Sasha's face when she'd left Ted's party. No matter what she did these days, Sasha seemed to enter her thoughts.

"Feel like talking about it?" Brenda said softly.

Chris felt a touch of pleasant surprise. She looked up at Brenda's elegant, fine-boned face. The two stepsisters had come a long way since their constant bitter fighting following the marriage of Chris's father and Brenda's mother. But the girls' recent acceptance of each other was still new enough for Chris that sometimes she forgot she actually had a friend under her own roof.

"Maybe it would help to talk," she said gratefully. She cut a piece of cheese and put it on top of a cracker. "Did you see what happened with Sasha and that guy she was with at Ted's party?"

"Are you serious, Chris? If I hadn't, it would have been kind of like missing the eruption of a volcano in the middle of someone's living room."

A few months ago, Chris would have taken Brenda's remark as a cynical jibe with bad intentions. Now however, she had gotten used to her stepsister's brand of hard-edged candor, and realized that under the sharp exterior was a sensitive, caring person.

"I guess it was the highlight of the party, huh?" Chris said gloomily. "I'm so mad at Sasha for bringing along some guy who'd go and mess up everyone's night like that. But. . . ." Her voice trailed off.

149

Brenda reached across the table and patted Chris's hand. "The cold war between you and Sasha is getting to you, right?"

Chris found herself appreciating her stepsister's straightforward approach. Chris too often had the tendency to bury a problem and hope it would go away. But lately she was finding that it was usually better to face it head on and try to find a solution. Listening to Brenda sum up the situation without beating around the bush made it easier to get it out in the open and talk about it.

"It's been that obvious?" she asked.

"For starters, it's kind of tough on the rest of us when you two head for opposite ends of the lunchroom, and we have to choose who to go sit with. That's number one. And then whenever a bunch of us are hanging out and only one of you is there, when the other one comes along the first one leaves pretty quickly. Sort of the way it used to be when Brad or I saw Phoebe and vice versa, you know?"

Chris nodded. It had taken Brad a long time to get over his breakup with Phoebe; and then it had taken Phoebe almost as long to get used to seeing Brad and Brenda as a new couple. Chris remembered the feeling of being helplessly stuck in the middle while her best friend, her stepsister, and Brad carried on a silent battle. And now she and Sasha were doing the same thing.

"The worst part of it is that I really miss Sash," Chris said forlornly. "But every time I think about the party, I get angry all over again, and it stops me from making up with her."

Brenda looked thoughtful. "Chris," she finally began, "I know a lot about getting angry and staying angry, and believe me, it doesn't get you anywhere. Like when I ran away last year — I was angry at the whole world."

Chris listened quietly. It was only in the last few months that Brenda felt she could confide in her about the terrible time she'd had following their parents' marriage.

"You know, I thought I had such a rotten deal," Brenda continued. "I felt so sorry for myself. But getting mad didn't change a thing. It just made me more miserable. Then one day Tony sat me down, you remember Tony, don't you?"

"Sure." Tony was one of the counselors at Garfield House, where Brenda had stayed when she'd run away.

"Well Tony sat me down and gave me this lecture about putting the past behind you and starting fresh. I didn't pay much attention, at least not immediately, but little by little I began to see what he meant. Maybe that's what you and Sasha have to do on a smaller scale."

Chris pushed a hand through her long, blond hair. "But that guy she brought ruined Ted's party," she protested.

"That's exactly what I'm talking about," Brenda replied. "What's done is done. Ted's party is over, and it's not going to get you anywhere to keep thinking about how things could have turned out differently. Besides, it's not fair to make Sasha responsible for what her date did."

"Well, it is her fault for bringing him," Chris insisted irritably.

"You know. Chris, people do make mistakes sometimes. Especially at parties, where there's all that noise and excitement and it almost seems like you're supposed to get out of control." She looked Chris straight in the eye.

Chris avoided her stepsister's pointed gaze. "You're talking about me at Laurie Bennington's party, aren't you?" She turned bright red just remembering that horrible night.

After a lifetime of doing what was expected of her and insisting that others do the same, always being the perfect student, daughter, and girl friend, everything that was bottled up inside her had come rushing out. For the first time, and the last, Chris had gotten drunk. So drunk that her friends had ended up carrying her out of the party. The only thing worse than her pounding hangover the next day had been humiliating memory of how she'd behaved.

Now Chris put her head down on the kitchen table. "Did you have to remind me?" she groaned.

"Chris, I didn't bring it up to make you feel lousy. . . ." Brenda toyed with a strand of dark hair.

Chris sighed and looked up again. "Oh, I know, Bren. And you're right. I suppose that kind of thing can happen to anybody."

"So you're going to get right on the phone to Sasha and straighten this mess out?" Brenda prompted.

Chris hedged. "Isn't it kind of late to call?"

Brenda glanced up at the kitchen clock. "Not if you do it this second."

"Okay! You win, Brenda." Chris trudged to

the phone. "But this doesn't mean I'm not still mad about what happened." She dialed the Jenkins' number. Brenda smiled encouragingly and gave her a thumbs-up sign.

"Hi, Mr. Jenkins? This is Chris Austin."

"Chris. We've been trying to call you all evening," Mr. Jenkins' voice came over the line.

Chris noted the worry in his voice. "Well, I just got home. Is Sasha — is everything all right?"

"I'm not sure," Mr. Jenkins replied. "You see, we don't know where Sasha is. Phoebe seems to be gone, also." His normally relaxed manner had been replaced by a tone of anxiety. "The Halls are here with us now, and we were hoping you might be able to tell us where the girls went this evening."

Chris felt her anger at Sasha melting in a flood of concern. "I don't have any idea where they are!" She saw Brenda look up.

"Sasha's disappeared," she said, covering the receiver with her hand, "and Phoebe's with her!"

Brenda's brow creased. "Did they call that guy, what was his name, Wesley?" she stage-whispered. "Maybe he'll know something."

"Mr. Jenkins," Chris said into the phone, "did you try Wesley's school? Maybe he knows where Sasha might be."

"Wesley? Who's Wesley?"

Chris inhaled sharply. Was it possible that Sasha hadn't told her parents about Wesley? Now that she thought about it, the Jenkinses would probably be less than thrilled that their daughter was dating a cadet. Chris could have kicked herself. She'd called up to make amends with Sasha, and she was winding up getting her into hot water with her parents.

"Chris?" Mr. Jenkins asked.

There was a long silence. "He's just this guy," Chris finally said.

"Chris, it's extremely important that you tell us everything you can. It's not like Sasha or Phoebe to go off without telling anyone. They might need our help," Mr. Jenkins implored.

Chris knew he was right. Sasha might end up being even angrier with her than she already was, but there didn't seem to be any other choice. "Wesley's a boy Sasha's been seeing, Mr. Jenkins. Wesley Lewis. He's a — he goes to Leesburg Academy."

"The military school?" Mr. Jenkins' worried words were now mixed with shock. There was a long, deadly pause. "Yes, I see," he finally uttered. "Well, thank you very much, Chris. I'll call the school and see what this young man has to say." His voice was tight.

"You're welcome," Chris said, feeling a bit like a traitor. "And, Mr. Jenkins, if it wouldn't be too much trouble, do you think you could call me when you find out they're okay?"

Mr. Jenkins assured her that he would, and hung up. Sasha might never want to speak to her again, but Chris had to know that she and Phoebe were all right. She wouldn't be able to shut her eyes that night until she was sure they were safe.

Chapter
16

Phoebe thrust her hands deep into her coat pockets, shivering against the freezing rain. She hadn't had time to change out of her sweat pants before running out of the house, and now the cold wind whipped right through the thin fabric. Sasha and Wesley were barely speaking to each other, Woody's prized sports car lay crumpled by the side of the road, and on top of everything else, she felt as if she was getting a cold. She sniffled miserably.

"Come on, Phoebe, we're bound to find something soon," Sasha encouraged. "Here, why don't you borrow my scarf for a while." She reached her hand up.

"Then you'll be cold."

"No, no, I'm fine," Sasha insisted, pulling off her lavender scarf. Suddenly, her arm froze in mid-motion. "Lights! Oh my god, look! There's something there, just down the road!"

The lights twinkling in the distance were like an oasis in the desert. Phoebe could just make out a sign, lit up over an overhead lamp. "It's a gas station!" she shouted, relief sweeping through her.

They all ran toward it with renewed energy, bursting through the station door to the warmth of a small, cluttered room next to the garage. Sitting in a broken-down swivel chair, drinking coffee from a styrofoam cup, was a burly, red-faced man with an imposing mustache. Phoebe had never been so happy to see anyone in her whole life.

"We had an accident all the way back down the road," she burst out, gesturing in the direction they'd come from. "The car's all smashed up and we don't have any way of getting home. . . ." Her voice rose in desperation.

The man didn't make a move. "Take it easy, young lady," he said, taking another swig of coffee. "Calm down and tell me what happened."

Phoebe relayed the details of the crash, Sasha and Wesley joining in, in a jumble of voices.

"But you're all okay." The man looked them up and down. "Well, don't worry. We'll get you kids home. Now first off, where were you trying to go?"

"Rose Hill." Sasha said. "Right outside of D.C.?"

"Yup." The man put his cup down on an old grease-stained table. "I know it. About sixty miles down the main highway. I can have my partner tow you there." He stood up. "It'll be a tight squeeze, but you can all ride up in the cab with him. Leo?" He stuck his head into the garage and called to his partner.

"Sash," Phoebe hissed, "I've only got three dollars on me."

Sasha fished around in her pockets. "I've got ten, eleven, let's see, eleven seventy-three," she said, putting some crumpled-up bills and change down on the table. "It would have been just enough for the bus fare home, with twenty-eight cents left over."

She shook her head. "Boy, I wish I were on that bus now. I mean, I wish I had been on that bus," she continued. "I'd be home now and everything would be fine. Well, almost everything." Phoebe saw her look at Wesley with a face that reflected as much hurt and sorrow as anger.

Wesley, too, wore a glazed expression as he pulled his wallet out of his pants pocket and counted off a crisp stack of bills. "Twenty-five," he said.

"Excuse me, sir," Phoebe ventured, as the red-faced man turned back to them, "but how much is this going to cost?"

"Well, let's see now, fifty-five miles. . . ." He scratched his head. "It'll run you about seventy, eighty bucks."

Phoebe gasped. She looked at Sasha and Wesley, panic rising in her throat. "Um, how about if we give you half of it now, and our parents give you the rest of it when we get there?"

"Doesn't make any difference to me, long as I get paid," the man shrugged. "You can give it all to Leo at the end if you want."

"Mom and Dad are going to absolutely love this," Phoebe muttered. At least, she thought to herself, she wasn't still out walking in the cold.

"I guess we'd better call them," Sasha said nervously. "The longer we wait, the worse it's going to be." She turned to the mustached man. "Do you have a phone we can use?"

The man shook his head. "Lines are out on account of the storm the other night. They were supposed to come by and fix 'em today, but they never made it."

"Oh, no," wailed Sasha. "Our poor parents, they must be about to give up on us."

"Look, after Leo hitches up that car of yours and gets on the road, you can ask him to stop at the truck stop off the entrance to the highway," the man said. "Use the phone there."

"Okay," Phoebe nodded. The truth was she was almost relieved the phone was out. She knew how worried her parents had to be by now, but the prospect of explaining everything to them was about as appealing as an algebra final.

A short, muscular man with a blue baseball cap came into the room. "Tow truck's all ready to go," he said.

"Okay," the mustached man replied. "You kids go ahead with Leo, here."

Phoebe thanked the first man, and she, Sasha, and Wesley followed Leo back out into the rainy night.

Half an hour later, Sasha watched Phoebe dial the Halls' phone number from the pay phone at the truck stop. She looked as if she'd just

158

swallowed something that tasted horrible, and clutched the receiver so tightly her knuckles were white.

Sasha knew just how Phoebe felt. Her own stomach was doing tense somersaults at the thought of getting on the line with her parents.

"Hi, Dad?" she heard Phoebe say nervously. There was a pause. "I'm fine. Yes, Sasha's with me." Another pause. "They are? Oh, no, you were? Dad, I'm so sorry." She put her hand over the mouthpiece. "Your parents are with them," she said to Sasha. "They were about to call the police."

Sasha bit her lip. This meant big trouble.

"It's kind of a long story," Phoebe was saying. "We were in a car accident. No, no one was hurt, but we have to get the car towed. Dad, can't I tell you when we get home?" Pause. "You do? Right now?" She looked at Sasha and ran the edge of her hand across her neck.

"We were on our way home from the cabin," she continued. "No, no we passed them on the road. Right. Well, see, I sort of lent it to Sasha and a friend of hers for the day, but then I heard you telling Mom about the Martins, so I took Woody's car and . . . Dad, I know! Please don't yell. Look, I said I was sorry."

Phoebe's voice was trembling now. "Don't you think I've been punished enough? We've been walking in the freezing cold all night, and Woody's car is ruined . . . yes, I *do* realize how worried you must have been. Dad, this is the first phone we could get to!" Her voice rose.

"I won't ever do anything like this again. Ever.

159

I promise." A tear trickled down her face. "Okay, so we'll talk about it when I get home." She sounded resigned now. "Yes. Uh-huh, I'll put her on."

Phoebe covered the receiver again. "I'm grounded," she pronounced miserably. "I hope you have better luck."

Sasha took the phone. "Hello?" she said cautiously. "Dad, listen, I'm really, really sorry for making you and Mom worry. I can explain."

"Please do," her father's voice came over the line.

She squared her shoulders. "See, I met this guy the day we were at Monticello."

"Wesley Lewis," her father said matter-of-factly.

Sasha gasped. "How do you know?"

"We were so worried about you, we called all your friends. When we finally got in touch with Chris, she suggested we try a young man it seems you've been spending time with."

Sasha felt her nervousness and exhaustion overpowered by a bright flare of anger. "Chris? Of course she'd tell! And what else did she say about him?"

"Sasha, she thought we knew about him already," her father said with a touch of exasperation. "Don't blame her. She didn't want to give us any information about him."

"But she did. I'll bet she told you where he goes to school, too."

"I asked her," Mr. Jenkins said flatly.

"That traitor!" Sasha exclaimed. "Just who does she think she is!?"

"Sasha." Her father's voice was stern now. "If there's anyone you should be angry at, it's yourself. Chris was as worried as we were, and only trying to help. You're lucky to have friends who care so much."

"Right, sure," Sasha said bitingly.

"You know, Sasha, it's not like you to be so unfair to your friends. And it's not like you to be dishonest or irresponsible, either. I have to say that I'm very disappointed in you," her father continued. "You know your mother and I don't like the idea of punishment, but I'm afraid that in this case I don't feel I have a choice. You can expect to be grounded, too."

Sasha gritted her teeth as she listened to her father. All this for a few lousy hours spent fighting with Wesley? It wasn't fair. She said a tight good-bye and banged down the receiver.

"Well?" Phoebe asked grimly.

Sasha gave her the thumbs down sign. "Same as you."

"How long?"

Sasha shrugged. "I guess they'll decide when I get home. Not that it matters. I mean, who would I go out with, anyway?"

She looked over toward the cafeteria counter, where Wesley was ordering something to eat. She couldn't help tracing his profile with her eyes. His handsome face still made her feel short of breath. Was it looks alone that had made her fall so hard for him? She'd thought it went deeper. She'd thought she loved him. Maybe she did. A part of her wanted to run up to him and throw her arms around him. But the other part held her back.

"You're still attracted to him, aren't you?" Phoebe asked simply.

"Oh, Pheeb, I don't know. I'm so mad and upset, I can't tell what I feel. First him, then we ruin Woody's car, then we both get grounded, plus the latest garbage with Chris. You know, she ratted on me and Wesley to my parents. Can you imagine anything lower and sneakier than that?!" Sasha demanded. "My dad said she didn't want to tell him, but I'll bet she was just waiting to get even with me for spoiling Ted's precious party. Geez, it wasn't even her own house."

Phoebe was quiet for a minute. "Sasha," she finally began, "we're in this mess together. But as far as Chris goes, I have to say I believe your father. Whatever Chris is, she's not a tattle-tale."

"Look, I know she's your best friend. . . ." Sasha felt herself growing annoyed with Phoebe also.

"She's your friend, too," Phoebe insisted. "Even though you guys had a rotten week. Sasha, think about it. With all the bad vibes coming out of this, you don't need to add to it, by declaring war on Chris."

"We're already at war."

"Well, then maybe you should declare peace," Phoebe said. "You're supposed to be the pacifist, after all."

Phoebe's words struck a nerve. "I haven't been behaving much like one lately, have I?" Sasha asked.

"It's okay, Sash." Phoebe slung an arm around her shoulder. "It's been a rough night for everyone."

162

"Brother, you said it," Sasha agreed. "And the worst part is, it's not over yet." She thought of her parents, waiting angrily at home, and kept hoping she would wake up to find that this was all a bad dream.

Wesley looked at his watch again, accidentally elbowing Sasha as she sat on Phoebe's lap, her head ducked in the cramped cab of the tow truck.

"Sorry," he grumbled. It was the first thing he'd said since the truck stop. He turned to the man called Leo. "Doesn't this thing go any faster?" he asked.

"Kid, we're pulling a solid ton of weight on the rear." He jerked his head back toward Woody's crumpled car, "and there are more of us up here than is legal. I can't exactly burn any rubber."

"Oh, what difference does it make anyway," Wesley muttered. "I've already blown my curfew by two hours. Boy, I'll bet they're cooking up a winner of a punishment for me."

"You and me and Sasha, too," Phoebe sympathized.

"Wesley," Sasha said, feeling timid about addressing him, "why can't you sneak in through that path you used last time?"

"They do a bunk check," Wesley said curtly. "They already know I'm missing, so sneaking in would make things worse. Besides, I've had it with all these lies and sneaking around." His words were accusing.

Sasha closed her eyes wearily. Why couldn't all this be over? The truck bumped up and down,

163

veering to the right as they exited the highway.

"You okay, Sash?" Phoebe gave her a pat on the back. "Look, there's the Ski Hut. We're almost home."

Sasha opened her eyes again and watched the familiar sights roll by. Fifteen minutes later they were on the access road to Leesburg, pulling up in front of the massive gates, the same gates where she and Wesley had said a passionate good-bye after their first date.

Sasha felt tears brimming in her eyes. She brushed them away brusquely, refusing to let Wesley see how upset she was. If he could dole out the silent treatment, she could, too.

She and Phoebe climbed down from the truck to let Wesley out. He thanked the driver, then jumped to the ground. Reaching into his pocket, he pulled out his wallet and handed Phoebe all the money in it. "For some of the towing expenses," he told her. "I'll make arrangements to get the rest to you next week."

"Great. Well, good luck," Phoebe offered.

"Sure," he replied defeatedly. He didn't even glance at Sasha.

She watched his broad back as he walked stiffly through the gates, never turning around. Tears formed again, and this time she let them escape down her cheeks. This morning she'd had such high hopes about her day with Wesley. Instead, it had turned out to be the worst day of her life.

Chapter **17**

"You and all your lenient talk!" Sasha's temper was hot. "You're the same as any other parents. You don't approve of the boy I was with, so you keep me prisoner in my own house! Gee, what a new innovative idea," she said sarcastically. She pushed away her breakfast plate, a few bites of whole wheat pancakes left on it.

"Sasha," her father said calmly, "it's true that I wouldn't have chosen a cadet as the ideal date for my daughter, but that doesn't have a thing to do with why you're being grounded. You lied to your mother and me, and by not telling anyone where you were going, you put yourself in what could have been a very dangerous situation. What if somebody had been hurt in that accident? Then what? Who knows how long it might have taken for someone to find you?" He took a sip of freshly brewed herbal tea.

"So you're going to keep me under lock and

key for the next month?" Sasha asked bitterly. "I thought you didn't believe in punishment."

"Sasha, going out is for someone who can do it responsibly," her mother put in. "Do you think you've earned the privilege?"

"Don't you see that I didn't have any other choice?" Sasha said in frustration. "If I'd come to you and told you I was spending the day with a boy from a military academy, I wouldn't have gotten one foot out the door."

"Honey, we might have been disappointed in your choice, but we've always taught you that every person is entitled to make his or her own decisions. Yourself included." Her mother poured more tea for herself. "You never even gave us a chance to show we meant what we said."

"Well, how do you think I'd have felt going off with someone I knew you disapproved of?" Sasha brought her plate over to the garbage can and scraped her leftovers into it.

"How do you think we felt having no idea where our daughter was?" her father asked. "We were afraid to even guess what had happened to you."

Sasha listened to his soft, level voice as she washed her dish and put it in the drain board. It was hard to argue with someone who was so calm and reasonable. Sometimes Sasha wondered how it would be if her parents blew up and yelled and screamed, and she yelled back, and they got it all out of their systems. She sighed.

"But, Dad, a whole month of being grounded? I'm going to go nuts." She wiped the plate and her silverware and put them away.

"You'll be surprised at how quickly a month will go by," her mother said.

All Sasha could do was to hope she was right.

"Phoebe?" the voice on the other end of the telephone said. "It's Woody."

Phoebe felt the muscles in her neck and back tighten, and a picture of the smashed silver Volvo flashed through her head.

"Woody, hi," she gulped, trying to sound normal. "Uh, when, um, did you get back?"

"Just this morning," he replied.

"Yeah? How was it?" Phoebe shook her leg up and down nervously as she sat at the kitchen table. She knew she ought to get right to the point and tell Woody about the accident, but she couldn't bear to break the bad news to him immediately.

"Oh, great. Really terrific," Woody said, but there was no enthusiasm in his voice. Phoebe had the strange feeling that he was nervous about something, too. But maybe it was only a reflection of her own state of mind.

"So, uh, how were all the plays?" Phoebe asked. "Did you see Griffin?"

Woody didn't answer her questions. He didn't ask about the car, either. "Listen, Phoebe, there's something I have to tell you, and I'd rather not talk about it over the phone. What are you doing right now? Is it okay if I come over?"

Now Phoebe was certain that Woody was also upset. Had he found out about the car from somebody else? But he said he'd just gotten back. There was no way he could have heard anything already. No, she knew it was still up to her to break the bad news to him.

"Sure, come on over. I've got something to tell you, too."

"Be there in five minutes." She heard the click as he hung up his phone.

Phoebe got up and wandered into the living room, stuffing her hands into the pockets of her pink overalls. What could Woody have to say? He'd been so brief, so serious over the telephone. Not even one of his usual wisecracking jokes.

She went over to the large bay window and stared out. It was gray, gloomy, and cold. Fitting weather for her first day of being grounded, Phoebe thought. Fitting weather to break the news to Woody about his most valued possession.

When she saw him coming up the walk, she went to the door, pulled it open, and gave him a hug. She was genuinely happy to see him despite the gnawing ache in the pit of her stomach when she thought about his car. "Come on in." She led him over to the living room couch. "Do you want something to eat or drink, or anything?"

Woody shook his head. "They gave us breakfast on the plane." He shrugged his shoulders. "At least that's what they called it. It was just a chewy bagel and some orange juice. Boy, that airplane food is enough to make you lose your appetite for the rest of the day. If it doesn't kill you first."

Phoebe gave a short laugh. "Lousy flight, huh? Is that why you sounded so down in the dumps over the phone?"

Woody's face turned grim. "Not exactly," he

said tightly. "Although it's true I'd rather be down on the ground driving than flying, now that I've got the Webstermobile," He brightened visibly as he mentioned his car. "Speaking of which, how'd she behave while I was gone?"

Phoebe bit her lip. "Woody, that's what I had to tell you about. There was a — well — we had a — an accident. . . ."

Woody sat straight up. "In my car? What happened? Who's 'we'?" His frightened words shot out like machine gun fire. "Was anyone hurt?"

"It was Sasha, Wesley, and I," Phoebe began. "We're all okay. But your car . . ." she took a breath, "the whole front right side was ruined."

There, she'd said it. But it didn't make her feel any better. In fact, watching Woody's face as the news seeped in, she wished she could melt right into the cream-colored carpet beneath her.

"H-how?" Woody stammered.

Phoebe launched into a recitation of the messy events of the previous day. When she got to the part about the accident, the scene flashed in front of her eyes, the sound of splintering glass and metal filling her thoughts. She gave a shudder, covering her face with her hands.

"Hey, Phoebe, everything's okay," Woody reassured her. "Just as long as no one was hurt, that's the important thing," he said magnanimously.

Phoebe nodded, pushing the horrible vision out of her mind. "It's true, but the car, Woody — I mean Sasha and I will pay for the repairs and everything, but you left it in my care and I. . . ."

"Don't worry about the car," Woody was gallant, though Phoebe noticed him swallow hard. "Wasn't doing much good anyway."

Phoebe knit her brows. "What are you talking about?"

"You know, in the image department. Didn't do a thing." Woody tucked his thumbs under his suspenders. "I thought it was going to turn me into an instant Don Juan, the Second," he joked weakly, obviously trying to hide how upset he was. "But no fish are biting, so to speak."

"But Woody, what about Kim Barrie? I saw you guys at Ted's party."

Woody's face lit up for an instant, but then his grin faded. "She's got a boyfriend in Pittsburgh," Woody stated flatly.

"She does? Gee, I didn't know that." Phoebe was quiet for a second. "But, Woody, don't forget that he's there, and you and Kimberly are here."

"It won't work." Woody was adamant. "She's great, but we're just friends, okay?" He gave his head a hard shake. "So, anyway, back to the car." It was clear that even that subject was preferable to the one they were on now. "How bad is the damage? Is it in a repair shop now?"

Phoebe took the hint and left the conversation about Kimberly behind. Something told her that, boyfriend or no boyfriend, Kimberly had had a wonderful time with Woody at Ted's party. The smile on his face had said it all. But Woody was making it plain that the topic was closed.

"Yeah, the car's garaged," she replied to his question. "At Calco's down on Whitney and State. Old Mr. Calco said his son would have a look at it tomorrow and give us an estimate, but he said fixing it will cost a few hundred dollars at the least. But don't worry about it. Sasha and I will get it done." Phoebe cringed. "Somehow." She tried to imagine how many baby-sitting jobs it would take to pay for all the damage.

"But it *can* be fixed?" Woody asked.

Phoebe nodded. "But you won't have it back for several weeks. Oh, Woody, I'm so sorry."

"Phoeberooni," he said gently, "please don't keep apologizing. It's just a car. The main thing is that you and Sash and Wesley are all right — even though those guys are having some problems." He frowned a little. "Too bad about that. Poor Sasha. But anyway, you're here, and you don't have a scratch on you. So don't get worked up about the Volvo, okay?"

Phoebe studied her dear old friend. She'd just wrecked the car he'd scrimped and saved for, the car he'd proudly shown off whenever he'd gotten the chance, and he was telling her not to worry about it, sincerely concerned for her safety above all else. She threw her arms around him in a warm, grateful hug. "Woody, you're the best!"

Woody's cheeks turned pink, and he combed his fingers through his curly dark hair as if he didn't know what to do with his hands. "Thanks, Pheeb."

"So, now it's your turn. You came over to tell me something," Phoebe said, "and instead, I've been laying all this bad news on you."

Woody picked at an imaginary piece of lint on his jeans. "I'm afraid my news isn't any better than yours." He plunged right in. "Phoebe, it's about Griffin."

171

Phoebe's heart jumped to her throat. "Oh, no! He has a new girl friend, right? He never wants to see me again." There was a pounding in her ears and it was hard to breathe.

"No, no. Nothing like that. I didn't even see him. And that's exactly the problem. He wasn't listed in the program, no one backstage had any idea who he was, and the bookkeeper at the producer's office said nobody by that name has anything to do with the production." Woody's voice was filled with concern.

The pounding turned to an all-over numbness. "But Woody, that's impossible!"

"It's true. He's not in the play."

Phoebe dropped her head into her palms. She had to try to think clearly. Griffin had called her right after the audition for the play. He'd barely been able to contain his excitement. But then, Griffin never was one for holding anything back. Or so she'd thought. In this case it looked as if he'd held back everything, including the truth. She picked her head up.

"Where do you think he is?" Phoebe was having trouble believing the whole story. She couldn't decide whether to be even more hurt and furious with Griffin than she already was, or to be anxious and nervous about him.

Woody shrugged his shoulders. "It just doesn't make sense. Phoebe, I know it's painful to think about, but when was the last time you spoke to him?"

Phoebe could remember it as clearly as if it had been five minutes ago. In fact it had been several months, and she told Woody so. "He said that with this job and all, he was going to be too busy for his old friends and the life he'd left behind in Rose Hill. He said his feelings for me hadn't changed but that — that — " Phoebe's voice wavered, and the words wouldn't come out.

"Well, you get the picture," she sniffed. "I had been all ready to visit him in New York, too. I mean, when he'd called the time before, right after the auditions, he told me he wanted me to come celebrate with him. I can't understand what happened!" Phoebe threw up her arms, her voice rising in despair.

Woody leaned back. "Pheeb, maybe none of us got to know Griffin as well as we thought, but it just seems so unlike him to lie or get sneaky, or whatever's going on here."

"Are you saying we should be worried about him?" Phoebe asked, a jumble of conflicting thoughts and emotions running through her mind.

Woody creased his forehead. "How do we know he doesn't need our help?"

Phoebe was enveloped by an icy cold. "I don't know, Woody. I can't help thinking that he could have found some way to let me know he really needed my help. I *did* talk to him. Maybe he just doesn't want to be found." Phoebe sighed, and the long, shallow breath caused her whole body to tremble. "Unless we find him, I guess we don't know anything at all."

Griffin's impish, brown-eyed face was etched in Phoebe's memory. She wrapped her arms around herself and shivered.

Chapter
18

Sasha sat cross-legged in the middle of her room, staring off into space. Her notebook lay open in her lap, a pen uncapped next to her. Her round script filled one page after another, but she could no longer write another word. Sad poems and melancholy stories were not the answer to her situation. She had to accept the fact that things were over between her and Wesley, and try to get back on her feet. She couldn't mope around forever.

She picked up her pen and made a thick black line under the last poem. THINGS TO DO, she wrote, in bold capital letters. 1. Work on new article for *The Red and the Gold*. 2. Finish story for Janie's birthday. 3. Find odd jobs to make money for repairs on Woody's car. She chewed at the end of her pen. That was a start. If she kept busy, she wouldn't have time to feel so sorry for herself. She added one more item. 4. Call Chris.

She looked long and hard at that last item. She was still furious at Chris, but she was no longer entirely certain that her anger was justified. Another talk with her father had convinced her that Chris had acted out of honest concern when she'd mentioned Wesley the evening before. And as for the night of the party, the more she thought about it, the less certain Sasha was that Chris was wrong. After all, she and Wesley were at total odds about the very same thing that Chris was so upset about — his fight with Marquette.

Darn Marquette! If only he hadn't decided to pick on her, maybe none of this would have happened. No! Sasha gave her dark braid a hard shake. She couldn't keep putting the blame on someone else. The fundamental differences between her and Wesley would have surfaced eventually, regardless of Chris, John Marquette, or anyone else.

She knew that. Why then, did it hurt so much? She couldn't stop thinking about Wesley: his face, his strong, sleek body, the tender way he'd held her. She still had the feeling that they could learn from each other's differences.

Sasha stop! she ordered herself. She had made up her mind to put the past behind her, and she was going to stick to that. She went back to the list in her hand. Okay, first things first. She got up and headed out into the hall to the upstairs telephone.

The Austins' phone kept ringing. Sasha counted ten rings, and then hung up. Everyone in the Austin household was probably out enjoying the weekend. Most likely, Chris was off having a great time with Ted somewhere, totally unaware Sasha was cooped up in this house, sadness pressing in on her from every direction.

Sasha sat down at the top of the staircase and leaned her head against one of the bannister supports. It was going to be a long, lonely month.

Downstairs, the doorbell rang. She heard her mother's footsteps echo off the hardwood floor in the foyer. The heavy front door creaked open. "Chris! Hello," her mother said.

Sasha sat up immediately. Chris had been thinking about her!

"How have you been?" her mother was asking. "I haven't seen you around recently."

Sasha swooped down the stairs. "Maybe because I haven't been a very good friend lately." She burst into the foyer where Chris was standing in her blue jogging suit and gave her a big hug. "I was just trying to call you," she said.

Chris, normally reserved, returned the hug freely. "You were? Oh Sash, I was so worried about you last night. When I heard you were missing — I don't know, I realized how much I've missed you. This whole thing between us is so. . . ."

". . . dumb," Sasha finished for her. "Chris let's forget the past week, deal?"

Mrs. Jenkins walked away quietly, leaving the girls alone.

Chris smiled, her classic features lighting up happily. "Deal," she agreed. "But I do want to hear about what happened yesterday. Did your parents do anything to you?" she whispered conspiratorily.

Sasha rolled her eyes. "I'm grounded for a month. It's a pretty sorry situation. Look, can you stay for a while? We can go up to my room and I'll tell you the whole story."

"Okay." Chris followed her up the stairs. "Sash? Listen, I wasn't a very good friend either." They entered the room and Chris sat stiffly on the edge of the bed. "I was so busy being mad at you for messing up at Ted's, that it took Brenda to remind me how easy it is to get out of control at a party like that."

Sasha knew Chris was also referring to the awful night she'd had at Laurie Bennington's party back in the fall. She held out her hand.

Chris took it. "I want you to know that I'm really sorry Ted had to ask Wesley to leave. I hope it didn't cause any trouble between you two."

Sasha swallowed hard against the lump that was forming in her throat. "It doesn't matter anymore. None of that matters." Haltingly, she told Chris about the disastrous trip she and Wesley had made to the Halls' cabin. When she was finished, her face was streaked with tears.

Chris didn't say a word, but she put her arm around Sasha and stroked her hair until she had calmed down. Sasha dried her eyes on the edge of her T-shirt. She was grateful to have Chris to talk to. If nothing else, at least things with Chris were right again.

Sasha knew Chris was trying her hardest to cheer her up. Chris passed along all the jokes Ted's football buddies had told him over the past week, and filled her in on the previous night at the sub shop, and kept one good record after another on the turntable of Sasha's stereo.

At first Sasha was simply going through the motions of having a good time, but by the third or fourth album the smile on her face was real. She and Chris strutted around the room, singing at the tops of their lungs to the new Cartunes' album. Sasha drummed her hands on the top of her dresser in time to the percussive beat.

"Sash, do you hear something?" Chris shouted above the music. "I think someone's knocking."

Sasha pulled her door open. Outside the bedroom stood her mother. "And they used to say that our generation played their music loudly."

Sash went over to the stereo and turned the volume down. "What's up, Mom?"

"You have a visitor, dear."

"Who?"

"Why don't you come down to the living room and see?" She smiled.

"Well, all right." Sasha wondered who was downstairs. Two visitors in one day. Maybe being grounded wasn't going to be as bad as she'd imagined. "Come on with me, Chris."

They followed Mrs. Jenkins down. "So, Mom," said Sasha, "who's the big surpr — " She stopped cold in her tracks when she saw the person sitting on her couch. Talking to her father, in full military garb, was Wesley.

"Sasha." He stood when he saw her. "And Chris. Hello," he said, polite yet reserved.

Sasha looked from Wesley to her father, then

back to Wesley, then to Chris. Sasha felt as though she'd been twirled like a toy top.

"Hi, Wesley," Chris said. She appeared decidedly uncomfortable, but she took a few steps toward him anyway. "I was — um — just on my way out, but I'm glad I got a chance to see you again. I was just telling Sasha that I — ah — I'm sorry about what happened last Saturday. I hope we can try to be friends." She extended her hand.

Wesley took it and they shook. "I hope so, too," he said. "And I'm also very sorry."

"Apology accepted. Well, see you around, I guess." Chris gave an awkward little wave. "See ya in school tomorrow, Sash. Bye, Mr. and Mrs. Jenkins. Oh, please don't get up, Mr. Jenkins. I can show myself out."

"Bye, Chris." Sasha watched her friend leave the room. Now it was just her parents and Wesley. Silence filled the air.

"I was telling your father about school." Wesley broke the ice. Sasha tensed up. What a subject to start in on.

"Sasha, there's no need to look so glum," her father said. "I've made my feelings clear to this young man, but he also knows that I never wanted you to hide your relationship with him from me because of who or what he is. If you want to see more of him . . . well, I can learn to accept that."

"Yes, me, too," her mother said. "Wesley, we're glad to have you as a visitor in this house." She smiled cordially.

Sasha shifted from one foot to the other, ill at ease and rather embarrassed. Her parents' well-meaning hospitality seemed a little silly now that her romance with Wesley was over. She was glad when they finally excused themselves and left her and Wesley alone.

"How are you feeling today?" Wesley began a bit stiffly.

"Okay, all things considered. I've been grounded for a month, but Chris came over and we made up." What a dumb thing to say. As if that weren't obvious. Sasha plunked down in the oversized, stuffed armchair.

"I'm glad," Wesley said simply. He sat back down on the couch.

"So . . . what happened when you got back to school?" Sasha fiddled with the hem of her Indian-print skirt.

"I had to report to the dean's office. My Saturday off-campus privileges have been rescinded for the rest of the semester."

Sasha whistled through her teeth. "Wow, that's pretty bad. I'm sorry to hear that. I really am."

"Thanks. I'm sorry about you being grounded, too." He paused, as if the next thing he had to say was difficult. "I'm also sorry about — well, about everything that happened yesterday. I wish it had worked out differently."

Sasha looked straight at him. "Me, too," she admitted.

Wesley toyed with one of the brass buttons on his uniform. "I guess this is a big day for apologies."

Sasha nodded.

"We really rushed into things, didn't we?" Wesley said.

Sasha gave a bitter laugh. "For once I agree with you. I think we were so busy feeling as if the whole world was against us, that we didn't give ourselves time to get to know each other, to be friends before we started being, well. . . ." Her sentence trailed off.

Wesley leaned forward. "You mean we needed to learn to like each other as well as love each other, right?"

"Exactly."

He got up and circled around the living room. "Sasha, do you think it's too late?"

Sasha watched him, his handsome face so serious, his long stride stiff with tension. "What do you think?" She held her breath waiting for his answer.

He walked over to where she sat, and stood directly in front of her. "I'd like to give it another try," he said shyly. "If you want to, that is."

Sasha let her breath out, an uncontainable smile appearing on her face. "I do want to. I want to very much. As long as we take it slowly, really slowly. It wouldn't be any good if we made the same mistakes all over again."

Wesley laughed, a big hearty laugh that filled the room. "Sasha, with you stuck in here for a month, me stuck on campus six out of seven days a week, and my parents usually around on the seventh day, I don't see how we could take it any other way besides slowly."

"I can't argue with you there." Sasha heard her own laughter mingling with his. She felt herself relaxing, and the knot that had been in the pit of her stomach for the past two days was disappearing.

A few hours ago she couldn't imagine how she was going to survive the next month, having to be alone with her thoughts for all those long afternoons and evenings. But now it didn't seem nearly so horrible. Not with Chris back on her side. And especially not now that she and Wesley had a chance for a fresh start.

"Should we shake on it?" she asked.

Wesley nodded.

Sasha felt the electricity of his gaze locking with hers. Their hands touched in a warm and tender grasp.

Chapter
19

Kimberly Barrie was thinking about Woody Webster again. She moved around the kitchen, adding a tablespoon of strong, black coffee to the chocolate melting over the double boiler. She pictured how he'd been waddling around the lunchroom on Friday as if he were carrying an extra hundred and fifty pounds on his tall lanky frame, a pencil stuck behind one ear stroking an imaginary beard.

"I know! Mr. Hardin!" she'd said as she walked by with her lunch tray.

"Mr. Hardin, what, young lady?" he'd asked through his nose, in a perfect imitation of the teacher's nasal voice.

"Mr. Hardin, sir," she'd giggled.

"And don't you forget it, young lady. That's the trouble with this generation — you've lost all regard for formality. Anything goes, don't you know. . . ." Woody had wagged his finger at her.

"Woody, that's great! You've got his speech down pat!"

"Pat? Did somebody say Pat?" His voice became low and gruff as he whipped the pencil out from behind his ear and snapped it in half.

"Mr. Patriano!" Kimberly had howled. She didn't have the strict history teacher herself, but every student at Kennedy knew his reputation for breaking pens and pencils if he caught you passing notes in class.

Stirring the chocolate mixture, Kimberly laughed out loud. Woody was so spontaneous, so much fun. She couldn't help comparing him with David again — David, always so self-contained and solemn. But as different as they were, both boys had a caring, sensitive side to them.

Those qualities were right out in the open with David; that was what had attracted Kimberly to him in the first place. But you had to dig to find Woody's more serious side. He didn't show it often. In fact, in the few weeks she'd known him, Kimberly got the feeling he made a point of covering it up around her by clowning around, the way he had at lunch the last time she'd seen him.

She wondered why. Perhaps it was because they were still pretty much strangers to each other. Maybe where some people would become quiet and shy, Woody played the funny guy. That was okay with Kimberly. She enjoyed Woody's being a funny guy immensely. But she also hoped she'd have the opportunity to get to know the other side of him better.

"Kimberly, darling?"

Kimberly looked up, startled from her thoughts

184

by her mother's voice. "Oh, hi, Mom. Just get home?"

Her mother nodded. "You look far away," she commented.

"Oh, I was just thinking about David," Kimberly replied, feeling a little guilty. Well, at least it was partially true. She wasn't sure what was stopping her from telling her mother the whole truth and saying something about Woody, but she could feel the beginnings of a blush creeping across her face. She turned toward the stove.

"You miss David, don't you?"

Kimberly automatically bobbed her head up and down.

"He called yesterday, didn't he?" her mother asked. "How is he?"

"Fine. He's preparing for another debate at the end of next week. When it's over, he wants me to come out and visit."

"Yes?" Mrs. Barrie walked over to the stove and peered into the top part of the double boiler. "Mmm, that looks good."

"Thanks. So I think I'll go if it's okay with you."

"I don't see any reason why not," her mother replied. "It's hard, isn't it?"

"What, the mousse? Actually it's a very easy recipe."

Her mother laughed. "No, silly, not the mousse. I mean being so far away from David."

"Oh." Kimberly took a half dozen eggs from the refrigerator and started separating the yolks from the whites. "Yeah, it's tough, but it was worse at first, when I didn't know anyone here.

185

I'm starting to meet some nice kids at school." Woody's face popped into her head again.

"That always helps," her mother said. "And you'll be seeing David in less than two weeks. That should help, too."

"Yes," Kimberly said firmly. "It'll be wonderful to see David again." But the boy she could not erase from her thoughts was Woody Webster.

Coming Soon...
Couples #6
CRAZY LOVE

Kim sighed again. This had to be the most romantic place in the world. Shafts of sunlight filtered through the thick branches spotlighting patches of the forest floor. There were clusters of brightly colored mushrooms, and pale, delicate toadstools on long, slender stems.

"You know," said Woody, breaking into her thoughts, "wouldn't this make the perfect place to stage a Shakespeare play, maybe *A Midsummer Night's Dream*? Can't you just see the sprites running around in these trees?"

Woody rushed around excitedly. "Perfect. Absolutely perfect," he mumbled, then ran over to another tree for a different angle. "Too wonderful." Finally he turned to Kim, completely unaware of her romantic fantasy. "Do you think the trustees of Rosemont would give me permission?"

"Woody Webster. You are the most frustrating person in the world," yelled Kim, charging at him. He dodged lightly out of her way, and playfully rumpled her hair as he did. Kim charged again. This time he ran behind a large pine tree. Kim rushed around one side and then the other, but each time he just escaped her grasp. Finally, she caught him off-guard and grabbed his shirt sleeve. They spun around and around then fell to the ground, Kim landing on top of Woody. Her face was inches from his. His eyes were shiny and devilish-looking. That sweet, funny smile, which had dominated her thoughts for so many hours, was now miraculously close. Before she even thought about the consequences, Kim felt herself leaning toward Woody. Their mouths met and his lips were as warm and tender as she had imagined.

*For help with family problems,
for confidence in making decisions,
for comfort in times of need . . .*

"Catherine Marshall reminds Christians that reliance on the Holy Spirit is essential. Each chapter gives evidence of people overcoming dire tragedies with the help of prayers to the Holy Ghost. Some are awesome, documented cases of miraculous cures, others are instances of regained faith and all are fascinating. . . . She writes unassumingly, simply and with palpable sincerity."
Publishers Weekly

"Catherine Marshall is one of America's finest Christian writers. . . . The book is dotted with evidence of her beautiful gift of painting word pictures. . . . The short devotional studies are carefully laid out, and thoughtfully presented. . . . It provides clear insights, simply set forth for those seeking a closer relationship with God, the Holy Spirit. . . . Penetrating and provocative . . . this book will beautifully guide."
Contemporary Christian Acts

CATHERINE MARSHALL

The
Helper

A Key-Word Book
WORD BOOKS, Publisher
Waco, Texas

First Key-Word Edition: December 1979

THE HELPER

A KEY-WORD Book
Published by Avon for Word Books, Publisher

ISBN: 0-8499-4137-7

Library of Congress Catalog Card Number: 77-92448

Printed in the United States of America

To
my son Peter
and to
Edith,
the daughter God gave me

Acknowledgments

I wish to express my appreciation to my secretaries, Jeanne Sevigny and Jean Brown, who as usual have patiently typed and retyped their way through the various versions of this manuscript; to Ruth McWilliams for her assistance in research and in copy-editing; for the special typing help of Louise Gibbons.

My special gratitude to my husband Leonard LeSourd, always an exacting critic and reliable sounding board; and to the close friends in both our Florida and Virginia fellowship groups, with whom I have shared the discoveries about the Helper recorded in these pages and the day-by-day living out of those discoveries.

C. M.

Contents

Foreword

In the early summer of 1944 I found myself curious about what seemed a strange subject indeed—the Holy Ghost. It was not that I had heard any sermon on this topic, or read a book, or been a part of some lively discussion group. Indeed, nothing overt had happened to spark this curiosity. It was rather as if I were hearing for the first time a replay of a lifetime of ecclesiastical garnishes that had hitherto floated past me—the endings of prayers, benedictions, christenings, communions, weddings and the like using the term "Holy Ghost" or "Holy Spirit." An inner spotlight now focused on this. Questions nagged and would not be silenced. . . . What was so significant about this spooky-sounding term? Why had the Church clung tenaciously to something seemingly so archaic? In short, what was this all about?

With the perspective of the years, I now know that God Himself had carefully planted the curiosity in me. For it was no passing whim. It did not go away, and it had ample emotional, intellectual, and volitional energy fueling it to keep me at a summer-long quest for answers to my questions.

I decided to go to the one place I could count on for final authoritative truth—the Bible. Scripture had never yet deceived me or led me astray. From long experience I knew that the well-worn words from an old church ordinance had it exactly right—the Bible still is "the only infallible rule of faith and practice."

At the same time I also knew that the search in Scripture could be no random dipping in; it had to be thorough and

11

all-inclusive. A Bible, a Cruden's Concordance, a loose-leaf notebook, pen, and colored pencils were my only tools.

All summer I gave a minimum of an hour a day to this. Using the various terms referring to the third Person of the Trinity, I looked up every reference in the Concordance, Old and New Testament. Morning by morning revealed new truths—new to me at least. Such as that in Old Testament times only certain prophets, priests, and kings were given the Spirit. Even then, the Spirit was given them only "by measure"—that is, a partial giving. So that was why Joel's prophecy,[1] fulfilled at Pentecost, was such startling news: in that great day the Spirit for the first time in history became available to *all* flesh, no longer "by measure" but in His fullness!

Or on another morning I discovered that John the Baptist, as the forerunner of Christ, was granted a unique gift—the Spirit from birth.[2] Jesus on the other hand, did not receive the baptism of the Spirit until He was about thirty years old at the time John baptized Him in the Jordan. Up to that time, Christ had performed no miracles or "mighty works." So even the Son of God Himself did not dare begin His public ministry without the power of the Spirit.

The messages kept piling up. I discovered that the fullness of the Holy Spirit is *not* something that happens automatically at conversion. His coming to us and living within us is a gift, the best gift the Father can give us. But the Father always waits on our volition. Jesus told us that we have to desire this gift, ask for it—ask for Him.

Something else shimmered through too. It's the Spirit who is the Miracle-Worker. When our churches ignore Him, no wonder they are so devoid of answered prayer. No wonder they have rationalized and developed an unscriptural position: the belief that miracles were only for the beginning years of the faith to get the Church started!

Rather, the truth is that Scripture assumes miracles. And the Helper (one of the names Jesus gave the Holy Spirit) always brings miracles in His wake, moves in the climate of miracles, expects them.

By now I was excited. I was also increasingly incredulous about the silence of the churches on this subject. How was it that I could not recall ever hearing a sermon on the Holy Spirit? Why was this not taught in Sunday School?

Naturally, I did not keep quiet about the search I was

on. My enthusiasm for my mounting discoveries was shared with Peter Marshall. It was happily inevitable that the study had to spill over into life. We asked for the great gift of the Spirit. Very quietly, by faith, we received Him— with immense richness and blessing added to our lives. The blessings have followed across the years and, for me, the unfolding joy of ever-new learning is still going on.

That was how, during the last years of Peter Marshall's life, two strong strands of teaching emerged in his ministry —a greater emphasis than ever on healing through prayer, and the beginning of an emphasis on the Holy Spirit. The healing renewal in the Church had begun in the Anglican Church in England and was at that time beginning to be reflected in Episcopal circles in America. But so far as Peter and I knew, there was no one who shared our new-found enthusiasm for the Holy Spirit's mission in our contemporary world. After all, this was twenty years before the tremendous revival of interest in the subject in the sixties.

Then in 1945 the editor of the Presbyterian monthly devotional magazine *Today* asked Peter to author an issue. Up to that time, each issue had been a miscellany of thirty or thirty-one assorted topics. Peter suggested to the editor that he and I coauthor the devotionals, and that they be the study of a single topic for the month. The editor agreed. The topic Peter and I chose was the Holy Spirit.

The resultant July 1945 issue of *Today* met with a surprising response. Copies were quickly exhausted, with readers writing in for more copies. In the next two or three years this issue was reprinted once, then again. As late as 1954 *Today*'s editor was writing in "The Editor's Visit" in the front of the April issue:

> Requests for back issues of *Today* on "The Holy Spirit," written by the Marshalls, keep coming to the Editor's office, but he is sorry to report that the supply is completely exhausted.

Those 1945 devotionals taken from the original summerlong study form the core of the material that follows. Since the Holy Spirit must and ever will be our Teacher, to that first material I have added more of His teaching and the insights He has given in the years since.

Back in 1945 Peter and I could never have foreseen the

amazing resurgence of the Spirit that began early in the sixties and by 1966-67 was in full swing. By ten years later, at least 500,000 members of mainline Protestant churches and 2,000,000 Catholics were involved in this renewal. Books on the subject began flooding from the presses.

Even with all this interest in the Holy Spirit, many church members are still wondering (just as I did back in 1944) whether this is another religious fad that will fade like all other fads. And whether its proponents are odd, eccentric people, just another brand of fanatics? Finally, whether this Helper can have any important bearing on his or her life?

If such wonderings are more than a passing vagary, the inquirer then speculates about where he can get reliable information about the Spirit. To such a seeker, I could give no better reply than that Dr. A. B. Simpson gave to some inquirers about the gospel of healing back in 1915:

> I sent them to their homes to read God's Word for themselves and ponder and pray . . . [because one must be] fully persuaded of the Word of God in this matter. This is the only sure foundation of rational and Scriptural faith. Your faith must rest on the great principles and promises of the Bible, or it never can stand the testing of the oppositions and trials that are sure to come. You must be so sure that this is part of the gospel and the redemption of Christ that all the teachings and reasonings of the best of men cannot shake you. . . .[8]

Dr. Simpson's advice is as sound and applicable to the baptism of the Spirit as to healing. The purpose then of the devotionals that follow is to go back to Scripture to discover what it would teach us about the Helper. Let the Bible speak to you where you are. You can trust it. Have no fear about resting your whole weight and, indeed, your very life on its message.

It is a shining promised land into which the Holy Spirit would lead all of us, that land prepared for the heirs—the beloved sons and daughters of the King. We do not have to wait for death to enter. It is for the here and now.

But the promised land won't come to us. Our entering in is volitional: it is necessary that we make up our minds and our wills to rise and enter.

When we do, the promise is sure,

Every place that the sole of your foot shall tread upon,
that have I given unto you. . . .[4]

No wonder the gospel is "glad tidings of great joy to all
men!"

Catherine Marshall

Evergreen Farm, Virginia
October 5, 1977

How to Use This Book

Since the Helper can never be packaged or programmed to fit any man-devised plan, the way to approach this book is with open expectancy. It has been written out of my own spiritual need to speak to those who share my longing for thirst-quenching quaffs of the Living Water.

The forty "helps," of course, are ideal for the forty days of Lent as a devotional guide—either for individuals or for study groups. But *The Helper* is also a book for all seasons just as the power of the Holy Spirit is needed every day of the year to help us cope with the problems and complexities of the difficult times we are living in.

For individual use, I recommend setting aside the same time each day, in the same quiet place, for reading, checking Bible references, and personal prayer. It helps to be very specific in one's prayer requests. This can become an exciting experiment by the keeping of a Prayer Log in which each petition is jotted down by date, with space left to record the date of the answer as well as details about how it came.

The little feature *His Word for You* at the end of each Help came from all the Scripture promises I began copying in a notebook about two years ago. This is the rationale that led me to begin searching out the promises . . .

If one of us were notified that a wealthy man had included us in his will, we would be eager to know what that man's "last will and testament" said.

It is not by chance that the word testament is used in Scripture—Old *Testament* . . . New *Testament*.

Our Father is very wealthy. And the news is out; the richest One in the universe has designated us among His

17

heirs. How eagerly we should be searching His will and testament to find out exactly what it is He has bequeathed us.

Anyone's inheritance always comes first in the form of a statement of intent, some promises on a piece of paper. Our inheritance from the Father follows the same order. Some of these promises have conditions attached, some do not. When we meet the condition, then the promise becomes a prophecy of what will come about. So it would be accurate to think of *His Word for You* as your personal word of prophecy, something to anticipate with greatest joy.

What a treasure these promises are! With the door of the treasure house open to us, why should we remain hungry paupers when we are heirs of the Father and joint-heirs with the Father's only-begotten, beloved Son!

Step out then to claim joyously each one of your bequests.

C. M.

Part One

Introducing the Helper

1 *Who Is the Helper?*

*And I will ask the Father, and He will give you another
... Helper ... that He may remain with you forever.*

*.... you know and recognize Him, for He lives with you
[constantly] and will be in you.*
                    (John 14:16, 17, AMPLIFIED)

Most of us begin by thinking of the Holy Spirit as an
influence, something ghostly, floating, ethereal that pro-
duces a warm and loving feeling in us. We betray this
misconception by using the impersonal pronoun "it" when
speaking of the Spirit.

But the Helper is no influence; He is rather a Person—
one of the three Persons of the Godhead. As such, He
possesses all the attributes of personality. He has a mind;[1]
He has knowledge;[2] He has a will.[3]

In addition, the Spirit acts and forms relationships only
possible with a person. Check for yourself these texts:

He speaks (Acts 1:16)
He prays (Romans 8:26,27)
He teaches (John 14:26)
He works miracles (Acts 2:4; 8:39)
He can be resisted (Acts 7:51)
He commands (Acts 8:29; 11:12; 13:2)
He forbids (Acts 16:6,7)

The Helper's work on earth today is also to administrate
the Church, Christ's body on earth. For instance, He sets

ministers over churches.[4] He distributes varying gifts and ministries to individual members of the Church,[5] and so on.

To crown all this, the Spirit, being a Person, is a Friend whom we can come to know and to love. One of His most lovable characteristics is that He deliberately submerges Himself in Jesus; He works at being inconspicuous.

This was illustrated recently at a banquet honoring a woman retiring from twenty-five years as head of the Sunday School Beginner's Department. Patiently, without self-consciousness, she had endured the speeches praising her.

Then she rose to speak. In three minutes, as the Spirit spoke through her, she preached one of the most eloquent sermons we had ever heard . . .

"All these years," she told us, "the children have been teaching me about Jesus. He's real to them, and they have made Him more real to me than I would have thought possible twenty-five years ago."

Her eyes were twinkling. "For instance, I remember the little boy who burst out with, 'If Jesus came right through that door now, I'd run right up and hug Him.'

"I owe such a great deal to the children. . . ."

As she sat down, we no longer thought of her—only of Jesus.

And that is typical of the Helper. Always there is a transparency in His personality so that Jesus can shine through. It is the Spirit's specific work to reveal facets of the Lord's personality rather than His own to us; to woo us and lead us to that Other, to glorify Him, to bring *Him* and *His* words to our remembrance.[6]

There are those who wonder whether the present-day movement of the Spirit may not be placing too great an emphasis on this Third Person of the Trinity. We need not be troubled about that. For the Helper always sees to it that He acts as a spotlight, ever focused on Jesus, so that we are not aware of the spotlight itself, only of that One who stands bathed in the brilliant illumination.

Thus an authentic hallmark of the believer baptized in the Spirit is that Jesus as a living Person becomes more real to him than ever before. That is the Spirit's glorious gift to you and me.

HELPFUL READING: John 16:7–31

HIS WORD FOR YOU: He is eager to answer us.
And it shall be that before they call I will answer, and while they are yet speaking I will hear.
(Isaiah 65:24, AMPLIFIED)

PRAYER: *Lord, I need the Helper today because I need to have the greatest gift of all, that You become real to me. There is not a single part of my life where I do not need Your help, Lord Jesus. Forgive me for those days when I haven't taken the time to talk things over with You. When I ignore You, I am the loser. Sometimes I tell myself that I am too busy to pray. That is self-deception. The truth is that I have a strange resistance to face You and to be honest with You. Lord, I give You permission to melt that resistance.*

Today I ask the Helper to nudge me into using the day's chinks of time to pray—when I'm driving or walking, or standing in line for something, or waiting my turn in the dentist's or doctor's office. So help me to practice Your Presence, Lord. Amen.

2 *Why Do I Need the Helper?*

*But you shall receive power when the Holy Spirit has come
upon you; and you shall be my witness in Jerusalem and
in all Judea and Samaria and to the end of the earth.*

(Acts 1:8, RSV)

Jesus was about thirty years old when He asked John the
Baptist to baptize Him. Behind Him lay "the hidden years"
of which we catch only glimpses in the Gospels. We do
know that until then He had lived a quiet life in the Nazareth carpenter shop and had attempted "no mighty works."

That day at the Jordan the Holy Spirit came upon Him,
permanently to make His home in the earthly temple of
Christ's being. Only then did Jesus dare to embark on His
public ministry.

In the same way, three years later the disciples were
instructed by their Master not to attempt to preach or to
teach or to witness until this same heavenly Dove had
implanted His fire in their hearts too . . .

> He commanded them not to leave Jerusalem, but to
> wait for what the Father had promised. . . .[1]

Only the Holy Spirit could give them the ability to communicate truth to other people; could supply them with in-
depth perception into the needs of others; could give them
a message; convict of sin; heal; administer the infant
Church—in short, equip them for service.

We in our century are certainly no less needy than our

Lord or those first disciples. For us to attempt any church work, any ministry or witnessing solely through man's devices, talents, and organizational machinery alone is as effective as trying to drive our car with water in the gasoline.

The year 1871 saw Dwight L. Moody apparently a great success as an evangelist. His tabernacle drew the largest congregations in Chicago. But according to Moody's own estimate of those years, he was "a great hustler" and this work was being done "largely in the energy of the flesh."[2]

Two humble Free Methodist women, Auntie Cook and Mrs. Snow, used to attend these meetings and sit on the front row. Moody could not help seeing that they were praying during most of his services. Finally he spoke to the women about it.

"Yes," they admitted, "we have been praying for you."

"Why me? Why not for the unsaved?" the evangelist retorted, a bit nettled.

"Because you need the power of the Spirit," was their answer.

After some weeks of this Mr. Moody invited the women to his office to talk about it. "You spoke of power for service," he prodded them. "I thought I had it. I wish you would tell me what you mean."

So Mrs. Snow and Auntie Cook told Moody what they knew about the baptism of the Holy Spirit. Then the three Christians prayed together—and the women left.

From that hour "there came a great hunger in my soul," Moody was to say later. "I really felt that I did not want to live if I could not have this power for service."

One late autumn day in 1871 Dwight L. Moody was in New York (on his way to England) walking up Wall Street. Suddenly, in the midst of the bustling crowds, his prayer was answered: the power of God fell on him so overwhelmingly that he knew he must get off the street.

Spotting a house he recognized, Moody knocked on the door and asked if he might have a room by himself for a few hours. Alone there, such joy came upon him that "at last he had to ask God to withhold His hand, lest he die on the spot from very joy."

From that hour Moody's ministry was never the same. He went on to England for what was to be the first of many evangelistic campaigns there. People thronged to North London to hear him.

"The sermons were not different," Moody summarized. "I did not present any new truths, and yet hundreds were converted. I would not now be placed back where I was before that blessed experience if you should give me all the world."

The evangelist was to live another twenty-eight years, and "to reduce the population of hell by a million souls." Through the Moody Bible Institute, the Moody Press, the Northfield Conferences, the Northfield and Mt. Hermon Schools, the vigor and power of his work continues to this day.

HELPFUL READING: ACTS 1:1–14

HIS WORD FOR YOU: He is out ahead opening the way.
Behold I am doing a new thing; now it springs forth; do you not perceive and know it, and will you not give heed to it? I will even make a way in the wilderness and rivers in the desert.

(Isaiah 43:19, AMPLIFIED)

PRAYER: *Lord, there are members of my family and friends who are hurting. They need You so sorely. Yet I don't know how to tell them the good news that You really are alive, that You love them, that help is available.*

Lord, I see that there is no way to get through to them unless You give me this gift of Your Spirit for service. I know that this is a "dangerous" prayer, but I ask you to create a hunger for that explosion of joy and love in my heart too. And I thank You for the sure promise that all of us who hunger and thirst for righteousness "shall be filled."[3] In Thy Name. Amen.

3   Have I Already Received Him?

And he said, "Into what then were you baptized?" They said, "Into John's baptism."

(Acts 19:3, RSV)

Paul was asking this question of the believers at Ephesus about twenty years after Pentecost. He made one thing very clear to these believers. He expected them to know the difference between John's baptism and Jesus' baptism.

The Ephesians' answer: "We have experienced only John's baptism." This meant that they had repented and received the forgiveness of their sins, but that they understood nothing about Jesus' enabling power for handling life in the present and the future.

So what was "John's baptism"? John the Baptist was the last of the Old Testament prophets. With John the era of the Old Testament closed forever. It had been a long dry period of the dispensation of law, with men trying to bridge the estrangement between them and the holy, just Jehovah by repentance, by obeying a multiplicity of laws, and by good works. The law could point men to the ideal,[1] but lacked power to help men keep the laws or to change character.

In crisp terms Jesus Himself assessed John the Baptist and the era just closing for us:

Truly, I tell you, among those born of women there has not risen one greater than John the Baptist; yet he

27

who is least in the kingdom of heaven is greater than he.[2]

"John is a great man, the greatest," Jesus was saying. "Yet the humblest disciple in the kingdom I am here to inaugurate has riches and privileges and graces, yes, and authority of which John never dreamed."

How could that be? Because man's efforts—even his best efforts—were at an end. In the new era of the kingdom, it would be God's Spirit *in* man doing the work.

So Paul sought to lead those Ephesian believers out of that Old Testament era of human striving into the glorious kingdom of the Risen One.

"Into what were you baptized?" is as pertinent a question today. It has prompted me to some sharp self-examination:

First, have I ever asked God for this gift, for Jesus' baptism of the Spirit, and claimed, by faith, Christ's promise?[3]

Have I any evidence of the Holy Spirit's work in my life? For instance, has the Spirit made Jesus real to me as a Person?[4]

Am I beginning to be able to hear the inner Voice of the Spirit? Does He tell me what to do for small decisions or major ones?[5]

Am I seeing in myself a new kind of love for other people? Is the Spirit giving me a tender concern and deep caring for persons whom I would ordinarily not choose as my friends?[6]

Am I experiencing the Spirit's help in the always tricky area of communication? For instance, am I experiencing times when the Helper gives my words wings into the heart of someone in trouble?

Am I experiencing the power of the Spirit? For example, to communicate Jesus' life to others, to bring them also into the kingdom?

Am I receiving the Spirit's definite help in how to pray about my deepest concerns?[7]

These are some of the strands of the Helper's work in the lives He fills. Am I, like the Ephesians, a stranger to His work?

HELPFUL READING: Luke 7:19–35

HIS WORD FOR YOU: Our Savior-King.

For the Lord is our judge,
the Lord is our law-giver,
the Lord is our king;
He will save us.

         (Isaiah 33:22, AMPLIFIED)

PRAYER: *Lord, I would not indulge in the kind of spiritual analysis that is still self-centered. Yet I know that Your truth means definiteness and clarity. The fuzziness that I've sometimes mistakenly taken for spirituality is part of my humanness, not Your Divine Order. I know that Your truth and Your life in me will mean real and noticeable progress.*

Lord, I need to have You lift my everyday life to another level altogether. I not only give You permission, but ask You to make in me whatever changes are necessary to receive Your Spirit. Amen.

4 No Need to Be an Orphaned Christian

"I will not leave you orphans."
(John 14:18, Swedish Translation)

An orphan is one who has known the warmth of a father's and mother's love, the security of home and hearthside, and is then deprived of these gifts.

Jesus' apostles were fearful of being in exactly that position. For three years the Master had been everything to them—beloved Companion, staunch Friend, never-failing Guide, provocative, exciting Teacher. When they wanted to know how to pray with results, they had but to ask Him. When Peter daringly tried to walk on the water, then became fearful and began to sink, he had but to stretch out his hand to have Jesus rescue him.

But lately, more and more often their Master had been speaking of His own death. "The time is at hand," He now told them. With dismay the apostles heard His soft "I go away."

Then Jesus, seeing their anxious faces, noting Peter's fearful question, "Lord, I don't understand. Where are you going?" hastened to reassure them. "I will not leave you orphans," He promised the little group. "I will *not* leave you comfortless. I *will* manifest Myself to you."

So Jesus was telling His followers, "Look, having broken into the time-space capsule of Planet Earth and lived for a time among you, you don't think I'm going to leave you there, do you? For in that case, what would those have who come after you? Only the written record of Me as an historical figure. No contemporary expression of God, the

Father, or of Me—Jesus—for themselves. No, I won't
leave it that way. I *will* come to you in the form of One
who loves you as I do and is able to care for you even as I
do now."

So it was that the apostles were about to enter a new
period in history—the era of the Holy Spirit, the third Person of the Trinity, after God, the Father, and Jesus, the
Son. This is the era that you and I are living in today.

It's no good our looking with longing to the Pre-Pentecost
time of Jesus' days of public ministry on earth and trying
to pretend that we are all still living in that other era. That
would be wishful thinking and what's worse, delusion—
living in unreality. But we do not need to look backwards.
What Jesus has provided for us today, in our time, through
the Helper is so much better.[1]

Jesus' promise to you and me is that the Helper will be
with us always, day and night, standing by for any protection we need and for every emergency. Our only part is to
recognize His presence and to call upon Him in joyous
faith.

Once the truth of this amazing comradeship gets firmly
imbedded in our mind and heart, we need never be afraid
again, or lonely, or hopeless, or sorrowful, or helplessly
inadequate. For the Helper is always with us, and altogether
adequate.

Perhaps it would help us to understand if we place the
Spirit's ministry in earth's time and space . . .

First Age	*Second Age*	*Third Age*
God, the Father.	God, the Son.	God, the Holy Spirit.
The law supreme.	Under grace.	Under election (a called-out people)
God spoke through a few prophets, priests, and kings.	Jesus teaching, healing, dying, rising again, glorified.	The restoration of a lost and defective world.
		The Holy Spirit sanctifies and works through the Church, Christ's Body.

Because the Holy Spirit is today present in His office on earth, all spiritual presence and divine communication of the Trinity with men are via the Spirit. In other words, while God, the Father, and God, the Son, are present and reigning in heaven, they are invisibly here in the body of the believer by the indwelling God, the Holy Spirit—the Helper.

Yet so long as we are ignorant of the Helper and His work, He cannot be fully operative in our lives. No wonder there is such vagueness and confusion in our minds when we speak or think of the Holy Spirit!

We have no greater need today than to be informed about the Helper. We need to know who He is, why we need Him, what He longs to do for us and our families, for our churches, and how we go about receiving Him. Otherwise we remain orphaned Christians—bereft of His love and of the magnificent fellowship, guidance and help He can give us.

HELPFUL READING: John 14:15–24

HIS WORD FOR YOU: He will direct our way.
And thine ears shall hear a word behind thee, saying, This is the way, walk ye in it, when ye turn to the right hand, and when ye turn to the left.
(Isaiah 30:21, KJV)

PRAYER: *"Jesus, without Thee we're orphaned and lonely,*
Come as our Teacher and Guide.
Leave us not comfortless, send us the Comforter,
Come to our hearts to abide."[2]

5 Could Anything Be Better Than His Presence?

It is to your advantage that I go away, for if I do not go away, the Counselor will not come for you; but if I go, I will send him to you.

(John 16:7, RSV)

How often we have envied those who saw Jesus in the flesh, who talked to Him and touched Him! Sometimes in the midst of some personal crisis we have thought wistfully, "If only I could hear His voice right now!"

It is the longing expressed so memorably in that classic children's hymn:

I wish that His hands had been placed on my head,
That His arms had been thrown around me,
And that I might have seen His kind look when He said,
"Let the little ones come unto Me!"[1]

We wonder how anything could be more wonderful than the physical presence of our Lord. Yet Jesus never spoke lightly or thoughtlessly. And here we have His solemn word in His Last Supper talk with His apostles that there *is* something better—His presence in the form of the Holy Spirit.

Moreover, in telling us this, Jesus used very practical businesslike terminology: it would be "expedient" for us, and to our calculated advantage, He said. What did He mean?

33

More, much more than the obvious fact that while Jesus
was in the flesh He was subject to the fleshly limitations of
time and space. Only those who managed to get within
arm's reach could touch Him; only a few thousand at most
could be within the sound of His voice.

But with the coming of the Helper, a new era would be
dawning. In the old era (Old Testament times up to the
Pentecost which Jesus was foretelling in this Last Supper
talk), the Spirit of God came upon only a few chosen
individuals, influencing them from above and without,
working from the outside inwardly.

In the new era, Jesus is telling us, His glorified presence
and His own resurrected life would be not only with us
but also *in* us,[2] progressively to transform us and our lives,
working from the inside outwardly.

As the Apostle John would later describe it:

> God's nature abides in him [us] . . . the divine sperm
> remains permanently within him. . . .[3]

This is the final outworking of that great Old Testament
promise:

> I will put my law in their inward parts, and write it
> in their hearts. . . .[4]

Here is a great mystery, difficult to put into words. It
becomes real and practical to us only as we walk it out.

Even in our time, we can observe two groups of Christians—those who have Christ beside them, *with* them, and
those who have the Lord Jesus *in them*.

The first group of Christians must still handle the knotty
problems of their lives on their own strength, with Jesus'
help. They get much help, of course, for a loving Lord will
always give us all we allow Him to give. So that's good, yet
not good enough.

The second group knows that they are as helpless as
Jesus said.[5] They also know that the "vine life" is the only
one that is going to bring heaven's power to earth and get
results: their life has to be inside the vine, an integral part
of its very cells and its life flow.[6] This inside life is what
the Spirit makes possible to us.

Recently, after a meeting where Jesus' teaching on this
had been explained, an Episcopal rector's wife approached

the visiting speaker. "I've been in the Church all my life," she said. "The vast difference between Jesus being *beside* us and His being *in us* had never even occurred to me. I *see it*! Light is bursting in all over!"

Now we begin to understand why Jesus said that the Helper's coming would be to our advantage. How we have underestimated and ignored this amazing blessing!

HELPFUL READING: John 14:15–17, 25–31

HIS WORD FOR YOU: Our faithful promise-keeping God. *And now, O Lord God, You are God and Your words are truth, and You have promised this good thing to Your servant.*

(II Samuel 7:28, AMPLIFIED)

PRAYER: *Dear Jesus, I begin to see that the Holy Spirit has been more a pious term to me than the great reality You intended Him to be. It staggers me to think that He is more wonderful than Your physical presence would be. Yet this is Your own solemn estimate of the Helper's worth.*

I also begin to see, Lord, that since the Helper is really Your presence in another form, what You were telling Your apostles—and me—is that You Yourself will be in me.

This is almost too momentous for me to grasp, Lord. That Divinity would deign to dwell in my poor humanity!

One thing I do know, Lord. My heart needs to be cleansed and set in order for such a royal Guest. I give You permission now to prepare my inner being. And Lord, help me to be open and receptive. Amen.

6 The Explosion of Power

A new spirit will I put within you. . . .
And I will put my Spirit within you. . . .
                 (Ezekiel 36:26, 27, AMPLIFIED)

Christianity was born into a world of trouble. The Roman world of the first century was awash in a rising tide of demoralization and evil. Today, we can see thought-provoking parallels between the period of the decline of the Roman Empire and our own time.

After His resurrection in many appearances, Jesus made it plain to His disciples that they were going to need His power to cope in such a disintegrating society. Therefore He instructed them to wait in Jerusalem until the Spirit came upon them.[1]

The result was the explosion of power recorded in the first few chapters of the Acts. This first Pentecostal outpouring of God's Spirit was then to be followed by other explosions of power across the centuries. Always these have come when evil was rampant, when men and women were depressed and in spirit-bondage, when the fires of faith burned low.

The twelfth century saw such a rekindling of the fire of the Spirit under St. Francis of Assisi. For forty years these fires burned brightly in Italy.

Then, when the Mother Church was in a period of particular decadence, the monk Martin Luther nailed his ninety-five theses to the church door at Wittenburg. Who could have guessed that such a tiny spark could have kindled the conflagration of the Protestant Reformation of the sixteenth century!

Other outpourings of the Spirit have followed: the Evangelical quickening of the eighteenth century led by John and Charles Wesley; the Great Awakening in the American Colonies of the same period; the American Pentecostal revival of 1900–1905 that began in Topeka, Kansas, then spread to Los Angeles, California, where it made forever famous the address 312 Azusa Street; the South Wales revival of 1904–1905 for which the Spirit used the twenty-six-year-old layman Evan Roberts.

Those who have studied in detail these intermittent outpourings of the Spirit since Pentecost tell us that all have certain elements in common . . .[2]

Nearly all have originated with the common people at a grass-roots level, outside the established church. The ever-present emphasis on repentance has usually drawn active, often bitter hostility from the Church.

All are characterized by a simplifying of the gospel and a return to Jesus Christ.

There is inevitably a great outpouring of joy and love.

Music always plays a large part, with much singing and fresh creativity resulting in new songs, hymns, and choruses.

All true moves of the Spirit result in moral and ethical reforms, and most have deeply affected the life and history of the nation in which they arose.

Thus the early 1960s saw the beginning of yet another return to the New Testament predominance of the Spirit, with that paramount importance which Jesus Himself gave to the Spirit. In the mid-sixties, almost simultaneously, the Jesus Movement arose among the young, the so-called Neo-Pentecostal movement appeared in the mainline Protestant churches, and there was the beginning of the Catholic Pentecostal movement at Pittsburgh's Duquesne University with four or five laymen. All these groups saw the Person of Jesus as mediated by the Spirit as the only Source of maturity and the deeper life; the only One who can enable us to cope with sin and the evil of these times we are living in; the One who guides, who heals, who empowers.

Within ten years some 400,000 members (a conservative estimate) of mainline Protestant churches in the United States were actively involved in this movement of the Spirit. By the end of the sixties the Catholic Charismatics formed the third—300,000 strong—major group of Pentecostal believers.

But so fast is this renewal now spreading that by the time of the worldwide 1977 Conference on Charismatic Renewal in Kansas City, Missouri (July 20–24), a surprising 50,000 Christians from more than a dozen denominations gathered there. The Catholics were out ahead with 25,000 delegates. There were 6,200 Protestants of mainline denominations; 17,000 non-denominational Christians; 2,000 Pentecostals; 400 Messianic Jews.

How can we explain a phenomenon like this now-worldwide burgeoning of interest in the Helper? How, except to see it as a sovereign move of God to help us all cope once again with the rising tide of evil on our worsening planet Earth!

So many centuries ago, the prophet Ezekiel clearly foretold the two steps that must always take place before any one of us can have the ability to cope with the evil in our world and to possess power for service. . . .

The first step is a readying and cleansing process. "A new spirit will I [God] put within you." That is, God will, through the Spirit, begin to renew and refresh our attitudes, convict us of sin, begin to teach us about obedience, change the thrust and climate of our inner beings. Thus He will be readying us for the crown and glory of His plan—that we, even in our flawed personhood, become the human temples of the Spirit. It was this cleansing and readying that the disciples had been experiencing during Jesus' earthly ministry and during the forty days and then the ten days they were waiting in Jerusalem prior to Pentecost.

But many Christians, because they have never been told that there is something more than regeneration and this "new spirit" within them, stop there. Among these are fine Bible students and church men and women active in the organizational work of their parish. Yet the excitement of the present-day, miracle-working Lord is missing because their eyes are still on what happened historically, back during Jesus' earthly ministry and in the early days of the Church. They have no concept of a living contemporary Lord living *inside* them, the believers, and working through them to redeem and heal others.

The second necessary step was clearly foretold by Ezekiel, "And I will put my Spirit *within* you." It is this further glorious experience that so many Christians are discovering freshly in our time.

Still the question comes, can we not receive all of this, both steps, at the time of our entering-in or being "born again"? Yes, we could, if we had the knowledge of what is available, along with the faith and capacity to receive all that. Certainly, there is no limit on God's side; He is always ready to give and give and give. On the day of Pentecost, three thousand people *were* able to receive both a new spirit and the Spirit on the same day.[3]

But most of us are not that open. In actual fact, we usually do experience being born again and then receiving the Spirit in two steps as Jesus' own apostles did, as the Samaritans did,[4] as the disciples at Ephesus did,[5] as did those present in Cornelius's house to whom Peter spoke,[6] and as many, many others have down the centuries since.

How important it is to know about this further joyful gift awaiting us and never to rest until we too have experienced our own personal Pentecost!

HELPFUL READING: John 7:33–39

HIS WORD FOR YOU: The final power of God.
Fear not, for I am with you. . . . Yes, from the time of the first existence of day and from this day forth I am He, and there is no one who can deliver out of My hand. I will work and who can hinder or reverse it?
(Isaiah 43:13, AMPLIFIED)

PRAYER: *Lord, I see now that my feeling altogether unworthy to be one of Your temples on earth is no excuse at all. For there is nothing I could ever do that would make me worthy to receive so great a gift. Any cleansing or preparation necessary must also be Your work in me.*
I do now, Lord, ask You to flood me on the inside with that new fresh spirit that can bid You welcome. Help me to

put no stumbling block in the way of this inner house-keeping and refurbishing and refreshing.

So ready me now to receive the most honored Guest in the cosmos—the Lord of glory. How I praise You that I am living in an era when such a stupendous miracle is possible! Amen.

Part Two

How Do I Receive the Helper?

1 Hungering and Thirsting for Something More

If you then, who are evil, know how to give good gifts to your children, how much more will the heavenly Father give the Holy Spirit to those who ask him.
(Luke 11:13, RSV)

Jesus delighted in comparing earthly fathers to His heavenly Father, and then in adding, "But how much more God!" The riches of heaven and of earth all belong to our Father, and He loves to shower them upon us. In Jesus' eyes though, the most precious of all possible gifts is this one of the Holy Spirit.

The first condition then, for receiving this gift so highly esteemed in Jesus' eyes, is our realization of the incomparable value of what we are requesting. For heaven's treasures are not given lightly. Nor will the Father tolerate tepid hearts[1] or honor halfhearted prayer requests.[2]

According to God's Word, without the Holy Spirit we do not have:

Personal awareness of God's love.

Conviction of who Christ is.

A message of real help to others.

The right words to speak in times of stress.

Any of the fruits of the Spirit, those lovable characteristics of the Spirit-filled life.

Real joy.

Renewal.

Guidance from God.

43

Comprehension of the thoughts and mind of God.	Healing (except what "nature" or doctors can give us).
Any help in our weakness.	The ability to like or to set our minds on things of the Spirit.
Freedom from slavery to sin and harmful habits.	
	An Intercessor with the Father.
Any of the gifts of the Spirit.	The Pledge of eternal life.

How then, without the Spirit, can we live anything but a half-life? Are we content to live at a spiritual subsistence level, ineffective and joyless? Realizing this truth can take us from lukewarmness to that hungering and thirsting that Jesus promises us will *always* be satisfied.[3]

Early in His ministry, Jesus had stressed the fact that it is only to the thirsty that He will give His living water:

"If any one thirst, let him come to me and drink. He who believes in me, as the scripture has said, 'Out of his heart shall flow rivers of living water.'" Now this he said about the Spirit, which those who believed in him were to receive; for as yet the Spirit had not been given, because Jesus was not yet glorified.[4]

Thus our thirsting and hungering for the Spirit is a necessary condition before we can be granted this gift.

So the world-famous preacher Dr. R. A. Torrey found it just prior to his baptism with the Spirit . . .

I had been a minister for some years before I came to the place where I saw that I had no right to preach until I was definitely baptized with the Holy Ghost. I went to a business friend of mine and said to him in private, "I am never going to enter my pulpit again until I have been baptized with the Holy Spirit and know it, or until God in some way tells me to go."

Then I shut myself up in my study. . . .

But Sunday did not come before the blessing came. . . . I recall the exact spot where I was kneeling in prayer in my study. . . . 1348 North Adams Street,

Minneapolis. If I had understood the Bible as I do now, there need not have passed any days. . . .[5]

Torrey's hungering and thirsting resulted in his asking for the gift of the Spirit with passionate persistence. That is the kind of asking with importunity that Jesus promised us would always be honored.

What then, is the next step in receiving this great gift? Simply that we ask our Lord for the Holy Spirit. Jesus' promise to give the Spirit "to those who ask him" is set in a passage (Today's Reading, below) that stresses importunity and persistence. He tells us to

. . . Ask and keep on asking, *and it shall be given you;* seek and keep on seeking *and you shall find;* knock and keep on knocking, *and the door shall be opened to you.*[6]

The Greek present imperative verbs "asking," . . . "seeking," . . . "knocking," denote a command, as well as continuing action. The asking required here is no timid tap on the door, but more like a rapping with the passion that results in bloody knuckles.

So dare to ask, first of all, for that gift of hungering and thirsting. Then when out of keen desire, you ask for the gift of the Spirit, you *will* receive Him because Jesus always answers the heart's sincere desire when that desire is in accordance with God's will.

HELPFUL READING: Luke 11:1–13

HIS WORD FOR YOU: How to get our prayers answered. *Now the confidence we have in him is this, that he listens to us whenever we ask anything in accordance with his will; and if we know he listens to whatever we ask, we know we obtain the requests we have made to him.*
(I John 5:14, 15, MOFFATT)

PRAYER: *Lord, I do not want to waste the years left to me on this earth. Nor do I want to go through life as a spiritual beggar, in rags, subsisting on the leftovers and the crumbs when I can be a child of the King, dressed in princely garments, feasting at Your banqueting table.*

Thank You, Lord, for making it so clear that rags and crumbs are not Your will; that Your giving, loving heart wants to dress me in the best robe, put a ring on my finger, and welcome me at Your table.

Yet Lord, I know that the gift of the Spirit is not for my joy alone; rather He is given as power for service. You alone can kindle in my heart the deep, fervent desire to be used like that. Take from me lukewarmness. Give me Your own holy passion. Thank You, Lord. Amen.

2 Accepting Jesus as the Christ

Therefore it is said, When He [Christ] ascended on high, He led captivity captive—He led a train of vanquished foes—and He bestowed gifts on men.
(Ephesians 4:8, AMPLIFIED)

We live in a time when our world is awash in prophets, gurus, and self-appointed messiahs with immense followings and wealth. Is Jesus then just one more prophet? Many stripes above the rest, to be sure, but still one of many? Each of us has to settle to the satisfaction of his own heart and mind the crucial question of who Jesus is.

Lest we dismiss this too readily, we also need to ponder our disinclination to accept Jesus' claim of exclusiveness in the sense of shutting out all others. Scripture's word on this is worth looking up. Statements like:

No one comes to the Father, but by me.[1]

and:

There is salvation in no one else, for there is no other name under heaven given among men by which we must be saved.[2]

Such statements give us pause today, for in our world they are considered dogmatic, not intellectually or socially acceptable. Some also feel that they are not even nationally

47

permissible because they go against our present interpretation of our Constitutional guarantee of "freedom of religion."

Thus each of us has an important decision to make here. Is Jesus really who He claimed to be—the *only* begotten Son of the Father, "very God of very God?" Is He entitled to be called "the Christ?" For the name *Christ* means "the Messiah," the One prophesied through all the centuries. After all, even men are sometimes called "lord," but there can be only one Christus—the Crowned One.

Until we catch a glimpse of the full glory of this crowned Christ, of the honors heaped upon Him, of the extent of the power the Father has placed in His hands, we can never grasp the significance of Jesus' question, "Who do you say that I am?"

For the Christ is the King of Kings, and the Lord of Lords.[3]

The Apostle John heaps up words to tell us that upon Jesus' return to heaven, He received power, and riches, and wisdom, and strength, and honor, and glory, and blessing.[4]

Not only our small planet Earth, but all of the cosmos has been put under His authority, subject to His word alone. This includes everything in the heavens, our earth and all of the planetary system, as well as the world below —that domain of evil spirits in rebellion against God's authority.[5]

But we miss the point of Christ's crowning until we see His coronation as another step in God's plan to lift us human beings out of the plight we have been in since the Fall. It staggers us to think that we, you and I, and our planet Earth are still today the passion of Christ's heart.

What happened at Pentecost is that the Holy Spirit was sent as Christ's coronation gift to us. Through the Helper, all of the crowned Christ's resources and riches and graces and wisdom and power became available to us humans in order that we might "reign as kings in life."[6] Could any plan have been more wonderful?

Jesus dramatized all of this for us in His incomparable parable of the prodigal Son.[7] What delighted the father's heart, pleased him most? Not the elder brother staying dutifully at home, toiling incessantly for the father. . . . "These many years do I serve thee, and yet—"

And yet the elder boy's heart had found no rest. He

knew no joy in all his labors. Nor obviously, had he made any progress in his Christian life, because he was jealous, full of grievances, grumbling, and self-pity. He was vindictive and unable to receive anything. So the elder brother did not please his father at all.

What delighted the heart of God was the prodigal who was willing to let his father do everything for him.

Amazingly, not a word of reproach or rebuke did the father speak when his wayward, wasteful boy came home. Instead, there was total acceptance, complete forgiveness, and all-out rejoicing that the prodigal was now ready to receive of the father's bounty. . . . "It was meet that we should make merry, and be glad."[8]

This is the gospel. This is the magnificent largess of the Father's heart, reflected in every way by the crowned Christ.

Are we then ready to accept Jesus as this crowned One, the reigning Christ of John's Book of Revelation, the all-powerful, miracle-working Lord of the universe?

This was the question my friend Madame Bilquis Sheikh struggled with one day ten years ago in her palatial country home in Pakistan.[9] Born of a wealthy family influential in government circles, she had been reared a devoted Muslim. Having been introduced to Christianity through a direct sovereign move of God, Madame Sheikh had reached out to talk to a missionary couple and to one nun. But she was still confused. How could she finally know which was truth —the Koran—or the Bible? And which was really the Anointed of God: Mohammed—or Jesus Christ?

She remembered that the nun had suggested, "Try talking to God as if He were your Father." But what Muslim could even think of talking to Allah like a father?

The next day, December 12th, was Madame Sheikh's birthday. She awoke thinking of her parents and of the extraordinarily happy birthday celebrations all through her childhood. Her father had never been too busy to receive his little "Keecha" in his study, to set aside whatever he was doing to help in any way he could.

Savoring these remembrances, her heart filled with gratitude, Madame Sheikh murmured a thanksgiving to her earthly father, "Oh thank you for being like that, father."

Then a shaft of understanding hit her. If her earthly father could be like that, then her heavenly Father—

Simmering with excitement, she sank to her knees by the bed and for the first time in her life shyly called God "My Father."

Something broke loose in her. He was there! Like a hand laid gently on her head. She could sense His presence, His love.

When Madame Sheikh rose from her knees three hours and many tears later, she had her answer—resoundingly. There on the table where she had left them, lay the Koran and the Bible side by side. Now she knew which was true —the Book that had led her to her Father and to that other One whose glory He will share with no other prophet— Jesus, the Christ.

HELPFUL READING: John 6:51, 54; 8:12, 28; 10:1–9, 33, 36; 14:6

HIS WORD FOR YOU: The permanence of work done in the Lord.

I know that, whatsoever God doeth, it shall be for ever: nothing can be put to it, nor any thing taken from it. . . .
(Ecclesiastes 3:14, KJV)

PRAYER: *Lord, I know that You were fearlessly dogmatic because You were simply speaking truth, telling it as it is. Just as two added to two must equal four, and no necessity for tolerance or broadmindedness can change that, even so there is no way to change the only route by which we humans can find our way to God.*

In a world where fuzziness and equivocation reign, I thank You for Your clarity and insistence on truth.

And Lord, my heart can't contain my gratitude that You are even now running down the road to meet me. Me— also a prodigal who has failed You so often. That You would dress me in princely raiment and prepare a banquet for me! This staggers me, Lord, and makes me very humble, and my love for You pours out in return.

Open my eyes now to the riches and fullness of Your magnificent plan. And Lord, this really is a daring prayer . . . I ask You to make me, like that other prodigal, a good receiver of all Your bounty. Amen.

3 Deciding to Obey the Good Shepherd

The Holy Spirit whom God has given to those who obey him.

(Acts 5:32, RSV)

The Lord gives the Holy Spirit to those who obey Him. This in no way contradicts the fact that God's gifts can be received only by grace (the unmerited favor of God) through faith, because faith (trusting God) and obedience are but two sides of the same thing.

Nor can trust ever end in just intellectual faith or lip service to faith. When it is the real thing, it will spill over into action—and that will mean obedience.[1]

For how can the Good Shepherd lead His sheep to green pastures and protect them from harm if the sheep refuse to follow the Shepherd? Our world today is such that the difficulties and evils each human being must walk through in his lifetime on earth are something like threading one's way across heavily mined terrain. Desperately, we need the all-knowledge and the all-power of the Good Shepherd. Yet there is no way He can help and protect us in the tender and minute way He longs to unless we trust His love enough to obey.

Kay Peters, wife of Dr. John Peters, the founder of that great organization World Neighbors, tells in an upcoming book of a night when she learned the hard way the importance of minute, unquestioning obedience to the Spirit's leading. After rigorous months of work on his doctorate at

51

Yale, John was teaching college classes with "moonlighting" teaching on the side for much needed income. A degree of exhaustion had set in.

In the middle of an exceptionally cold winter's night, Kay awoke to hear her husband getting out of bed. The inner voice of the Spirit spoke a clear, strong warning to her, "Go with John."

But as most of us would, Kay allowed her mind to get in the way. "Why, I never go to the bathroom with John. Why should I go now?"

So instead of obeying, she asked, "John, what's the matter?"

"I think I'm catching a cold," was the reply. "Just going to see if I can find some medicine."

Reassured, Kay quenched the warning voice inside her and snuggled more deeply into the covers.

Suddenly, from the bathroom came the sound of a terrifying crash. Leaping out of bed and dashing for the bathroom, Kay was aghast at what she saw. John had fainted and fallen in the tub. In the process the ceramic tile soap dish had been torn from the wall. The broken pieces had deeply gashed the side of his face and torn loose the lower part of his right ear.

Her husband was unconscious. Like a broken doll, his long body was draped incongruously over the side of the tub. His face rested on the bottom with a wide stream of blood already pulsing down the drain.

Although it turned out that Dr. Peters had had a concussion and did lose a great deal of blood, this emergency was in the end beautifully handled by the healing work of the Spirit. For God, unlike us, holds no grudges when we fail to obey. His only desire is to *help us*.

Long after the crisis was past and the Peterses were praising God for the way it had turned out, Kay was still pondering:

When was I going to start obeying consistently? If I had done so before the accident occurred, the whole tragic episode could have been avoided. I had to sing my song of rejoicing in a minor key.

When Jesus promised the Holy Spirit, He stressed (at least three times) that this gift was for the obedient. Here are some statements to look up and ponder: John 14:15, 16, 21, 23; Acts 5:32.

Often we stumble because we sense that we are like the apostles before Pentecost: they wanted to obey, but had not the ability to do so. There is then the temptation to reason, "Even though I mean to obey Jesus now and tell Him so, how do I know that I'll be able to obey Him in the future? I don't trust myself. So how can I ever meet this condition of obedience in connection with asking for the Spirit?"

Even on this seemingly impossible level, there is good news. When we obey the light we have now, set the rudder of our will to heed and follow the loving help the Spirit wants to give us in the future, and tell Jesus so, we find that He counts our willingness and purpose as obedience. From then on, the glad tidings are that the Spirit Himself will increasingly supply us with the *ability* to obey. God is ahead of us here, as always. He knows both our mistrust of ourselves and our weakness in obedience, so the glad promise is that we shall be able to obey, only

> [Not in your own strength] for it is God Who is all the while effectually at work in you—energizing and creating in you the power and desire—both to will and to work for His good pleasure and satisfaction and delight.[2] *Phil. 2:13*

Let us then not allow any discouragement about ourselves to halt our determination for the Spirit's full presence and help in our life. How can we *not* want to obey when we begin to comprehend the magnitude of the Helper's love and complete goodwill for us!

HELPFUL READING: Acts 9:10–19

HIS WORD FOR YOU: My heart, His home.
The (Holy) Spirit [Himself]—indwelling your innermost being and personality.
May Christ through your faith [actually] dwell—settle down, abide, make His permanent home—in your hearts! May you be rooted deep in love and founded securely on love....

(Ephesians 3:16, 17, AMPLIFIED)

PRAYER: *"Take, O Lord, and receive my entire liberty, my memory, my understanding, and my whole will. All that I am, all that I have, Thou hast given me, and I will give it back again to Thee."* Amen.

(Saint Ignatius Loyola)

4 Inviting Jesus as the Baptizer

He . . . Upon Whom you shall see the Spirit descend and remain, that One is He Who baptizes with the Holy Spirit.

The Comforter . . . Whom I [Jesus] will send to you. . . .
(John 1:33; 15:26, AMPLIFIED)

Scripture makes it clear that Jesus Himself is the only One who can baptize us with the Spirit. That is why there must always be the first step of commitment to Jesus (being "born again") before we can receive the fullness of His Spirit.

These facts shed light on a little vignette in John's Gospel. In one of Jesus' first post-resurrection appearances, He appeared and spoke to His apostles who had gathered behind locked doors for fear of the Jews.

Peace to you! [Just] as the Father has sent Me forth, so I am sending you.

And having said this, He breathed on [them] and said to them, Receive (admit) the Holy Spirit![1]

The incident has been a puzzling one since we know that the fullness of the Spirit could not be given until Pentecost. By "breathing upon them" was not Jesus dramatizing for His apostles the fact that the Spirit could be imparted only by *His* breath, His very life?

55

He knew that when the day of Pentecost finally came, the apostles would recall this scene and would then understand that always the Spirit must be connected with His own Person.

We twentieth-century Christians can receive the Spirit no other way, except by Jesus, the Baptizer . . .

In 1963 the Episcopal rector Graham Pulkingham was sent to the Church of the Redeemer in the East End of Houston, Texas. It was a poverty-stricken slum area with a racial mixture of blacks, Mexican-Americans, and poor whites. Six churches of different denominations in this area had already given up and moved away.

It looked as if the Church of the Redeemer was about to meet the same fate. Within seven months of Graham's arrival, the parish had lost seventy-five families and a third of its revenue. The vestry voted to close the church except for one Sunday morning service.

But the gigantic needs of the East End community lay heavily on the young rector's heart. The sheep were starving and astray. Who was going to feed them? And *how?*

Then Graham heard of David Wilkerson's work in the slums of Brooklyn. There the situation was even worse than in Houston's East End. Yet there the sheep were being fed. Miracles were happening with the narcotics pushers, the prostitutes, and the teenagers who were mainlining drugs.

In mid-August of that year the way was opened for Graham to spend four days with David Wilkerson. For the first three days, he saw all the different facets of David's work in the Brooklyn slums. The afternoon of the fourth day found Graham in the book-lined library of an old house with Dave and two other men. Out of the blue, Dave turned and said to Graham, "I bear witness about you— kneel down, I want to pray." The young rector knelt and the three men laid their hands on his head.

Let Graham tell what happened then . . .

Soon . . . all awareness of the men and their prayers, of the room, and even of myself was obliterated by the immense presence of God's power. . . . The very foundations of my soul shook violently. . . . *Those prayers for a powerful ministry are being answered! Right now! Great God, can it be?*

In a moment of breathless adoration, all my longing for love was satisfied and my inner being was swept clean of defilement. . . . I bowed my head to the ground and still kneeling, wept convulsively.

"We can go now, the Baptizer's here," said Dave Wilkerson to his companions, and they departed.

Sometime later I rose to my feet with a strange buoyancy. The Baptizer had done His work, and I knew that from then on my ministry would be of Godly power.[2]

So it turned out. In the years that followed, the Church of the Redeemer reopened its doors and its heart to the East End folk. What has happened is a thrilling story. I have been there and have seen this former slum area transformed now into a Christian community so vital that it is making news all around the world.

Jesus' own bestowal of the gift of the Holy Spirit made all the difference!

HELPFUL READING: John 7:34–39

HIS WORD FOR YOU: How beautiful He is!
How beautiful upon the mountains are the feet of him who brings good tidings, who publishes peace . . . who says to Zion, Your God reigns!
(Isaiah 52:7, AMPLIFIED)

PRAYER: *Lord Jesus, I thank You that all of the Father's good gifts are now Yours to bestow on us, Your children, including the greatest gift of all, the Spirit Himself.*

I begin to see that without the Spirit my personal life and my church's life are as inert and dead as lifeless clay. Show me now anything in me that would hinder or block my receiving this new life. Cleanse my heart, Lord, and prepare it to be a fit dwelling place for You. In joyous anticipation. Amen.

5 Being Willing to Be Put to Work

But whosoever will be great among you, shall be your minister:

And whosoever of you will be the chiefest, shall be servant of all.

For even the Son of man came not to be ministered unto, but to minister. . . .

(Mark 10:43–45, KJV)

Jesus' resurrection appearances included long talks with His disciples and some explicit orders: they were to "tarry in Jerusalem" until the descent of the Helper into their lives. The purpose of this tarrying? So that they would have the Helper's wisdom, guidance, and power to become His witnesses, beginning in Jerusalem, then in ever-widening circles.[1]

Note that Jesus did *not* tell them or us that the gift of the Helper is for our own spiritual development or perfection. Nor is it even for getting rid of our selfishness by dying to self. Nor for our happiness or joy or euphoria in new freer-form fellowship. Not even so that we can get our prayer needs met.

All of those results will follow as dividends, provided we accept Jesus' top priority—witnessing to the world out there (now under Satan's dominion) in loving service. Indeed, so long as we seek the baptism of the Spirit with ourselves primarily in mind—for *our* Spiritual growth, for *our* peace of mind and joy, for *our* prayers answered—then the Helper always withholds a measure of himself.

The Holy Spirit will not come to us in His fullness until we see and assent to His priority—His passion for ministry. Are we ready to give ourselves to others? He will accept no excuses about our inadequacy in this way or that. Giving us adequacy is *His* business. That's what His coming to us is all about. So—are we ready to be His "living sacrifice" to carry His love to His needy children—anytime, anywhere?

The Helper has used a failure of mine in this regard to teach me how much He means business about service. One night about two years ago I was alone in our home, so had carefully locked all doors. Close to midnight, I was ready for bed and about to turn out the lights.

Suddenly, there came a loud knocking on the front door. Asking who it was through the still-closed door, I heard the voice of an acquaintance whose sister was dying of cancer in a nearby town.

As the midnight visitor and I then talked face to face, I learned that she had come to ask me to drive with her then, that night, to pray at her sister's bedside. There were some complications, including the fact that she had not telephoned the sick woman's husband to tell him of this nocturnal visit. So I demurred, asking if I could go to the bedside the following day. Reluctantly, my visitor agreed and left.

But the following morning the sick woman was moved to the hospital. That day when I got to her room, I found that she had sunk into deep coma. No one was around—no member of the family, no hospital personnel. Quietly I sat there and prayed for her, but there was a sinking feeling of anticlimax. She died later that day.

Questions kept pounding at me. . . . What would have happened had I gone on that night? Only God knows. But at least the sick woman would have been conscious. Was there an important word the Helper wanted her to hear?

So the Spirit has used this incident to teach me. With incisiveness, He has put His finger where it hurts: "Not enough flexibility or promptness in obeying Me. So you drive to another town in the middle of the night. Forget sleep. Forget your convenience. Even ignore certain amenities, as you see them. When I say 'Go,' I'll take care of the amenities too."

In searching out the Helper's dealings with some towering Christian figures around the turn of the century—

Dwight L. Moody, R. A. Torrey, C. I. Scofield, J. Wilbur
Chapman, A. B. Simpson, Billy Sunday—I find that they
were given an emphasis on the "gift of the Holy Spirit for
service" or what they called "soul-winning service." This
relates directly back to Jesus' orders to be His witnesses all
over the world.[1]

Moody's statement is representative of this group:

> In some sense, and to some extent, the Holy Spirit
> dwells in every believer, but there is another gift which
> may be called the gift of the Holy Spirit for service.
> This gift, it strikes me, is entirely distinct and separate
> from conversion and assurance. God has a great many
> children who have no power, and the reason is, they
> have not the gift of the Holy Ghost for service. . . .
> They have not sought this gift.[2]

How sad if the modern movement of the Spirit is better
known for chorus-singing, hand-clapping, lifted hands, and
great mass meetings than for service.

Since the Helper is Jesus' own presence among us, we
can be certain that in our time, as always, He will still be
girded with a towel, washing our feet, lovingly ministering.

And we—are we better than our Master?

The fullness and overflow of the Spirit will come to us
only as we too say "Yes" to Him, reach for the towel and
the basin of water, and get to work.

HELPFUL READING: John 13:3–17; 21:11–17

HIS WORD FOR YOU: To those in need of rescuing.
*Strengthen the weak hands, and make firm the feeble
and tottering knees.*

*Say to those that are of a fearful and hasty heart, Be
strong, fear not! Behold, your God will come with ven-
geance, with the recompense of God; He will come and
save you.*

(Isaiah 35:3, 4, AMPLIFIED)

PRAYER: *O Lord Jesus, I can see that my adventures
with You haven't even begun until I am willing to go to
work for You. All my excuses and rationalizations of inadequacy are no good: that's really saying that You are in-*

adequate to work through me as You please, once I am willing.

So Lord, here I am. I know that it's a hazardous prayer because You will rush to answer it—but take me, use me.

I see it now! Even as You bring those staggering needs to me and to those with whom I am in close fellowship, that's when You will give us faith-strengthening demonstrations of Your present-day power.

As You plunge us in over our heads, that's when we will be given the particular gifts of the Spirit we need.

Lord, Your ways are incredible. You are incredible—and I love You. How great You are! Lord, I worship You. Amen.

6 *Repentance and Baptism: Rising to New Life*

When they heard this they were cut to the heart, and said to Peter and the apostles, "Friends, what are we to do?"

"Repent," said Peter, "repent and be baptized, every one of you, in the name of Jesus the Messiah for the forgiveness of your sins; and you will receive the gift of the Holy Spirit."

(Acts 2:37, 38, NEB)

As in imagination we listen to Peter preaching this, his first sermon[1] after the startling events of Pentecost, we can scarcely believe what we are hearing. This confident, articulate, impassioned, fearless man is *Peter?* The same big rough fisherman who habitually said and did the wrong thing and was so cowardly that at his Master's crisis-moment he crumbled even under a few questions from a servant girl!

But this is a new Peter. The old timid, ineffective man is now submerged in and filled with the Holy Spirit. And with startling results! Every word of this first sermon goes to its target and so convinces and convicts his listeners that on the spot three thousand of them become followers of Jesus.

In our time we need to know what exactly Peter meant by preaching the necessity "to repent." We are told that the word means "to turn around" or "to change one's mind." But to change our minds about what? About our appraisal of the old life we have been living so far.

Peter was a case in point, and we can see ourselves reflected in him. In the old days he had had plenty of drive, abundant energy and determination, some obvious talents, even good motivation—he meant well. Yes, and the burly, gruff fisherman deeply loved his Master and wanted to please Him.

Yet none of that was good enough. So this new Peter had repented of his old life and his effort to handle it on his own. That is, his appraisal of that old self before Pentecost had long since been a crisp "no good." After all, Peter and the other one hundred nineteen gathered in the Upper Room were asking the *Holy* Spirit to come and live in them, and holiness and cleanliness cannot live in a sin-ridden slum.

Rees Howells, Welsh coal miner (1879–1950) whom God mightily used in the ministry of prayer-intercession, has written of the first time he met the Spirit. It was as real an experience as Rees' meeting with the Savior had been three years before . . .

He said to me, "As the Savior had a body, so I dwell in the cleansed temple of the believer. I am God and I am come to ask you to give your body to Me that I may work through it. . . ."

He made it very plain that He would never share my life . . . but there were many things dear to me and I knew I couldn't keep one of them. . . .

He put His finger on each part of my self-life, and I had to decide in cold blood. He could never take a thing away until I gave my consent. . . . He was not going to take any superficial surrender. . . .[2]

So real was this repentance period for Rees that the process took five days and many tears, during which he lost seven pounds.

The Spirit may point out to any of us a wide gamut of sins—any unforgiveness or resentment harbored in the heart—no matter how seemingly justified; estrangements; any still-hidden dishonesty or unfaithfulness; indulgences; our particular use of self-will; and certainly, any involvement with the occult, however innocent or far back. This would include fortune-telling, spiritualism, horoscopes, playing with Ouija boards, drugs that opened the unconscious to spirit powers, and any involvement with cults directed by any power other than Jesus Christ. Any such uncovered sin needs to be confessed, followed by our acceptance of God's forgiveness, and a renouncing of Satan and all his works.

Sometimes the Spirit will then go to the other end of the spectrum and point out something seemingly trivial saying, "That also must go." This can be puzzling. Would God concern Himself with a seeming triviality? The experience of other Christians down the ages can help us here. Their writings tell us that there is no such thing as a small or trivial sin because all sin is an act of self in rebellion against God. And the Spirit knows that repentance becomes real to us only as He makes it very specific.

Yet because the Helper is always a realist and insists on being thoroughgoing, He is after much more than throwing out some sin-debris here and there.

Again, Rees Howells' experience illustrates this. After the Spirit had pointed out to Rees those things to be jettisoned, then . . .

> Like Isaiah, I saw the holiness of God, and seeing Him,
> I saw my own corrupt nature. It wasn't sin I saw, but
> my nature, self . . . that thing which came from the
> Fall. . . .[3]

So how can we deal with something as basic as the sin-nature with which we were born?

Usually, we try to rid ourselves of selfishness or irritability and a temper that erupts, or whatever, by confessing and repenting of our sin, setting our will against it, and working at getting rid of our bad habit—with God's help, of course.

But that is not Scripture's prescription for our deliverance. The problem is that this is our fallen nature acting, and that nature—no matter how patched-up, improved, or disciplined—can have no part in God's kingdom.[4]

In this impasse, Scripture has glad news for us:

> We know that our old (unrenewed) self was nailed to
> the cross with Him [Jesus]. . . .[5]

and

> Are you ignorant of the fact that all of us who have been baptized into Christ Jesus were baptized into His death?⁶

With the Cross, God wiped out the old creation that was flawed in Eden. The gospel's momentous news is not only that Jesus died on that Cross, but that you and I and our flawed natures also died with Him.

Here is a homely illustration of this. . . . If I place a dollar bill between the pages of a book, then burn the book, the dollar bill goes up in flames along with the book. Just as surely, each of us humans, together with all the sins we would commit in our lifetime, along with our capacity for sin—the sin principle in us—died on that Cross.

How can I be certain of this? Because God says so. This great truth is all over the New Testament. In addition to the passages above, here are some further statements with which to satisfy your own mind and heart: Galatians 2:20, Colossians 3:3, II Timothy 2:11.

Not only that, even as I was "in" Christ on His Cross, so I also rose with Him,⁷ have been set in the heavenlies with Him, and I am now complete only in Him.⁸

So this means that God will not allow us (being dead—defunct) any Christian experience in our old fleshly nature, nothing apart from Jesus. God is not going to drop into our laps, as a package commodity, unselfishness or a loving disposition or any virtue.

Instead, He has promised me Jesus' resurrection life in me. Thus it will be Jesus' selflessness and patience and love manifested in my life—not my own.

So now as I let go my old tired efforts at self-improvement and step out to trust Jesus' fresh, exhilarating resurrected life in me, to my amazement, I find solid ground beneath my feet.

Perhaps you have wondered about the meaning of those adult Believer's-Baptisms in backyard swimming pools or at the edge of the ocean. Many of those participating are Christians who were christened as babies. Now that the Helper has revealed to them what being baptized into Jesus' death really means, they long to experience leaving their old self under water with the joy of rising to a new life in the Spirit.

Who but a loving heavenly Father could have thought of that!

HELPFUL READING: Acts 8:25–40

HIS WORD FOR YOU: He never condemns us.
Therefore, [there is] now no condemnation for those who are in Christ Jesus.
              (Romans 8:1, RSV)

PRAYER: *Lord Jesus, I do need a housecleaning on the inside. It takes courage for me to ask this: bring to my remembrance anything I need to confess to You. I want to get rid of all the debris. Especially my resentment against _____, and my stubborn unwillingness to love _____. I give all this negativity to You. You take it, Lord.*

And how grateful I am that I don't need to be encumbered with my sin-nature, that it too was nailed to Your Cross. But Lord, this is not yet real to me. I ask the Helper to grant me a personal revelation of this great truth to bring it alive for me.

Show me now how to claim my new life in You, Lord Jesus, and to walk hour by hour in that fresh new dimension. And thank You for the feeling of adventure! Amen.

7 Accepting God's Grace

*The wind blows . . . where it will; and though you hear its
sound, yet you neither know where it comes from nor
where it goes. So it is with every one who is born of the
Spirit.*

(John 3:8, AMPLIFIED)

We have seen that there are definite steps to be taken if
we are to receive the baptism of the Spirit. There must be a
real thirst resulting in specifically asking Jesus Himself for
this gift. There must be repentance, forgiveness, and a
break with one's old life. There must be the set of the will
to obedience, and the desire and intention to use one's life
(no matter what one's vocation or profession) for ministry
to others.

To these must be added one more condition—the fact
that there is no way we can receive the Spirit except by a
present-tense faith. For nothing any of us could ever do or
stop doing can earn this or any of heaven's gifts. Forever
and forever they are given only by grace—which is the
unmerited favor of a loving Father.[1]

Yet once we realize how unworthy we are to ask the
Helper to come and live inside us, then on what basis can
we find the faith to ask for and receive this gift of gifts? It
is a relief to realize that the basis for faith here has nothing
to do with us and everything to do with the Lord Jesus.
Scripture makes it plain that the coming of the Spirit at
Pentecost (and ever since) is the result of Jesus' exaltation,
glorification, and crowning in heaven.[2]

Watchman Nee, preeminent Bible expositor, expresses it
succinctly: "The Holy Spirit has not been poured out on

you or me to prove how great we are, but to prove the
greatness of the Son of God."[3]

In other words, the outpouring of the Spirit is earth's
evidence and proof of what happened after Jesus' ascension: not only of the magnificence of His crowning in
heaven, but of His very real coronation power. Paul strains
for words in trying to describe this:

> When he raised him [Jesus] from the dead and made
> him sit at his right hand in the heavenly places, far
> above all rule and authority and power and dominion,
> and above every name that is named. . . .[4]

Then since Christ's power, meant to be mediated
through the Spirit, is our triumphant Lord's gift to us, how
tragic if any of us fail to appropriate it!

Once I had realized all of this after I had spent the
summer of 1944 studying the Scripture about it, I knew
how impossible my Christian walk would be without the
Helper. I also saw that even in the Acts accounts there was
wide diversity in how different individuals received the
Spirit. Sometimes He would come through the laying on of
hands or after the sacrament of baptism, sometimes not.
Some received the gift of tongues at the moment of their
Spirit-baptism, others did not. It was obvious that the Spirit
cannot be pigeonholed or preguessed or manipulated, and
that we had best not try. Jesus gave Nicodemus the perfect
analogy: who can preguess or control the wind?

So, since at that time I had no group to lay hands on
me, very quietly and undramatically I asked for the gift of
the Spirit. The setting was my bedroom with no other
human being present. I knew too that when we accept one
of heaven's gifts like that—so quietly in the now—we cannot demand instantaneous proof that the Lord has heard
and answered. For that would be walking by sight, not
faith at all.

Still, being a practical person, I couldn't help wondering
how long this blind-faith period would last. What about
Jesus' promise made on the eve of His glorification at the
dawning of the era of the Helper, that He *will* manifest
Himself to us?[5]

That Jesus should have promised to reveal Himself to us
in this new era is not surprising. After all, the Helper is a

Person whose work is to point to and reveal Jesus. And, I reminded myself, any person dwelling with us would inevitably reveal himself by his personality traits—his ways, deeds, and words.

As I searched out the experience of other Christians on this (such as Dwight L. Moody, Charles G. Finney, R. A. Torrey, John Wesley, Sammy Morris—the African boy, Evan Roberts, A. B. Simpson, Watchman Nee, and many in our own time), I learned that some had had manifestations of the Helper's presence—such as feelings like a series of electric shocks, waves of liquid love pouring through one's body, feelings of impossible joy, speaking a heavenly language—while others had not.

Scripture makes it clear that the Helper is not fond of spectacular ways of exhibitionism. After all, no trumpets herald the pinky-gray opalescent dawn. No bugles announce the opening of a rosebud. God speaks not in the thunder or the roaring wind, rather in a "still, small voice."

So I knew that although I should not deny their validity, I should guard against demanding a highly emotional or dramatic experience as initial proof of my baptism in the Spirit. Our triumphant Lord does not need to prove anything. If Jesus wanted to grant me some dramatic evidence, fine. But I would wait for *His* timing on any manifestation at all of the Helper's presence.

Nothing overt happened that first day. I experienced no waves of liquid love or ecstatic joy. But then in the next few days, quietly but surely, the heavenly Guest made known His presence in my heart. He began talking to me at odd moments throughout the day. Sometimes even as I would open my mouth to speak, there would be a sharp check on the inside. I soon learned that the Helper sought to prevent careless words or critical words or even too many words. Nor would He tolerate even a trace of sarcasm, or faithless words of doubt or fear.

So day by day came the evidence that after I had asked the Helper to enter and take charge, He had done exactly that.

This evidence mounted. The Helper now sought to guide me even in life's small decisions in order to smooth my way or save me time and futile effort. I also found, as has many another, that the manifestation of His presence on which the Spirit places highest value is the power to witness effectively to others of Jesus.

He then entered into my prayer life and began directing that. He became the major creative Agent in my writing. In the months that followed and indeed, on down the years, He would methodically bring one area of life after another under His control—health, finances, ambition, reputation. I soon realized that the baptism of the Holy Spirit was no one-time experience, rather a process that would continue throughout my lifetime. True, there was that initial infilling. But how well I knew that I had not thereby been elevated to instant sainthood. In my humanness, self kept creeping back in, so I needed repeated fillings if I were ever to become the mature person God meant me to be.

Not only that, I would discover that the special gifts of the Spirit along with the fruit of His presence—His character within us—are also marvelously authentic evidence of His presence.

And the very dramatic manifestations? Some of those were to come later. Some I have never yet experienced. Yet that September would come the crown of all—the presence of the Risen Lord, the literal fulfilling of "and I will love him [her] and manifest myself to him."[6]

HELPFUL READING: John 3:1–21

HIS WORD FOR YOU: Our Father's good will for us.
What father among you, if his son asks for a loaf of bread, will give him a stone; or if he asks for a fish, will . . . give him a serpent . . . ?

If you then, evil-minded as you are, know how to give good gifts . . . to your children, how much more will your heavenly Father give the Holy Spirit to those who ask . . . Him!

(Luke 11:11, 13, AMPLIFIED)

PRAYER: *Lord, I have accepted the challenge of Your great promise. I have asked for the gift of the Helper. I have bidden Him welcome as He enters my heart to take possession. So now, by faith, I accept Your sure promise that this is done, that I have received the Spirit.*

I wait patiently now for these tokens of the Helper's presence that shall reveal that He is not only with me but in me.

Help me too never to fall into the trap of thinking of

the Helper as a servant to do my bidding; rather create in me the willingness to be Your servant, Lord, for Your work to be done through me. Then only will I know the fullness of the Helper's presence. In Your strong name, I pray. Amen.

Part Three

How the Helper Meets My Everyday Needs

1 *He Saves Me Time*

Walk as children of light . . . and try to learn what is pleasing to the Lord.
           (Ephesians 5:8, 10, RSV)

Often we think of God as One concerned only with our spirit's welfare, not with the affairs of everyday life—like how we handle the hours of our day. We are inclined to resist the Spirit's inner nudges because we suspect that what God wants "for our own good" would be about as welcome as castor oil.

The truth is quite the opposite. Yet it is only a daily experimental walk with the Spirit that will prove this to us. He is concerned about our spirit's health and growth, but He is also attentive to what is of present, practical importance to us. We will find that it is to our intelligent self-interest to become sensitive to the Helper's loving directions. These come in several forms: urges, promptings, uneasiness . . . stops. We have all known these.

So often I have experienced it. One evening my husband Peter and I had planned to see a particular movie. It turned out to be a disappointing evening in every way. Long queues made it impossible even to get near the theatre. Then a store which we thought we might visit proved to be closed.

On the way home, having been frustrated at every turn, Peter and I compared notes and found that earlier, each of us had had a strong inner feeling that we should not go. But neither had verbalized this, fearing to disappoint the other, especially since there was no reason to give except

the inner direction. We learned an important lesson that
evening about the Spirit's desire to spare us frustration and
wasted time.

The well-known author Agnes Sanford relates a similar
type of experience. She had an important engagement in
Richmond, Virginia. Several hours previous to departure
time, however, Agnes was aware of a strong "stop" from
the Spirit. Since her mission was the Lord's work and she
could see no reason for such guidance, she disregarded it
and started.

Before the train reached Richmond, there was a wreck
on the track ahead. The train stopped in time, but the
passengers were forced to sit up all night as they waited for
the track to be cleared. "Afterward," Agnes said, "I realized that the inner Voice had been trying to warn me of
this."

We need the practice of daily experimentation in hearing
the Spirit's voice. Since not all inner desires, urgings, or
even voices are from God, He has graciously given us a
number of ways of testing out such inner directions.

It is important to remember that the inner Voice will
never bid us do anything shady, dishonest, impure, unlov-
ing, or selfish in the sense that it hurts another. Nor will
He ever tell us anything contrary to Scripture because God
will not contradict Himself.

Then too, as often as possible this kind of guidance
should be checked out with a fellow Christian. Finally, one
of the Helper's special gifts is that of the discerning of
spirits. He has promised that each church fellowship con-
stituted by Him will have one or more individuals to whom
He has given this needed gift for the benefit of all in the
fellowship.[1]

However, I found that in the everydayness of life when
there was not time for this more thorough checking, and
when the inner guidance did not obviously violate any of
God's loving laws or hurt another, it was important to obey
and thus experiment with it. That was how I learned to
recognize the Helper's voice.

Nothing will so strengthen our faith and convince us of
the tender love of God and of His concern for even the
minutiae of our lives as this daily walk in the Spirit.

HELPFUL READING: Acts 10:17–24; 27:1–3; 9–11

HIS WORD FOR YOU: He will turn troubles into highways.
> And I will make all my mountains a way, and my highways shall be raised up.
> (Isaiah 49:11, RSV)

PRAYER: *Lord Jesus, so often I ignore or ride roughshod over these strong inner feelings supplied by the Spirit. What is lack of trust in You, Lord, change that. Give me Your own confidence in the Father's never-failing love and goodwill.*

What is willfulness in me, Lord, change that too. For nothing could be more foolish than thinking I know better than You do. Help me this day, no matter how busy I get, to listen and to obey. Amen.

2 He Guides My Actions

*The Holy Spirit said, "Set apart for me Barnabas and Saul
for the work to which I have called them." . . . So, being
sent out by the Holy Spirit, they went down to Seleucia.*
(Acts 13:2, 4, RSV)

The setting for the Spirit's special message to Barnabas
and Saul (Paul) was the first little Christian Church in
Antioch. This city was one of the most corrupt in the
Roman Empire at a time when corruption, poverty and
flagrantly gross sins were rampant.

Paul and Barnabas had been ministering together in the
Antioch church for only a year. The work seemed such a
tiny, flickering light in the great pagan city. Yet here was
the guidance of the Spirit directing the little new church to
give up its two top leaders.

The fellowship's human reaction might well have been,
"But—but Paul's and Barnabas's work has only begun
here. How can we get along without them? Besides,
shouldn't young new recruits be the ones to be sent out for
their training rather than our most capable leaders?"

Yet that was not the reaction of the Antioch fellowship.
Instead, they fasted and prayed, asking the Spirit, "Have
we heard You correctly?" Having confirmed that they had,
they then laid hands on Barnabas and Paul and sent them
out with everyone's blessing.[1] They trusted the Spirit to
take care of His own in Antioch and of His still-struggling
church there.

From my own experience and that of many others, I
know that the Spirit's guidance is just as real in our cen-

tury as it was in Paul's day. As a college girl attending
Atlanta's Westminster Presbyterian Church where Peter
Marshall pastored, I first heard him tell the story of this
same kind of guidance in his life . . .

Born in the industrial town of Coatbridge, Scotland, he
felt the call of God on his life at age twenty-one. His "tap
on the shoulder" came one night at the Buchanan Street
Kirk after a call for recruits by the London Missionary
Society.

At the time Peter thought that "the Chief" (as he liked
to call God, the Father) was calling him to China. As
events turned out, all doors which would have led to China
were closed one after the other: it seemed that God had an
altogether different plan for Peter Marshall.

At this juncture his cousin, Jim Broadbent, was led to
present to Peter the idea of his emigrating to the United
States to enter the ministry. The young Scot was stubbornly
resistant to his cousin's suggestion but agreed to pray
about it.

Three weeks later Peter still had no answer. Then
one Sunday afternoon as he was walking through a
rhododendron-lined lane in the Sholto Douglas Estate, the
Chief gave him his marching orders.

"I was walking along that lane puzzling over the decision
before me," he was to say later, "when all at once I *knew*.
The answer was a clear-cut strong inner conviction, quite
unmistakable, that God wanted me in the United States of
America."

So on April 5, 1927, Peter Marshall arrived at the Bat-
tery off Ellis Island; from there he went to Elizabeth, New
Jersey; then surprisingly, south to Birmingham, Alabama;
to Georgia's Columbia Theological Seminary; from thence
years later, to the Nation's capital where he would become
a major spokesman for the Chief.

"My own choice was to go to China," we college students heard him say that day in Atlanta. "But the Holy
Spirit had other plans. If God is to use us as His hands and
feet and voice, it is just as necessary for Him to guide us
geographically as in any other way. It *does* matter to God
where we are at any given time."

The Spirit cannot guide us, however, as long as we insist
on finding our own way. It is as if we, groping along in the
dark, are offered a powerful lantern to light our path, but

refuse it, preferring to stumble along striking one flickering match after the other.

Instead, first we have to ask the Spirit to lead us; then by an act of will place our life situations and our future in His hands; and then trust that He will get His instructions through to us.

Second, seeking to control everything ourselves by the same kind of wire-pulling and door-crashing practiced by those who know nothing of God's leading, can have no place in the Spirit-led life. Such manipulation merely impedes the Spirit's work on our behalf.

I can affirm from experience that allowing the Helper to guide one's life is an exciting, fulfilling way to live. His plans for each of us are so startlingly superior to anything we can imagine.

HELPFUL READING: Acts 8:26–40

HIS WORD FOR YOU: Formula for a significant life.
Humble yourselves—feeling very insignificant—in the presence of the Lord, and He will exalt you.—He will lift you up and make your lips significant.
(James 4:10, AMPLIFIED)

PRAYER: *Dear Lord, I scarcely understand my own reluctance to take hands off and let You manage my affairs. Do I actually think that You, the sovereign, omnipotent God, cannot get along without my help! Lord, forgive me for presumption like that.*

But sometimes I find it harder to wait on You, being bidden not to do anything at all except trust You, than it would be to rush ahead trying to arrange things myself. I need Your help with this. I ask for patience. Above all, I ask for the faith to believe that my future is important to You.

Thank You that my times are in Your loving hands. Amen.

3 He Protects Me

*But safe he lives who listens to me;
from fear of harm he shall be wholly free.*

*God is to us a God of deliverances and salvation, and to
God, the Lord, belongs escape from death. . . .*
(Proverbs 1:33, MOFFATT; Psalm 68:20, AMPLIFIED)

If we were willing to accept the Spirit's help and to listen
to His voice, many of the evils, difficulties, and accidents
that befall us would be avoided. I believe this to be an
important answer to the question so often asked, "How
could a loving God allow such-and-such a dreadful calam-
ity to happen?"

Across the years I have heard so many true incidents of
escape from death by following the Spirit's instructions
that it is difficult to choose among them. All have this in
common: someone in a crisis situation was able to hear the
Spirit's quiet interior voice and moved to obey, thus escaping death.

One evening over dinner in a New York City restaurant
a friend told this story. . . . Several years previously she and
her two young nephews were aboard a plane at Orly Air-
port (Paris) waiting to take off for London. "As I sat
there," the friend told me, "suddenly that quiet but very
clear and authoritative Voice told me to take my nephews
and deplane at once. No explanation was given. I obeyed
and even managed to get our baggage pulled off." She
paused, looking me directly in the eyes. "That plane
crashed. All aboard perished."

"What a story!" I marveled. "And what courage it took for you to obey that!"

But what about the other passengers, we wonder? One thing we know. God is no respecter of persons. He loved them as much as He loved my friend. Then did the Spirit try to get a message through to one or more mechanics? To the pilot? To other passengers too? No doubt. Though there can be no definitive answer, surely we need to ponder the important interplay between man's free will and the Spirit's mission to guide and protect us.

Another friend, the Reverend Joseph Bishop of Rye, New York, has related this story. . . . For years Joe had befriended and ministered to Ruth, one of his parishioners and a cerebral palsy victim from birth. Ruth could get around only with the aid of an ingeniously equipped, motorized wheelchair built for her by her father. But the crippled body was presided over by a highly gifted mind. With the constant love and encouragement of her family and her pastor, Ruth had graduated from Drew University.

Several years followed, with Ruth helping with the church's weekday Nursery School. But Ruthie's greatest longing was to be able to hold a regular job, earn her own way in the world. In her case, since she had difficulty even feeding herself, her dream seemed impossible of attainment.

Late one afternoon Joe was returning home from his church office. At his front steps the Spirit spoke to him. It was "a compelling, irresistible, mandatory call to go to see Ruthie. I had not planned to do so." Yet down to her house he strode as fast as he could walk.

Joe let himself in by the side entrance and called out Ruthie's name. He found her in a back room weeping and alone. Ruth had been in deep depression with feelings of suicide.

That afternoon both Ruth and Joe found themselves stunned, overwhelmed by the realization of God's love and caring. What had begun as a possible tragedy ended up as praise.

Ruth went on to get a Ph.D. at the University of Illinois and is now on the staff of a state hospital in Iowa. God even provided Frances, a devoted, mentally limited companion, to care for her. Frances needed Ruth's fine mind and Ruth needed Frances's strong arms and legs.

Such true stories dramatize for us how one's survival can depend upon our receiving into our hearts the Helper. At the moment of being "born again," each of us is given the ears in our spirit (a new receiving set) to enable us to hear His voice. But it's as if the receiving set is faultily connected up and is bringing in intermittent messages with much static and dead air until we have received the infilling of the Spirit.

We need to practice listening and obeying in the daily round. Only then will we be prepared to hear His directions for crisis situations.

HELPFUL READING: Acts 16:6, 7; 22:17–21

HIS WORD FOR YOU: The Lord helps and delivers in time of trouble.

When you pass through the waters I will be with you, and through the rivers they shall not overwhelm you; when you walk through the fire you shall not be burned or scorched, nor shall the flame kindle upon you.
(Isaiah 43:2, AMPLIFIED)

PRAYER: *Dear God, You are my Father, I am Your child. I put my hand in Yours, thanking You that Your will is to keep me safely until my work is completed here. Thank You for the tender care that would speak to me through the Holy Spirit. I do so want to learn how to hear and to be obedient. Open my ears of the spirit. Remind me to listen many times a day. And oh Lord, give me an obedient heart. In Jesus' name, I pray. Amen.*

4 He Is with Me in Everyday Situations

Likewise the Spirit helps us in our weakness.
(Romans 8:26, RSV)

The literal rendering of the Greek word *Paraclete* can be interpreted variously as "One at hand" or as "One by our side" . . . "One alongside to help" . . . "One who may be counted upon in any emergency."

Jesus' succinct statement of our human plight tells us clearly enough why we so desperately need the Holy Spirit as Helper:

Apart from Me—cut off from vital union with Me—you can do nothing.[1]

Actually, when we human beings feel most capable of handling life on our own, invariably that is when we are most in need of Jesus' help mediated to us by the Spirit. Nor is this just spiritual need. It is a practical, workaday assistance that the Helper longs to give us.

One day I was trying to copy a magazine picture of an attractive hour-glass-shaped curtain for the glass in our kitchen door. It looked easy. But in vain I labored over the fabric for three hours, growing more frustrated, baffled, and irritated by the minute.

Challenged by my failure, I then called in a friend, only to find that she too was unable to come up with a workable pattern. Finally, I decided to give up the whole project. Thereupon I turned to other household tasks.

At that point, very quietly, the Helper took over. "Do it this way," He told me, and proceeded to give me simple, practical instructions in the form of a series of pictures in my mind. The technique He suggested had not once occurred either to me or to my friend. It worked easily, perfectly.

Some of the Spirit's help is also aimed at releasing us from many of the time-consuming details of daily life—not to make us lazy, but so that we can be free to take on more important tasks for Him and to help other people. Indeed, when we allow the Spirit to move through us to the needs of others, we are going to be so busy as sorely to need the Spirit's very practical help—finding where to repair an important tool, locating a misplaced article, or saving money on food or clothing purchases.

One day I felt a nudging to take a particular book to a next-door neighbor who was in bondage to fears of all kinds. But the Helper said quietly, "There is no need to take it over right now. Wait a while, and she will come to you."

So I turned to other tasks. Within an hour the neighbor appeared at our front door. I gave her the book and discovered that she had in hand a recipe for a special dish I had been wanting to make.

The time and effort saved in such experiences would be a gift enough. But there is also immense joy and exhilaration and faith-building in these hourly, daily demonstrations of the Helper's presence—God "tabernacling with us."

HELPFUL READING: Matthew 10:29–31; 17:24–27

HIS WORD FOR YOU: Our every need will be met.
And my God will liberally supply (fill to the full) your every need according to His riches in glory in Christ Jesus.
(Philippians 4:19, AMPLIFIED)

PRAYER: *Dear Lord, that You should be interested in every detail of my everyday life seems almost too good to be true—and yet too wonderful not to be true. I have sorely needed Your reassurance about this. You know how often I've wondered whether I should bother the Lord of the universe with the trivia of my little life. Now I accept Your word that the fabric of daily life is woven of such details and trivia, and that how I handle this is important to You and to the kingdom. And since You are concerned with the fall of each sparrow, how much more are You concerned about me! How I thank you, Lord! Amen.*

5 *He Is My Remembrancer*

But the Counselor, the Holy Spirit, whom the Father will send in my name, he will teach you all things, and bring to your remembrance all that I have said to you.
(John 14:26, RSV)

The early days of my walk in the Spirit were full of exciting discoveries. After all, the gospel narratives are startlingly brief. There is so much *not* told us, so many gaps. Mostly, we are given principles as guidelines, but the question always is, how does this work out in everyday life? How do I apply this in my workaday world?

Jesus' words about the Spirit teaching us all things and bringing to our remembrance all that Jesus has said, are one such guideline. My exciting discovery was that Jesus' promise is much more inclusive than we have thought or dreamed. Once started on my walk in the Spirit, I found that the Helper had quietly become the living Repository of my memory and my mind—that incredibly intricate human brain that still baffles all scientists—the Chief Librarian of my lifetime storehouse of memories, thoughts, quotations, all kinds of specific data.

He was now in charge of the whole, and I could trust Him to find and bring up out of the voluminous "stacks" of memory whatever I needed. There were those everyday gaps in memory when I could not recall a person's name or the name of a street or a book or a verse of Scripture. The Spirit was eager to come to my assistance. When I asked Him for this help and then released the problem from my mind, usually not immediately, but within hours, the Helper would deliver the answer.

Then I experienced His delight in showing me what to do about misplaced articles for which I was hunting.

Subsequently, I came upon yet another facet of the helper's role as our Remembrancer. This is pointed out in Jesus' promise that when we are . . .

brought before kings and governors for my name's sake . . . Settle it therefore in your minds, not to meditate beforehand how to answer; for I will give you a mouth and wisdom, which none of your adversaries will be able to withstand or contradict.[1]

Though the promise refers specifically to the crisis situations of Christians caught in persecution, an experience in the summer of 1963 showed me how all-inclusive this promise is too.

It happened towards the end of a trip through the South Seas to Australia. The British Commonwealth edition of my book *Beyond Our Selves* had just been released, and I had been asked to make some bookstore, press, and television appearances in Sydney and Melbourne. Among these was the televised program "Meet The Press" seen all over Australia and noted for its tough approach.

No hint of the questions was allowed ahead of time. The visitor faced a panel of press men and women who could ask anything they wished, and who had acquired a reputation for ruthlessness. I sensed that my husband Leonard (we had been married in 1959, ten years after Peter's death) and several friends who had accompanied me to the studio and who would be monitoring the program in a private room, were afraid for me. They knew that as an author, I am a "paper person" always with a pencil in hand. And paper people are rarely noted for carrying specifics in their heads. So how would I fare since no notes could be used or referred to on "Meet the Press"?

Before the program began, quietly—within myself—I asked the Helper to take over. "This panel isn't exactly 'kings and governors,' " I told Him, "but they might as well be. Since there's no way I can meditate beforehand on how to answer, this is the perfect setup for You to handle. I am helpless; You are adequate. Please manage everything for me."

And He did! Never have I had a prayer more gloriously answered. The first part of the answer was that the representatives of the press were not antagonistic. But on top of that, the Helper revealed Himself a brilliant Rememberer. I heard myself calmly giving dates, place names, quoting portions of Peter Marshall's Senate prayers verbatim, even (most surprising of all) providing some sports data—I, who pay little attention to professional sports!

So I could never doubt that this was all the Spirit's work. Such relaxation and exuberance entered in, that my time with "Meet the Press" became pure joy all the way—fun for me and for the interviewers.

Try the Helper as Your Remembrancer. Experiment with small, everyday needs first. As you learn how adequate and trustworthy He is, as you relax and trust Him more and more, you will find Him a Companion of inestimable worth.

How did we ever live without Him!

HELPFUL READING: I John 2:24–29

HIS WORD FOR YOU: Our wonderful burden-bearing Lord!

Blessed be the Lord, Who bears our burdens and carries us day by day, even the God Who is our salvation!
(Psalm 68:19, AMPLIFIED)

PRAYER: *Lord, I confess that I have been reluctant to admit You into my daily life in relation to small, intimate needs. I had not thought that the Lord of the universe, high and lifted up, should be bothered with my little problems. Yet here You are making it clear to us that the Helper will be as close to us as our own thoughts, supplying even needed information and reminding us in a critical moment of Your words of promise and blessing.*

Thank You too for putting Your finger so incisively on a deeper reason for my reluctance to admit You to the minutiae of my life. I have been afraid of the fair exchange You are asking of me: the Helper will supply everything— even these small needs—in exchange for my whole life. Not only does He want to use me, He wants an exuberance of giving on both sides.

Lord, melt away any pockets of resistance left. Don't let me hug any part of my life to myself.

Show me today how to take at least one definite step of trusting the Helper. Thank You, Lord. Amen.

6 He Gives Me New Desires

And all of us . . . are constantly being transfigured into His very own image in ever increasing splendor and from one degree of Glory to another; [for this comes] from the Lord [Who is] the Spirit.

(II Corinthians 3:18, AMPLIFIED)

The Helper can indeed change our desires and our tastes and our habit patterns.

Some years ago I had a friend in Washington, D.C., Winifred Hanigan, who had established a unique dress business. For a yearly fee, she would consult with a client about her clothing needs for her life-style, then handle all shopping and fitting for her. Since the nation's capital is full of small-town people in need of sudden sophistication, Winifred's service was a godsend to wives of officialdom and the diplomatic service.

Janet was a friend of mine, a Kansas girl working on Capitol Hill. She knew that she was hopelessly deficient in clothing taste and know-how, yet she did not have Winifred's fee. Our friend took Janet on anyway.

The first concern was acquiring basics. A necessary basic for Janet's job and the Washington climate, Winifred told her protégé, was a fine three-piece tweed outfit—suit and coat. A beautiful British tweed, mostly in deep reds, was selected and ordered.

When it arrived and Janet picked up the outfit, she cried all the way from Winifred's shop to the bus stop on Connecticut Avenue. The tweeds were ridiculously expensive. They cost all of Janet's salary for two weeks. And she wasn't even sure she *liked* the outfit!

Then we watched a strange thing happen. As Janet wore the clothes made of the beautiful tweed, she noticed her own taste being transformed. The purchase turned out to be one of the mainstays of Janet's wardrobe for eight years. The tweeds were not worn out even then.

But all this could not have happened without Janet putting herself in Winifred's hands, trusting her enough to obey her.

This is a homely illustration, an analogy of the process by which the Spirit changes us. But He can't do this until we trust Him enough to put ourselves in His hands. . . . "For all who are led by the Spirit of God are sons of God," Paul solemnly tells us.[1]

Then immediately Paul points out that this does not mean "a spirit of slavery to put you once more in bondage to fear. . . ." Rather, this is "sonship—in the bliss of which we cry, Abba! . . . Father!"[2]

When Janet submitted herself and her taste to Winifred, exactly as a son or daughter submits to a parent, then an astonishing process was set in motion: her taste was "transformed . . . by the . . . renewal of [her] mind—by its new ideals and its new attitude. . . ."[3] And this is exactly the way the Spirit deals with us when we submit ourselves as sons.

Further, just as Janet found that she could trust Winifred's taste, even so we find the Spirit possesses the kind of taste that we can trust implicitly.

We have only to look around us at the beauties He wrought as One of the Agents in the creation of our world to know that here is One of impeccable taste, our world's finest Connoisseur. Anywhere we turn in nature we see the demonstration of this—from the lowliest roadside buttercup to the intricately engineered iridescence of seashells like the chambered nautilus or the Pacific triton's trumpet; from the proud beauty of the preening male cardinal to the flashing brilliance of the tiny hummingbirds; in every foaming, curling wave of the ocean and every star in the sky.

True, in ourselves we are not quite ready for such perfection. At points each of us wants to drag along in the mud of mediocrity. Our taste has to be educated upwards as Janet's had to be. But we have nothing to fear in this process.

We can trust the Spirit in His work of renewing and transforming us into sons and daughters fit for the King.

HELPFUL READING: Ephesians 4:22–32

HIS WORD FOR YOU: God finishes what He began.
The Lord will perfect that which concerns me: thy mercy, O Lord, endures forever: forsake not the works of Your own hands.
(Psalm 138:8, AMPLIFIED)

PRAYER: *Lord, I sense that I haven't even begun to grasp the extent of the transformation You want to make in me. Yet I thank You that these changes do not mean that I will be any less myself. I begin to see that it's rather my tendency "to be conformed to the world" that blurs and all but wipes out my individuality. Your "transforming" enhances the real me.*

Lord, by an act of will, I ask You to undertake on my behalf that transformation. Give me the ability and the grace to be quick to hear, to bend with the wind of the Spirit, to obey. In Jesus' name. Amen.

7 He Changes My Undesirable Habit Patterns

*I indeed baptize you with water unto repentance: but he
that cometh after me ... shall baptize you with the Holy
Ghost and with fire.*

... that we ... might walk in newness of life.
(Matthew 3:11, KJV; Romans 6:4, RSV)

It is as *sinners* that we receive Christ for salvation and
are baptized in water. It is then as *sons* that we receive the
baptism of the Spirit. Notice how clearly John the Baptist
(as quoted by Matthew above) makes this distinction.
After we have been received by Jesus and are then heirs of
the Father, along with Him, then Jesus Himself (He alone)
can baptize us with the Spirit. Not until we have entered
into both of these experiences can we walk in full newness
of life. Our "born again" life is never our own natural life
raised to its highest development. Rather, it is that life
scrapped, dead, "crucified with Christ." Then to take the
place of that old natural life, the Divine life condescends to
its lowliest home—your heart and mine. Until the Spirit is
thus tabernacling with us, the newness of life of which the
Apostle Paul so often spoke will be mere theory and will
elude us.

But once we have been born again and have received the
Spirit, then what is the newness of life like? What can we
expect?

Some of the changes involve deep and extensive inner

transformation. Study the fifth chapter of Galatians and note the element of change which Paul depicts and his list of high character traits which should be common to all who receive the Spirit: love, a great joy and gladness, an even temper and patience, kindness and a generosity in our judgment of our fellows, faithfulness (hanging in there), gentleness, self-control and self-restraint.[1]

When we allow the Spirit to develop in us these gracious traits, then like the boy Jesus growing up, we too will "increase in wisdom . . . and in favor with God and man."[2]

Other changes the Helper will make in us will then vary from person to person. Some will be more superficial, yet specific and noticeable changes in tastes and in habit patterns. One girl, who had been barely tolerant of other people's pets, found herself loving dogs. Another lost her taste for heavy makeup. Yet another, who had often gone to see X-rated movies (especially foreign ones), now found these distasteful to her.

A man was no longer interested in escaping into reading detective stories for interminable hours. Another man, a compulsive viewer of televised sports, found this of sharply decreasing importance to him. An Atlanta friend who for years had habitually looked forward to his late-afternoon bourbon and water was astonished to find himself not wanting the drink.

In His changing of our desire-world the Spirit will deal with each of us differently. Given that, any church or religious group that seeks to place us back "under law" with lists of "Thou shalt nots" is denying the Spirit's work and interfering with it.

We watched the unique individuality of the Spirit's work with our friend Betty in Delray Beach, Florida. For years she had been struggling to stop smoking. She felt convicted about a child of the King being in bondage to some grains of tobacco wrapped in a paper tube. Yet Betty felt helpless to get free of this and was therefore discouraged.

One night she had a short vivid dream. She saw the face of the speaker at a recent meeting who had mentioned the smoking problem. Then a hand and arm with a lighted cigarette between the fingers came into view. In the dream the fingers began vigorously tamping out the cigarette. There the dream ended.

The next morning the dream was still vividly present to Betty. She wondered if its meaning could be as obvious as it seemed. Pondering this, she automatically reached for her package of cigarettes. A single cigarette was left in the package. Betty lighted it, but she soon found that it tasted different—not at all good. With disgust she tamped the cigarette out exactly as in the dream. She has had no desire to smoke since.

This is the gracious work of the Spirit.

HELPFUL READING: Galatians 5:16–24

HIS WORD FOR YOU: A prescription for getting rid of a bad habit.

But this shall be the covenant that I will make with the house of Israel; After those days, saith the Lord, I will put my law in their inward parts, and write it in their hearts. . . .

(Jeremiah 31:33, KJV)

PRAYER: *Lord Jesus, how I thank You that the freedom into which You call me does not seek to change me by forcing me to do what I do not want to do, rather changes me on the inside by giving me new desires. Only a love like Yours could ever have thought of such a gracious plan. For I find it no burden to do what my new desires want to do.*

So I open myself to You and give You permission to change me as it pleases You. Lord, I anticipate the adventure that lies ahead. Thank You, Lord, thank You. Amen.

Part Four

How the Helper Ministers to Me at a Deep Level

1 *He Convicts Me of Sin*

If I go, I will send him [the Helper] to you. And when he comes, he will convince the world concerning sin . . . because they do not believe in me. . . .

(John 16:7–9, RSV)

If a group of knowledgeable Christians were asked, "By what signs can one recognize that he has just received the Spirit?" we might get a variety of answers: "I felt a great inrush of love and joy," or, "My whole body tingled with a great warmth; I wanted to shout—and did," or, "I spoke in a heavenly language for the first time."

Yet the answer Jesus gave to His apostles during His Last Supper talk was altogether different: "When the Helper comes, He will convict the world of sin."

Why, we wonder, since Jesus was sending the Spirit to help us and to be our Comforter, would the Spirit's first priority be to convict us of sin? That sounds so stringent, anything but comforting.

And what sin did He mean? When we speak of sin, we think of lying, cheating, greed, slander, a vicious tongue, temper, cruelty, sexual promiscuity, adultery, murder and the like, whereas, when Jesus spoke of the convicting work of the Holy Spirit, He did not mention those sins. In fact, He used the singular "sin," then went on to define sin as unbelief—"Because they do not believe in me."

Jesus' viewpoint here is clearly not ours, since most of us rarely think of unbelief as being sin. In fact, sometimes we are actually proud of it, calling unbelief resistance to superstition and foolish credulity, thinking of our skepticism as sophistication, the result of our being educated out of prejudice—the blind acceptance of unproven premises.

At best, we view unbelief as a disability we really can't help—"I'm sorry, I wish I could believe. But you know I have to be honest. After all, I can't work faith up in myself."

Neither sinking down before unbelief helplessly nor bowing before it in intellectual pride solves our problem here. In both instances we are left exactly where we were before.

Then why does Scripture not only call unbelief a sin, but the fountainhead of all sin, the sin that encompasses all other sins?

Because by our unbelief we reject Jesus Christ, who He is, all He stands for, what He came to earth to do.

It was of this root sin that the Spirit convicted three thousand men on the Day of Pentecost through the second sermon Simon Peter ever preached. Bluntly, Peter had charged them with rejecting the Lord of Life—"whom you crucified and killed by the hands of lawless men." Whereupon they were "cut to the heart" and anxiously inquired, "Brethren, what shall we do?"[1]

How often I have heard preachers tell their congregations that we today "crucify the Lord afresh." This same thought is also in that lovely spiritual, "Were You There When They Crucified My Lord?"

Yet until recently something about that thought eluded me. Then the Spirit showed me that every time I reject Jesus' ability to handle any problem or problem area of my life, I am rejecting Him as the Lord of Life as truly as did the three thousand on the Day of Pentecost. He claimed to be the Savior, to be able to save us from any sin, any bondage, any problem. By disclaiming that, with regard to any one of my problems, I am calling Jesus a liar and a charlatan—a fake prophet—as truly as did those who long ago howled for His death before Pilate and who drove in the nails.

At that point I am also back in the Garden of Eden standing beside Adam and Eve giving heed to the serpent —"Don't believe God. He's really trying to deceive you and take away your happiness. After all, you know your own situation best. Don't be afraid to follow your own best judgment."

Whenever I follow the serpent's twisted, convoluted advice, instantly I reveal the root of my sin-nature. It has many tentacles, among them my rebellion against God, the

self-will of my determination to have my own way, and my
arrogance. How ridiculous we human beings are when we
set the pathetic limitations of our finite minds and petty
judgment over against the infinite wisdom of our Creator!
We can see this in regard to our own children. We can
simply judge better than they can. . . . "No, you may *not*
ride your bike in the heavy traffic downtown." . . . "Stop it,
Johnny, you'll pull that chest over on yourself." . . .
"Debbie, *no!* You cannot play with matches." But how
blind we are to the fact that we grownups are in an even
more untenable position in relation to our Heavenly Father.

Even so, we hear our amazing Lord telling us, "Neither
do I condemn you." Here too, His viewpoint is very different from ours. Even as we are inclined to center down on
legalistic and fleshly sins, so we usually assume that we are
in for massive doses of judgment and condemnation.

Not so!

For God sent the Son into the world, not to condemn the world, but that the world might be saved
through him.[2]

The difference here is that we think of sin as the breaking of laws, whereas Jesus thinks of sin as being bound.
Why would anyone with goodwill condemn a poor man
bound with chains or tied with heavy rope? Would he not
rather want to free him?

That, Scripture tells us, is the plight of us all before we
meet Jesus because

All have sinned. . . .
If we say we have no sin, we deceive ourselves,
and the truth is not in us.

Every one who commits sin is a slave to sin.[3]

And Jesus came to earth, He announced at the beginning of His public ministry, for the express purpose not of
condemning us, but of releasing all of us sin-captives.[4]

Therefore, until we see ourselves as bound in many specific areas and in need of freeing and saving, obviously we
will have no need of the Savior. Our danger then will be
that of approaching Jesus not as a Savior but as a Santa
Claus for the good gifts He can give us.

The truth is that none of us can go anywhere in the

Christian life so long as we are chained with unbelief. For in any area we look, until we believe that Jesus is the Savior of our life for whatever our problem is—health or sex or money or job or strained or severed human relationships or whatever—there is nothing He can do for us. And we will then stay bound on a level plateau, getting nowhere until the Spirit convicts us too of unbelief as the sin it is, until we begin to see God's grief for our lack of trust in the Lord of life, and allow Jesus to deal with this sin in as summary a fashion as He deals with all sin.

So long have most of us thought fuzzily about unbelief that there is relief in knowing of this clear-cut remedy for our sin. The steps are clear: we must stop all excuses; confess our lack of trusting Jesus as sin; give the Spirit permission to bring us to repentance about this, even at the emotional level; claim God's promise of forgiveness and cleansing.[5]

Then, to our delight, we shall find a fresh and new faith springing up in us like the bubbling up of a spring of clear water.

HELPFUL READING: Acts 2:14–21.

HIS WORD FOR YOU: Jesus—God's eternal "Yes."
For all the promises of God find their Yes in Him [Christ].

(II Corinthians 1:20, RSV)

PRAYER: *Lord Jesus, Sovereign Lord, into whose hands the Father has given all power, I lift up my heart and my life to You.*

Lord, so often I must have grieved You with my lack of trust. Your loving, giving heart has wanted to shower good gifts on me and my family and friends, yet I have been too bound by the sin of not believing even to lift my hands to receive the gifts.

Lord Jesus, forgive me!

I do confess my unbelief as the sin it is. And I ask You now to forgive me and to cleanse me of this black sin. I thank You that the "cleansing from all unrighteousness" You have promised includes the gift of Your own implicit trust in the goodness, the mercy, and the present-day power of the Father.

Thank You, Lord. Amen.

2 *He Values My Personhood*

Now the Lord is that Spirit; and where the Spirit of the Lord is, there is liberty.
(II Corinthians 3:17, KJV)

Many people are afraid of the Helper. Often unspoken is the fear, "If I assent to the Spirit, won't He then just take over and make me do all sorts of kooky things?"

But from a great pool of Christian experience comes the answer. No, the Helper never violates anyone's free will. He, like each person of the Trinity, has supreme respect for our personhood. He will never trample upon that or take us any further than we are willing to go.

In this regard the Holy Spirit and all powers of darkness stand in complete antithesis. Satan despises our personhood and steadily seeks to suck all freedom of will from us. Satan wants us in slavery to him; the Helper wants our freedom.

This is at once an awesome measure both of the value that God places upon the creatures made in His own image and of the humility of Jesus who "stooped low, made himself of no reputation, and took upon him the form of a servant."[1]

The Spirit faithfully reflects both attributes here: (1) the freedom of choice of the human will is one of the most precious gifts God has given us. Therefore, the Helper waits upon the assent of our will. And, (2) in line with Jesus' own humility, the Helper waits to see how much welcome we will accord Him; how open we are to His help, so that through us He can help others. This amazing humility means that the Spirit actually puts Himself at the

103

disposal of our volition. In that sense, He even submits Himself to our human weakness and frailty.

The supreme value Jesus places on our freedom of will was dramatized for me during my encounter with the Risen Lord that memorable night, September 14, 1943, at my parents' home in Seaview, Virginia.

I had already been ill many months, and was not getting better. Discouragement was deep. Before falling asleep, I had given up my own struggle for healing. I had already tried everything. Nothing had worked. So with many tears, I cast myself on the mercy of God. The relinquishment was complete.

At about 3:30 A.M. I was awakened from a sound sleep —very wide awake. Suddenly—He was there. Jesus, standing on the right side of the bed. The room crackled and vibrated.

Since I have detailed this experience elsewhere, I want to emphasize here just one aspect of the electrifying moments that followed. At the end, Jesus gave me this simple directive, "Go, and tell your mother."

Even in that moment of command, I was acutely aware of Jesus' regard for my personhood and of His hands-off attitude as regards my free will. There was no stampeding, no crowding. The choice to obey or not to obey was clearly mine. That's the way Jesus wanted it to be.

In a flash, I understood how it had been with that rich young ruler in the gospels. . . . "Go, and sell what you have . . . and follow Me." With him too, as with me that night, there had been Jesus' hands-off attitude, "You decide." Mark's account of this incident tells us that Jesus beholding the young man, loved him.[2] Even so, Jesus had stood silently by, love in His eyes, yet had watched the young man turn his back and walk away.

Not understanding why He wanted me to tell my mother, I still knew that I must obey anyway. My healing began at that point of blind obedience. In retrospect, I realized that it was not for my mother's sake that Jesus had given me this directive, but for my own sake: I had to bend the will and obey.

Since that night I have understood that this reverence for the freedom of life God Himself has given us is a position neither the Father, nor Jesus, the Son, nor the Spirit will ever abdicate.

So what does this mean in our walk with the Helper?

The startling truth is that He will come to us and fill us only to the degree that we are willing to be filled. He insists upon being a welcome guest in our hearts and beings, never a trespasser or an interloper or a squatter.

In fact, we can, whenever we choose, turn this sympathetic, courteous Guest from the door of our heart. We can also so grieve Him with wrong attitudes that He simply withdraws. . . .[3]

When the truth of this final humility of God dawns upon us, it puts an end to any fear about losing our selfhood to the Helper.

It also places a fearsome responsibility upon *us*. How much do we want Him? How much of Him are we willing to receive? What limitations are we placing upon Him?

It follows that even after our initial baptism of the Spirit, as our willingness and receptivity increase, we will also experience repeated fillings. These will come as we step out in ministry. Special filling and special outpouring will be given for tough situations, extremities we alone could never handle. This has been the experience of many individuals across the centuries.

HELPFUL READING: Matthew 19:16–22

HIS WORD FOR YOU: Take a deep breath of the fresh wind of the Spirit.

> *The Spirit of the Lord is upon me, because the Lord has anointed me . . . to proclaim liberty to the captives . . . to grant a garland of beauty instead of ashes, the oil of joy for mourning, the garment of praise instead of a heavy, burdened-and failing spirit. . . .*
>
> *Everlasting joy shall be theirs.*
> (Isaiah 61:1, 3, 7, AMPLIFIED)

PRAYER: *Lord, I see now that my fear of the Spirit has also, in an odd way, been a dodge for placing the responsibility of my life and growth on You rather than seeing that the degree of my openness to You rests squarely on my shoulders. Often I have deceived myself—"Whatever God wants to give me, it's up to Him"—when all the time, the door of my heart was shut, with most of the shutters drawn.*

Lord, thank You for always knocking on the door and never crashing it down. Lord, Helper, it is my will to open the door wide to You. Enter, Lord, and be my honored Guest. What joy to welcome and receive You! Amen.

3 He Teaches Me about Tears

*And I will give them . . . a new heart—and I will put a
new spirit within them; and I will take the stony [unnaturally hardened] heart out of their flesh, and will give them
a heart of flesh [sensitive and responsive to the touch of
their God].*

(Ezekiel 11:19, AMPLIFIED)

Jack is a fine professional man with serious family problems. He has many Christian friends who love him and his
family and who want to help. Yet Jack is trying to carry
his heavy burden all alone, the stiff-upper-lip way. Why,
we have wondered, does he insist upon isolating himself?
Why will he not ever unburden his heart and mind when
he needs to so desperately?

Then one day I found out why. "I was reared an Anglican," Jack told me. "Pretty starchy, I guess. I'd like to
come and see you and your husband. Honestly, I would.
But I know I couldn't do it without getting emotional—*and
that just wouldn't do.*"

I looked at Jack in astonishment. He would actually
then pass up the talk-therapy and the prayer-therapy needed
because he was afraid of tears!

An incident like this dramatizes how warped our values
can become and how completely we have misunderstood
about tears for men as well as women. The Spirit would
teach us that tears are the pearls of God's kingdom.

Some years ago a close friend, whom I'll call Sam, asked
for and received the gift of the Helper in his life. Sam had

always been mistrustful of any emotionalism, especially in religion. His father had been a dignified seminary professor. In Sam's house the emphasis had always been on a strictly intellectual approach to Christianity. Even old Sunday School or evangelistic-type hymns were too emotional for Sam's taste.

But after the Helper came into Sam's life, immediately we noticed a startling change: anytime our friend spoke of Jesus, we would see tears in his eyes. Suddenly, for the first time, Jesus was a Person. Not only that, a dear Person.

Nor was Sam embarrassed or apologetic about the moisture in his eyes, though sometimes he would laugh at himself a bit. But Sam knew that something had changed him down deep at the heart-level. The hardness there before had been softened, "made responsive to the touch of God," as the prophet Ezekiel expressed it. And Sam knew that he could be glad about tears like those.

Scripture often warns us that a hard heart is the sign of major trouble between us and God. Our eternal spirit is then in real jeopardy . . .

Jesus told us that hardness of heart is the major cause of divorce.[1]

It had been hardness of heart that kept the Israelites wandering in the desert for forty years, and cost the entire generation that left Egypt the Promised Land.[2]

We are warned that toying with sin or deliberately harboring even small sins in our lives results in an accretion of the hardening process in us.[3]

Jesus made it clear that even for the "good people" the pride of self-righteousness results in serious hardening of the heart.[4]

This hardening process then, should be something to fear above all else. And the opposite of this stony heart is the warm heart of flesh that the Spirit puts within us. The warm heart is going to result in tears sometimes— unashamed, unabashed—because now we recognize the Source.

It was true for Jesus, and He is our pattern here as in all things. . . .

He wept over the city of Jerusalem because it was a city filled with hatred and violence, not knowing the things that belonged to its peace.[5]

He wept at the tomb of his friend Lazarus out of sympathy for His dear friends.[6]

Indeed, as we begin to live and to walk in the Spirit, we find that quite often tears precede some of God's greatest miracles. In such instances, the tears are the evidence that the Spirit is there, moving in power.

Four-year-old Troy Mitchell of Ontario, Canada,[7] had been born with eczema and a chronic asthmatic lung condition. The best medical care available had still not handled the running, oozing sores and cracked lesions resulting from the eczema.

In 1968–69 there had been miraculous healings among several of the Mitchells' friends when they had gone to Kathryn Kuhlman's services in Pittsburgh. Troy's parents and grandparents decided to drive the little boy the five hundred miles to Pittsburgh.

The group got to the auditorium about 9:00 A.M., two hours before the service would begin, and almost immediately, Sharon, Troy's mother, began to weep—for no particular reason. After the service began at eleven, Sharon was crying harder than ever, to the embarrassment of those with her.

Midway through the service, Miss Kuhlman stopped and said, "Someone here is being cured of eczema."

The Canadian group paid no attention. They did not connect this with Troy at all. Sharon continued to weep.

Ten minutes later, Kathryn held up her hand again, "I'm going to have to stop this service yet again. Someone here is grieving the Holy Spirit."

Maggie Hartner, Miss Kuhlman's observant helper, was walking the aisles. She stopped beside the Canadians and asked who they were praying for and what was wrong. When eczema was mentioned, she exclaimed, "Well, for goodness' sake. I've been hunting you all over the auditorium. *Haven't you heard what's been going on?* Please check your child."

Sharon's tears stopped instantly. She jerked Troy's shirt over his head. Every sore on his body was healed. The scabs had turned to powder and dusted to the floor. Even an especially bad draining sore on his left arm was covered with fresh skin.

Troy has never had a return of the eczema. His two Ontario doctors, Doctors Montgomery and McLeod, have both documented the healing.

Sharon's tears, which she had not understood at all, had been the Spirit's insignia, the sign that He was present and at work.

Admittedly, there is weeping that is not of the Spirit, just of the soul or the emotion—tears of rage, of frustration, of self-pity, or as a bid for attention. But very soon we come to know the difference and to value honest emotion as a sign of a heart in which the Helper dwells.

HELPFUL READING: Romans 12:15, 16; Hebrews 3:7–19

HIS WORD FOR YOU: A bright promise for the depressed.

But God, Who comforts and encourages and refreshes and cheers the depressed and the sinking. . . .
(II Corinthians 7:6, AMPLIFIED)

PRAYER: *Lord, I recognize that most of the time my fear of showing emotion is simply pride—silly false pride. This too is a part of self that I would lay on Your altar. Let me never be afraid to mingle my tears with those of my friends and neighbors. If this is the price I pay for a soft, warm, loving heart in which You dwell, then Lord, I pay it gladly, so gladly.*

In Thy name, Amen.

4 *He Is My Comforter*

As one whom his mother comforteth, so will I comfort you. . . .

And I will pray the Father, and he shall give you another Comforter, that He may abide with you for ever.
(Isaiah 66:13; John 14:16, KJV)

Few of us ever completely outgrow a longing for the comfort of a mother's love when we are hurting. The broken heart can be an open, raw wound. What is dangerous to us and grieves the Spirit above all else is to steel ourselves when emotions well up inside and allow hardness to creep in as a steel-plate protection.

"Let Me handle the hurt for you," the Spirit tells us. There have been many such moments in my life, but one which, though I have written about it before, illustrates best this side of the Helper's tender ministrations to us.

In the early morning hours of January 25, 1949, my husband, Peter Marshall, had awakened with alarming pain in his chest and down both arms. The doctor had come, an ambulance was called, and Peter had been taken to the hospital. I had no way of handling this crisis except to drop on my knees beside the bed.

But my knees no sooner touched the floor than I experienced God as a comforting Mother—something altogether new to me. There was a feeling of the everlasting arms around me and at the same time, waves of tenderness like warm holy oil being poured over me. It was the infinite

110

gentleness of the loving heart of God, more all-pervading than any human mother's love could ever be.

Later was to come the more masculine side of God's caring when He knew that I would need more than tenderness. Then He would give me the first installment of the other side of His comfort—not only loving consolation, but *strength*.

At the moment I interpreted this experience to mean that Peter's heart would be healed. Later, I realized that God had granted this special help so I could understand with a final knowing that He had been with us, a participating Presence through every moment of Peter's homegoing. For at 8:15 that morning, the news came. Peter's heart was forever stilled.

Then it was that I experienced the kind and quality of "comfort" God gives us today through the Holy Spirit. If His comfort were limited to pity or commiserating with us (as much human sympathy is), it would lead us to self-pity—and that's no help at all. Rather, the Spirit's comfort puts courage into us, empowers us to cope with the strains and exigencies of life. The word is *Paraclete*, meaning "alongside, to help in every emergency." And the "comfort" He brings comes from the Latin word *fortis*, meaning "brave." It is a strong, courageous word. Thus the Spirit becomes our "Enabler"—no feather cushion, rather steel in the backbone equal to every sorrow and perplexity and disappointment.

So I found Him in those days following Peter's death. I was not myself. This was not my strength—but the Spirit's. He carried me over and above all circumstances, so that miraculously, *I* could be used to impart strength to a sorrowing congregation and to many in the nation's capital to whom Peter had been a tower of strength.

Yet despite the "fortis" side of God's comfort, I shall always cherish those moments when the Mother-tenderness of God enfolded me.

Years later I would come across passages on this Mother-heart of God in the writings of Hannah W. Smith, the Quaker. In an old book, long out of print, she wrote a lyrical chapter called "The Unselfishness of God" . . .

But now I began to see that if I took all the unselfish love of every mother's heart the whole world over, and piled it all together, and multiplied it by millions, I would still only get a faint idea of the unselfishness of God. . . .

Hannah Smith saw that in the light of this mother-side to God's love for us, even the term "lost" becomes comforting. For . . .

Nothing can be lost that is not owned by somebody, and to be lost means only, not yet found. The lost gold piece is still gold with the image of the King upon it; the lost sheep is a sheep still, not a wolf; the lost son has still the blood of his father in his veins. . . .

Who can imagine a mother with a lost child ever having a ray of comfort until the child is found? Is God then more indifferent than a mother? In fact I believe that all the problems of our spiritual life . . . would vanish like mist before the rising sun, if the full blaze of the mother-heart of God could be turned upon them. . . .

In the Helper we have the perfect balance of God's love—infinite tenderness on the one side, infinite strength on the other. This One with the magnificent dual-sided personality is the Comforter who will be with us forever, every step of the way through this life, no matter what difficulties or sorrows life hands us.

For this we have Jesus' own word. And that never fails!

HELPFUL READING: John 14:26; 16:12–15

HIS WORD FOR YOU: Jesus, our Everlasting Supporter. *It is before his own Master that he stands or falls. And he shall stand and be upheld, for the Master—the Lord—is mighty to support him and make him stand.*
(Romans 14:4, AMPLIFIED)

PRAYER: *Father, I thank You that You have so lovingly provided a way to meet my every need, that You and You alone satisfy all the deep and hidden hungers of my heart. You know how much I hurt. You see my unshed tears. I even battle bitterness sometimes, Lord. Take that away and give me Your comfort instead.*

How I praise You for Your gentleness with me. But even more, that You send me the Enabler to supply the strength I do not have, to undertake for me. Thank You, Lord. Thank You. Amen.

5   *He Teaches Me to Pray (I)*

The Spirit himself intercedes for us . . . according to the will of God.

(Romans 8:26, 27, RSV)

Why cannot an omnipotent God, knowing our needs, supply them without waiting for our prayers?

He could, of course, but that is not His plan for his children on earth. Instead, He has dared to arrange it so that He is actually dependent upon us in the sense of our prayers being necessary and all-important to the carrying out of His will on earth.

When Jesus' apostles realized that their prayers were *that* important, they pleaded, "Lord, teach us to pray, as John taught his disciples."[1]

Jesus then gave them the Lord's Prayer as the perfect pattern prayer. It is a form (though with immeasurable depths), an outward structure or technique of communicating with the Father.

On the apostles' side, the patterned prayer was all that they were able to receive at that time. Jesus knew that there could be no entering into the full secret of answered prayer until the coming of the Helper.

Looking forward to that great watershed event, during His Last Supper talk their Master spoke especially of the joy of answered prayer ahead:

"Up to this time, you have not asked a . . . thing in My name [that is, presenting all I AM] but now ask and keep on asking and you will receive, so that your joy . . . may be full and complete."[2]

"Up to this time" refers to Jesus' imminent glorification and the Helper's coming at Pentecost. At that time God's plan of redemption would be complete: God the Father would receive our petitions at the throne of grace and mercy; the glorified Jesus would be our Advocate and High Priest to present our case and plead our petition before the Father; the Spirit would be the prayer-Helper within us to show us how to prepare our prayer-petitions so that they would be made according to the will of God, and so would always be answered.[3]

Unquestionably, all of us need massive help with praying aright. So set is our flesh against praying at all that the Helper's first task is to create in us even the basic desire to pray. He is the One who also spotlights for us the prayer-need or topic for prayer by creating a "concern" within us.

Then the Helper has to uncover for us the essence or kernel of what it is we really want. Usually, the true desire at the heart of our prayer-petition is buried under debris that obscures and muddles the real issue.

It is also the Helper's task to show us the blockages in the way of a given prayer-petition—any self-seeking, our desire to control, any resentments and unconfessed sin, etc.

He is also the One who gives us His own prayer faith; also His fervor to replace our tepid love and caring—and so on and on. No wonder we so desperately need the Helper as our prayer Director!

As we recognize our ignorance about praying aright and our helplessness, and actively seek the Spirit's help, our prayer life becomes the anteroom to amazing adventures.

So we have been finding it in a fellowship group of which I have been a member for several years. Doris, a young married woman, a good friend of several in the group, was very ill. The doctors gave little hope.

One evening as Frances, one of the group, was preparing dinner, the Helper spoke to her quietly but urgently, "Doris needs prayer." In her mind's eye Frances could see our entire group of about fourteen people gathered with Doris. Yet she had no idea whether Doris would be willing to receive prayer help.

Frances' obedience however, brought results: two eve-

nings later the whole group gathered. Doris came happily,
along with her sister who was visiting her.

Since the Spirit had asked for and engineered the meeting, He was there in power. He brought out into the light
Doris' girlhood terror and hurt through her stepfather's
sexual abuse. Her sister's presence was necessary to verify
all of this and to add details. This childhood trauma had
warped Doris' relationship with her husband and with all
males and undoubtedly was a factor in producing a serious
physical illness.

That evening we watched the Spirit orchestrate through
our prayer a beautiful healing of the memories. Jesus lifted
from Doris the weight of a lifetime. The evening ended in
such glory that we thought Doris' physical problem had
also been healed.

Not so. As it turned out, the glory was our loving part-
ing with Doris and her send-off into the next life. She died a
month later.

In retrospect, we could only conclude that the Spirit,
knowing what lay ahead, was unwilling for Doris to begin
her new life encumbered with Satan's wreckage. She went
to meet her Lord freed and cleansed and joyous.

All around us are those caught in bondages, imprisoned
in fears, hampered by disease to whom Jesus longs to bring
His release and His joy. But He waits on *our* prayers. It's a
solemn thought.

HELPFUL READING: Acts 9:10–19

HIS WORD FOR YOU: My delight is in Him; His delight
is to help me.
> *Delight yourself also in the Lord, and He will give you
> the desires and secret petitions of your heart.*
> (Psalm 37:4, AMPLIFIED)

PRAYER: *Father, this is the promise I make to You: when
the Helper prompts me to pray, I will drop what I'm doing
and pray; when I feel a concern for someone, I will talk
with You about it and seek Your direction. Keep me alert
to the Helper's tug at my sleeve, and give me, Lord, as a
gift, a high level of willingness to obey and to follow
through.*

I praise You for the gigantic network of prayer and con-

cern and love wrought by the Spirit in us Christians all over the world. I praise You that this stretches even across the barrier of what we call death. I praise You for letting me see the importance of prayer through Your eyes—as the richest resource of the Kingdom, one of the Helper's most treasured gifts to us. Praise You, Lord! Amen.

6   He Teaches Me to Pray (II)

May the . . . Father grant you the Spirit of wisdom and revelation . . . illuminating the eyes of your heart so that you can understand the hope to which He calls us, the wealth of his glorious heritage in the saints. . . .
(Ephesians 1:18, 19, MOFFATT)

The Apostle Paul's passionate prayer is that we, God's people, begin to understand "how rich is the glorious inheritance our Father has bequeathed and stored up for us." From the moment that we are born again, we have the right to call Him "Abba, Father," we "who once were no people and now are God's people."[1] And from that moment on, Paul assures us, all the graces and riches and spiritual treasures and answered prayers we shall ever need in our lifetime have already been deposited to our account . . .

Blessing . . . be to the God and Father of our Lord Jesus Christ . . . Who has blessed us in Christ with every spiritual [Holy Spirit-given] blessing in the heavenly realm![2]

There is a good reason why Paul used the past perfect tense here—God "has blessed us" ~eady—the riches have already been deposited to our account and are waiting for us. In our earthly life a son usually has to wait for his father's death before inheriting the portion of his father's estate due him. But in the spiritual life, the death that brought us our inheritance took place two thousand years ago at Golgotha.

When the eyes of the understanding are really opened to see this fact, it altogether changes our prayer life. No longer is there any need of pleading with God to change an undesirable circumstance or to grant us something we need. Since the answer has already been stored up for us, our prayer petition rather needs to be for revelation—"Lord, open my eyes" to see what's there. We are asking Him to let us see at least briefly into the world of spirit, like granting us X-ray eyes for a peep into the treasure room where the golden treasures are stored. Our prayer request is for a sovereign move from the Godward side, *not* in a shifting or change in outward circumstance, but in an inner revelation. From then on, prayer becomes waiting on Him for that insight.

When the insight comes, then faith—"the substance of things not seen"—follows as surely as the sun rises each morning. This "knowing" is altogether different from all pull-yourself-up-by-your-own-bootstraps faith techniques. How often I have tried to quell my own doubts by rebuking negativism and concentrating on the positive—and have tried to call that faith. Yet all such self-help gimmicks are light years away from Jesus' quiet knowing that wrought mighty miracles.

The difference between Jesus and us here is that our Lord seems to have had instant knowing in any particular case because His spiritual eyes were steadily open to revelation. Over and over, patiently, Jesus explained this. . .

> I assure you . . . the Son is able to do nothing from Himself—of His own accord; but He is able to do only what He sees the Father doing. . . .[3]

This seeing what the Father is doing is revelation. Or again . . .

> I am able to do nothing from Myself . . . but as I am taught by God and as I get His orders. . . . As the voice comes to Me, so I give a decision. . . .[4]

Once again, the hearing and knowing is revelation.

In the life of Jesus, the Gospels give us no instances of miracles until after the Spirit came upon Him at the time of His baptism by John the Baptist. This suggests then that even for the Lord Himself the Spirit was the indispensable

link in Jesus' revelation (followed by His knowing) in
relation to the problem before Him—the leper or the blind
man or the sick child.

And Jesus is our perfect pattern, the Pioneer of our faith
here as in all things. So when the Helper lays a concern on
our heart, our part is to ask Him to open our spiritual eyes
and give us the revelation needed.

The next move will then be the Helper's. For us, as for
Jesus, the Helper is the bearer of the needed revelation, the
One who enables us to see the prayer concern as Jesus sees
it. Since the answer to our need is already there, as the
Helper pulls aside the shrouding curtain to reveal to us
what is there, this will necessarily result in faith-knowing.
And at that point the miracle happens.

So our friend Kay Peters discovered some years ago
when her seven-year-old son Don awoke one morning feeling ill.

"Where does it hurt, Don?" his mother asked.

The lad motioned to his jaw and neck. "And here too,"
he said, moving his hands along the inside of his thighs.

Fear gripped Mrs. Peters. Mumps! There was an epi-
demic at his school. Mumps could have dangerous consequences in males!

Kay Peters had prayed many times for people who
needed to be healed—with remarkable results. But as she
started to pray for Don, one thought stopped her—did she
have the right to pray for "natural" childhood diseases?

Immediately, she knew what she had to do—simply ask
Jesus. When she did, the answer was not long in coming:
"Disease is never natural. Health is natural and normal,
what I want for My children. The idea of any childhood
diseases being natural or acceptable is one of Satan's lies,
passed down from generation to generation."

Joy leapt in Kay Peters' heart. Then almost instantly a
counter-thought intruded, as though to knock down the
joy. . . . "Better have mumps now than later."

But why should her son ever have the mumps? Hadn't
Jesus just said—? That couldn't be God's message. The
revelation came—that was Satan! He was telling her not to
believe Jesus. The father of lies had tipped his hand.

Ignoring Satan's negative suggestion, the mother not
only prayed for her son, but added, "And may he be im-
mune from the mumps forever."

With that she received quiet instructions from the inner

Voice: she was not to ask Don how he felt, and she was to observe him carefully.

Very soon it became apparent that the observing was in order that she would miss no part of the miracle. In a few minutes Don began chattering and laughing. Soon he was rolling on the bed. Then he began somersaulting. "Mother, I feel *good*. I don't know *when* I've felt so good! Mother, God heard your prayer and I'm all *well!*"

Don slept soundly that night, and by the next morning there was no trace of soreness or swollen glands. He went on to school that day, and Kay Peters reports that Don, long since a father himself, has never yet had the mumps.

HELPFUL READING: II Kings 6:14–23

HIS WORD FOR YOU: Claim Your Inheritance!
He has granted to us his precious and very great prom-
ises, that through these you may escape from the cor-
ruption that is in the world because of passion, and be-
come partakers of the divine nature.
(II Peter 1:4, RSV)

PRAYER: *Lord, I have come to You as a beggar believing*
myself poverty-stricken, lacking, when the fact is I am a
child of the King, heir to all Your riches—including every
insight and revelation I need for each prayer request. How
foolish I must seem to You, Lord! And how my spiritual
poverty-complex must grieve You.
I want so much to sit at the Helper's feet in the School
of Prayer and be taught by Him. Show me now how to
apply these glorious truths in my own life. And make me
a good pupil! In Thy name. Amen.

7 He Convinces Me of Eternal Life

In Him you also . . . were stamped with the seal of the long-promised Holy Spirit.

That [Spirit] is the guarantee of our inheritance—the first fruit, the pledge and foretaste, the down payment on our heritage—in anticipation of its full redemption. . . .
(Ephesians 1:13, 14, AMPLIFIED)

Jesus provided us with few details about life after death. When He gives us the Comforter though, His pledge is that we shall live forever with Him. Furthermore, the Spirit also supplies us with a little foretaste of what that life will be like.

The experience that was my foretaste of immortality occurred in the early morning hours of that September day back in 1943 when suddenly I knew that the Risen Christ was standing beside my bed. The room was charged with electricity, as if the Dynamo of the universe were standing there, as indeed He was!

This was not a vision. I saw nothing with the retina of my eyes. Yet I "saw" every detail clearly with the eyes of the Spirit. In the next few moments I experienced the reality of the spiritual body and learned that it has every faculty of the physical body, though with greater sensitivity and some dimensions added.

There was the total encounter of person to Person. The vividness and impact of Jesus' personality in its myriad facets broke over me like waves cresting on a shore: His kingliness (I wanted to fall on my knees and worship), yet the down-to-earthness of His light touch, His sense of humor, and His loving "You are taking yourself much too seriously. There's nothing here I can't handle."

It was perfectly apparent that He knew every detail of my situation and of the household, as also of my mind and thoughts. He rebuked me for nothing. Rather, the thrust of His personality challenged me out of the physical hole of illness to rise and walk on into the future.

Since that experience, I can never doubt the reality of a life after this one. But now I also understand how essential it is that our inner spirit, so deadened by sin, be touched by the only One who can bring us alive. For how can we enter the next life without our bodies until the faculties of our spiritual body are activated and brought alive?

I also understand better after that night something about what the post-resurrection appearances of Jesus must have been like. I have concluded that our spiritual bodies will have memory (not forgetting anything we know now), mind, will, emotions, personality. I will still be myself. I will know others as themselves, "even as also I am known." There will be nothing shocking in the transition, only a continuation of who I am now.

That memorable night I learned that with my spiritual body there will be instant (and accurate) transferral of thought, words, exchanges from person to person, without the necessity of using the vocal cords or of hearing with the eardrums. In other words, the spiritual body is real, even more real than the physical body.

In the years since that memorable night I have found other ways in which the Spirit is the foretaste and down-payment of immortality. As we begin to live and walk in the Spirit, we find that each wonderful gift He gives us is a sample of that which will be multiplied a thousandfold in the life to come.

There, we shall love as He loves; here, we have a small measure of that love for Him and for each other.

There, we will have the joy of unbroken communion with that amazingly provocative, magnificent Personality; here, only moments and facets of His presence are real to us.

There, we shall have full knowledge; here, the Spirit of Truth gives us bits of knowledge, perception, wisdom, and guidance.

In heaven, there will be no more pain or sickness or disease; here and now, the Spirit sometimes does heal our diseases; upon occasion He is inexplicably blocked from doing so.

There, we shall be done with sorrow; here the Comforter heals our broken hearts and, in the midst of our sorrow, gives us His joy as His pledge of our inheritance.

HELPFUL READING: I Corinthians 15:42–50

HIS WORD FOR YOU: His pledged word, the surety of eternal life.

I assure you, most solemnly I tell you, the person whose ears are open to My words . . . and believes . . . on Him Who sent Me has eternal life. And He does not come into judgment . . . will not come under condemnation— but he has already passed over out of death into life.

(John 5:24, AMPLIFIED)

PRAYER: *My Lord and my God, I thank You that I do not have to wait until death to taste the Spirit's wonderful gifts. I praise You that our immortality begins the minute we ask You to touch us and resurrect our dead spirit. How great it is to have day by day, the Helper's samplings and first fruits of life that will go on and on.*

Give me such fullness of the Spirit as shall make my life here and now, my home and my church, bits of heaven on earth. Amen.

Part Five

The Outpouring
of the
Helper's Generosity

1 Joy

You received the word in much affliction, with joy inspired by the Holy Spirit; so that you became an example to all. . . .

(I Thessalonians 1:6, 7, RSV)

Joy is one of the fruits of the Spirit promised us.[1] Yet perhaps some of us have misunderstood this word. We may think of joy as the exhilaration of prayers being miraculously answered; of the happiness of life going smoothly because of God's blessing on it; or the emotional euphoria of the singing and rejoicing of God's people in invigorating fellowship.

While God often graciously grants us these blessings, the joy of the Spirit is something deeper. The promise is not that the Christian will have only joyous circumstances, but that the Helper will give us the supernatural gift of joy in whatever circumstances we have.

We can see the working out of this in Luke's account of the infant Church. These first Christians had plenty of problems! After Pentecost Peter had no sooner preached his second sermon than he and John were arrested.[2] Following that, a group of apostles were jailed and flogged.[3] Then Stephen was stoned to death.[4] Christians were hunted out and hounded from their homes.[5] James, believed by some scholars to be the Lord's half-brother, was beheaded.[6] Then Peter was imprisoned by Herod, who intended to execute him.[7] And so on and on.

Yet in the midst of all this, the Acts account is peppered with statements about the irrepressible joy of these first Christians. . . . "They partook of their food with gladness."

. . . They were "constantly praising God." . . . "And the disciples were filled with joy and with the Holy Spirit."

And as we watch Paul and Silas being arrested in Philippi, "struck many blows," then thrown into prison with their feet in stocks, to our astonishment we see the Helper's joy taking over in this situation:

> But about midnight, as Paul and Silas were praying and singing hymns of praise to God, and the [other] prisoners were listening to them. . . .[8]

Those other prisoners must have been listening with incredulity, for there is nothing natural about singing and praising while one's feet are chained in stocks. Obviously, genuine joy in such circumstances is impossible for us humans; it is clearly supernatural.

But Jesus never promised us a gift of human joy delivered to us like a package. Rather, His promise is:

> I [Jesus] have told you these things that *My joy and delight may be in you*, and that your joy and gladness may be full measure and complete and overflowing.[9]

It is His own Joy that is pledged us. Through the Spirit, the risen and glorified Lord will Himself take up residence in our cold hearts, and along with Him comes His joy.

Why have we not understood about Jesus' joy? Why has Christendom distorted Scripture by insisting so repeatedly upon the picture of our Lord as "a man of sorrows and acquainted with grief?"

Of course He was *acquainted* with grief since He had come to earth in the flesh for the specific purpose of destroying all of Satan's grief-wreckage. Jesus spent His days going about looking into pain-racked eyes and in summary fashion—with delight—releasing men and women from the enemy's bondages. These were joyous tasks because the Lord of life loathed sickness and disease and broken relationships and insanity and death. So day by day, He left behind a string of victories.

And the greatest victory of all lay ahead—the Cross. Isaiah, in writing of the Messiah to come as being a "man of sorrows and acquainted with grief," was foretelling the agony of that Cross. Yet even there

Jesus . . . for *the joy that was set before Him* endured
the cross. . . .[10]

And how is it that we have not taken seriously one of the
most beautiful pictures of Jesus in the New Testament? . . .

Thou hast loved righteousness, and hated iniquity;
therefore God, even thy God, *hath anointed thee with
the oil of gladness above thy fellows.*[11]

So the writer of Hebrews is telling us that Jesus of
Nazareth was possessed of more gladness and more joy
than all other human beings.

But there is even more. Jesus has promised us not just
the extraordinary gladness other men saw in Him while He
walked the earth. We, being supremely blessed by living in
this era of the Holy Spirit, also are pledged the joy of the
victorious, resurrected and glorified Lord.

Looking forward to Pentecost, Jesus said to the eleven
apostles (and to us):

In a little while you will no longer see Me, and again
after a short while you will see Me . . . because I go
to my Father. . . .

But I will see you again and [then] your hearts will
rejoice, and no one can take from you your joy.[12]

In that day of the Spirit's coming to earth there would
be every cause for rejoicing and for continuous praise, for
Satan would be finally worsted, with the victory of the
Cross complete. This supernatural joy then, is the Joy of
the Spirit.

Recently, we witnessed the Spirit bring the gift of His
joy in the midst of cruel circumstances. Mary and George
Greenfield are an attractive couple who began attending
our Monday night church fellowship group in Delray
Beach, Florida. There they received the Baptism of the
Spirit.

Six days after that event their only daughter Patty (a
college sophomore) was abducted during a holdup of the
Cumberland Farms Dairy Store where she worked.

By the next day hundreds of people were praying for

Patty's safety. Yet some of us who attempted to pray for Patty's safe return (including her parents) experienced a check or block, something that was puzzling and hard to interpret at the time.

On the following Monday night (two days after Patty's disappearance) during the singing of "Amazing Grace," George Greenfield's tears began flowing. At that moment, George knew that his daughter was with the Lord. Along with the news came a strong assurance that even poured itself into words, "Don't cry, Dad. I'm okay."

Two days later Patty's body was found by a local detective. Subsequently, police arrested two young men who confessed to the killing.

When a sheriff's detective, an FBI agent, and the Greenfields' minister came together to tell them the sad news, they found the Greenfields' attitude astonishing: they already knew and had been prepared. Though these parents did not understand the "why" of the senseless murder any better than any of us, and while they grieved for their lovely daughter, there was total calmness and no bitterness toward the killers. The newspaper reporters swarming over the case were at a loss to explain the inner strength and sense of victory in the Greenfields—qualities they had never before encountered in such circumstances.

When my husband and I telephoned George and Mary from Evergreen Farm in Virginia where we had gone for the summer, the Greenfields ministered to us over the phone.

Those who attended the memorial service for Patty will never forget the power and beauty and, yes, the shining joy of the Lord that was present. One person described the service as a paean of deeply-felt praise!

Others over the centuries have groped for words to explain the Spirit's gift of joy. Here is how Dr. R. A. Torrey put it after the very sudden death of his lovely, intelligent little nine-year-old daughter Elizabeth from diphtheria:

The next morning . . . as I passed the corner of Chestnut Street and LaSalle Avenue, I could contain my grief no longer. . . . I cried aloud: "Oh, Elizabeth! Elizabeth!" And just then the fountain that I had in my heart broke forth with such power as I think I have never experienced before, and it was the most joyful moment that I have ever known in my life.[13]

How then, do we get the Spirit's joy? Recognize that it is more likely to come not when things are going well, but whenever we are faced with adversity or problems. This is our opportunity to claim part of our inheritance as a child of the King.

In order to do that, we have to allow Jesus to give us *His perspective on our situation.* Illness, ill will, accidents, poverty, injustice, broken homes are still with us because in our world there is still much mop-up work left from Satan's wreckage. Once a Christian asks for and receives the gift of the Spirit, he has enlisted in the mop-up crew. Then he will be the target not only for his share of the difficulties that are a part of our humanness ("In the world, you *have* tribulation . . ."[14]) but also those special darts Satan reserves for all Spirit warriors. The special darts were exactly what the first Christians were up against.

Jesus' perspective also includes the long view. Our human view is myopic because it is so self-centered. He insists that we see ourselves as one tiny link in a long line of God's men and women enlisted in the mopping-up process and looking forward not only to a celestial city, but to a time when earth itself will become the kingdom of God ruled by Him, the victorious Christ.

So what is your problem? No matter how bad it is, claim Jesus' own perspective, His own joy in the midst of it. Then really open yourself to that joy and be ready to receive the surprise of your life.

HELPFUL READING: Acts 16:19–34

HIS WORD FOR YOU: Jesus always triumphs.
  But thanks be to God, who in Christ always leads us in triumph.
                                          (II Corinthians 2:14, RSV)

PRAYER: *Lord, You and I know that I am facing some difficult circumstances in my life, especially my concern about _____. As I ask for Your perspective and Your thoughts on this problem, I begin to see that worry and fretting and taking thought on all the negatives is not being the realistic pragmatist I had thought. In fact, You are telling me that when I wallow in "what-ifs" and discouragement and self-pity, I am ignoring You altogether.*
  As I turn to You, Lord, at this moment and spread this

grief-problem out before You, I hear You say, "There's nothing here I can't handle. Why are you so troubled?"

Your joy shines through Your words, Lord. Let Your joy be mine too. I open my heart to it. Amen.

2 *Faith*

*Now faith is the assurance (the confirmation, the title-deed)
of the things [we] hope for, being the proof of things [we]
do not see and the conviction of their reality—faith perceiving as real fact what is not revealed to the senses.*
(Hebrews 11:1, AMPLIFIED)

The call to faith is all over the New Testament. We are
told that "without faith it is impossible to please" God.[1]
Nor can we receive anything from God or get anywhere in
the Christian life without faith. And in one of the greatest
blank-check promises Jesus left us, He pinned everything
to faith:

And whatever you ask in prayer, you will receive, if
you have faith.[2]

Yet there is a sense in which this imperativeness of faith
simply discourages us. For most of us sense that we *do*
have doubts; we lack the total knowing and assurance that
is faith.

So what is this faith required of us?

We are told that faith is

The substance of things hoped for, the evidence of
things not seen.[3]

The word "substance" suggests an object—physical
property—while the original word in the Greek carries the
sense of action. Therefore, this might be better translated,

133

Faith is the substantiating of things hoped for.

How do I substantiate something or make it real in my
experience? My rock garden at Evergreen Farm in Virginia
is a perfect spot for the delightful flower, impatiens. There
in that partially shaded spot, the eye-ravishing clumps of
pink and cerise and salmon spread and thrive.

Were I blind, those beautiful colors would still be there
on the hillside, but I would lack the faculty to verify for
myself the pink and the cerise and the salmon.

Even so, our human problem is this: so long as we are
in these bodies, we lack the equipment to substantiate divine facts. Our five natural senses are useless in the world
of spirit.

In this impasse, faith comes to our rescue. God has
ordained it so that faith is the one faculty capable of bridg-
ing the chasm between our limiting humanness and God's
real world of spirit. Faith then, becomes our inner spirit's
eyes, ears, touch, even wisdom and understanding. Only
over this bridge of faith can God's real facts about the
particular blessings we need out of God's rich storehouse
be so substantiated to you and me personally that they
become real in our experience.

Yet the fact of those gifts and blessings I need out of
God's storehouse[4] did not spring into being at that point in
time when I first realized them. They have been there waiting for me all along, just as the colorful clumps of impatiens have all along been there in the rock garden. Were I
without sight to verify the impatiens, then neither my skepticism nor unbelief about the plants, nor my belief, would
affect the fact that the flowers *are* there.

Even so, the fact of God's supply for me was solidly
there, was a fact all along. That is why faith always has to
be in the present (denoting completed action), as contrasted
with hope which is always in the future.

It was this "presentness" of faith that Jesus was teaching
us when He said:

So I tell you, whatever you pray for and ask, believe
you have got it, and you shall have it.[5]

So how do you and I get faith—like that? Most of us
Christians have tried a variety of ways: rebuking doubts,

repeating affirmations, reading Scripture and claiming particular promises, sharing the faith-building experiences of others through the printed or the spoken word.

All of these have value. Yet there is a better way. For it would be possible to use all the faith-building techniques imaginable and still bypass a direct confrontation with the Person of Jesus. Nothing is so important in His eyes as each of us establishing and then activating a personal relationship with Him.

Thus Jesus requires that I come directly to Him to get the faith I need for the substantiating of divine facts to my natural mind. This substantiating *is* revelation, and revelation is the Helper's assigned work in our world.[6]

Seeking such revelation means that in relation to any prayer need, I go to Jesus and ask, "Lord, speak to me about this. What do You want to tell me about it? Lord, pull aside the veil of flesh and give me a peep into the world of spirit. Let me see this situation through Your eyes. What would please You about it? I await Your word on this."

At this point, I am not asking for a change in outward circumstances, just for that inner revelation. Then I wait and listen and watch.

When that insight is given—Jesus' very personal word to me—then faith, "the substantiating of things not seen," automatically follows. And in the wake of that quiet knowing (that "perceiving as real fact what is not revealed to the senses"),[7] external events change. Faith has wrought the miracle of answered prayer.

Our friend Jamie Buckingham tells of such a miracle in his life. At age thirteen he had overheard a nocturnal conversation from his parents' bedroom praising his brother Clay, "I'm so proud of Clay. He's the finest son we have."

The oversensitive Jamie interpreted this, "I love Clay more than I love Jamie." Twenty-five years later Jamie was still struggling with the door slammed shut that night between him and his mother. So resolutely had the door been slammed and padlocked, so deep was the unforgiveness that it had affected Jamie's relationship with all women.

Jamie did not know then to ask for God's revelation on the closed-door problem between him and his mother. In this case, one day the Helper stepped in and graciously gave the insight anyway:

"Let me show you something about those kinds of doors. . . . None of them are real. Once a door like that is bathed in the blood of my son Jesus, it disintegrates. True, it may look as if it is still there, but it's only in your imagination. I have set you free."[8]

This revelation resulted in knowing that his prayer of twenty-five years was answered. The problem was solved. It remained only for Jamie to live out in actions his love for his mother. That turned out to be easy. The word of revelation was correct: there was simply no barrier or problem there.

Only—he needed not have waited twenty-five years. The rich and beautiful answer was there all along.

HELPFUL READING: Matthew 8:5–13; Romans 1:16, 17

HIS WORD FOR YOU: God's storehouse contains everything I need.

Blessing . . . be to the God and Father of our Lord Jesus Christ, the Messiah, Who has blessed us in Christ with every spiritual (Holy Spirit-given) blessing in the heavenly realm!

(Ephesians 1:3, AMPLIFIED)

PRAYER: *Lord, I have been troubled about this situation with _____. My distress about it nags at my mind. Now, Lord, I lay this situation out before You and ask You to speak to me about it. Is there a revelation You can give me? I would like to see this with Your eyes, Lord, so I ask You to take the veil off mine.*

By faith, I thank You ahead of time for Your insight and Your instruction as to how You want me to pray.

I await Your word, Lord. Amen.

3 *Love*

God's love has been poured out in our hearts through the Holy Spirit. . . .

(Romans 5:5, AMPLIFIED)

As soon as we are old enough to enter a Sunday School room, we are taught the simple but powerful words,

"Jesus loves me! this I know,
For the Bible tells me so—"[1]

Certainly a most basic teaching of the Christian faith is this sure knowing of the Master's love for each one of us.

There is a better way, though. Knowing of Christ's love through Scripture is head knowledge. Yet my awareness of His love for me must be more than head knowledge before it warms my heart, touches my emotions, and brings me to my knees in grateful adoration.

Perhaps the greatest distance any of us ever has to travel is that long trek between the head and the heart. Just so, the love of Jesus is something that I must *experience,* and only the Holy Spirit can make me feel that great, tender love.

When the Holy Spirit does pour His love into our hearts like that, how do we respond? How do we, in turn, express our love for Him?

In as many different ways as there are varieties of human beings. . . .

By taking our first steps toward understanding of what

137

real praise is, we learn that prayer can be adoration of Him, not just asking for things.

We begin to sing and praise Him with our voices in hymn and anthem and simple choruses, even as the Psalmist David did so long ago.

We express our love by lavishing the alabaster box of ointment on Jesus' feet, as Mary did.

Brother Andrew[2] of Holland did this too. He gave all the clothes in his suitcase to his Christian brothers in Cuba who were suffering severe economic persecution. And just before the plane took off for the Netherlands, Andrew took the shoes off his feet and handed them out the plane door to a minister in need of shoes.

We express love too by finding the practicable working out of Jesus' "If a man loves me, he will keep my word."[3] I have a friend who has accepted this injunction literally. For her, the touchstone of every action she takes is simply, "My Lord, what decision in this matter would most please You?"

The young author, Ann Kiemel,[4] goes on a love mission three days each week. Mondays, Tuesdays, and Wednesdays are the days she gives her time, her strength, and her substance to the people in her cosmopolitan Boston waterfront neighborhood—the street sweepers, the waitresses, the delivery boys, the secretaries, the housewives, the janitor of her building. Always, her message is that she has a great Lord and that He loves her so much that He has sent her to tell the waitress or the janitor or the secretary that Jesus loves them too.

For always and always, Jesus' question "Do you love Me?" or "Lovest thou Me more than these?" is followed by His "Then feed my sheep" . . . "Feed my lambs."[5] It is a love that we cannot keep to ourselves. If we do, it withers and dies.

This love is not something we can manufacture in ourselves. The motive power to share His love by sharing the essence of *us* with others in true spirit-to-spirit communication has to be a work wrought in us by the Spirit. Only the Spirit can kindle His fire in our cold hearts.

Sarah Van Wade discovered this when faced with the fact that David, her alcoholic ex-husband, had stopped drinking, had accepted the Lord, and wanted to remarry her and be a father again to their four children. Her first reaction was, "I'd rather die than be married again to David. How could I live with a man I loathe?"

But Sarah had no peace about this. Since she had come to depend completely on the Lord to help her rear four children and provide income through writing, she knew her attitude displeased Him. In a fit of despair, she lay on her bed weeping and praying. "Please, Lord, I'll do anything for You. Don't ask me to go back to David. The children and I are so happy here."

Then Sarah suddenly realized she had told a lie. She was content with her new life as a writer, but the children were not. They had accepted the divorce, but they were not happy without their father. After another storm of tears, Sarah gave in.

"Okay, Lord, I'll see David. I can't stand him for the way he hurt us, but I'll be willing to do what is right. Since I have total deadness for him, You would have to love him through me."

Sarah's willingness to be an instrument for the Lord's love was the key to the reuniting of this family, a story memorably told in their book *Second Chance*.⁶ To Sarah's surprise David had really changed. There was a new gentleness in him and a new strength. The Helper not only gave Sarah the gift of a fresh love for her husband which she thought she could never have, but created a new spirit of love in a family where before there had been only bitterness and hatred.

Before Pentecost Peter and James and John and the other apostles had plenty of head knowledge about Jesus. They had fresh, intimate, precious memories of three years with Him. They were as well informed of what Jesus had taught as men could be. They loved Him too.

Yet they were fearful men, frozen into immobility, hiding behind closed and locked doors, incapable of sharing their Master at all, or of feeding any of His lambs lost in a pagan world. They were uninspired men, their inner spirits like the bedraggled sails of their fishing craft hanging limp and motionless on a windless sea—going nowhere.

Until—until the wind of the Spirit filled those sails, billowing them out with such vigor that thenceforward the apostles were not only inspired men, but sent-out, driven men. Surely there is no higher drama anywhere than to look at the Before-After pictures of Jesus' apostles. And this same Before-After drama is what the Spirit wants to recreate in us today.

No wonder we dare not do without the Spirit's work in our lives!

HELPFUL READING: John 21:1–25

HIS WORD FOR YOU: The giving love of God for us.
He who did not withhold or spare [even] His own Son but gave Him up for us all, will He not also with Him freely and graciously give us all [other] things?
(Romans 8:32, AMPLIFIED)

PRAYER: *Lord, I confess that I have been long on head knowledge of You and woefully deficient in heart knowledge. I have loved You intellectually, but not with the warmth of my heart's adoration. I had not realized, Lord, that Your being loved freely and spontaneously by the creatures You have made is important to You. I had not understood that this is what worship is!*

Lord, I want to love You like that. I ask the Spirit now to be my Teacher. I ask Him to do the work in me, to kindle that kind of fire in my heart. Praise You, Lord. I do love You! Amen.

4 *Vitality*

It is the spirit that gives life, the flesh is of no avail. . . .
(John 6:63, RSV)

Food, vitamins, sleep, rest, relaxation, fresh air, exercise are not the only media of physical restoration. There is another—that of a minute-by-minute supply of vitality and strength given by the Holy Spirit.

We are told that

> . . . if the Spirit of him that raised up Jesus from the dead dwell in you, he . . . shall also quicken your mortal bodies by His Spirit that dwelleth in you.[1]

This is just another facet of our helplessness and of His adequacy. For us to experience this quickening, there must be a reliance on His strength rather than on our own natural vitality.

Dr. A. B. Simpson was a famous New York clergyman whose life roughly spanned the nineteenth century. Always frail physically, while still in his twenties he developed serious heart trouble. Speaking at even three services a week—two on Sunday, one on Wednesday—was excruciatingly hard for him.

Then at thirty-seven, Dr. Simpson's damaged heart was healed by Jesus, a healing verified by the doctors. Thereafter his pastoral, evangelistic, and literary work increased manifold. Yet always for the rest of his life, he was conscious that he was "drawing his vitality from a directly supernatural source."

During the first three years after Dr. Simpson's heart was healed, he kept count and found that he had preached more than a thousand sermons and often held twenty meetings a week. As he put it:

> On a day of double labor I will often be conscious at the close, of double vigor. . . . Nor is this a paroxysm of excitement to be followed by a reaction, for the next day comes with equal freshness. . . . This is nothing less than "the life of Christ manifested in my mortal flesh."[2]

Dr. Simpson founded the still-flourishing Christian and Missionary Alliance and steadily, until his death at seventy-six, turned out prodigious quantities of creative work.

This same physical restoration has also been the secret of the vitality of the beloved Dutch Christian Corrie ten Boom.

During World War II in the Dutch village of Haarlem, the ten Boom family courageously hid a succession of Jews and helped them to escape the Nazis. The entire family was eventually hauled off to Ravensbruck Concentration Camp. Corrie was the only member of her family to survive the long imprisonment.

My husband and I were guests at her eighty-fourth birthday dinner in Miami some time ago. Corrie was still sharp of mind, keen of wit, and as active as ever. For some years she has had angina. Yet when these pains and heart spasms come on her, she goes off by herself to be alone with her Father. Quietly, she waits for Him, knowing He will either take her to be with Him or fill her cup with vitality for more service.

What has come year after year is nothing less than the life of the Spirit transmuted into even the cells and tissues of her body.

HELPFUL READING: II Corinthians 4:6–16

HIS WORD FOR YOU: Life flows from His Presence.
For thus saith the Lord God, the Holy One of Israel: In returning and rest shall ye be saved; in quietness and in confidence shall be your strength. . . .
(Isaiah 30:15, KJV)

PRAYER: *Lord, I would claim the promise of Your Word that Your own life "is manifested in our mortal flesh." I begin to understand that when the Spirit is moving, He adds energy. So I ask now for that quickening power to revitalize each cell of my body. Take away all fatigue. I open myself to receive Your newness of life. Thank you that I will begin to see life with fresh, clear eyes. In Thy power alone, I make this prayer. Amen.*

5 *Healing*

So I say to you, Ask and keep on asking, and it shall be given you. . . .

And these attesting signs will accompany those who believe: in My name . . . they will lay their hands on the sick, and they will get well.

(Luke 11:9; Mark 16:17, 18, AMPLIFIED)

I am a very slow learner spiritually. Sometimes it takes me years to grasp a lesson the Helper is trying to teach me. Thus I have long pondered why I was not instantly healed of my lung disease by Jesus' presence in my bedroom that September night in 1943. That was definitely the turning point in my illness; from that night there was steady improvement. Yet to many Christians the slow-return-to-health route does not seem to honor the Lord as much as dramatic instantaneous healing.

I also asked myself: did an instantaneous or a gradual healing hinge solely on the level of my own faith? This is a theology of healing often taught. Yet to believe this places a burden of guilt on the sick person. The sufferer is already oppressed by disease; he does not need the added burden of guilt.

In our time the Helper is now giving us quite a different explanation: many authentic healings through prayer are a gradual process rather than a one-time miracle. The complete healing thus takes time and persistently repeated prayer work. And this slower timing, by the way, is consistent with all normal processes of the body, as well as of everything in nature.

Interestingly, the Helper is currently bringing this truth to the attention of a number of people scattered over the Church at large and not necessarily in contact with one another. Thus the Reverend Tommy Tyson, evangelist-teacher from North Carolina, has stumbled upon what he calls "the soaking prayer." This means that the person being prayed for is gently bathed in the prayer-atmosphere for a considerable time. In this case, those praying conceive of Jesus' life and power as pouring steadily into the affected area.

Another is Father Francis MacNutt,[1] active for ten years in the Catholic Charismatic Renewal. He now asks for a frank appraisal of the results for those prayed for. . . . Is the pain gone? Is there movement in the affected part of the body? Is there some or much improvement? From many such experiences Father MacNutt's best rough summary is that after prayer 75 percent feel demonstrable results. Of that total, 50 percent feel improvement but the need of further healing.

Teenager Bunni Determan was one who needed persistence in prayer. Bunni had to wear a neck brace because of severe scoliosis, which is an S-shaped curvature of the spine. In June 1975, after a group including Father Mac-Nutt and Bunni's mother (a professional nurse), prayed with the girl for about ten minutes, some improvement could be seen. Encouraged, they continued the soaking prayer for two more hours. By then most of the curvature at the top of the spine had straightened out.

At this point in his healing work, Father MacNutt often has to withdraw, and the patient's family and friends in a local prayer group take over the prayer-work. Thus everyone concerned becomes involved in a growing and learning experience. With Bunni the healing has continued as her mother and teenage friends have continued to pray. The girl is now out of the neck brace and her spine is about 90 percent straight, despite the fact that the medical prognosis on scoliosis is usually progressive deterioration.

If the soaking prayer seems costly in time and effort (and it is), a prayer-effort of eight or ten hours for someone like Bunni compares very favorably with the medical effort of weeks and even months spent in hospitals, the outlay of thousands of dollars, the pain and trauma of operations, long series of X-ray or cobalt tretaments, plus medication that goes on and on.

I wonder now why I ever expected five or ten minutes of prayer to cure everything. Or why any of us have accepted the principle often taught that to pray more than once for a healing betrays a lack of faith.

The Lord taught the opposite. In two separate parable-stories on prayer He commends dogged perseverance. (See the suggested Helpful Reading that follows.)

Jesus also left us the example of the blind man for whom even He had to pray twice.[2] After laying His hands on the man's eyes and praying, Jesus asked, "Do you see anything?"

The man's reply was, "Yes—something. But people look queer, like—well, trees walking around."

Then He put His hands on his eyes again, and the man looked intently [that is, fixed his eyes on definite objects], and he was restored, and saw everything distinctly—even what was at a distance.[3]

Asking questions like "Do you see anything now?" and looking for results actually stimulates faith. When Father MacNutt marked Bunni's spinal S-curvature in red ink, and all those praying could see a noticeable straightening after ten minutes of prayer—even if only a little—everyone was jubilant. Faith then sprang forth to undergird the group for more praying.

The joyous news is that we do not need to wait for the special mission of the healing evangelist. God wants all His people to believe in His goodwill for health and to step out and experiment in prayer. He wants to use all of us.

In early summer 1977 I had a telephone call from an Episcopal priest, the Rev. James Monroe, of Fort Lauderdale, Florida. Danny, the five-month-old baby son of a young couple in his church, had been in a Miami hospital since birth. Only eleven pounds, he could not breathe outside of the oxygen tent. He was being fed intravenously. The fear was that lack of oxygen might have caused brain damage and possibly destroyed his eyesight.

The child's parents were believers and had come to Jim seeking help. He had prayed with them but Danny was not better. Jim Monroe wanted so much to help. Did I have any suggestions?

"Have you anointed the baby with oil and laid hands on him as you prayed?" I asked.

"No, I haven't. Only prayed with Danny's parents. Strange—why didn't I think of anointing with oil? I'll *do* it!"

Six weeks later I received this happy report:

> I am delighted to tell you that little Danny is doing marvelously. After I talked with you, his mother and I went together to the hospital. I gave him unction for healing. Since that time he has steadily grown strong. On this past Thursday he breathed normally without oxygen for the first time in his life. He has begun to take food normally in small amounts without tube feeding. His eyesight which we feared to be seriously impaired now seems normal and his little muscles are gaining strength daily. Soon he will be home.
>
> Danny's a *beautiful* baby—big blue eyes, medium brown hair. We give thanks to God daily for exercising His healing power.

The priest added that he was going to persist in prayer for Danny that God would also heal the little boy's memories of those difficult months.

Then I knew that the Helper had been pointing Jim Monroe to persistence in prayer along with the rest of us. Surely, here is one of the keys to the new breakthrough in healing we have been seeking.

HELPFUL READING: Luke 11:5–13; 18:1–8

HIS WORD FOR YOU: He will turn troubles into highways.
> *He who believes in Him . . . shall never be disappointed or put to shame.*
>   (I Peter 2:6, AMPLIFIED)

PRAYER: *Lord, I think of* _____ *who is in dire need of Your healing power. Surely, my concern is but a crumb off the loaf of Your encircling love and concern. Yet I confess, Lord Jesus, that I have been content to pray for* _____ *in private and have never yet gone in person as Your feet and hands and voice with Your promise of healing.*

For so long I have hidden behind my unworthiness and my small faith. I see now that You are asking me not to measure or weigh my faith, just to step out on what I have.

Thank You for this message that Your strength and Your power go with even Your humblest disciples. Since there is added power in agreement in prayer, show us now those You have chosen to go with me to _____. And Lord, grant now as we go that encouragement and improvement in _____'s situation that will signify Your blessing.

You are still the Healer, Lord Jesus; we are only the instruments in Your hands. We praise You that all power in heaven and in earth is still Yours today. Amen.

6 *Peace*

My peace I give to you; not as the world gives do I give to you.

And the peace of God, which passes all understanding, will keep your hearts and your minds in Christ Jesus.
(John 14:27; Philippians 4:7, RSV)

The peace that Jesus gives us through the Comforter is not dependent on any outside circumstances. It is given right in the midst of great activity or stress or trouble or grief while the storm rages all around us.

Peter Marshall was fond of describing God's peace with a favorite story. . . . At one time a famous artists' association announced a contest. All pictures entered in the competition were to depict "peace." The winner would be awarded a large sum of money.

Paintings of all sorts were submitted. There were serene pastoral scenes; placid lakes; an intimate cottage scene, cheerful and snug before a cozy fireplace; untrammeled vistas of freshly fallen snow; a painting of a tranquil, windless dawn in muted opalescent colors.

But the painting selected by the judges for the first prize was very different from all the others. It depicted the height of a raging storm. Trees bent low under lashing wind and driving rain. Lightning zigzagged across a lowering, threatening sky. In the center of the fury the artist had painted a bird's nest in the crotch of a gigantic tree. There a mother bird spread her wings over her little brood, waiting serene and unruffled until the storm would pass. The painting was entitled very simply, *Peace*.

"That," Peter would point out, "is a perfect picture of the peace God has promised us."

So many have experienced this gift of the peace that "passes all understanding." . . . The young preacher, Malcolm Smith, was in Manhattan's Sloan Kettering Hospital being prepared for surgery early the next morning. Physicians had diagnosed the bleeding mole on his back as deadly melanoma—a malignant tumor.

That evening a strange nurse appeared in the ward. "I've seen many people die," she told Malcolm Smith, "but I've never seen a preacher die." She was half-smiling, half-sneering. "I've always wanted to see if they really believe what they preach. What does it feel like to be dying, preacher?" And she turned on her heel and left.

The taunting words kept ringing in Malcolm's ears. . . . "What does it feel like to be dying, preacher?"

Then a male nurse came in to shave all of Malcolm's chest and back. As he realized how extensive the surgery was to be, terror rose to stick in his throat and engulf him in waves. But let Malcolm himself tell it . . .

The terror screamed, "You prayed and you weren't healed." The thought mocked me. Fear surged and receded like an ocean tide. And like the incoming tide, it always came closer, never withdrawing quite as far as before.

Suddenly a thought came clearly through the tumultuous, encroaching fears: *You have been promised the peace of God under all circumstances. Claim what is yours.*

Malcolm knew that the Lord had spoken. Immediately, he climbed out of bed and headed for the bathroom, the only place where there was any privacy. There he sank to his knees on the cold tile floor.

Instantly, he felt overwhelmed by the love of God and the greatness of God. He felt no need of pleading or begging. Instead, praise and worship of God for being Who He Is poured out in a torrent. And the praise was followed by the glorious gift of God's peace. All fear was gone, evaporated. Malcolm slept soundly that night.

After the surgery the next day the doctors returned their verdict: the wart had indeed been malignant, so they had also removed the lymph glands. Radium therapy was being planned.

Yet two days later a puzzled doctor announced to Malcolm that analysis of the lymph glands had proved them free of cancer. "Somehow there's been a mistaken diagnosis." The doctor appeared to be embarrassed. "Almost never happens. Anyway, you're in fine health and we need this bed. You can go home now."[1]

It is not possible for any of us to go through life without encountering some crises that spawn emotions we cannot handle on our own. But we have to *know* about our inheritance as a child of the King in order to be able to claim it. "The peace that passes all understanding" is an especially precious part of that inheritance that not a one of us can do without.

HELPFUL READING: Galatians 5:22–24; Philippians 4:4–8

HIS WORD FOR YOU: The Lord has heard and will deliver.

Though I walk in the midst of trouble, You will revive me: You will stretch forth Your hand against the wrath of my enemies, and Your right hand will save me.
(Psalm 138:7, AMPLIFIED)

PRAYER: *Lord Jesus, even in these lovely days sometimes I find fear in my heart as I wonder what the next few years will bring. We are living in uncertain, troubled times. How I thank You that Your gift of peace does not depend on circumstances at all.*

I praise You that You have hidden me, Your child, as in the hollow of Your hand, and that the Father's great hand rests over all. I praise You that this citadel of rest and peace is mine whenever I need it and ask You for it. Let me feel this, Lord, so that my spirit relaxes into Your peace. Thank You, Lord, thank You. Amen.

7 Other Tongues

And they were all filled with the Holy Spirit—they began to speak in foreign tongues, as the Spirit enabled them to express themselves.

(Acts 2:4, MOFFATT)

One of the Helper's characteristics is that He is practical and pragmatic. We expect just the opposite. "Holy Ghost" or "Holy Spirit" sounds so other-worldly, so high-flown.

But the Helper's mission during this era of the Spirit is to us earthly creatures still in the flesh. We are the ones who are always pretending that we are more "spiritual" than we are. The Helper, on His side, deals with us in a rational, realistic, down-to-earth manner.

One of Jesus' specific commands for this era of the Spirit was to "go into all the world and preach the gospel to every creature."[1] The Helper knew that the minute the disciples took this seriously, they would run into language barriers. Jerusalem was more of a melting pot than some areas of New York City are today. So with his usual practicality, the Helper moved to solve that problem.

In the miracle that followed on the day of Pentecost,[2] fourteen separate languages and dialects are mentioned as being used by these unlettered men and women, with other dialects flicked at. This was the gift of "other tongues." Later, another aspect of the same mystery would appear—a heavenly language, sometimes not a known one, yet always subject to the speaker's will.[3]

Certainly more controversy has swirled around this gift than any of the others. The common misconception that the gift of tongues is ecstatic, unarticulated babbling is not

the New Testament position. Rather, Paul seems to assume
that any heavenly language always would have an interpretation, if we had faith to believe that and could but make
connection with an interpreter. Therefore his advice about
use of the gift in private and his warnings against misuse of
the gift in public are based on this premise.[4]

Everything Paul has to say about tongues reflects a
common-sense, balanced view. On the one hand, he refuses
to give this one gift undue emphasis or importance; on the
other, he will not reject it.

Then do we have authenticiated instances of "other
tongues" in our time? Yes, we do. Many instances. Of
those I know, here is a true incident told me by my friend
Betty Malz of Pasadena, Texas. Betty is the tall, attractive
author of that memorable life-after-death experience, *My
Glimpse of Eternity*.

A considerable portion of her childhood was spent in
Attica, Indiana. Betty's father ministered in the little frame
Rosedale Church. Rosedale saw many astonishing answers
to prayer and many of God's miraculous gifts bestowed. As
for instance, what happened some years ago one hot summer evening to Betty's quiet, shy mother, Fern Perkins,
who scarcely ever raised her voice in church.

The congregation was suffering with the heat, so the
church's double doors opening onto a little porch were
wide open to catch any breath of air stirring. In the middle
of the service two things happened simultaneously. . . .

Inside the church Betty's mother was suddenly told by
the inner Voice to stand up and pray in her heavenly
language. Fern Perkins' natural reserve and reticence about
such a thing were swept aside by a compulsive inner pres-
sure: she *had* to obey.

As she did, outside the church an elderly Greek coal
miner, his miner's cap and lantern still on his head, was
walking by the church as he headed home from work. This
man was in deep discouragement. Coal mining had been
the only job he could find. The pay was small and the
hours long. He never saw the light of day: he went to work
before sunrise and returned after dark. To add to his discouragement and loneliness, he had found no one in the
community who could understand his Greek, and he spoke
little English.

As he plodded along past the Rosedale Church, suddenly
through the open doors he heard a woman's voice speaking

perfect Greek. At last! At last someone with whom he could talk!

Impulsively, the man sped into the church, spotted the woman from whose lips still came that beautiful modern Greek. Ignoring the stares of the worshipers, he began excitedly jabbering to Mrs. Perkins in his native tongue. Of course Betty's mother could not understand a word he was saying.

By now the church was in an uproar. Gradually, the truth dawned on both sides. It was a miracle straight out of the Book of the Acts because the miner himself was able, haltingly, to translate the message that was manna to his spirit. As Betty recalls, it was something like this . . .

God loves you. God has a purpose for your life and for your family. He has the power to forgive sins, to bring you joy and hope and loving purpose. He *will* give you a path to travel that will bring joy and peace to you and to those you love so dearly.

When the man realized that his new friend did not naturally speak Greek, and that God had taken hold of her tongue and spoken this through her, he dropped to his knees, and with tears pouring down his cheeks, began praising God. Then and there the miner gave his life to Jesus.

From then on, he and his family not only attended Rosedale Church regularly and made a host of friends there, but several other families were drawn into the church because of this one miracle of the Helper's gift of "other tongues."

HELPFUL READING: Acts 2:4–21

HIS WORD FOR YOU: The rock like characteristics of the Kingdom.
   And all His decrees and precepts are sure—fixed, established, and trustworthy.
      They stand fast and are established for ever and ever, and are done in [absolute] truth and uprightness.
         (Psalm 111:7, 8, AMPLIFIED)

PRAYER: *Lord, I ask You today for the Helper's gift of present-tense faith because past-tense faith suffices not at all for the needs of today. I see that I can be thoroughly "orthodox" and agree that the early Church long ago experienced Your power in miraculous ways, yet have this affect my life not at all.*

With my mind, I know that "You are the same yesterday, today and forever."[5] Then why do I keep limiting You today? I ask you to break this barrier in me—now. Give me an open, expectant will and heart that goes out to meet You, still the miracle-working Lord, right now.

I worship You, Lord Jesus. I praise You that You are still the Lord of heaven and of earth, with all power. Amen.

8 *Miracles*

Holding the form of religion but denying the power of it. . . .

All power is given unto Me [Jesus] in heaven and in earth.
(II Timothy 3:5, RSV; Matthew 28:18, KJV)

What does Timothy mean when he refers to "holding the form of religion but denying the power . . ."?

It is time to be plain about this. The Holy Spirit insists upon taking us into the realm of the miraculous. Unless we can follow Him into this world of miracles there is no way that we can receive the fullness of the Spirit.

The Bible from Genesis to Revelation is peppered with examples of the supernatural intervention of God. By that is meant an act invading our time-space planet over and beyond what we humans have come to expect in the concept of nature as a "closed system." By "closed system" we mean natural law observable and definable, rigid, rather than being pliable and regulated by the sovereign God.

Here is the dictionary definition of "miracle":

An event or effect in the physical world beyond or out of the ordinary course of things, deviating from the known courses of nature.[1]

As for Jesus' attitude toward the supernatural, His is an insistent bugle call to the faith that there is no human need His Father cannot meet: no disease, no matter how hideous or far advanced, no cruel circumstance His Father cannot handle.

In Jesus' total trust in His Father we can see at least three strands: first, "Power belongeth to God."[2] Jesus believed this so totally that over and over He moved out to stake His life and His entire reputation on the validity of this fact.

This is perfectly illustrated in the story of Jairus, ruler of a synagogue, who approached Jesus begging Him to come to his home and heal his desperately ill twelve-year-old daughter. At that moment a messenger arrived to tell the sad news, "Your daughter is dead: do not weary and trouble the Teacher any further."[3]

Would any of us have gone to the dead girl to pray for her recovery? Scarcely! To do so would make us look like a fool, or worse, insane.

And our human reasoning always gets in the way in a situation like this: "What if prayers aren't answered? Won't that destroy the faith of the girl's parents and many other people too?"

Obviously, no such doubts entered Jesus' thinking. He went straight on to Jairus' house, took the child's cold limp hand in His, and with calm audacity said, "Child, get up!"

And she did open her eyes and get up, to the stunned amazement of everybody.

The second strand of Jesus' faith and trust in the Father was His insistence on God as having all love. Over and over, He compared God to the most loving human father we know or can imagine. Anything that ordinary human love longs to bestow—taking away pain, restoring sanity, pouring out joyous gifts, providing food and housing or any other material resource needed, directing us to the right job, giving ideas and inspiration and wisdom, restoring severed relationships, preventing premature death—all this and more, Jesus insisted, the Father's love wants to give us.

But the first two strands would not be enough to help us, if God had not left to Himself the liberty of stooping to intervene in human affairs. This third strand is that He does reach down to answer our prayers. Were He, in fact, rigidly encased and bound by the natural laws of the universe He Himself had called into being, then the miracles as recorded in the gospel narrations could never have happened.

Quite the contrary, Jesus knew perfectly well about natural law—seedtime and harvest, famines, tempests, hunger and starvation, disease and death. All this made not one whit of difference to Him. Very simply, Jesus' faith was that His Father was over and above all natural law; He was omnipotent over anything in earth or in heaven. He could and would stoop to relieve human need unhampered by any rival power.

Then when we leave the Gospels and go on to the Acts, the disciples gathered at Pentecost and became, to a person, "witnesses to His resurrection."[4] Not all the one hundred twenty who gathered in the Upper Room had been present in the garden on resurrection morning. That did not matter. The important thing was that they accepted unequivocally the bodily resurrection of their Lord from the dead. He had been dead. He was now alive. Not just spiritually. Not just a ghost. Physically alive, as they themselves were alive.

This acceptance changed their viewpoint about everything. In the face of this stupendous miracle-fact, any other miracle was possible and probable. Then God could do *anything!* Believing *that,* they were prepared to let the Spirit use them to stand the Roman world on its head.

And we too must believe in the resurrection as those first-century men and women did, with no effort to spiritualize it or explain it away. Practically speaking, this means that we make a clear-cut decision of our wills no longer to duck the impossible situations in our orbit. Like Jesus on the way to Jairus' little daughter, we too, knowing full well our helplessness, must walk right on, opening ourselves and the "impossible" circumstances to the miracle-working power of the Spirit.

When we dare this, the promise still stands:

Every place upon which the sole of your foot shall tread, that I have given you. . . .[5]

Forever and forever, this is the Helper's challenge.

HELPFUL READING: Mark 5:22–43; Luke 8:41–56

HIS WORD FOR YOU: God's giving knows no limit.
If God is for us, who can be against us? The God who did not spare his own Son but gave him up for us all, surely He will give us everything besides!
(Romans 8:31, 32, MOFFATT)

PRAYER: *Lord Jesus, I see human need all around me. I can't help thinking of _____ and _____ . They are desperate. Only a miracle can handle their situations.*

Suddenly, I have a new viewpoint of miracle-working faith, Lord. It does not mean that I have any power or instant piety of my own. Or that You have handed me a big slug of confidence or emotional euphoria that I might mistakenly call faith.

What faith does mean is that I'm willing to be used of You for _____ and _____; and that I believe You when You tell me that You Yourself, the risen and glorified Lord, will be present and in me when I go to _____ and _____ to bring the power of God to earth exactly as You did long ago.

As I go forth to these friends, the work will be Yours, not mine. The results will be Yours too.

Lord, guide me now. Shall I pick up the phone? Tell me the first step.

Thank You, Lord. Amen.

Part Six

The Helper
and the Church

1 Has My Church the Spirit?

And He has put all things under His feet and has appointed Him the universal and supreme Head of the church. . . .

Which is His body, the fullness of Him who fills all in all— for in that body lives the full measure of Him who makes everything complete. . . .

(Ephesians 1:22, 23, AMPLIFIED)

In the post-resurrection days before Jesus' ascension to the right hand of the Father, He charged His disciples not to try to form a church or to attempt any work for Him until they had received the Spirit. They were to wait in Jerusalem until they were endued with power, commissioned for service.[1]

The reason was obvious. Here were one hundred twenty disciples—mostly uneducated fishermen and tradesmen, along with some humble women—so filled with fear of the Jewish hierarchy on the one hand, and the power of Rome on the other, that they hid behind locked doors.

Looking at them cowering there, we might wonder whether Christianity had any chance at all. Poor, terrified, broken crutches they seemed! What chance would such unlettered and untalented folk have against entrenched Jewish tradition and the screaming eagles of Rome's might?

But Jesus had a plan. The one hundred twenty were to become Christ's Body on earth. That Body came into being at Pentecost. Thus Pentecost is the birthday of the Christian Church.

From that day the Holy Spirit was given an altogether new office. Into His hands was placed the administration of

every detail of the life of the Church. The plan was that
from Jesus' ascension into heaven until His return to earth,
He would be our Paraclete in heaven, there to be the "head
over all things for the church."[2] The Holy Spirit would be
our Paraclete on earth to administer and order the "building up of the body of Christ"—the Church.[3]

That is why, apart from the Spirit, the Church of Christ
has no viable life. Any Christian church that ignores the
Spirit is an apostate church. Moreover, the *full* blessings of
Pentecost can only be experienced by the fellowship of
believers in the Church, never by the solitary Christian.

In explaining this to the Ephesian Christians, Paul did
not say that the Church is *like* a body, but that it *is* the
Body of Christ. And that "the full measure of Him who
makes everything complete lives only in that Body."[4]

Practically, this means that not only in worship, but in
prayer and in service and ministry to others, we cannot get
along without one another. For instance, Jesus often gives
pieces of the insights needed for prevailing prayer to several members of the Body. As for ministry, He would not
normally give all of the gifts of the Spirit to one individual.

As for the how of Christian maturity, there can be no
growth or deeper life for any of us separated from our
fellow-Christians. Individualism and our old life of inde-
pendence are no good, Jesus tells us, simply because we
will die if we continue that way: no branch can live unless
attached to the Vine. And the Vine has not a single branch,
but many branches.

Once we see the necessity of this kind of Christian fellowship, our next task is to find the right Body of Christ
for us. As given us in Scripture, here are some questions to
help point the way. . . .

Where does my church stand in regard to the Holy
Spirit?

Am I and my fellow church members really functioning
as Christ's Body on earth?

Does the Person of Jesus occupy a central and preeminent place in the preaching and life of my church, as over
against emphasis on loyalty to the church as an organizational and denominational entity?[5]

Does my church recognize in any way the offices that
the Spirit would like to fill, such as pastors, preachers,
teachers, evangelists, prophets, healers, miracle-workers,
helpers, administrators?[6]

To what extent is my church a practicing body of the "priesthood of all believers?" (Or are we still mostly a spectator church relying on the professional church staff?)[7]

Are strangers who come to my church impressed with the atmosphere of joy and praise and genuine worship? Does the singing reflect that joy?[8]

Is there deep caring for one another, as shown by the sharing of material resources as well as spiritual experiences? Are there any needy in my church whose necessities are not being met?[9]

Are any of the sick being healed?[10]

Are we in our church seeing lives being steadily turned upside down, reclaimed for Jesus? Are there recovered alcoholics? Broken homes mended? Estranged children reconciled? Drug addicts and mental patients cured? Lost people who find a new purpose in life?[11]

Are we in our church experiencing power over sin in our daily lives? For instance, are we progressively shedding ego hang-ups, hurt feelings, selfishness, lack of love? Are we being convicted of the sin of unbelief by the Spirit?[12]

HELPFUL READING: Revelation 3:13–22

HIS WORD FOR YOU: Mountains of obstacles melt before him.

> *Then he said to me, This is the word of the Lord to Zerubbabel, saying: Not by might nor by power, but by my Spirit, says the Lord of hosts.*
>
> *For who are you, O great mountain of [human obstacles]?*
>
> (Zechariah 4:6, 7, AMPLIFIED)

PRAYER: *Lord Jesus, I confess disappointment, sometimes even disgust about my church. If the infighting in churches, between Christian groups, and in Christendom generally sickens me, how heinous must all this lack of love be to You, Lord.*

Yet I know that discouragement or disgust is not right. Nor is giving up on the Church. For she is Your Body on earth. And no matter how stained her garments, we have Your promise that "the gates of hell shall not prevail against her," and that finally, the Church will be presented to You in glorious apparel.

Meanwhile, Lord, I make two requests. Please straighten out my attitude about my church. Make it right before You. And show me, Lord, a first constructive step that I can take on behalf of my church, Your Body, in this place.

I await Your direction, Lord. Thank You! Amen.

2 *He Brings Reconciliation*

Now I beseech you, brethren . . . that there be no divisions among you; but that ye be perfectly joined together in the same mind and in the same judgment.

God, who . . . gave us the ministry of reconciliation. . . .
(I Corinthians 1:10, KJV; II Corinthians 5:18, RSV)

What is the Church? It is not the building. That we know. Nor is it an organizational or denominational structure.

The New Testament definition of the Church is the Greek word *ekklesia*[1] with two facets of meaning: "the called out ones" and "those called together."

There is also Paul's vivid analogy or synonym for the word *Church:* "the body of Christ."[2]

So a group of the called-out ones who have been tapped by the Lord to live and work and pray and minister together, comprise the Church, the Body of Christ in any given place. To these have been entrusted one of the passions of Jesus' heart, His ministry of reconciliation.

Since the Helper will always faithfully reflect Jesus' own Spirit and viewpoint, His most fervent desire would also be the Helper's. We can be certain then, that wherever the Spirit is allowed to enter, He will always be indefatigably working at the mending and re-fusing of broken relationships.

So where do Christ's followers stand with this matter of reconciliation?

In the first-century Church immediately after Pentecost,

Jesus' prayer for oneness and unity was gloriously answered:

> And the multitude of them that believed were of one heart and of one soul: neither said any of them that ought of the things which he possessed was his own; but they had all things common.[8]

Here was no forced sharing as in state socialism or communism. Rather it was altogether voluntary, based simply on the caring of these men and women for one another.

And the oneness today? We have to concede that the fragmentation of Christ's Church is a scandal. The Church's divisions and cliques and infighting are one of the biggest stumbling blocks to the acceptance of Christianity of those outside the Church. Our factions and our resentments, one to the other, dishonor our Lord as nothing else can.

Not only that, the separateness and divisions drive the Helper away. Quietly, He simply departs. Our beautiful church building is left to us, along with our tranquil, perfect worship forms. The church organizational machinery carries on as usual—the church boards, the regular meetings of this and that. Everything appears to be intact: we will, we think, go out "as at other times before" when all the while we have no notion of the tragic truth: "we wist not that the Lord was departed from us."[4]

Yet there are bright spots in our day too. The Spirit is on the move with, as always, incredible results.

My husband Leonard and I have watched at close range a modern example of reconciliation which has come out of Washington's Watergate scandal. Obviously, Watergate produced intense distrust, violent resentment and anger—a climate of hostility and hatred involving many in the nation's capital. Among them, former Senator Harold Hughes, a political liberal and such a vigorous critic of President Nixon that he was a top man on that administration's enemies list. Thus Hughes became a particular target for Chuck Colson, Nixon's "hatchet man."

Colson thought Hughes a menace to the nation because of his violent and outspoken opposition to Nixon policies.

Hughes thought Colson the epitome of evil as the leader of the White House gang. In politics, Chuck Colson stood for everything that Harold Hughes hated.

Then in an incisive way the Holy Spirit moved into Chuck's life, cleansing him, changing him, bringing him to his knees.

Years before, Hughes had already had the same experience. It had happened at a time when Harold had been contemplating suicide because of despair over his anger about life and his drunkenness. Jesus had been Rescuer and Savior to him in every sense.

Then came the dramatic moment when Harold and Chuck were brought together through an intermediary, Doug Coe, head of the Washington Fellowship Group.[5] In order to take a little of the heat off, Doug had decided to make it a quiet evening with wives at the home of Al Quie, Minnesota Republican Congressman. Doug had also invited a former Democratic Congressman from Texas, Graham Purcell and his wife, Nancy. The setting was the Quies' paneled family room with the group gathered around a mammoth brick fireplace.

In the midst of the others, Colson and Hughes were rather like two boxers waiting in their separate corners for the sparring to begin. Then abruptly Harold began the action. "Chuck, they tell me you've had an encounter with Jesus Christ. Would you tell us about it?"

So Chuck described what had happened that memorable summer night near Boston when a life-long barrier between him and his God had been broken down. To his surprise, Colson felt no embarrassment in talking about this, the most intimate experience of his life, yet he was supremely conscious of his inadequacy.

Here is Chuck Colson's own description[6] of what happened as the spirit in Hughes heard his spirit testify of Jesus Christ:

For a moment there was silence. Harold, whose face had been enigmatic while I talked, suddenly lifted both hands in the air and brought them down hard on his knees. "That's all I need to know. Chuck, you have accepted Jesus and He has forgiven you. I do the same. I love you now as my brother in Christ. I will stand with you, defend you anywhere, and trust you with anything I have."

I was overwhelmed, so astonished in fact, that I could only utter a feeble, "Thank you." In all my life

no one had ever been so warm and loving to me outside of my family. And now it was coming from a man
who had loathed me for years and whom I had known
for barely two hours.

Then we were all on our knees—all nine of us—
praying aloud together. . . .

These men became close friends, part of an intimate
Christian fellowship, though even today they have differing
points of view politically.

Later on would come another night at Fellowship House
in Washington, D.C., when the Helper brought together in
one room four incredibly disparate individuals—Eldridge
Cleaver, once a prime target of the Nixon administration
as well as of the Justice Department as Black Panther
leader; the former head of the Ku Klux Klan (pledged to
keep blacks in total submission through terror tactics);
Colson; and Hughes. After years of rebellion, all four men
had made dramatic surrenders to Jesus. Where in all the
world could four such unlikely candidates for Christian
fellowship have been found? Yet that night saw the four
praying together. This is the reconciliation that the Spirit
brings!

As we witness the miracle of it we realize that true
oneness of mind, heart, and spirit is not something we can
program or manipulate; it is the priceless gift of the Spirit.
Then let us not deceive ourselves that it can be achieved by
shaking hands or hugging a neighboring worshiper at a
scheduled point in a church service. Or by making small
talk with someone over a cup of punch in the so-called
fellowship hour.

These can be good beginnings, but the true reconciliation Jesus is asking of us is not fellowship game-playing: it
means patient listening to another's point of view in an
effort to understand; painful apology perhaps, and in the
end it always involves sharing life deeply on a continuing
basis with our own *ekklesia*—those who have been called
together by the Spirit Himself.

HELPFUL READING: Matthew 5:24; 18:15; Ephesians
4:1–8; 23–32

HIS WORD FOR YOU: God's people claim their inheritance of peace.

Let Christ's peace be arbiter in your hearts: to this peace you were called as members of a single body. And be filled with gratitude. Let the message of Christ dwell among you in all its richness. Instruct and admonish each other with the utmost wisdom.

(Colossians 3:15, NEB)

PRAYER: *Lord, I need You in my home and in my church. Without You, we are separate human beings going our separate ways.*

This day come into the heart of each of us who lives here and into every room in this house. Only with Your presence will it be a home.

And Lord, my church is very needy. We go through the motions of worship, we brush one another politely on the way out. But what a sad parody this is of the oneness You want for us!

Lord, let Your ministry of reconciliation now begin in me. Tell me now where I can begin to erase misunderstandings. What can I do today to affirm another human being, to encourage someone discouraged? Let me be a bridge between You, Lord Jesus, and one of Your children who is hurting. And take away from me the selfishness that I like to call sensitivity.

We need You in this place, Lord. Abide with us today. Amen.

3 He Cleanses the Body of Christ

Therefore, putting away falsehood, let everyone speak the truth with his neighbor, for we are members one of another.

And do not grieve the Holy Spirit of God. . . .
(Ephesians 4:25, 30, RSV)

Each of us has faced the dilemma: a fellow-Christian or a member of our family is "overtaken in a fault." Perhaps there is moral slippage, or anger and unfairness to a child or a marriage partner, or a slide towards alcoholism, or a vicious tongue causing rifts in the office or the church. We care deeply about the erring one. What are we to do? What is *our* responsibility?

In past centuries the local church often disciplined such a one. I have been astonished to read in old nineteenth-century records (for instance, of Washington, D.C.'s New York Avenue Presbyterian Church) of a drunkard or an adulterer having been actually summoned before the Session for questioning and corrective discipline.

Currently, in certain Christian groups there is something of a return to this group correction. Passages like I Corinthians 5:1–6 and Titus 3:1–10 have convinced us that bad leaven really can contaminate the whole; that the Spirit of *Holiness* cannot tolerate evil that invites Satan to enter a family unit or a church; that therefore we *do* have a responsibility not to shut our eyes to sin; that ignoring wrongdoing never deals with the problems caused by evil.

Thus some of these groups try to convict the wrongdoer by "light" or truth sessions with, in some instances, severe spiritual and psychological damage. Two clergymen in one such group were plunged into nervous breakdowns from which they were many months recovering. In another instance the head of one community has taken it upon himself to point out the sins of members and to administer not only correction but punishment—with disastrous results.

Surely, the lesson here is the truth Jesus made clear in His Last Supper talk: it is the Spirit's province, and His alone, to convict of sin. "When *He* comes, *He* will convince the world of sin. . . ."[1]

When we try it on our own, we are seeking to usurp the Helper's place. The result of attempting in the flesh to convict another of sin is wreckage—defensiveness, anger, estrangement, loss of self-worth, defeatism, depression—whereas, when the Spirit does this corrective work, it is "good" hurt, the kind that leaves no damage, that never plunges us into despair or hopelessness but is always healing in the end.

Do we then have no part or responsibility in this? Yes, we do. A close look at Jesus' words immediately preceding the passage already mentioned . . .

But if I depart, I will send him *unto you.*

followed by

When He comes, he will convince *the world* of sin. . . .[2]

shows us that God does intend to use human beings as channels for the Helper in the conviction of sin—as also He uses us with intercessory prayer, with the teaching and preaching ministries, with healing, and all the rest. To get to the needy world all around us, the Spirit has to use those whose bodies are already His living temples. His plan then is to work through the Spirit-baptized believer individually as well as through the Church Body.

Over and over we see the working out of this plan in the Acts' narrative. The Spirit used Simon Peter's Pentecost sermon to bring three thousand to conviction of sin.[3] Again Peter was used in the case of Ananias and Sapphira.[4] Philip was the Spirit's human conduit for the correction of Simon the sorcerer.[5] Later we see the Spirit working through Paul to correct Simon Peter himself,[6] and so on.

Jesus Himself had laid a solid base for such correction: "If your brother sins, rebuke him,"[7] and "Go and tell him his fault."[8]

Yet this remains a difficult assignment for which we desperately need the Spirit's help. Most of us either want to shirk altogether being used by the Helper for any correcting or disciplining work, or else we become judgmental and try it on our own without love. Continually, we need to beware of our incorrigible human blindness to our own faults as contrasted with the way we see other people's faults as if under a giant magnifying glass.

When we do begin to accept responsibility for others around us, what safeguards should we establish?

(1) We have to be convicted by the Helper of our own sin first before He can use us for others. Especially of our sin-nature and of the root sin of unbelief.

(2) We have to be willing to be used for the Helper's convicting work, and tell Him so. It helps to remind ourselves often that Jesus' purpose is never to condemn men, but always to free them for happiness and rich fruit-bearing for Him.

(3) Many a Christian down the centuries has found that the Spirit cannot use him for the conviction of another until he is willing to become involved in that other's life, to do anything or make any sacrifice. We need to face up to this. This is love in action and it can be costly.

(4) We need to be sure that a loving relationship exists between us and the person to be corrected. If there is already anger and resentment, the correction will only tend to make the situation worse.

How can we know whether we are moving with God's love, or in fleshly judgment? Tests to apply here are a tender grief for the guilty one, with a jealousy for God's honor before men and a deep strong faith in Jesus' power of deliverance in the wrong situation.

(5) We need to undergird the correction first with prayer, asking the Spirit to do the work. This is all-important. We need to pray also for the Spirit's own love and gentleness, and to ask close friends to be in prayer while we are administering the correction to another person.

We have only to brush guidelines like these to realize that our real trouble is not caring enough and not taking time for the prayer that would link us to Him who can solve all problems.

HELPFUL READING: Matthew 18:15–22; I Thessalonians 5:12–22

HIS WORD FOR YOU: How to deal with those who wrong us.

> *Beloved, never avenge yourself, but leave it to the wrath of God; for it is written, "Vengeance is mine, I will repay, says the Lord."*
>
> (Romans 12:19, RSV)

PRAYER: *Lord, how can I who am still so flawed be used for the correction of anyone else? I ask You to save me from the cowardice that makes me unwilling to be used at all, and from a holier-than-thou spirit that would attempt any part of this on my own strength.*

I do see the point of correction: By our sin, we have given Satan ground on which to stand and we bring more wreckage to our lives, to our homes, our businesses and our churches. Thank You for the Spirit's power in cleaning up the ground and expelling Satan.

You alone, Lord, can make me usable to You for this work. Make me a willing instrument in Your hands. In Your strong name, I pray. Amen.

4 *He Brings Unity*

*I do not pray for these only, but also for those who believe
in me through their word, that they may all be one; even
as thou, Father, art in me, and I in thee, that they also may
be in us, so that the world may believe that thou hast sent
me.*

*Now the company of those who believed were of one heart
and soul. . . .*

(John 17:20, 21; Acts 4:32, RSV)

Jesus' Last Supper talk with His eleven apostles was
over. Well He knew what lay just ahead for Him—
ignominious betrayal, rejection by His own people, ruth-
lessly cruel mauling and manhandling followed by a lingering death.

Yet just before He resolutely walked out over the Brook
Kidron to the Garden of Gethsemane, He paused for what
we know as His High Priestly Prayer.[1] Jesus' thoughts
were not on Himself or the physical cruelties just ahead;
His concern was for us who would "come after."

So much was this oneness of heart and mind and spirit
Jesus' passion that He reiterated this petition four separate
times. He was leaving the world, He said, to return to the
glory of heaven. He knew that all would be lost without
that unity. Therefore, into the hands of the Helper—the
Emissary to earth he was about to send—He placed the
responsibility for the carrying out of this prayer request.

When we look at the fragmentation of the organized
Church today, all might seem to be lost. So many denomi-

nations and splinter groups! Scarcely a local church without infighting and factions. Little real Christian unity even yet between racial groups—blacks and whites, or differing nationalities, or disparate economic classes.

Such minuscule progress towards unity dramatizes for us what does *not* work. Making laws will not do it. Education does not bring unity either. Not even rallies, marches, strikes, and blatant propaganda can effect true oneness. In the United States black-white segregation has seen two decades of laws and education and every external device, but even yet we make painfully slow progress.

So how is the answer to Jesus' High Priestly Prayer to come about? Scripture makes it plain that the Holy Spirit is the only real unifying agent in our world. This was one of the first discoveries of the one hundred twenty men and women after Pentecost. As though to dramatize His unifying mission, the Helper first wiped out language barriers.[2] Economic differences and possessiveness were then dissolved.[3] National and religious taboos and theological exclusiveness were in turn leveled by the Spirit.[4]

And in the midst of these miracles

> The company of those who believed were of one heart and one soul. . . .[5]

and

> They partook of food with glad and generous hearts, praising God and having favor with all the people.[6]

The same kind of miracles take place in our time wherever we will allow the Helper to work. It was a thrilling experience to sit at the center of the Arrowhead Stadium in Kansas City, Missouri, at the 1977 Conference on Charismatic Renewal and see 50,000 pairs of arms raised, 50,000 voices crying, "Jesus is Lord"—Christians—Catholic, Messianic Jew and Protestant from every major denomination worshiping in unity.

South Africa, torn asunder by the starkest racial disunity on our planet, was represented by Archbishop Bill Burnett, by the Reverend Charles Gordon, and others. These men told us of the wildfire spread of the Spirit in Africa today where 25 percent of the white Anglican and Presbyterian clergy are now Spirit-baptized. They see this move of the Spirit as Africa's only hope for survival without total holocaust and a Communist takeover.

Apart from the Spirit, *apartheid* (Afrikaans for "separateness") rules in South Africa. There, whites are only 17 percent of the total population. The blacks must live in separate townships (such as Soweto near Johannesburg) where less than one-third of the blacks' homes have electric lights; less than one-tenth, running water. Seething hatred is rampant.

Yet the Spirit can dissolve even such formidable barriers as these. Charles Gordon, minister of a church in Durban, told how the Helper directed them to send word to the blacks that they would be welcome at the regular weeknight services held in white homes.

In discussing this prospect, someone remarked to Mrs. Gordon, "And probably, a big black Spirit-filled man will come up and hug you." Charles was astonished to see the blood drain from his wife's face. With an ashen face, she questioned, "You aren't serious, are you?"

"I'm being partly facetious, I suppose," the friend replied, "but it really *could* happen, you know."

"The strange part is," Charles told us, "my wife attended a very liberal college, and she has extremely broad views on issues like race. Yet she had no control over that inherited, built-in reaction."

After the meeting was in full swing the following week, a knock came on the door and two black men entered. All seats were taken. After a hushed, tense moment, two young men rose to offer the visitors their seats.

At the close of the meeting, one of the blacks, a tall, burly man, crossed the room and exuberantly lifted Mrs. Gordon off the floor, praising God as he hugged her.

"And do you know," Charles told us wonderingly, "my wife seemed to be completely composed. Isn't that amazing!"

Before leaving for their own townships, the visitors told the assembled group, "Word came to our compound that there are people who love even blacks. We came tonight to find out if it was true. And it is!"

The passion of Jesus' heart for oneness will be fulfilled—but only by the Helper's work in our world. After all, this oneness is of man's inner spirit, and only the Spirit can melt our hard hearts and our stubborn insistence that we are right and everyone else wrong. Only the Spirit can change the climate of our inner spirit so that we are able to receive and welcome a dissentient human being into our hearts.

HELPFUL READING: Ephesians 2:14–22

HIS WORD FOR YOU: Jesus always opens prison doors.
Now the Lord is the Spirit, and where the Spirit of the Lord is, there is liberty—emancipation from bondage, freedom.
(II Corinthians 3:17, AMPLIFIED)

PRAYER: *Lord Jesus, show me any wrong attitude in me that would impede the answer to Your passionate prayer for unity and oneness.*

I think of _____ and _____ who, I know, bear grudges and resentment against me. They are Your children too and You love them as much as You love me.

As You know, Lord, all my efforts at righting these situations have failed. Now I see why only the Helper can convict any of us humans at the heart level and bring about reconciliation.

So now, O Holy Spirit, I turn this task over to You. As You work in _____ 's heart and _____ 's, keep me alert and sensitive so that when the moment of reconciliation comes, I will gladly go more than my half of the way to meet my friends.

By faith, I praise You for this new unity ahead. Thank You, Lord. Amen.

5 *Channels for His Power*

Truly, truly, I say to you, he who believes in me will also do the works that I do; and greater works than these will he do, because I go to the Father.

(John 14:12, RSV)

This is one of the most staggering promises Jesus ever made. When we consider the works He did—curing the sick, healing leprosy, opening blind eyes and deaf ears, restoring crippled limbs, curing palsy and arthritis, returning the violently insane to normalcy, yes, and even raising the dead—then was Jesus seriously promising that we—you and I—would not only do these same works, but even *greater* works? Could He be serious?

As we read the Acts we find that His early apostles did take this preposterous promise at face value and proceeded to act upon it. No doubt they discussed among themselves precisely what Jesus had meant by *greater* works. But in the meantime they *were* healing the sick and the crippled.[1] They *did* raise the dead.[2]

Those first-century disciples were able to be channels for such amazing miracles because they took seriously the all-important link between Jesus' "works" and theirs that most of us are missing today: the Holy Spirit was the connection between the humanity of Jesus and the Father.

After their Master's resurrection, they understood finally His divinity: He really was "the only-begotten Son of the Father." But all along, these men who had walked the roads of Palestine with Him had realized the reality of Jesus' humanity in a way that we have still not grasped.

180

He was real flesh and blood. They watched Him get hungry and thirsty and often very weary from the jostling, demanding crowds. Then too, they knew that "He was tempted in every way as we are. . . ."[3] Nor were these temptations easier for Jesus to resist than they are for us, for Satan always shrewdly sees to it that only the higher reaches of subtlety and finesse are presented to more spiritual persons. We could admire from a distance a Lord who could not sin; we can give our heart's devotion only to a Savior who understands our every weakness because He has been there too.

The Apostle Paul would express this true humanity of his Lord in unforgettable words:

Though he was divine by nature, he . . . emptied himself by taking the nature of a servant.[4]

How real this "emptying" was, Jesus sought again and again to impress upon His followers. He was insistent that they grasp this all-important fact that was to be the bridge from His life to ours. . . .

I am able to do nothing from Myself—independently, of My own accord; but as I am taught by God. . . .[5]

I do nothing from Myself—of My own accord, or on My own authority—but I say [exactly] what My Father has taught Me.[6]

Whatever I speak, I am saying [exactly] what my Father has told Me to say and in accordance with His instructions.[7]

The Father that dwelleth in me, he doeth the works.[8]

He was saying, "I have no power in Myself. The emptying is complete. Believe Me, I am only a channel for my Father's power. In exactly the same way (after I have ascended to My Father, after I am no longer the empty servant but the glorified Lord and the crowned Christ), then you also will be channels for My power. It was the

Spirit who made it possible for Me to do my Father's works. It is the same Spirit (whom I will send to you) who will make it possible for you to do My works."

Surely *that* is why He was looking forward to an era of greater works. We do not yet know all that this means, but one thing is clear: as the number of Spirit-baptized Christians multiplies, eventually there can be many thousands doing His works.

Then why are we not doing them? It is noteworthy that one of the first serious heresies of the infant Church of the late first century and early second century was Docetism—the denial of the real humanity of Jesus. The fact that miracles began to die out about that time has usually been attributed to declining faith. True, no doubt. But behind the anemic faith lies a significant fact. As the years went on, Christians no longer saw Jesus as their "Brother" as the early disciples had. Increasingly, He became a figure sculpted in marble, painted in oils with a gilded halo, encased in stained-glass windows.

By being in awe of such an inaccessible Jesus, they sought to honor Him, but in also dropping out the Holy Spirit, the third Person of the Trinity—that all-important link between His humanity and ours—they really dishonored Him.

The promise is still there for us—that we can "do greater works." The Spirit as Teacher is eager to lead us on and out into new dimensions, yes, even of the supernatural. Do we have the faith to believe and the courage to act?

HELPFUL READING: Mark 16:15–20; Acts 1:4–11

HIS WORD FOR YOU: God never changes.
For God's gifts and His call are irrevocable—He never withdraws them once they are given, and He does not change His mind about those to whom He gives His grace or to whom He sends His call.
(Romans 11:29, AMPLIFIED)

PRAYER: *Lord Jesus, I begin to see that while You walked the earth in human flesh, the Spirit taught You and was Your link with the Father, just as now He wants to teach me and be my link with You. I understand better now in what sense You really are my Brother.*

How I thank You, Lord, that I don't have to be "worthy" of any of this. How could I be? Instead, what I ask for is the willingness to empty myself of me even as You were willing to be emptied. I know it's a daring prayer, Lord. Give me the courage for it. Amen.

Notes

Foreword
1. Joel 2:28, 29.
2. Luke 1:15.
3. A. B. Simpson, *The Gospel of Healing* (Harrisburg, Pa.: Christian Publications, Inc., 1915), pp. 178, 75.
4. Joshua 1:3 (KJV).

I. Introducing the Helper

Chapter 1 Who Is the Helper?
1. Romans 8:27.
2. I Corinthians 2:10, 11.
3. I Corinthians 12:11.
4. Acts 20:28.
5. I Corinthians 12:8–11; Ephesians 4:7–12.
6. John 16:13, 14.

Chapter 2 Why Do I Need the Helper?
1. Acts 1:4 (AMPLIFIED)
2. William R. Moody, *The Life of D. L. Moody* (New York: Fleming H. Revell Co., 1900), pp. 146, 147, 149; and R. A. Torrey, *Why God Used D. L. Moody* (New York: Fleming H. Revell Co., 1923), pp. 51–55.
3. Matthew 5:6.

Chapter 3 Have I Already Received Him?
1. Galatians 3:24.
2. Matthew 11:11 (AMPLIFIED)
3. Luke 11:13.
4. John 15:26.

5. Romans 8:14.
6. Galatians 5:22; James 2:8, 9.
7. Romans 8:26.

Chapter 4 No Need to Be an Orphaned Christian
1. John 16:7.
2. A. B. Simpson, *When the Comforter Came*, (Harrisburg, Pa.: Christian Publications, Inc.).

Chapter 5 Could Anything Be Better Than His Presence?
1. "The Sweet Story of Old," Jemima T. Luke, 1841.
2. John 16:7; 14:17.
3. I John 3:9 (AMPLIFIED).
4. Jeremiah 31:33 (KJV).
5. John 15:5.
6. John 15:1–8.

Chapter 6 The Explosion of Power
1. Acts 1:1–5.
2. This interesting analysis is summarized from James Burns' *Revivals, Their Laws and Leaders* (London: Hodder & Stoughton).
3. Acts 2:37–41.
4. Acts 8:14–17.
5. Acts 19:1–7.
6. Acts 10:44–48.

II. How Do I Receive the Helper?

Chapter 1 Hungering and Thirsting for Something More
1. Revelation 3:15, 16.
2. Luke 18:1–8.
3. Matthew 5:6.
4. John 7:37–39 (RSV).
5. R. A. Torrey, *The Holy Spirit* (New York: Fleming H. Revell Co.), p. 198.
6. Luke 11:9 (AMPLIFIED).

Chapter 2 Accepting Jesus as the Christ
1. John 14:6 (RSV).
2. Acts 4:12 (RSV).
3. Revelation 19:16.
4. Revelation 5:12.
5. Colossians 2:10; Ephesians 3:10; 4:8–10; I Corinthians 15:24.
6. Romans 5:17 (AMPLIFIED).
7. Luke 15:11–32.

8. Luke 15:32 (KJV).
9. Bilquis Sheikh, *I Dared to Call Him Father* (Lincoln, Va.: Chosen Books, 1978).

Chapter 3 Deciding to Obey the Good Shepherd
1. James 2:17–22.
2. Philippians 2:13 (AMPLIFIED).

Chapter 4 Inviting Jesus as the Baptizer
1. John 20:21, 22 (AMPLIFIED).
2. Graham Pulkingham, *Gathered for Power* (Plainfield, N.J.: Logos International, 1972; and New York: Morehouse-Barlow Company, 1972), pp. 75, 76.

Chapter 5 Being Willing to Be Put to Work
1. Acts 1:8.
2. W. H. Daniels, *Moody, His Words, Works, and Wonders*, p. 396.

Chapter 6 Repentance and Baptism: Rising to New Life
1. Acts 2:14–39.
2. Norman P. Grubb, *Rees Howells, Intercessor* (Fort Washington, Pa.: Christian Literature Crusade), pp. 38–40.
3. *Ibid.*, p. 29.
4. I Corinthians 15:50.
5. Romans 6:6 (AMPLIFIED).
6. Romans 6:3 (AMPLIFIED).
7. Ephesians 2:5, 6.
8. Colossians 2:10.

Chapter 7 Accepting God's Grace
1. Galatians 3:1–5.
2. Acts 2:32, 33.
3. Watchman Nee, *The Normal Christian Life* (Fort Washington, Pa.: Christian Literature Crusade, 1964), p. 88.
4. Ephesians 1:20, 21 (RSV).
5. John 14:21.
6. See Devotional, "He Values My Personhood," in Part IV.

III. How the Helper Meets My Everyday Needs

Chapter 1 He Saves Me Time
1. I Corinthians 12:4–10.

Chapter 2 He Guides My Actions
1. Acts 13:3.

Chapter 4 He Is with Me in Everyday Situations
1. John 15:5 (AMPLIFIED).

Chapter 5 He Is My Remembrancer
1. Luke 21:12–15 (RSV).

Chapter 6 He Gives Me New Desires
1. Romans 8:14 (AMPLIFIED).
2. Romans 8:15 (AMPLIFIED).
3. Romans 12:2 (AMPLIFIED).

Chapter 7 He Changes My Undesirable Habit Patterns
1. Galatians 5:22, 23.
2. Luke 2:52 (RSV).

IV. How The Helper Ministers to Me at a Deep Level

Chapter 1 He Convicts Me of Sin
1. Acts 2:23, 37 (RSV).
2. John 3:17 (RSV).
3. Romans 3:23; I John 1:8; John 8:34 (RSV).
4. Luke 4:18.
5. I John 1:9.

Chapter 2 He Values My Personhood
1. Philippians 2:7.
2. Mark 10:21.
3. Ephesians 4:25–32.

Chapter 3 He Teaches Me about Tears
1. Matthew 19:8.
2. Psalm 95:8; Hebrews 3:7–11.
3. Hebrews 3:13; Ephesians 4:17, 30–32.
4. Mark 3:5; 8:17; Romans 2:1–5.
5. Luke 19:41, 42.
6. John 11:34–36.
7. Jamie Buckingham, *Daughter of Destiny* (Plainfield, N.J.: Logos International, 1976), pp. 163–67.

Chapter 4 He Is My Comforter
1. Hannah Whitall Smith, *My Spiritual Autobiography* (New York: Fleming H. Revell Co.) pp. 211, 215, 216 (now out of print).

Chapter 5 He Teaches Me to Pray (I)
1. Luke 11:1 (RSV).
2. John 16:24 (AMPLIFIED).
3. I John 5:14.

Chapter 6 He Teaches Me to Pray (II)
1. I Peter 2:10 (MOFFATT).
2. Ephesians 1:3 (AMPLIFIED).
3. John 5:19 (AMPLIFIED).
4. John 5:30 (AMPLIFIED).

V. The Outpouring of the Helper's Generosity

Chapter 1 Joy
1. Galatians 5:22.
2. Acts 4:3.
3. Acts 5:18, 40.
4. Acts 7:58–60.
5. Acts 8:3.
6. Acts 12:2.
7. Acts 12:3, 4.
8. Acts 16:25 (AMPLIFIED).
9. John 15:11 (AMPLIFIED).
10. Hebrews 12:2 (KJV).
11. Hebrews 1:9 (KJV).
12. John 16:16, 17, 22 (AMPLIFIED).
13. R. A. Torrey, *The Holy Spirit* (New York: Fleming H. Revell Co.), p. 95. For the full story, see pp. 93–95.
14. John 16:33 (RSV).

Chapter 2 Faith
1. Hebrews 11:6 (RSV).
2. Matthew 21:22 (RSV).
3. Hebrews 11:1 (KJV).
4. Ephesians 1:3.
5. Mark 11:24 (MOFFATT).
6. John 14:26; Luke 21:12–15; John 16:14, 15, etc.
7. Hebrews 11:1 (AMPLIFIED).
8. Jamie Buckingham, *Risky Living* (Plainfield, N.J.: Logos International, 1976), pp. 89–91.

Chapter 3 Love
1. Words by Anna Warner; music by William B. Bradbury.
2. Another portion of Brother Andrew's story is told in *God's Smuggler* by Brother Andrew with John and

Elizabeth Sherrill (New York: The New American Library, 1967).

3. John 14:23 (RSV).
4. For more on this author, read *I'm Out to Change My World* by Ann Kiemel (Impact Publishers).
5. John 21:15–18.
6. David and Sarah Van Wade, *Second Chance* (Plainfield, N.J.: Logos International, 1975).

Chapter 4 Vitality
1. Romans 8:11 (KJV).
2. A. B. Simpson, *The Gospel of Healing* (Harrisburg, Pa.: Christian Publications, Inc., 1915), pp. 170, 171.

Chapter 5 Healing
1. Francis MacNutt, *The Power to Heal* (Notre Dame, Ind.: Ave Maria Press, 1977) pp. 39–45.
2. Mark 8:22–26.
3. Mark 8:25 (AMPLIFIED).

Chapter 6 Peace
1. Malcolm Smith, *Turn Your Back on the Problem* (Plainfield, N.J.: Logos International, 1972), pp. 87–89.

Chapter 7 Other Tongues
1. Mark 16:15 (KJV).
2. Acts 2:7–12.
3. Acts 10:44–48; 19:4–7.
4. I Corinthians 14.
5. Hebrews 13:8.

Chapter 8 Miracles
1. *The New Random House Dictionary of the English Language.*
2. Psalm 62:11.
3. Luke 8:49.
4. Acts 1:22.
5. Joshua 1:3 (AMPLIFIED).

VI. The Helper and the Church

Chapter 1 Has My Church the Spirit?
1. Luke 24:46–49.
2. Ephesians 1:22 (RSV).
3. Ephesians 4:12 (RSV).
4. Ephesians 1:23 (AMPLIFIED).

5. Colossians 1:18.
6. Ephesians 4:8–12; I Corinthians 12:28, 29.
7. Isaiah 61:6; I Peter 2:5; Revelation 1:6.
8. Romans 14:17.
9. Acts 4:32–35.
10. I Corinthians 4:20.
11. II Corinthians 5:17; I Peter 1:23.
12. John 16:8–11; Acts 2:37.

Chapter 2 He Brings Reconciliation
1. Acts 5:11.
2. I Corinthians 12:12, 13.
3. Acts 4:32 (KJV).
4. My two-word-change paraphrase of Judges 16:20.
5. My personal knowledge of the situation described here came through Leonard LeSourd's close involvement with Colson in editorial work on the book manuscript of *Born Again* and the friendship with him that has resulted.
6. Charles W. Colson, *Born Again* (Lincoln, Va.: Chosen Books, 1976), p. 150.

Chapter 3 He Cleanses the Body of Christ
1. John 16:8 (RSV).
2. John 16:7, 8.
3. Acts 2:14–41.
4. Acts 5:3, 9.
5. Acts 8:9–24.
6. Galatians 2:11–16.
7. Luke 17:3 (RSV).
8. Matthew 18:15 (RSV).

Chapter 4 He Brings Unity
1. John 17.
2. Acts 2:4–12.
3. Acts 2:44, 45; 4:33, 34.
4. Acts 10; 11:1–18.
5. Acts 4:32 (RSV).
6. Acts 2:46, 47 (RSV).

Chapter 5 Channels for His Power
1. Acts 3:1–8; 5:15, 16; 8:6, 7; 14:8–10.
2. Acts 9:36–41; 20:9–12.
3. Hebrews 4:15.
4. Philippians 2:6, 7 (MOFFATT).
5. John 5:30 (AMPLIFIED).
6. John 8:28, 29 (AMPLIFIED).
7. John 12:50 (AMPLIFIED).
8. John 14:10 (KJV).